BETHANY J MILLER

Sunshine Daydream

First edition

ISBN: 978-1-7344810-1-3

This book was professionally typeset on Reedsy.
Find out more at reedsy.com

This book would not have been possible without the unconditional, unwavering support of my favorite Deadhead, Mike. Thank you for pushing me, believing in me, listening to this book at least a hundred times, and always being down to shake your bones.

*

Thank you to Linda Fausnet, Rebekah L Fraser, Tara L. Roi and The Greater New Haven Writer's Group, who never let me do anything less than my very best.

*

Jill Karkella at China Cat Creations, thank you for working diligently to help me create a perfect cover.

*

And to all my fellow Deadheads, life's a hell of a ride and I'm so glad to be on the bus with all of you.

*

A portion of the proceeds from the sale of this book will be donated to Archive.org, as the giant catalog of Grateful Dead shows they make accessible to the general public for free is an invaluable resource as well as a true joy for any Deadhead.

Author's Note

In the spring of 1991 I left home to follow the Grateful Dead. I'd have happily stayed on tour forever, if my life and the death of Jerry Garcia hadn't interrupted me. Instead, I stepped away, focused on raising a family and being a respectable adult. But in the back of my drawer, behind the collection of t-shirts I'd amassed as a gymnastics/robotics/football mom, the tie-dyes were still lurking.

Sunshine Daydream began as an attempt to come to terms with the life I'd left behind. But as I researched the shows Bailey and her friends go to, listened to each them over and over on Archive.org or watched them on YouTube, determined to get every historical detail correct, I was transported back to that magical time when the only thing that mattered was getting into the show.

Rather than coming to terms with what I'd left behind, I wanted it more than ever. After more than 20 years away, I went to a show.

The first thing I noticed was how very different everything was. There was no more "lot" as I knew it. Vending was done in venue-approved booths, not out of people's trunks. Most everyone had a ticket. No one offered me doses. And I didn't know anyone.

But as much as things had changed, some had stayed the same. When Bobby came out on stage and the first notes of "Eyes of the World" echoed through the stadium the crowd went wild. The grey-haired guy next to me offered me a hit of a legally obtained joint, the twenty-something kid on my other side sang every word to every song. When the woman in front of me turned around during "He's Gone" and we sang that we were going to steal each other's faces, I knew I was home.

The Grateful Dead scene as I knew it may be gone, but the vibe is still there. In bars where bands cover songs written before they were born, at multi-day music festivals where clean cut college kids dance next to brothers and sisters with dreadlocks to their waists, at stadium shows where middle-aged moms and grey-haired grandpas talk about what it was like back in the day, and in the hearts of every Deadhead.

Chapter 1

Teague was half way through the preliminary draft of the prenup when he stopped. He couldn't write this contract. He considered how to phrase what was going to amount to a refusal to work with this client as he dialed the extension for the firm's senior partner.

"This is Phillip."

"Phillip, this is Teague. I'm working on the Constantine prenup and I've got some concerns." He began pacing, his long strides taking him across the small space much too quickly. "Some of the things he's looking to do are illegal, and some I'm not comfortable with."

There was a pause, the sound of papers shuffling. "You are aware of who this is. What this particular client means to this firm."

He loosened his tie. "I am, and I do. Which is why I feel that another attorney may be better suited to—"

Phillip cut him off. "I expect the preliminary draft of the Constantine prenup on my desk by the end of the day." The line went dead.

Teague set the phone back in the cradle and sank into his chair. He pulled out a yellow legal pad, intending to re-read the client's instructions and take notes. Instead, he drew triangles in the margin.

This wasn't what he'd had in mind when he'd chosen his specialty. He'd intended to make sure men were fairly represented, that they were allowed visitation rights to their children, that vindictive wives didn't play the sympathy card and walk away with everything. Basically, he wanted to be the lawyer his father hadn't had.

He hadn't realized how horrible people could be to each other. There were days when he'd sit in his office long after everyone else had gone, trying to work through other people's issues so he didn't have to bring them home. Ironically, his attempts at not bringing problems home were causing major problems *at* home.

The phone rang, startling him out of his thoughts. "Hello?"

"Teague?"

"Cole?" He could tell immediately, by the desperate tone in his brother's voice, there was a problem. "What's wrong?"

"I'm in jail. You gotta help me. I'm so fucked."

He leaned back in his chair. The only surprising thing about Cole being arrested was that it hadn't happened before. "What'd you do?"

"Nothing."

Taking a deep breath, reminding himself that this was his brother and he was required by the laws of family to help, he clarified, "What were you arrested for?"

"Possession with intent to sell." Panic tinting his voice, he added, "They're saying fifteen years. It'd be 2005 by the time I got out. *Two-fucking-thousand and five.*"

"Who's saying fifteen years?"

"The judge."

Teague sat up straighter. "You've already been to court?"

"This morning."

His mind suddenly reeling, trying to remember everything he'd ever learned about criminal law, he asked, "Tell me exactly what happened."

"I was walking home yesterday, and these fuckin' cops start harassing me, and next thing I know they're throwing me in the car, arresting me on bullshit charges."

2

"They read the formal charges this morning?"

"Yeah, but I'm telling you, they're bunk."

"Did you enter a plea?"

"Yeah. I told them I was innocent. I wasn't selling anything to anyone."

He grabbed the legal pad and started making notes. "You pled not guilty. Did you tell the judge you were going to hire an attorney?"

"I told him you were one. That's why they let me call you."

"Okay. I'll get someone over there. Where are you?"

Fear coming through the phone loud and clear, he said, "Vermont. I've been staying at the house up here."

Teague dropped his pen, watched it roll across the pad. This was suddenly a hell of a lot more complicated. "Shit. Cole, listen, I'm going to have to..." He needed to think.

"You're gonna get me out, right? They set bail."

That was out of the question. Not loving the idea of telling Cole he didn't trust him, he used the easiest excuse he could. His girlfriend. "I can't do that. Marlena'll kill me. Just sit tight and stay out of trouble until I can figure this out."

As soon as he hung up, he began pacing again. *Criminal defense is not your thing. You're gonna have to hire someone. How the hell are you going to pull that off? You don't have any contacts in Vermont, and no good way of making any. If you ask around here, everyone will know by tomorrow that your brother's in jail for dealing drugs. Fuck! Cole's dealing? Jesus. It's gotta be a mistake. But it's not and you know it. Does Mom know? Shit, I'm gonna have to call her.*

There was no way in hell he was calling his mother until he had a plan.

If I had a Vermont phone book I could— Forget it. That'd just be a name. Same if I use the Lawyer's Reference catalog. The most I'd get is a specialty, and just because they practice criminal defense doesn't mean they're any

3

good. Something like this, fifteen years, you gotta meet them in person, make sure you're comfortable with them.

He stopped pacing. *Shit, I'm gonna have to go up there myself. The house is five hours, at least, from here. If I drive up tonight, I can start making calls first thing in the morning. Marlena's fundraiser is tomorrow and if I miss it she's gonna freak. But Cole's pretrial is next Friday, I don't have time to waste. If I go up in person it also means someone else gets assigned to the Constantine fucking prenup. That's a plus. Do you even want to do this? Cole's dealing fucking drugs. He belongs in jail. But if I don't do something Mom'll never forgive me. Christ, this sucks.*

Back at his desk, Teague took out his wallet and flipped through credit cards to the picture Cole had given him for Christmas. The black and white image of all four brothers, shirtless, smiling, with their arms around each other, had been taken during the summer they'd spent in Vermont, just before their parents split. Teague wondered where Cole had found it. Probably Vermont. Cole'd had plenty of opportunity, since he was the only Gallagher who'd used that house in the last twenty years.

As he slid the picture back into his wallet Teague made a decision. He didn't agree with his brother's choices, or his lifestyle in general, but Cole was still his little brother. He had to do what he could to help him.

He had to go to Vermont.

* * *

It had been bad enough going to HR, explaining that he needed a couple days, maybe a week, off from work. Listening as the office manager reassigned his most pressing cases to other attorneys and answering questions about his clients' needs. He'd given out the phone number at his mother's house in Vermont to everyone who was helping him, just in case there was a question.

Now he was going to have to explain this to Marlena.

He sat in his car and stared at the front of the townhouse. Marlena had bought it before they'd met. She'd liked the eat in kitchen, with its sleek white cabinets, and she'd liked that there was a balcony off the bedroom upstairs. She could have bought a house, but she hadn't wanted to worry about shoveling snow or mowing the lawn.

When he'd first moved in they'd talked about buying something together. Someplace with an open floor plan where they could entertain, and maybe a yard for kids. Climbing out of the car, he knew there was little chance of that happening now. He'd been warned that if he didn't make her his first priority it was over.

As soon as he stepped into the foyer she called from the kitchen, "You're late."

He slipped his shoes off and set them on the rack in the closet, hung his coat, and headed down the hall. He stood in the doorway and watched Marlena for a moment. He loved the way her dark hair, cut very short in the back, showed off the curve of her neck. She stood on her toes as she reached to pull dishes out of the cabinet.

"Let me get that for you." He moved to help.

"I've got it." She grabbed the dishes, turned and set them on the table with a bang. She crossed her arms over her chest. "Teague, we talked about this. You get out of work at five."

The way she pressed her lips together, he knew he was in trouble. "Babe, I couldn't help it."

"Yes, you could. You're a lawyer, not a doctor. No one's going to *die* if you leave on time."

"This time it's different."

"Yeah? How."

"Cole called. He's in trouble."

She rolled her eyes. "I'm sure. How much did you send him?"

"Not that kind of trouble. He's in jail, for possession with intent to sell."

"Shocking."

He clenched his fists. "Marlena, this is serious."

Her lip curled as she said, "Why do you sound surprised? Did you really not know what he was doing?"

He'd known Cole did drugs, but he hadn't considered he may be dealing. And when he'd told him the charges were bunk, Teague had believed him. Even if he wasn't completely sure of what "bunk" meant.

Marlena continued, "I'm sure someone at your firm can handle it."

"That's the thing." He explained, "He's in Vermont. I'm going to have to go, in person, to hire someone."

Her eyes narrowed. "You're going to Vermont."

"Yes."

"When?"

"As soon as I can pack a bag."

She enunciated each word as she asked, "And how long will you be gone?"

This was the part he was dreading. "A few days?"

She slowly uncrossed her arms, put her hands on the table between them and leaned forward. "Teague, you know how hard I've worked on tomorrow night's benefit dinner. How many donor's asses I had to kiss, how many of my parent's friends I had to beg into coming. How is it going to look if you're not there?"

"It'll look like I had a family emergency."

"Not acceptable."

"I have to go."

"You don't *have* to do anything."

"What am I supposed to do? Just leave Cole sitting in jail?"

She snapped, "Cole *belongs* in jail."

6

"He's my brother."

"Ted Bundy had a brother, too. Do you think he should have bailed him out of jail?"

Appalled, he said, "How the hell can you compare Cole to *Ted Bundy?*"

"How the hell can you choose your fucked up, hippie freak, druggie brother over *me?*"

"How the hell can you ask me to choose between you and Cole?" Disgusted, he said, "I'm going to pack."

She yelled down the hall at his back, "Pack everything, because if you leave this house you're not coming back."

He ignored her. His brother needed him. He wasn't going to be some douche bag who left his family to fend for themselves, or who demanded that they choose between people.

He threw a garment bag on the bed and packed slacks and Oxfords. He wondered briefly if Marlena was serious. Just in case, he pulled out a suitcase and added a couple pairs of jeans, a few polos, and whatever else he thought he'd need for a few days away. As an afterthought he threw in his address book, the novel he'd been reading for the past year, and the football jersey he wore on Sundays.

Looking around the room, he decided there wasn't anything else he wanted. He'd paid for most of what was there, but nothing else was *his*. He zipped the suitcase and brought both bags down to the foyer. He slipped the brown shoes he'd chosen that morning back on and tucked the black ones in the side of his suitcase.

"You're such a fucking asshole."

He looked up to see Marlena, arms crossed, leaning against the wall.

Straightening, he considered trying to make this right. But the Constantine prenup flashed thought his mind. It wasn't that they were trying to protect their assets, or that they were going into a marriage expecting it to fail. *Relationships shouldn't require conditions. If he loved her, and she loved him, they'd work out whatever shit came up— together.*

He pulled out his keys and unclipped the one for the condo. He bounced it in his hand a few times, then handed it to Marlena.

She stared at him, shock on her face.

He opened the door, picked up his bags, and walked out.

Chapter 2

The tape player on top of the refrigerator was a poor substitute for seeing the Grateful Dead live. Bailey sang along anyway, about midnight sun and silver kimonos and diamond eyed jacks.

She measured sugar into a big stainless-steel bowl, added salt and baking powder. When she'd opened her coffee shop four years earlier she'd taped the index card with her mom's handwritten instructions to the freshly painted cabinet above her workspace. After making muffins nearly every morning since, she cracked eggs, poured milk, and added blueberries without having to consult her mom's precise script.

As she scooped batter into tins, "China Cat" gave way seamlessly to "I Know You Rider." The words echoed through her. When she'd first heard those lyrics she'd had no idea how much she'd someday miss having riders. Especially Jesse, although she didn't consider her boyfriend to be a rider even when he chipped in for gas. They'd been together way too long for that. *Since the beginning. It's always been you and Jesse. He'll be back soon. Maybe today. A lot of family go home after the New Year's shows.*

She smiled a little to herself as she remembered the first time someone had referred to her as family. It'd been at Red Rocks, a few months after she'd left home to follow the Dead. She hadn't even known the guy who'd said it, but the feeling of being accepted as a

Deadhead had stuck with her. *Are you family, still? You haven't been to a show in months.*

She'd skipped News Year's in Oakland, it was too hard to take time off to drive cross-country. And the previous fall she'd only managed three nights in Philly. *You can go back. You* are *family, and nothing can change that.*

The timer dinged. She pulled the first tray of cookies from the oven, slid the second tray in, put the muffins on the lower rack, and shut the door. Once the timer was reset and the first cookies transferred to a cooling rack, she prepped the third and final tray.

The tape player popped open. Instead of flipping the cassette over, she shut it off and headed into the main room. Delilah padded softly past her, nuzzling her big black head against Bailey's hand. She briefly thought how funny it was that people were afraid of rottweilers. Delilah was the sweetest dog ever. She rubbed the dog's side before turning the knob on the stereo. She almost started the tape in that player, then opted for the radio. Maybe in a while she'd switch back to the Dead, but right then she needed to listen to something that didn't stir so many memories.

Tom Petty was singing about rolling joints. She sang along as she started coffee. Once she had the first pot brewing, she went out into the seating area.

Morning sun streamed through the big windows at the front of the shop, reflected off the glossy tops of the light oak tables with their matching chairs, and brought brightness to the seating area in the front corner. Bailey straightened the deep blue and burgundy throw pillows on the couches, knowing it was a lost cause. By the end of the morning rush they'd be in total disarray again.

That was fine. She wanted people to make themselves comfortable. To play the board games she'd piled on the coffee table, to read a book or two, or to just hang out and do nothing.

Satisfied that everything was ready, she flipped the sign on the door to "Open."

* * *

Bailey took advantage of the late afternoon lull to clean. She threw out cups that had been left on tables, wiped up cream and sugar spills, and pushed chairs back where they belonged. Behind the counter she added to the growing list of supplies she needed to order while she kept one eye on the street, looking for the school bus. A light snow had begun to fall and she worried about the roads.

When her niece, Aria, came in Bailey came around the counter and grabbed her in a bear hug. "Hi, sweetie! How was school?" She kissed her cheek and set her down, running her hand down Aria's long, light brown hair.

"Good. We had gym today and we played leap frog."

"Sounds like fun. Do you have homework?"

Aria rolled her eyes dramatically. "Yes. We always have homework. It's supposed to make us 'sponsible."

Bailey thought it was insane to have homework in kindergarten. "Go start it please and I'll bring you a snack."

Aria went to a table and unpacked her bag, pausing to pet Delilah when she wandered over. The dog lay at her feet, where the crumbs usually fell.

Bailey brought a cookie and a glass of milk to the table. "Do you need anything else?"

"No, Auntie, thank you."

"If you do, come get me." She went back to work, checking on Aria between customers.

When Rain came in, shaking snow from his long blonde dreadlocks, she leaned across the counter and kissed his cheek. Of all her friends, she missed him the most when he was gone. "Hey now. Where've you been?"

"Here and there. I caught the shows in Oakland." He gave her an easy smile, his deep blue eyes lighting up. "New Year's Eve they opened with 'Sugar Mag', then went into 'Touch of Grey.'"

She rolled her eyes. "I hate that fucking song. And 'Sugar Mag' should always be followed by 'Sunshine Daydream.'"

His smile growing, he said, "I know, but they made up for it. They rolled out a 'Dark Star', then *ended* with 'Sunshine Daydream' and did 'Midnight Hour' for the encore."

"Wish I coulda been there." "Dark Star" was a rarity, and any time it made it into the rotation was cause for celebration. Hoping against hope, she asked, "Did anyone else come back with you?"

"Na, I hitched."

"Fuuuck, that sucks."

He shrugged, "It wasn't that bad. I hooked up with family to Chicago. Then I caught a ride with a trucker all the way to Springfield, then Matt came and picked me up." Rain always spoke quietly, but as he leaned closer to Bailey he lowered his voice even further. "Matt told me about Cole."

That had been the biggest topic of discussion all week. "It sucks, he totally doesn't deserve to be in jail."

"No doubt."

She said, "I heard they set his bail really high."

"They think he's a flight risk."

"Would you hang around, if it were you?"

"Hell no."

"Me, neither. If I were Cole." She asked, "What do you think's gonna happen to him?"

"His brother's some big shot lawyer, coming up from Connecticut. I'm guessing he'll work something out."

Surprised that no one else had mentioned that, she asked, "How'd you hear that?"

"Matt was in court on Tuesday with my sister, when Cole was arraigned. They set his pretrial for next Friday." He shook his head sadly. "Fridays are bad. That usually means they're not planning on letting you go."

Bailey scrunched her eyebrows together. "Really?"

Rain shrugged. "That's what my old man always said." The bells above the door jingled as people came in. He glanced up at the menu boards. "Bail, can I get a large organic blend?"

She poured the coffee. As she handed it to him, she asked, "Where are you staying?"

"With Matt. They've got some shit to do around the farm and I'm gonna give a hand."

"So you'll be around for a while?"

"For a bit."

There was a flutter in her stomach— definitely interest in the way he was looking at her. "Don't be a stranger."

"I won't."

He took his coffee and sat with Aria. The little girl gave him a huge hug. Bailey took care of the next customers and half-watched the two of them, Aria bouncing in her seat as she told Rain something. It made Bailey feel good that her friends went out of their way to be kind to her niece, considering she spent so much time at the shop. After a while Rain hugged Aria, waved to Bailey, and left.

When Katelyn came in to relieve her, Bailey took Aria and Delilah upstairs. The convenience of living above her shop had been the deciding factor when she'd chosen this location, although she'd wanted to be downtown anyway. She'd always loved the old brick buildings that surrounded the town green, with their high ceilings, huge windows and unique features. Her building had vintage tin ceilings, something that just wasn't done anymore.

She opened the door of her apartment to the lingering scent of sandalwood incense. She slipped her Birkenstocks off, leaving them by the door with all the other shoes, and crossed the hardwood floor barefoot. She turned lamps on as she went, lighting the chocolate walls and cranberry couches with a warm glow.

On the other side of the living room she flipped through tapes, reading labels. "Any special requests?"

"Foxboro last year?" Aria spun slow circles in the space between the coffee table and the couch, her arms wide and her skirt flaring around her.

Bailey grinned. "You just want that because you were there."

"Not-ahhh." Aria stopped spinning and gave her the most adorable smile. "They ended with 'The Mighty Quinn' and you like that one."

She countered, "Yeah, but they did 'Sugar Mag' without 'Sunshine Daydream' and that's so weird." She began looking for that tape anyway, because Aria had asked for it and because she liked nearly every song they'd done that night.

"They did it on New Year's."

She figured that was what Aria and Rain had been talking about, but she asked anyway, "How'd you know that?"

"Because everyone knows." She started spinning again, slowly enough that she could ask, "Do you think Jesse will bring tapes from New Year's?"

The casual reminder that her boyfriend had left her behind again stung. After the shows in Philly she'd gone home to Vermont to take care of the shop and Aria. Lacking those responsibilities, Jesse had finished out the tour. Cole, Sage and a few others had come back in early November. Jesse hadn't.

Keeping her back to her niece, Bailey said, "I don't know. It depends on when he comes back, if the tapers have made copies yet and if he can get them."

"How come he's not back?"

She found the right tape and stuck it in. "I don't know."

"Rain's back. And Sage. I saw him yesterday."

Bailey turned around slowly. "Sage has a car. And Matt went down to Springfield to get Rain. If Jesse's on his way he probably has to hitchhike, and sometimes that's really hard."

"Why don't we just go get him? Like Matt got Rain?"

Bailey sighed, knowing Jesse would show up when he was ready. "I don't know where he is, or what he's doing. He might be on his way, or he might chillin' on the west coast so he can catch the shows in February." Not into discussing this any further, she asked, "What do you want for dinner?"

"Hmmm." Aria made a show of giving it a lot of thought, with her hand on her hip and a finger over her lips. "Stir-fry?"

"Perfect. I'll get the rice going and you can pick veggies." Bailey led her into the kitchen. Even in the fading light of late afternoon the room was bright and sunny, the yellow of the cabinets echoing the sunflower pattern of the wallpaper. She pulled the cord on the ceiling light anyway, liking a lot of light when she cooked.

Aria got a cutting board, set it on the table and started carefully chopping the vegetables the way her aunt had taught her. After a while, she asked, "Auntie? Are you going on spring tour?"

Over her shoulder, she said, "That's a ways away. I haven't decided."

"Can I come? If you go?"

"Not this time, sweetie. You've got school." She felt bad. Aria was used to being part of Bailey's life, including going to shows, and school was really getting in the way. It was an adjustment for both of them.

Pouting a little, she said, "Yeah, that's what Nannie said, too."

Surprised, Bailey turned to actually look at Aria. "You asked Nannie

15

if you could go on tour?"

"Yeah. Just the east coast shows, though. Cuz that's what you do, right? When me and Mallory grow up we're gonna get a van, like yours, and do *all* the shows."

She smiled at the thought of Aria asking her Nannie if she could go on tour. Not that Baily's mom would have been surprised by the question. Most everyone Bailey knew had spent at least some time on tour, and Aria had spent a whole lot of time with Bailey and her friends. But still, it was interesting that Aria apparently thought it was a normal thing to do. She asked, "And what does Mallory's mom say about that?"

"She says we'll see." Aria looked at Bailey from the corner of her eye. "That's what grown-ups say when they mean no."

Smiling at the blunt assessment, Bailey went back to cooking.

* * *

After dinner Bailey and Aria snuggled on the couch, reading. When Bailey's mom, Ellen, got there they stacked the books on the coffee table while Aria got her shoes.

Quietly, hoping the little girl didn't hear, Bailey told her mom, "I heard Aria asked if she could go on tour."

Ellen glanced at her granddaughter and smiled. "She did." She looked back to her daughter. "She wants to be just like her Auntie Bailey."

Bailey wasn't sure how she felt about that. As much as she loved being on tour, living on the road could be a hard life. Not necessarily what she wanted for her niece. Speaking louder, so Aria heard, she told Ellen, "Her homework's done. We had veggie stir-fry for dinner, and she somehow managed to weasel ice cream out of me."

Aria grinned at the last part as she carefully tied her shoelaces. She grabbed her bag and took Ellen's hand. "Bye, Auntie Bailey."

Bailey gave her a quick hug and kiss, "See you tomorrow." She watched her mom and niece as they went down the stairs, Aria already chattering away about her day.

Once they were gone and the dishes were done, Bailey called Delilah and went back downstairs. By this time of the night everyone in the shop was family. They kicked back on couches and sat around tables, or stood in groups talking. Delilah lay in her customary corner and Bailey sat on the couch next to Rain. He hugged her in greeting. "Hey, sistah."

"Hey now." She leaned against him, letting him keep his arm around her shoulders. It was nice to sit quietly after having to talk to customers all day. It was nice, too, to feel Rain's fingers trace along her skin.

Eventually everyone left, except Rain. Bailey locked the doors, shut off the lights, and walked back to where he was leaning against the wall at the bottom of the stairs, waiting. He touched her hair, played with the hair wrap, making the silver bells tinkle softly. "Hey."

"Hey." She ignored an unexpected surge of nerves as Rain's blue eyes met hers. They'd been friends a long time, nothing would change that.

He brushed his hand over her cheek, rested it on her neck. He leaned toward her, kissed her gently.

She led him upstairs. She pointed at the stereo as she sat on the couch. "Do you want to put something on?" She watched his back, loving the way his dreads hung nearly to his waist. She twirled her own hair. She'd been close to letting it dread once. A long time ago.

After a minute he put a tape in the player and came to sit next to her.

"What'd you pick?"

He took her hand. "You'll see."

The music started and she grinned. She recognized "Alabama Getaway" immediately, and it was easy enough to guess what he'd chosen. "Rochester War Memorial, 1982?"

"Damn, Bail, you're good."

She shrugged. "That was our first show."

He nodded. "It was."

"That was such a great tour." Those were the days she so desperately missed, when it'd always been her, Jesse, Rain and Sage. "It feels like a million years ago."

He laced his fingers into hers. "It's been *eight years*."

"That's insane." She put her head on his shoulder. "We shouldn't even be old enough to be able to say that."

She felt him smile against her head. "No shit, huh?" He laughed softly. "I still remember you with pig tails tied with ribbons."

"And I remember when you were Walter."

He snorted. "I swear to god, if you ever tell anyone that..." He trailed off.

Barely a whisper, she said, "I'd never do that."

Just as softly, he said, "I know." He let go of her hand and slid his fingers over her shoulder, tangled them into her hair.

She leaned into him, kissed him firmly.

Delilah nudged her leg. Pulling back from Rain, she gave the dog a quick scratch between her ears. "Go lay down."

She put her head in Bailey's lap.

Bailey gently pushed her off, stood and held her hand out to Rain. He took it and she led him to the bedroom. She shut the door, leaving the dog in the living room.

She slid her hand under his shirt, feeling his smooth skin. Closing her eyes, she put her head against his chest as he ran his fingers through her long, soft hair.

He unbuckled one side of her overalls, letting the strap dangle. She shuddered with pleasure as he caressed her hip. When he undid her other buckle and let her pants fall to the floor, she stepped out of them and pulled him towards the bed.

"Dire Wolf" played, just loud enough to hear through the door. She hummed, the music always a part of her.

Tingles of pleasure ran through her as Rain trailed his fingers over her shoulder, across her collarbone, traced her breasts, making her nipples harden. She touched his side, watched her winter-pale fingers against his skin, still tanned from his time in California, as she ran them along his hip. He moved above her.

Gently, she stopped him. "Wait." Reaching into the nightstand, she grabbed a condom.

Needing to feel close to him, she ran her hands over the smooth skin of his shoulders, down his sides, and gently pulled his hips, guiding him. Her eyes closed as she concentrated on the pressure of him pushing into her.

Warm breath, expelled with a low moan, tickled her shoulder. Slowly at first, so she felt every thrust and withdrawal, then harder, faster, he took what he needed until he strained against her. Arching to meet him, she tightened her grip on his hips, felt sweat break out over his skin as he throbbed inside her.

He wrapped his arms around her, his jagged breath slowing to normal. He ran his hand over her cheek, turned her face to his and kissed her. "Do you have another condom?"

She stayed on her back while he did what he needed to. Once he was ready, he ran his fingers up her thigh, touched her inside. With each movement he brought her closer to fulfillment. "Rain, ummmm, Rain." His name slid from her lips, disappearing into the space between them. Pleasure radiated from where he touched, pulsed through her in waves coming closer and closer together. "Now, please."

Nearly there, she heaved against him, her body tightening uncontrollably around him. She stopped breathing, her entire consciousness focused on him inside her. *"More."* He pushed, groaning with the effort, as she came on him.

Spent, they lay in the dark together. He kissed her shoulder as he slipped his arm around her waist. She twined her fingers with his and held him close. She drifted, listening to the comfortable rhythm of his breathing, and to the music that had been the background to nearly everything she'd ever done.

Chapter 3

The incessant ringing drove Teague out of bed. He stumbled downstairs, wondering why the answering machine didn't pick up. And why the hell there was no phone upstairs. He tripped over a work boot in the middle of the living room floor and nearly toppled onto the coffee table. He bolted to the kitchen, sure he'd never get there in time, and grabbed the phone. "Hello?"

His mother's unmistakably cold voice responded. "It's about time."

He rubbed sleep from his eyes. "Hi, Mom. I'm fine, thanks for asking."

"Obviously you're fine. You answered the phone." In typical Priscilla fashion, she added, "The *fourth* time I called."

"I was sleeping."

"It's after nine o'clock."

He sank into the nearest chair, closed his eyes and leaned back, then jerked away. The vinyl chair was freaking cold. He sat straighter so his bare back didn't touch. "I didn't get to bed until two this morning."

"So what you're telling me is you've yet to do anything about this... *situation?*"

"Cole just called me yesterday. What exactly do you expect me to have done?"

"You're the lawyer. You tell me."

What the hell did I do to deserve this. "Today I'm going to put together a list of possible attorneys and make appointments."

"I'd prefer if you took care of this yourself."

For the third time, he told her, "I can't represent him. I'm not licensed to practice in Vermont. And even if I was, I'm not qualified to do this."

"You did go to go law school, did you not?"

"Yes, I did. And I studied criminal law, just like every other law student. But I've never practiced it. Asking me to defend Cole would be like asking a proctologist to deliver a baby."

"And you think there's someone there, in *Vermont*, who is going to do a better job than you?"

"Yes, Mom, I do. For starters, laws vary state to state. And the lawyers here have working relationships with the prosecutors and judges. Cole needs every advantage he can get, and he needs an attorney who is experienced in cases of this magnitude."

"*This magnitude*? It was *marijuana*."

He didn't bother to remind her it had been *a lot* of marijuana. "Are you really willing to risk him being in jail for the next fifteen years?"

After a moment she snapped, "Fix this," and hung up.

He stared for a moment at the harvest gold, rotary dial desk phone, the same one that'd been there the summer they'd spent in the house. He remembered his oldest brother, Shea, hadn't been happy about spending a month in Vermont and had forfeited his allowance for a year to be allowed to call his girlfriend in Connecticut once a day.

The phone wasn't the only thing that was the same. The kitchen walls and all the cabinets were still avocado green and the appliances were burnt orange. It was like the sixties had vomited, and no one had bothered to clean it up.

Teague remembered his mom telling his dad a house in Vermont was a good investment, so close to the ski slopes. They'd be able to rent it out to the snow bunnies. Teague had been so young, he'd wondered why rabbits would want a house. And if they'd pay for it in carrots.

They'd never rented it out, though. His mother and the four boys had stayed in it one excruciatingly boring summer. Since then the only use it got was when Cole stayed there. His mom hadn't cared that the house wasn't generating revenue. She'd only cared that she could tell her friends they had a vacation home in Vermont. And that she'd made her ex-husband pay for it.

She'd probably been planning her divorce even then. It was what Teague would have counseled a client to do if she were planning a divorce years in advance. Make sure she didn't work, that she gave up her own life to take care of her husband and the kids, that she had lots of nice things.

The idea that his mother had probably done exactly that made him sick.

He stood and stretched. He should probably call Shea and Callum, let his older brothers know what was going on. First, though, he needed caffeine. He opened cabinets one by one until he found a Mr. Coffee. It was covered in dust.

He set it in the sink, then wondered if it was a good idea to run water over an electrical appliance. He mumbled, "Probably not," and instead set it on the counter. The sponge crammed behind the faucet looked nasty. He found a new one, still in cellophane, and carefully wiped down the coffee maker.

While it sat to dry, he started to look for coffee.

Marlena kept theirs in a canister on the counter, so he'd always know where to find it. Marlena was good at things like that. He was probably going to miss that about being with her.

After going through every cabinet twice he had to finally admit there was no coffee. Which made sense, considering that the coffee maker had been dusty.

Frustrated, he went back up to the room he was using. He'd just have to get showered and dressed, and go find the nearest Dunkin' Donuts.

* * *

Bailey finished the dishes and went to check in with Katelyn. "I'm gonna give Rain a ride over to Matt and Lucy's, and pick up supplies. Do you need anything?"

Katelyn paused, a sleeve of cups in her hand, and gave her a questioning look. "Since when are you and Rain a thing?"

"We're not."

"Yeah, okay." She rolled her eyes.

Bailey leaned against the back counter and folded her arms over her chest. She was aware of Katelyn's thoughts on her relationships.

Katelyn set the cups down. "Bailey, whatever deal you and Jesse have, it's…" She trailed off.

"Everything doesn't have to be so serious. Just because you and Liam take your relationship that way doesn't mean everyone does."

"Bailey, Rain isn't some guy just passing through."

"We're all just passing through."

Not amused, she asked, "How does Rain feel about it?"

"How does Rain feel about what?" Rain said, coming in from the back.

Katelyn looked up guiltily. "Double brewed coffee."

"Rain has never had double brewed coffee, but he'd be totally into trying it."

Bailey smiled, at Katelyn getting caught, and at Rain's third-person response. "Katelyn, do you need anything from the store?"

Katelyn looked from Rain back to Bailey. "Can you check for breakfast popsicles? Mallory's on an anti-breakfast kick and they're

24

the only thing she'll eat in the morning."

Rain asked, "You let your kid have popsicles for breakfast?"

"I can't send her to school on an empty stomach." Sounding very defensive, she added, "Besides, Lucy makes them with strawberries from Matt's greenhouse, so they're healthy."

"Wish you were my mom." Rain turned to Bailey. "Ready?"

Bailey asked Katelyn, "Are you good here?"

"Yeah, I got it."

Bailey poured a large organic blend and handed it to Rain. To Katelyn, she said, "I'll be back."

Rain took the cup and went back the way he'd come. Bailey started to follow, but Katelyn stopped her. "Bailey, I didn't mean to pry."

There was nothing she wanted to say to that. "I'll see if they have the popsicles for Mallory."

Outside, Bailey opened the door of her van and waited for Delilah to settle into her spot on the bed. She'd always wanted a Volkswagen, but they were too small so she'd ended up with a Chevy. It had captain's seats in the back for Aria and the sides curved outwards. Once she and Jesse had pulled the third row of seating out and built a platform it was just big enough to fit a full size mattress across the back. She didn't often sleep in it, she could afford hotels, but it was still nice to have the option.

Once Delilah was in, Bailey climbed into the driver's seat, started the ignition, then turned to look at Rain. He'd sat in her passenger seat more times than she cared to remember. Him, Jesse, whoever else they'd picked up along the way who managed to call shotgun. Not just in her current van, but in the Chevy Vega she'd had when they'd first left home.

Rain asked, "You okay?"

"Yeah." She smiled slightly. She put the van in reverse and checked the mirrors. "What does Matt have you doing?"

"He's working on upgrading one of the greenhouses, so I've been cutting PVC."

"Sounds like fun."

He shrugged. "I do what I can for them."

They sat in comfortable silence until she pulled into Matt and Lucy's. Once she'd parked, Rain headed to Matt's greenhouses, and Bailey went into the store.

She waited in line while a young woman with a chubby baby on her hip bought goats milk and maple syrup, and as an elderly gentleman bought a bag of apples. When she got to the counter, Bailey smiled at the girl who greeted her. "Hi. I'm Bailey. You should have a crate for me?"

The girl looked completely puzzled. "Um, today's not a pick up day."

Used to Lucy's ever-changing student-staff, she said, "It's not a farm share. It's a commercial account."

"I'll have to get Lucy."

"No worries."

The girl went to the back room and Bailey wandered through the store. She picked up a package of dried strawberries and a bag of fresh spinach. She was always amazed at the variety of things Matt grew. Sometimes she thought he was like King Midas, except everything he touched turned to a high-yield plant. She liked that idea. She'd weave it in next time Aria asked her to make up a Princess Willa story.

While she browsed the freezers, looking for Mallory's popsicles, the front door opened. She glanced over to see if it was someone she knew. It was just some guy, in a tan dress coat. His dark hair was gelled, held back with sunglasses. Even from across the room Bailey could see the Oakley "O" on the leg. *His glasses probably cost more than my first car.*

It was most definitely not someone she knew. She turned back to the freezer.

Lucy's current help was still in back. As the guy waited, he drummed his fingers on the counter. Bailey could hear it across the store.

The girl came back out. "Can I help you?"

His tone was impatient. "I need coffee."

"I'm sorry, we don't have coffee."

"Is there a Dunkin' Donuts somewhere?"

"Ummm…"

Bailey started towards the counter, intending to give him directions. Before she'd gone two steps Lucy was there. "The best coffee around is Bailey's, downtown."

"I want the closest place to here."

"Sure. That'd be Rich's Citgo. Take a right out of the parking lot, about two miles down."

He turned and stalked out. Bailey picked up two packages of popsicles and brought everything up to the counter. "Hey, Lucy."

"Hey now." The older woman smiled in welcome. "How's things?"

"Good. I hear Matt's working on a project."

"Isn't he always?" She grinned. "I can't complain. He lets me do my thing, and he does his."

"Can you add this to my bill?"

Lucy turned to the new girl and explained, "When we have commercial customers—"

* * *

It was past noon by the time Teague parked his BMW in the driveway. This place was ridiculous. The closest store he'd been able to find was half an hour away. The only place to get coffee was a gas station, and it was crap. He'd bought two cups anyway. He grabbed the coffee and bag of groceries and headed inside.

As he had been the night before, he was struck by the scent of the house as soon as he opened the door. It was kind of musky and earthy. It sort of reminded him of incense at church.

He set the coffee cups on top of the accent table next to the front door, pulled out a muffin from the bag of groceries, and broke a piece off. It was dry and crumbly. He was glad he hadn't tried to eat it in the car.

He swallowed the first bite and washed it down with lukewarm coffee as he looked around. The living room was huge, taking up three quarters of the first floor. It stretched from the exterior wall on the left to the kitchen on the right, and was open from the front all the way to the back. Windows on the far wall looked out at snow-covered trees. It would have been a beautiful room, except it was as atrociously sixties as the kitchen.

The wall to the left, which would have been perfect for a fireplace, was instead dominated by a freestanding wood stove. It looked like Darth Vader's helmet, if it had been made for a giant, and painted blood red. Even the stovepipe was red, which made no sense, because the rest of the room was pale blue.

The walls were done in blue wallpaper covered with brown flowers in a repeating pattern. So was the ceiling. Teague stared at it, wondering who the fuck wallpapered a ceiling. He figured it was probably the same person who installed wall to wall shag carpet in the same blue as the walls.

It seemed somehow ridiculously appropriate that the couches and arm chairs were dark yellow velvet. Maybe because that rounded out the primary palette.

He could practically see Cole sitting on the couch, in one of the tie-dye shirts he insisted on wearing. There was no doubt that he'd sat there. The coffee table, a heavy looking dark wood thing, had a stack of dirty dishes and half a dozen beer bottles on it. And in the middle, a glass pipe. If it hadn't been drug paraphernalia it would have been beautiful, with blue and purple swirls running from the bowl up the stem.

Teague had never understood the appeal of pot. The few times he'd smoked, it hadn't been anything to write home about. And, although he'd had opportunity, he'd never had the urge to try anything else. He rarely even drank beer. *Even Marlena thought you were too freaking straight.*

He stepped forward, picked up a little glass bottle. This looked like something a lot more serious than pot. He turned it over in his hand, read the label, mumbled, "Patchouli." He opened the bottle. It smelled like the house, just stronger. He put the cap on and set it back on the table.

He felt stupid, having thought for a second it was a crack vial. Not that he'd ever seen a crack vial.

This was the first time it had ever occurred to him that a lack of experience with illegal drugs might be a detriment. He looked around again. Even if the bottle had only been hippie perfume, the glass pipe was most certainly not for tobacco. And there was no telling what else might be laying around the house.

Not my problem. He was there to hire a lawyer, then he'd be free to go home. A couple days at most.

He took the bag of groceries into the kitchen. If he wanted to get out of there anytime soon he had calls to make.

Chapter 4

Bailey hit snooze. Rain tightened his arm around her and mumbled, "You okay?"

"Mmmmm. I have to get up."

"That sucks."

"Yeah, it does." She eased out from under his arm. If she'd been alone she'd have turned a light on. She wouldn't do that to Rain, though. Especially not at five in the morning. In the dark she pulled open a drawer and felt around. Her fingers brushed corduroy. That had to be a pair of overalls. And the soft cotton in the drawer above was a shirt.

By the time she had the second buckle on her pants done Rain was snoring. She crept out, closing the door softly behind her.

Delilah was waiting when Bailey came out of the bathroom. She took a minute to give her a belly rub. "Come on, girl. Me and you've got work to do." She started down the stairs, the dog charging ahead.

She let Delilah out, stood for a moment watching her. It was still odd to see Delilah without her brother, Samson. It'd been months since he'd died, but Bailey sometimes caught herself looking for him. She left the door open a crack for Delilah and turned to the tape player.

She picked a cassette at random and hit play. "Bertha" started. Bailey rolled her eyes. One of her teachers in high school had always called her Bertha, no matter how many times she'd corrected him. It had driven her nuts, especially when her sister had heard about it and begun to tease her, too. She'd never been able to like the song because of the association.

She began setting ingredients in a line on the counter, singing under her breath. There was background noise on this recording. The first tendrils of dread wormed into her mind. There were very few tapes in her collection that had people in the audience talking. Lots of cheers between songs and after certain lines were sung, sometimes hoots of sheer excitement, but not usually the murmur of voices over the tracks.

She dropped butter into the bowl for cookies. "Greatest Story Ever Told" started, guitar backed by a soft snare drum, and the unease in her stomach grew. "Bertha" followed by "Greatest Story" with audible background noise? It could only be July 13, 1984.

She considered changing the tape. Instead, she clenched her jaws and began creaming butter. She was going to get past it this time. It had been six years. She *had* to move past it. Then, the screech cut through the song.

She spun around, hit stop.

She leaned against the refrigerator, bit her knuckle as she fought back tears. Six fucking years, and she still nearly threw up every time she heard it.

The sound hadn't really been a screech. It sounded almost like a harmonica, or a train whistle. Some mistake from the sound board, most likely. It had been a second, a blip that she wouldn't even remember from any other show. Especially one that ended with a "Dark Star" encore. She'd come out of that show flying so high on adrenaline, she hadn't needed drugs.

It wasn't until the next day, when she'd stood in line for the pay phone, had made a rare call home, that she'd found out her sister was gone. And it wasn't until Jesse had brought that tape home that she'd remembered that sound.

Late at night, unable to sleep as she so often had been back then, her mind had made the connection.

The show had started at seven. They almost always did.

That was ten on the east coast. The time the restaurant Peyton had gone to closed its doors, the time she'd climbed into her convertible Volkswagen Cabriolet.

By then Bailey had been surrounded by thousands of Deadheads, blissfully immersed in Bobby's voice, singing about Moses wearing spurs while riding a quasar, in need of a left-handed monkey wrench.

Peyton had been alone in her car, on a dark country road, driving way too fast. She'd certainly have been singing, too. She'd have chosen something from "Les Miserables" or "The Phantom of the Opera" though.

The coincidence, the sound on the tape at exactly that time, was too much. It didn't matter that her rational brain knew the two had nothing to do with each other, for Bailey they would forever be intertwined.

Shaking, she slid the tape back in the case. She didn't know why she even kept that show. She couldn't listen to it, had never made it past the point when she knew what night it was. Determined not to make that mistake again, she put the tape in a junk drawer, shoving it all the way to the back.

She should have done that years ago.

She pulled the box of tapes off the shelf and read the names. "Something good. Come on, Bailey. Pick something else." She grabbed Springfield '85, jammed it in the player and hit the button. It was half-way through the tape, nearing the end of "Slipknot!" She'd have loved to start from the beginning, but she couldn't wait for it to rewind.

As she continued creaming the sugar into the butter, the first notes of "Franklin's Tower" filled the kitchen, and her mind. She'd thought, for a long time, the name of the song was "Roll Away the Dew". The Dead were great at naming songs for something obscure, instead of the one line everyone knew.

The familiarity of her routine was soothing. She moved through her morning, focusing on the here and now, forcing the past to the background of her mind.

She opened the door at six-thirty to let in customers who were lining up outside, despite the frigid Vermont weather. A young couple wearing ski jackets were first through the door. The girl grinned and gripped the guy's hand with both of hers as he placed their order.

Bailey made coffees and packaged cookies for a couple guys in brown canvas Carhartt jackets. She asked, "Working outside today?"

The taller one answered, "Comes with the territory."

"Stay warm." She handed them their orders.

When Rain came downstairs she gave him the organic blend without having to ask what he wanted. As he took it, he told her, "Lucy's picking me up, and I'm gonna catch a ride back with Kayla later. So, I'll see you tonight?"

She liked that he was coming back. "I'll be here."

When there was a lull she tidied up, washed the dishes from the morning's baking, and browsed a catalog of restaurant equipment. There was a page of blenders, and a list of things to make with them. She didn't serve alcohol, so daiquiris were out, but smoothies were a possibility. *No one around here has them, except that place in the mall, Orange Julius.*

The bell above the door jingled. She set the catalog and her list aside and greeted a sister with beads threaded into her dreads. "Hey now. What can I get'cha?"

"Do you have echinacea tea?"

"I do."

By the time she served the tea there were three more people in line to distract her from whatever thoughts she didn't want to have.

* * *

In Connecticut Teague would have had his pick of dozens of attorneys in his immediate area. In Vermont, there were six who advertised criminal defense in the entire Yellow Pages. Two had declined to take the case over the phone. He'd met with three of the others and hadn't been comfortable with any of them. There was something about meeting in someone's living room, or converted garage, that didn't instill confidence in him.

His final appointment was at an actual office, in an actual town. A city, by Vermont standards. He'd skipped Rich's Citgo, hoping there'd be a Dunkin' Donuts.

If there wasn't, he'd be shit out of luck. He thought he'd left early but it took *for-ev-er* to get anywhere. There were no highways, and the back roads all curved between high, rounded mountains with nothing but an unbroken blanket of trees on them.

He started to think he'd done something wrong— there was no way the town was this far away. Then he came around a curve and in front of him was a picturesque town nestled between the hills.

At the first real intersection he scanned the buildings as he waited for a traffic light. The town green was to his left, with streets on all four sides. On each street, across from the green, was a row of two- and three-story buildings, mostly brick, and all with storefronts at street level.

There was a Woolworth's at the end of the block across from him and a boxy looking grocery store that dominated the block to his left. A pizza place sat next to a women's clothing store, and a head shop stood prominently between a record store and something called Beads, Etc..

There was no sign of the iconic orange and pink Dunkin' logo. At the end of the first block he waited for a mom to hurry her two bundled-up children across the street, turned left to continue around the green, and continued to scan his surroundings.

Then he saw it— a sign proclaiming that the store below it was Bailey's. That was the name of the place that woman had given him, before she'd told him about the gas station. Even if she'd been exaggerating about it being the best coffee around, it had to be better than Rich's Citgo.

The closest available parking space was half a block away. He considered driving around the green again, then glanced at the clock on the dash board. He didn't have time to try for something closer. The moment he got out of the car he regretted the decision. Bitter cold seeped through his slacks and found its way down his collar. By the time he got to the coffee shop he was shaking. He yanked the door and stepped inside.

Immediately he realized he'd made a mistake. The place had deep purple walls decorated with old Jimi Hendrix and Janis Joplin concert posters, and the Grateful Dead was playing in the background.

This was exactly the kind of place Cole would love. He'd fit right in with the long-haired guys sitting on couches in the front corner, talking to girls wearing flowered skirts and sandals. *Sandals* in January. And some of the girls had jeans on, under their dresses. Because it was too cold for a dress, but they wanted to wear it anyway? That was ridiculous.

The beginnings of a caffeine-withdrawal headache squeezing his temples, he decided he'd just get his coffee and be out quick. He stood in line and listened to the customers in front of him order organic tea and fair trade coffee, whatever that was. He jiggled his keys in his pocket.

The girl behind the counter chatted with the guy in front of him. With her baggy overalls and worn t-shirt he mistook her for a teenager. But the corners of her hazel eyes crinkled slightly when she smiled and Teague knew she had to be older than that.

If she did something with her straight brown hair she would have been cute. Except she had a stud in her nose and as she moved little silver bells jingled from the end of blue and purple string tied into her hair.

Realizing she was talking to him, he jerked his eyes away from her hair and looked at her face. "Sorry?"

Smiling, she said, "Early, huh? What can I get you?"

It wasn't early. It was going on ten. Instead of pointing that out, he said, "Coffee. Large."

"What kind?"

He glanced up at chalk boards mounted on the wall, covered in neatly written descriptions of an overwhelming assortment of coffee and tea. Looking back at the woman, he said, "Black."

She looked at him for a long moment. He started to worry. Maybe this place only served hippies. Or maybe this was one of those places where they wouldn't serve you unless you ordered by name. As far as he was concerned, there was no difference between Kona and Kenyan, he just wanted a freakin' coffee.

Then she turned and poured his drink. He began to relax.

As she put the cup on the counter, she asked, "Can I get you anything else?"

The menu board listed muffins, made with local ingredients. He asked, "What's in the muffins?"

"Today they're blueberry."

That didn't *sound* like weird-ass fair trade hippie food. He said, "I'll take one."

She bagged the muffin and rang up the sale. He handed her his credit card. She politely declined. "I'm sorry, cash only."

Frustrated with every goddamn thing, he snapped, "Forget it," and turned to leave. He'd just hope the lawyer's office offered him coffee.

The girl said, "Here, it's on me."

He turned back. "Sorry?"

"You look like you could use the coffee." She gave him an understanding smile.

He didn't want to take anything from anyone, least of all some hippie chick. But he needed that coffee, and he was holding up the line. He could practically feel the annoyance of the people behind him. Finally, he said, "I'll come back later with cash."

She pushed the bag containing the muffin towards him. "No need. I hope your day gets better."

Unsure if this was really okay, he took the cup and the bag and headed for the door.

He wasn't even outside when the guilt started. He had no right taking handouts. He wouldn't have, if there hadn't been a line behind him, and if that girl hadn't been so insistent. And if his head hadn't been pounding.

He took a sip of the coffee. Then another.

Weird-ass hippie crap or not, whatever she'd put in his cup was amazing.

The lawyer's office was just a few doors down. Teal paint peeled from the door under a weathered black sign with the Scales of Justice painted in gold on it. The signs of neglect didn't indicate a conscientious attorney.

Resigned to wasting his morning interviewing another ill-suited lawyer, he stepped through the door of *Whitney and Finkel, Attorneys at Law.* He introduced himself to the receptionist, "Attorney Gallagher, here to meet Attorney Whitney."

The woman looked like a grandmother, with snow white hair held back on one side with bobby pins. "Nice to meet you. Have a seat, I'll let him know you're here."

She picked up the phone and he turned to survey the half dozen chairs in the small waiting area, their maroon upholstery showing age. He chose one and sat. He stared straight ahead, feeling like the receptionist was looking at him. He could imagine her at the water cooler, telling the other women that she'd met the lawyer whose brother was a drug dealer.

His stomach rumbled. *Can't sink much lower than brother of a drug dealer. Might as well eat the muffin.* Feeling like a kid sneaking candy, he broke off a piece. It was moist, full of berries, it practically melted in his mouth. He nearly moaned, it was so good.

"Attorney Gallagher?"

Startled, he jerked his head up. "Yes?" He hoped he hadn't moaned. He wasn't actually sure.

"Follow me, please." As the woman started down the hall, she glanced back at him. "Can I get you a coffee?"

The idea of law office coffee paled in comparison to what he had in his cup. "No, thank you. I stopped on my way here." He raised the paper cup, showing her the "B" on the front.

Conspiratorially, she said, "I don't blame you. Bailey's is the best." She led him to a conference room. "Why don't you go ahead and finish your breakfast. I'll wait a minute before I send him in."

"Thank you." He sat in one of the black leather chairs and set his bag and cup on the long wooden table. He considered not finishing his breakfast, but the way the woman had said it, he felt like he had to. Like not eating would disappoint her.

Just as he finished a middle-aged guy came in. He gave the impression of a linebacker, despite that he wore a suit. The grey at his temples accentuated the youthfulness of his face. "My mother tells me you've been to Bailey's this morning."

Teague stood, feeling more than a little embarrassed at getting caught eating. "I was."

"Good choice." He held out his hand. As Teague shook it, he said, "Call me Bill."

"Teague. Thank you for taking the time to meet with me, Bill."

Settling into the chair across from Teague, Bill folded his hands on the table and said, "Tell me about Cole."

Teague sat back down. "I don't know details. Just that he was arrested on Monday for possession with intent to sell."

Bill waved him off. "I know the charges. Tell me about your brother."

Unsure how he was supposed to answer, he didn't say anything.

"Does he work? Go to school? Play an instrument?"

"No. He doesn't do any of that." He said the only thing he could think of. "He follows the Grateful Dead."

Leaning back in his chair and folding his hands together, Bill said, "We have quite a few Deadheads around here. Some of the nicest people you could ever know. They also have some of the best drugs around, and in the eyes of the law drugs are drugs, even when it's just pot."

Teague had no idea how to respond.

Bill smiled. "Not what you were expecting?"

"Not really."

Bill leaned forward, putting his arms on the table. "The first thing we have to do is find out exactly what really happened, and if Cole is in fact guilty. If he is, the best course of action may well be a plea bargain. But I looked over the police report, spent some time trying to put pieces together, and I'm not sure your brother did anything wrong."

Picturing the glass pipe on the coffee table, the rolling papers he'd found in the silverware drawer, he said, "He's definitely doing things wrong."

"My job isn't to pass judgment on Cole's choices. It's to secure the best possible outcome for him in this case. I'm not gonna lie to you. The police report details some pretty crazy shit. It may be that the best we can hope for is a lighter sentence. He has no prior record, he's got strong family ties, and I'd be very surprised if he has any behavior issues while he's in custody. We can try for five years, with probation after that. But before I go that route, I'll need to know the truth."

Teague liked that Bill wasn't giving him bullshit lines about how he'd won every case he'd ever tried. He'd already done research, and he knew about Deadheads. He wasn't what Teague had imagined, what he'd been looking for when he'd started, but he knew in his gut he was the right choice. "What do you need to get started?"

Chapter 5

As soon as Aria was through the front door, practically dragging Ellen behind her, she said, "Auntie Bailey, can I watch cartoons?"

"Morning, Aria. Not yet. We're going shopping." Bailey grabbed her coat from the rack by the back door.

Ellen looked frazzled as she told Bailey, "We've had," she glanced at Aria, "a rough morning. She hasn't had breakfast yet."

Bailey assured her mom, "I've got it."

"Thanks." Ellen looked grateful. "Aria, I'll see you this afternoon. Be good for Auntie Bailey, please."

Aria folded her arms and pouted.

"Aria, would you like a muffin?" Bailey slipped her coat on.

"No."

"Okay. Then you can wait to eat until we're done with our errands." She took Aria's hand and followed her mom out the door.

On the sidewalk outside, Ellen gave Aria a hug and a kiss. "I'll see you tonight."

Giving her a mad face, Aria grudgingly said, "Bye, Nannie."

Ellen turned towards her car, and Bailey gently pulled Aria the other direction.

As they passed the travel agency two doors down from her shop, Bailey asked, "What's up, sweetie?"

"Danielle from school says her mom lets her watch cartoons in her

41

pajamas on Saturday morning." She stomped a clump of snow. "But I have to get up and get dressed, cuz Nannie has to work. And now I gotta go shopping?"

She understood what it felt like to have to do something you didn't want to. "Well, I suppose if you really don't want to come, I could ask Ann Marie if you can stay at the shop with her."

"Really?"

She glanced down at her niece. She couldn't really do that. It was one thing for Aria to be there with Bailey. It was completely different for Bailey to leave her niece with an employee, during her shift. "I could. But then, who would beg me for ice cream?"

"I could beg before you leave."

Smiling at Aria's ingenuity, she said, "You could. But what if I forgot, since you weren't right there to remind me?"

Aria rolled her eyes. "You wouldn't forget. *You* care about what I want."

The way she stressed 'you' Bailey knew there was a problem. She stopped and squatted next to Aria so she could look at her eye to eye. "Is this about cartoons?"

"I never getta do anything the other kids do. It's not fair."

"Is there something specific you want to do?"

"Danielle gets to watch TV all the time, and I don't know what she's always talking about, and even Mallory watches *Ducktales* and..." Her lip trembled, "I can't cuz after school I gotta be with you. And I tried to tell Nannie but she said it was just a TV show, and not any reason to cry."

She searched Aria's face, trying to look at the whole thing from her perspective. "Was this this morning, when Nannie was getting ready for work?"

"Um hm. Because I just getted to see the song at the beginning, and she made me turn it off."

"That must have been frustrating." She sighed. "Can I think about this, and see if we can come up with a solution?"

"Really?"

"Yeah, really. Nannie has to work, and so do I. But what you need is important, too." She stood and started walking again, crossing the street diagonally and continuing down the row of stores that fronted the south side of the town green. "You know, when I was your age I used to do Saturday shopping with my dad. We'd go to the hardware store first, because he was always doing projects."

"Like painting?"

"Sometimes, but not the kind of painting me and you do. He liked to build things, like the book cases at Nannie's, and the bird feeders in the back yard. So sometimes he needed paint, or wood or finishing nails, or a lot of other things. Then, after that, we'd stop in to see my grandma for a minute." She had to pause until the lump in her throat passed. "My dad always had a little something for his mom. A book he knew she'd like, or some new yarn. She liked to knit, so she always loved it when he brought yarn."

"Nannie knits."

"She does. She made the hat you're wearing, didn't she?"

"But she let me make the pompom." She glanced up at Bailey, her cheeks pink from the cold.

Bailey tugged lightly at the purple hat. "You did a great pompom." They were coming to the end of the second block, and the first stop on their trip. "We're going into Woolworth's today."

"What for?"

"To see how much a blender costs, if it's more expensive here or from a catalog."

When they stepped inside, Aria pointed at the lunch counter. "They have ice cream there."

For years Bailey had intentionally avoided the lunch counter at

Woolworth's, and ice cream in general. "They do." She almost pulled Aria towards the blenders. But she remembered how grown up she'd felt, sitting on the tall stool with the red vinyl on the top, having ice cream with her dad. It had been the best part of Saturday shopping. *Aria deserves to eat ice cream. This is your hang up, not hers.* "Do you want some?"

Aria's jaw dropped. "Ice cream for *breakfast*? Yes!"

Bailey led her to the counter and sat down. She pretended not to see that Aria struggled to climb up on the stool. She also ignored the triumphant look when she managed it. Once Aria was settled she asked, "What kind of ice cream do you want?"

"What do they have?"

The waitress came over. "Good morning. Can I get you coffee to start?"

Bailey said, "Actually, we'd like ice cream."

Raising a penciled eyebrow, she said, "Sure."

Aria asked, "Do you have chocolate? With whipped cream?" She snuck a glance at Bailey, then added, "The kind in a can?"

Bailey smiled into her hand. Aria wasn't usually allowed to have whipped cream from a can, and definitely not at nine in the morning.

"Sure thing." The waitress looked to Bailey. "And for you?"

Her dad had always ordered strawberry. She always had too, because he had. "Chocolate and whipped cream sounds perfect. Do you have fudge, too? For both? And chocolate sprinkles?"

"You got it. Those'll be right up."

Sitting there, looking down at Aria, Bailey couldn't help thinking how much her dad would have loved the little girl. How he would have taken her for ice cream every Saturday. *You should not have come here.* She pushed down that feeling.

This was for Aria, who was there, alive and vibrant, and not bogged down by memories of people who had died before she could have known them. Aria, who needed her aunt, because she'd never have her mom. Bailey looked away, quickly wiping tears from her eyes. *Jesus, sistah, get your shit together.*

Aria twisted back and forth on the stool a few times. "Why do you need'a see how much a blender is?"

Glad of the distraction, she said, "I thought in the summer I'd make smoothies, like they have at the mall, because it's hot and people don't always want coffee."

"Oh." She swung her feet. "You could make milkshakes, too. With a blender."

"We better make sure we get a good one, then."

"Definitely." Aria looked so serious, it made Bailey grin.

The waitress brought their sundaes. "Can I get you ladies anything else?"

"I think we're good, thank you." Bailey picked up her spoon and began to scoop ice cream.

Aria giggled and whispered, "She called us ladies."

"Why is that funny?"

"That's what you call old people." She took a bite of whipped cream.

Curious, Bailey asked, "You don't think I'm old?"

"Well, I mean, you are. But not like her." She pointed at the waitress, whose grey roots were showing at the top of her unnaturally orange hair.

"How old do you think I am?"

Aria tipped her head, thinking. "Fifty...hundred?"

Bailey snorted. "Not even close."

Between bites of ice cream she asked, "How old are you?"

"Twenty-five."

"That's old."

"Thanks, kid."

"Did my mom come with you and your dad shopping?"

Aria hardly ever asked anything about Peyton. "No, baby. Your mom had voice lessons on Saturdays." All the time Peyton had spent doing things— voice lessons and theater practice and choir— had been time Bailey had spent with her dad. *He loved you. You know damn well he didn't leave you on purpose.*

"Why did she need voice lessons?"

Realizing that probably didn't make a lot of sense to a six year old, she said, "Your mom wanted to be a singer." Not into trying to explain opera, she said, "Like on the radio."

"Oh." Aria ate a scoop of ice cream. "Did Jerry have to take voice lessons?"

She laughed involuntarily, then said, "I'm pretty sure he didn't." To stave off the inevitable, she added, "Not Bobby, Phil, or any of the other guys, either."

"So how'd they get on the radio?"

"They were just lucky, I guess."

* * *

Aria started up the outside stairs, headed for Bailey's apartment. Bailey called her back as she opened the door that went directly from her back patio into the coffee shop's kitchen. "Come this way, please. We're going to check on the shop before we go up."

In the kitchen, Bailey told her, "You can leave that bag here for now and go get a muffin."

Aria set the bag of groceries she'd carried on the counter and skipped into the shop. Bailey set her own bags on the counter and let Delilah out. By the time she followed Aria, the little girl was already seated on a couch, having an animated conversation with a woman with long red hair.

Bailey stepped behind the counter. "Hey, Ann Marie. Everything going okay?"

"We're running low on raw sugar. I added it to your list." She leaned close and lowered her voice. "That guy over there," she glanced at a customer then quickly back to Bailey, "was asking for you."

The yuppie guy from the day before, the one who hadn't had cash, was reading a newspaper at the table in the front corner. "What's he want?"

"I don't know. But he said he'd wait for you to get back."

"He asked for me specifically?"

"Not by name. He said he was looking for the woman with the hair wrap, who had been working here yesterday morning." She laughed a little. "He didn't say hair wrap, though. He said 'the thing, with the bells, in her hair.'"

Bailey remembered the feeling she'd had, like she knew him from somewhere. *Aria's father?* Peyton had never told anyone who he was, and Bailey had long ago given up on figuring it out. But once in a while it crossed her mind. *He's exactly the kind of guy Peyton'd have gone for. The gelled hair, the Oakley sunglasses. I bet he drives a BMW.* She'd almost decided to go over to his table when he looked up. Their eyes met and this time there was the definite spark of recognition.

He made his way over. Bailey met him at the end of the counter. *His eyes are brown. Aria's are blue, which has to come from her father.* Having already known it was a ridiculous idea, most likely brought on by the fact she and Aria had been talking about Peyton that morning, she dismissed it easily. *There is something, though, about his eyes.*

"I wanted to thank you for yesterday, and to pay you back." He pulled cash from his pocket.

Bailey leaned against the counter. She had no intention of taking his money. "I appreciate that, but there's no need."

He continued to hold the money out.

She considered him for a long moment. *He probably* does *drive a*

BMW. She took the money. "Thank you." He started to turn away. She almost let him. Then, on a whim, she asked, "Do I know you?"

He turned back, looking as puzzled as she felt.

She clarified, "I mean, from somewhere else? Before yesterday?"

"No." He went back to his table and began gathering up his newspaper.

Chapter 6

Teague had intended to go to Rich's Citgo. Instead, he'd somehow ended up at Bailey's and he was now enjoying a perfect cup of coffee.

He leafed through the morning paper. Apparently the town council was looking to purchase open land, to protect the area from over-development. That was freakin' hysterical, considering that there was basically nothing between his house and town except trees. There was a craft bazaar at the First Congregational Church next weekend, and a local kid was competing in the state level spelling bee.

Laughter rolled through the room. He looked up, to the couches in the opposite corner. There were a bunch of hippies sitting around. Maybe the same ones as the first day he'd been there. Maybe not. They all looked the same to him. Long hair on both the girls and the guys. Clothes that didn't match, or fit. It would have driven him crazy if his jeans dragged, especially since there was snow on the ground.

They all looked perfectly comfortable, regardless of the fit of their clothes.

He looked back down at his newspaper, turned the page, and froze. Cole's mug shot stared at him. *Jesus, he* looks *like a fucking drug dealer.* His tangled hair hung past the sign he held and his beard was fuller than the last time Teague had seen him, but it was his brother's eyes that did it. They had the same sketchy look criminals always seemed

49

to have in mug shots.

There was a half-page article with the photo. Teague read it, his stomach churning more with each paragraph. He'd known some of the information, but there was much more than he'd been given when he'd called the police department. Cole had been picked up just yards from the entrance of an abandoned farm, where *someone* had set up an illegal growing operation. A trail of footprints in the snow led to the greenhouse, where hundreds of plants in all stages of maturity were being cultivated. It seemed pretty obvious that "someone" was Cole, and he'd been out to check his crop.

It was a triumph for the DEA. They'd been watching the operation, waiting for the perpetrator to show up. One of the officers who'd been part of the investigation was quoted as saying the war on drugs was in full swing and this was proof the government was winning.

Christ, he'd been lucky Bill had been willing to take Cole as a client. It was a slam dunk for the state.

* * *

It was driving Bailey insane. Every time she looked at that yuppie guy, the familiarity tickled her brain.

Mostly it was his eyes. The deep brown, surrounded by dark lashes, the unique way they went up a little at the outer corners. She wondered what they'd look like if he ever smiled.

It was possible that he was someone she'd gone to high school with. Or maybe she'd seen him around. Other than the two years she'd spent on tour, she'd lived in town her whole life. She knew a lot of people.

He'd been sitting at the corner table all morning, was on his second coffee, and she couldn't stop thinking about it. There was only one other person there— Sage, taking a nap on one of the couches.

Normally during a lull she'd have wiped down tables. Instead, she poured herself a cup of coffee and walked over to the yuppie.

"May I?" He looked up. She indicated the seat across from him and sat. "We haven't formally met. I'm Bailey."

Surprise flashed over his features, quickly replaced by a frown.

"I hope you're enjoying your coffee."

Cautiously, he said, "I am, thank you."

"Are you new to Vermont?"

He folded his hands over his newspaper. "I'm just visiting."

"Are you here for work, or play?"

He cleared his throat. "I'm here on family business."

"You have family here?" That seemed promising. Maybe she *had* seen him around.

"Sort of." He stared at her. It was not a friendly look.

Family business could be just about anything, from a wedding to a funeral. She remembered how it had driven her crazy when people wouldn't stop pestering her after her dad had died. Feeling really bad for bothering him, she said, "I hope things work out for you."

The muscles in his cheek tightened visibly as he clenched his jaw.

She wanted to say that if he needed anything to let her know. But that was stupid. She didn't actually know this guy, or what his family business was. Instead, she asked, "Will you be back in tomorrow?"

He glanced around, then settled his gaze back on her. He didn't say anything.

This wasn't getting her anywhere. She stood, started to walk away, then turned back. She almost asked his name, but already he was back to reading the paper.

* * *

Teague had to call his mother. If he didn't give her an update soon she'd call him, and probably be pissed he hadn't called her. When she answered he got straight to the point. "I found a lawyer. He's going out to talk to Cole today. The pretrial is set for Friday, I'll call you when I get out of court and let you know what's happening."

"Have you been to visit your brother?"

Her accusing tone put him on the defensive. "No. Before you can visit an inmate they have to put you on their visitors list, then the warden has to vet you. There's forms, requests for information, everything will have to be sent state to state, it's going to be a long time before I can see him." Then he added, "You can go. Parents and spouses don't need to be vetted."

"As you are fully aware, I'm at the house in Vero Beach. I can't exactly drop everything and fly up to Vermont."

Yeah, but you expected me to drop everything to save him. "I'll let you know when I have more information."

He set the receiver back in the cradle and tried to figure out how long it would be until he'd be able to see Cole. *Monday night they'd have held him at the police station, and everything would have revolved around his arraignment on Tuesday. He'd have been transferred to prison after court. Most likely he'd have made his visitors list that night with they did his intake. The applications are probably already in the mail. And he'd have sent mine to Marlena's. Damn it. I'm going to have to call her.*

He picked the phone up, listened to the dial tone, and set it back down. Twice. "Fuck, just do it."

If he didn't talk to her there was a good possibility she'd just throw the application in the trash, if she hadn't already. He picked the phone up again and dialed.

She answered on the third ring. "Hello?"

He cleared his throat. "Marlena, hey. It's Teague." *Dumbass, she knows who you are.*

Her tone went instantly icy. "The things you left behind are boxed up. You can get them tomorrow."

"I can't get there tomorrow. Maybe next week—"

"Tomorrow. I'll be here between ten and noon. After that, it's all going out on the curb. Oh, and you need to call work." The line went dead.

She boxed stuff? What'd I even leave there? He pictured the condo, mentally walked through it. He'd left all his suits, and whatever other clothes he hadn't taken. A box of papers— income tax returns, the paperwork for his car loan, bank statements. A coffee mug his niece had given him for Christmas.

Is it really worth it to face Marlena for some suits, a bunch of papers and a coffee mug? Maybe I can wait until she puts everything outside, then take it. But I'd have to drive all the way back there. And that doesn't solve the actual issue. I need that application.

The phone began to beep loudly. He pressed the button on the top of the base, then let it go. He called back and was happy that the machine picked up. "Marlena, Cole doesn't know I'm in Vermont, so he probably sent a visitors application there. I know you're pissed, but I'd really appreciate it if you could forward it to me." He gave the address and hung up.

He began to dial his office. His fingers, though, dialed his oldest brother, Shea. He colored triangles in the margins of his notepad as the phone rang, then as he explained to Shea's receptionist who he was.

Finally, his brother came on the line. "Teague? What's up?"

"Hey, Shea. Have you talked to Mom lately?"

"Not since Christmas. Why?"

He said, "Cole's in jail, in Vermont."

"What for?"

"Possession with intent to sell."

"Can't say I'm surprised." He paused, then added, "I don't really know what I'm supposed to say. Or ask. Or do."

Teague smiled at Shea's uncharacteristic awkwardness. "Nothing, really. I just thought you should know."

"I assume you're taking care of it?"

"I've hired someone. I don't do this kind of thing."

"Does Dad know?"

"I haven't called him, and I can't imagine Mom did either."

He laughed bitterly. "No. I'm sure she hasn't. Are you going to?"

Teague sighed. "Yeah. Callum, too." He colored in another triangle. "If you need to get in touch with me, I'm staying at the house in Vermont."

"Let me know if there's anything I can do to help."

He almost blew that off. Then he had an idea. "Ya know, actually, there is." He explained about Marlena, and the boxes of his stuff, and was relieved when Shea said he'd send one of his interns to pick it all up. He thanked Shea and hung up.

Now he had another issue, though. Calling his father wasn't something he'd considered. Their relationship basically consisted of very short conversations on major holidays, and Teague liked it that way.

Hoping to make it short and sweet, he dialed his father's number. The answering machine picked up. *Perfect.* He prepped a message while he listened to the outgoing one, then said, "Hi, Dad. It's Teague. I thought you should know Cole was arrested, he's in jail in Vermont. I'm staying at the house up here, if you want to call me back." He spieled off the number and hung up. Hopefully his father wouldn't call back.

He checked the time, figured what time it was in San Francisco. Callum didn't have a set work schedule, so anything after ten in the morning was fair game. He got his brother's answering machine and left a message.

He sat at the kitchen table for a long time, thinking. He really should call work and check on his cases. There was the couple who were fighting over custody of their dog. And the wife who was holding her soon-to-be ex's bowling ball hostage.

Then there were the people with actual issues. The one where the wife had given up her career to care for her mother-in-law full time. The couple who had used a sperm donor, and now she said he had no rights to the child because it wasn't actually his. It wasn't legal, but the mom was keeping the little girl from seeing the man she'd always known as her dad.

Teague would have loved to represent both those cases, if he'd been on the other side. *That dad doesn't deserve to be kept from his daughter. Damn it, that was specifically the kind of shit I wanted to prevent.*

He wasn't calling work.

Instead, he was going to clean. He couldn't continue stepping over that boot in the living room forever.

He started with the pizza box on top of the TV, then picked up the overflowing ash tray that had been on an end table. There was what looked like half a joint in it. Cole would probably be pissed if he threw it out. He dumped the ash tray, joint and all.

Once he'd had a guy who'd cited 'refusal to clean' as the reason for filing for divorce. Teague had thought that was the most bullshit reason ever. If he'd been able, he'd have divorced Cole.

* * *

Bailey pushed chairs in, threw out trash, fanned out a stack of magazines on top of a bookcase. She cleared tables, stacking newspapers customers had left in case someone else wanted to read them. The yuppie had left his paper, folded with the center out. She unfolded it, smoothed the pages in the middle.

Cole's mug shot looked back at her, to the right of the story of his arrest. She sank into the chair, her chest squeezing painfully. He looked so scared.

She couldn't blame him.

She knew only the most basic information. The article gave so much more. Tears clouded her vision as she realized how much trouble he was in.

When she finished, she set the paper down and leaned back in the chair. It didn't make sense. The police had been watching that place for months. But Cole had been gone all summer. He hadn't come back until after fall tour had ended.

Any plants he'd started the last time he'd been around would have died while he'd been away.

She picked up the paper, looked at the mug shot again. He had such beautiful eyes, it was a shame to see them looking so…

Holy fuck.

The realization was so powerful she nearly dropped the paper.

Those eyes. She knew she'd recognized them.

The yuppie had the same eyes.

Chapter 7

Teague attempted to reposition himself on the wooden bench as Bill, Cole's attorney, settled at the defendants' table. Cole, in handcuffs and leg irons, was led in from a door off to the side. He scanned the room, his eyes seeming darker than usual in his unnaturally pale face. When he found Teague he seemed to relax a bit. Casting his gaze down, he allowed himself to be led to the seat next to his lawyer.

Seeing Cole in ill-fitting, navy blue prison garb, looking so completely dejected, was a shock.

The last time he'd seen his brother had been at Christmas. He'd been the same as he always was, happy to be home, talking about places he'd been and things he'd done, always wanting to know what everyone else was doing. *And we didn't listen. Not really, anyway. We all wanted him to be gone, because he's embarrassing, with his long hair, his stories of sleeping outside, his lack of a job.*

Teague's stomach churned with the realization that Cole wouldn't be home for Christmas next year, or for many years to come. The next time he'd be there for a holiday everything would be different. Their niece and nephews wouldn't run to Uncle Cole, excited to have someone willing to play pirates or knights in shining armor with them. They'd possibly be married, with kids of their own. *This is real. Christ, Cole's in jail and they're going to keep him for fifteen years. And I'm going to let them.*

57

Cole waived his right to a jury and the next court date was set.

The judge asked Cole if he was able to post bail. Guilt bloomed, huge and hard in Teague's stomach. It wouldn't have been any problem for him, or their mother, to arrange for Cole to be released. But they'd agreed it was too risky; he'd be gone before the ink on the check was dry. So he watched in silence as his brother was remanded to the custody of the State.

Cole didn't look at Teague as he was led back though the side door, his shoulders slumped in defeat.

* * *

Teague sat in the corner at Bailey's and stared into his coffee. After leaving the courthouse he'd sat in his car for a full twenty minutes telling himself he could *not* bail Cole out, no matter how badly he wanted to. Cole was guilty, and he was going to have to pay his debt to society.

It had still been a struggle. He'd deserted his little brother when he'd needed him most.

One of the guys on the other side of the room asked loudly, "Bail! Turn this up?"

The background music got louder. Teague knew this song. A version of it had been in a movie Marlena had dragged him to. The one with Tom Cruise, where his brother was an idiot savant. *You are the biggest piece of shit. Tom Cruise didn't desert his brother.*

The people on the couches sang loudly, pointing at each other across the coffee table and yelling, "Hey now!" along with the music. One girl got up and started dancing.

"May I?"

He jerked his gaze to Bailey as she sat across from him without waiting for an answer.

She folded her hands around a big blue mug. "You're Cole's brother."

He stared, stunned. "How'd you—"

"It was your eyes. I knew the first time I saw you they looked familiar." She smiled a little. "Cole told me once they were Scandinavian eyes." The smile was replaced by concern. "Have you seen him?"

Of course she knows Cole. "No."

She searched his face, then said, "I'm sorry, I didn't mean to bother you." She stood. "If you do see him, could you let him know everyone's thinking about him? I don't know if it'll help, but, anyway..." She turned and walked away, went behind the counter and did something at the back so he couldn't see her face.

You really are the biggest piece of shit. All she did was ask about him. You could have at least been nice. What if she's his girlfriend? She'd deserve to know what to expect.

He went to the counter, where she was watching the people dancing. "Bailey?"

She turned, a smile fading from her lips as she folded her arms.

Guilt wormed into his stomach. "Cole's pretrial was this morning. His lawyer says the state is confident they'll get a conviction, and they're planning to make an example of him." He finished, "I'm sorry, it doesn't look good."

"What's your name?" Gently, she added, "Unless you want me to just call you Cole's brother."

There was concern etched on her face, in the lines around her eyes and the tight set of her lips. He answered, "Teague."

"Teague." She repeated it, as if experimenting. "That's nice. What does it mean?"

"You make a habit of asking strangers what their names mean?" As soon as the words were out of his mouth he wished he could take them back.

She just smiled, though, and said, "You're not a stranger. And yeah, sometimes I do."

That seemed so weird, he asked, "Why?"

She held his gaze. Her eyes were the most intriguing combination of green and brown. "I had a history teacher who made us do a report on the origins of our names, which we had to present to the class. It was fascinating, especially because so often the meaning of a name seemed to fit the ideals of the parents, and had nothing do with the child. But the way the kids felt about their name sometimes shaped their entire life, especially if they didn't like it."

His curiosity piqued, he asked, "So what does Bailey mean?"

"Bailiff." She smiled a bit. "I don't mind my name, or the meaning. Although I'm pretty sure my parents didn't know what it meant when they chose it."

"Why did they choose it?"

"When my mom was pregnant with me she heard some lady in the grocery store scolding her daughter, Bailey. She liked the name."

The smile that spread over his face was as unexpected as this entire conversation. "So you were named after a misbehaving child?"

"Yeah, I was." Her smile grew, too. "What about you?"

"I don't know what my name means, only that my parents were going for all Irish names. My older brothers are Shea and Callum. Although I think they gave up by the time they got to Cole." Thinking about his brother, the heaviness that had started to lift settled back. "As soon as I can see Cole I'll let him know you're thinking about him."

"Thank you." Her smiled was replaced by a much more somber expression.

He felt compelled to ask, "Are you going to be okay?"

Her eyebrows drew together for a moment, then her expression cleared. "Family's kind of... I mean, Deadheads are... It happens. You get used to it. What about you?"

Reflexively, he said, "I'm fine."

She looked into his eyes for a moment, then said, "Thanks, for letting me know about Cole."

"Yeah, of course." He didn't really know what to say, nothing seemed appropriate. But he didn't need to say anything. Bailey turned away, went over to the group of people on the other side of the room and started talking.

Teague ignored the glances thrown his way as he dropped his cup in the trash and left.

As he settled into the car, he wondered what Cole's name meant. *That's stupid. It's not like it matters.* But the thought was there, and it grew as he drove. Maybe their names were appropriate, maybe not.

If they'd been named for who they were, Cole's name would mean 'dreamer'. When the other boys had been outside playing football, or building forts or climbing trees, Cole had been content to stay inside playing with Matchbox cars or toy rockets. Teague could still hear him talking to himself, making up stories of how he was going to fly to the moon and make friends with all the aliens. He'd come home from school one day with a drawing of what he thought an alien looked like, and he'd spent all of dinner showing his older brothers and telling them about all the amazing powers the alien had. They'd humored him, as they always did, asking for more and more details. After a while their mother had stated, in her usual cold tone, *'They've already landed on the moon, and there's no little green men there.'* Teague could still feel her disapproval as they finished dinner in silence.

We had a lot of dinners in silence. Cole's imagination wasn't the only thing their mother disapproved of. Shea's need to turn everything into a competition, Callum's quick witted humor, and Teague's insatiable questions all annoyed her. It had been so obvious that she disliked children, he'd often wondered why she'd had four of them.

He parked the car and climbed out. As he stepped onto the porch he heard the phone. He jammed the key in the doorknob and prayed he'd get to the kitchen before the caller hung up.

At least there was no boot to trip over anymore.

He grabbed the handset. "Hello?"

"Teague?"

"Hey, Wendy." Recognizing the young paralegal's voice, his mind raced as he tried to change gears. "What's up?"

"I was just wondering if everything was okay. And when you thought you might be back."

He began to pace. "I'm not sure. Things aren't going quite the way I'd expected."

"You should call Phillip and let him know what's going on with you. I was in HR filling out a vacation request form, and I heard him saying the last he heard from you was when you tried to pawn off the Constantine prenup, which he wasn't happy about. He thinks you made up the story about a family emergency to get out of it. And he said if you're not back on Monday morning they're going to start scheduling interviews."

He didn't know what to say. He settled on, "Thanks for letting me know."

"Teague, are you okay? I mean, this isn't like you at all."

No shit. "Yeah, I'm okay. I really am dealing with family issues."

"Call Phillip."

After he hung up, he sat at the table and stared at the phone. The easiest thing to do would be to go home. Call Shea and see if he could crash there until he found a new place, go back to work and straighten out whatever he needed to, and get on with his life.

Except knowing he'd have to deal with his clients made him want to vomit. People spewing their spin on their lives, intent on hurting the person they'd once loved, not caring who got caught in the crossfire. The week before Christmas he'd gotten one of his clients full custody of his kids. He'd done it by forcing the wife to admit to the judge that she'd spent part of the previous year in a psych ward. When she explained that it was because she'd been the driver in the car accident that had killed her father, Teague had used that to further advance the idea that she was an unfit mother, though he'd known damn well that the accident had been caused by a tractor trailer truck losing its brakes.

When he'd walked out of the courthouse the woman was kneeling with her children, her arms around them, her shoulders shaking as she tearfully explained she'd see them as often as she could. The children had looked shell-shocked, and the husband smug.

So much for doing the right thing.

He'd never been a big drinker, had ignored the bottles he knew were above the refrigerator. But they were there. And the idea of letting all this go for a little while was extremely appealing. Especially because he remembered distinctly that there'd been a bottle of Jameson.

Fuck it all. He didn't even bother getting a glass.

Chapter 8

Teague chose the table farthest from the windows. The light hurt his head. If he'd been at home Marlena would have told him he deserved this for drinking too much. *She'd have been right. Guess that's one plus to this whole mess. I don't have to listen to a list of my shortcomings every time I make a mistake.*

On the other side of the room laughter erupted. There was always laughter from over there. He wondered what was so funny, and what it would be like to be in on whatever it was. To have friends who—

"Hey, Teague." Bailey sat across from him. "Are you okay?"

His brow furrowed. "Why?"

"You just look like you're having a rough day." She smiled kindly.

"I'm fine, thanks." *That's probably the world's biggest lie.*

She must have known, because after a moment she said, "I'm sorry you have to go through this."

He shook his head. "This has nothing to do with me."

She picked up a napkin, began folding and unfolding it. After a moment, she said, "Cole was here that morning, before he got arrested. Everyone who hadn't gone to the New Year's shows was, because I didn't want anyone driving drunk." She looked up at him, her expression earnest. "I keep thinking if I'd driven him home that day, or if he'd been able to get a ride with someone else, he wouldn't have gotten arrested."

He wished his head wasn't so foggy. "What does him being here have to do with him getting arrested?"

"I read the police report, in the paper. It said they arrested him on the road, in front of an abandoned farm. I let him walk home." She set the napkin down, smoothed it out. "If I'd driven him, he wouldn't have been there, and they wouldn't have arrested him."

Sure he'd misunderstood, he asked, "Cole walked home from here?"

"Yeah."

"It takes twenty minutes to get here in a car."

"Yeah."

"It's miles of twisting back roads."

Her eyebrows drew together. "Yeah. And?"

Incredulously, he asked, "Why would anyone walk that?"

"Because no one was going out that way and he didn't want to wait for me to be able to bring him."

He knew Cole didn't have a car, but he'd never thought about what that meant on a day to day basis. "Did Cole walk here and back often?"

She shrugged. "Probably."

He rubbed his hands over his face, forcing his hungover brain to work. Dropping his hands, he said, "One of the things they're holding against him is that he had no valid reason to be in the middle of nowhere, in the freezing cold on New Year's Day. But if he was on his way home, wouldn't he have just told them that?"

She snorted. "Have you ever tried— Forget it. You wouldn't understand."

"Understand what?"

She looked at him for a long moment before she said, "Teague, cops don't listen to people like Cole and me."

"That's not—" He couldn't argue. He'd doubted much of what Cole said himself.

"So, here's the thing. Cole couldn't have been growing plants."

"Why not?"

"Because it takes a lot of work." Smiling a little, she said, "I love your brother, but he's not exactly the most organized person. Or the most reliable."

"No shit. I spent this entire week cleaning up the mess he left." He shook his head in dismay. "I found a cereal bowl in the bathroom closet."

"Exactly. I mean, my mom's already ordering seeds, so she can start them in the house in March and have them ready to move outside in May. Can you see Cole doing that?"

Shocked that she'd talk about that out loud, he asked, "You mom's growing pot?"

Laughing, she said, "Tomatoes, Teague. And cucumbers, broccoli, eggplant. She has a huge garden."

His face burning with embarrassment, he said, "Oh."

"The point is, that article, in the paper? It said the greenhouse was full of plants. But even if Cole had managed to start seeds, he couldn't have maintained them. He wasn't around enough."

He had no idea what his brother did, or where he went. "Where was he?"

"On tour."

This was the thing he'd never been able to get his mind around. "Why would anyone want to see the same concert over and over?"

"Every time the Dead play it's different."

He didn't really care that much about the Dead. He was more interested in figuring out if there was something to what Bailey was saying. "Okay, so, when was he gone?"

"He caught a ride with me to Foxboro, so that was July 2. I was back here by the middle of July, but as far as I know Cole finished summer tour, then went out west." She turned to the group of people sitting on the couches. "Hey, Sage?"

A guy with shortish brown hair, standing up everywhere like he'd just gotten out of bed, turned around. "Yeah, babe?"

"You did the west coast shows in August, right?"

"*Shore* did."

"Who'd you ride with?"

"These cats from Venice."

"Did'ya see Cole?"

"Could'a. You know how it is." He grinned before turning back around.

Bailey turned back, "I can check around, but I know he was out there. And he was definitely at The Spectrum in October, because he had floor space with me. And he was in Miami, because they did a 'Dark Star' and he was psyched he'd been in."

"What's a dark star?"

She gave him a funny half-smile. "It's a song. The Dead hardly ever play it, so when they do it's a big deal."

He didn't care much about the dark star thing, and he didn't know what floor space was, but the rest was promising. He'd have to call the lawyer, first thing Monday morning.

"Teague?"

Bailey had asked him something. "Sorry, I was thinking."

"I asked if you want to come hang out. Tonight, after I close. I thought maybe you'd like to meet Cole's friends?"

He glanced at the other side of the room. "Thank you for the offer. It's not necessary, though."

"No, it's not. But you're welcome to come, if you want."

* * *

Teague settled at his kitchen table and unwrapped the grinder he'd picked up on his way home. One of the best things about eating alone was that he could use the paper wrapping as a plate. *Marlena would be horrified.* Not that he cared what Marlena thought.

The faucet dripped. "I should probably do something about that." With no one there to hear him, his voice sounded too loud.

His father would have done it himself, while his mother stood over him going on and on about how they could afford a plumber. He briefly entertained the idea of calling his father to ask how to fix it. Instead, as soon as he was done with his dinner, he drove back into town.

It looked different at night. The Christmas lights were still up on the green, giving the trees and the gazebo in the center a cheerful glow. The warm lights of storefronts spilled onto the sidewalks where a handful of people scurried through the cold to their destinations.

As he got out of the car in front of the hardware store, he noticed that on the adjacent block there was a used book store. He headed there instead.

He'd never been in a used book store but had the vague idea it would be musty and ruled over by an ancient librarian type woman. He knew he was wrong the moment he opened the door and the teenager at the counter greeted him with a friendly smile. There was no unpleasant odor and the floor to ceiling shelves were neat and tidy, arranged by subject. There were overstuffed chairs set into nooks here and there, next to tables with Tiffany lamps set on them.

He browsed the rows of books, remembering that he still had a novel he hadn't finished but thinking maybe he'd pick up something to read anyway. The problem with that novel was that Marlena had gotten it for him because it was what everyone was talking about, not because it was something he was interested in.

Skipping over the romance section, which was easily double the size of any other section, he skimmed titles of mysteries, then sci-fi, and onto thrillers.

Of all the Gallagher boys, the only one who had ever been a reader was Cole. After Shea and Callum had gone off to college and the house was substantially quieter, Cole would often tell Teague about what he was reading. One of his favorites had been *Lord of the Rings*. There didn't appear to be a copy of that on the shelves. There was, however, a copy of *The Talisman* cowritten by Stephen King and Peter Straub and he remembered Wendy from work saying she'd loved it.

Deciding it was worth a buck even if he never finished it, he moved on to the 'How To' section. He found a plumbing book, then came across one on remodeling older homes. His home could definitely use some remodeling.

On his way back to the car his eyes were drawn to Bailey's. Maybe he'd blown off her invitation to hang out too quickly. Even if he didn't fit in, it could be interesting to see what Cole's life was like. He dropped the books in the passenger seat of his BMW and continued around the block.

Pausing at the door, he watched the people inside; friends talking, laughing, being together. They wore corduroys or overalls, or jeans that were too lose, paired with tie-dyes and bulky knitted sweaters in bright colors, and shirts with pictures of dancing bears or skeletons. The yellow oxford he'd put on that morning, the tan slacks he hadn't given any thought to, would be so completely out of place.

That must be how Cole feels when he comes home.

He turned away.

Chapter 9

Bailey moved through her day making small talk with friends and regulars, greeting strangers as if they were old friends, and the whole time keeping an eye out for Teague. She wasn't surprised he hadn't taken her up on her invitation to hang out on Saturday night. However, she *was* surprised he hadn't come in on Sunday.

Maybe he went back to Connecticut. He'd have to at some point. He definitely had a job, and possibly a wife, maybe even kids.

Then he was coming through the door, getting in line. His eyes met hers and a small smile tugged at the corner of his mouth. She smiled in return. When he got to the counter she had to resist the urge to lean over and kiss his cheek, as she did with all her guy friends.

"Hi, Bailey."

"Hey now. I was starting to think you'd gone back home." His expression darkened. She added, "I'm glad you didn't."

The darkness cleared. "Can I get a coffee, please? And a muffin."

She filled his order, wondering what she'd said to upset him. After he'd settled at his regular table she glanced around the room, made sure everyone looked content, then went to join him. "You didn't come in yesterday."

"I was busy."

None of the conversations she'd had with him had been easy, she hadn't expected this one to be different. She had the feeling, though, that maybe he was glad of the company, even if he didn't show it. "Doing something good, I hope."

"Not really." He settled back into the chair. "I was deciding what I wanted to do with the rest of my life."

She raised her eyebrows. "That's a pretty big decision for a Sunday."

There was a light in his eyes that hadn't been there before. "I guess it is."

"What did you decide?"

He cleared his throat. "I decided I'm not ready to decide. So instead, I'm going to hang around here for a while and fix up my mother's house."

Curious, she asked, "You don't have to go back to Connecticut, for work or anything?"

"I," he rubbed the back of his neck, looking uncomfortable. "No."

There was definitely more to that, but she didn't want to push.

Without any prompting, he said, "I called Cole's lawyer this morning and talked to him about what you said. How Cole wasn't around to take care of plants."

"Yeah?"

Sighing, he said, "He knew that already, and it doesn't help. Cole doesn't leave any sort of provable trail. He doesn't have a checking account or credit cards, he uses cash for everything. He gets places either by getting rides with friends or hitchhiking. He stays in hotels sometimes, but he never checks in under his own name. The only hope we have of proving he was gone for the majority of the time would be to have reliable people testify that Cole was with them. And—" he stopped, looking worried.

She supplied the rest. "Family aren't the kind if people who are considered reliable."

"I'm sorry."

"It's fine. You probably wouldn't be able to talk anyone into testifying anyway." Her heart hurt, knowing that Cole was innocent and there was nothing she could do about it. "If there's anything I can do, please let me know."

Looking oddly nervous, he said, "Actually, there is something I need. Although it doesn't have to do with Cole."

"Name it."

"A plumber?" His face went beet red.

"Liam. He can do anything."

"You trust him?"

"Yeah." Puzzled, she asked, "Why?"

"I mean, is he *family*? Because," he looked supremely uncomfortable, "I can't let just anyone in."

Grinning, because Cole may have been innocent of the charges against him but he sure as hell wasn't innocent, she said, "Yeah, Teague. No worries."

"It's kind of urgent. Not an emergency, there's not water pouring all over or anything. But I can't use the kitchen sink."

"I'll get his number for you. If—"

He narrowed his eyes at her. "If what?"

She smiled slightly. "If you promise to come hang out tonight."

* * *

Teague opened the refrigerator, brought out two bottles of Sam Adams and offered one to Liam. "Thanks for coming out."

Liam waved him off. "Glad to help."

"What do I owe you?"

He held up his beer. "This should cover it."

"You were here an hour, right?" Pulling his wallet from his back pocket, Teague counted out what he thought was fair, added an extra $20, and set it on the counter.

"Bro, seriously. We're good." He finished his beer and set the bottle in the sink. "Bailey said to tell you seven tonight." He picked up his tool box and left, leaving the cash on the counter.

Resigned to having to go to Bailey's no matter how uncomfortable it was, Teague went up to his room and stared at the row of slacks and pastel shirts hanging in his closet. Everything he owned was completely inappropriate for hanging out at Bailey's.

He owned one pair of L.L.Bean jeans. They fit properly, the cuff landing half an inch above the ground, but they'd have to do. After some though he decided to borrow a shirt from Cole. At the other end of the hall, in the bedroom no one was using, he sifted through piles of laundry, glad that he'd washed all the clothes that Cole had left scattered throughout the house. His brother had an insanely huge collection of shirts. That was a good thing, since Teague didn't want to wear anything that had any type of tour on it. He'd never seen the Grateful Dead, hadn't ever listened to their music on purpose. There was no way he was going to wear one of their shirts. He considered a tie-dye, but they seemed so bright. Finally, he found a white shirt with a picture of turtles dancing in front of a train station. It wasn't anything he'd normally have chosen, but it wasn't horrible.

The entire way to town he tried to talk himself out of going. This was ridiculous. He was a lawyer, for Christ sake. He'd gone to four years of college, three years of law school, completed an apprenticeship, passed the Bar.

He was still talking himself into turning around and going home when he got to Bailey's. The door was locked but, just like last time when he'd been there after closing, the room was full of people. This time, though, he knocked.

A girl in a long, flowered dress let him in. "Teague, right?"

"Yes."

"I'm Katelyn." She locked the door behind him. "Next time you can come in the back."

"Sorry. Bailey didn't tell me."

"No big." She looped her arm through his. "Come on, I'll introduce you." She pulled him over to a loose circle of people. "You already know Liam."

He reached around Katelyn, held out his hand, "Hey, Teague. How's the kitchen?"

He shook Liam's hand. "So far so good."

Katelyn pointed to people, gave names that Teague knew he'd never remember.

A girl with shoulder length brown hair was saying, "It was like a parking lot. All because of one traffic light."

"You'd think they'd make the only road going into a place like that more than one lane." A stocky guy with black hair shook his head.

"Yeah, but bro, seriously, I made a fucking fortune selling water to people stuck in their cars."

"And Jerry was *on*. Man, unbelievable sets at those shows."

Teague had no idea what they were talking about, and he wasn't about to ask. He glanced around, wondering where Bailey was. From behind him someone started singing to the song on the radio, and all of a sudden people all over the room were joining in.

Bailey came out from the kitchen and turned the volume up. Katelyn moved closer to Liam to make room for Bailey next to Teague. "Glad you came." She tugged his shirt gently. "Nice shirt."

He started to say something about it being Cole's, but she had already turned her attention to the other people in the circle. Teague moved, let the circle close where he'd been. He didn't belong here, in Cole's clothes, with Cole's friends. Slowly, he backed towards the door. Bailey'd seen him, that was enough.

"Hey, brah." Startled, he looked down at a tiny pixie of a girl with blonde hair hanging straight to her waist. "You're Teague."

"I am."

She tipped her chin down and gave him one of the most provocative looks he'd ever seen. "I'm Kayla." A slow smile spread across her face. "Nice to meet you, finally."

"It's nice to meet you, too."

"Come on, we're going to play cards and we need another person." She slipped her arm around his waist. Despite that she came barely to his chest, she steered him easily to a table in the back corner. She took a seat next to a girl who was maybe sixteen and said, "Teague, this is Ruth," she turned to the other woman at the table, "and Lucy."

As he sat he was surprised to realize he recognized the older woman. He said, "Lucy, we've met. You gave me directions, to find coffee."

"Looks like you found it." She was probably about as old as he was. Her hair was dark blonde, with no signs of grey, but her face had a more mature look than Kayla or Ruth's. She turned to Kayla, "I hope Matt wasn't boring you with his incessant talk of hydroponics."

"Are you kidding?" Kayla gave her a huge smile. "It was fascinating."

As she shuffled the cards she said, "Sometimes I think plants are the only thing he thinks about." She glanced up and said, "He even talks about it in his sleep."

Ruth added, "Instead of Playboy, Matt keeps seed catalogs in the bathroom."

Lucy laughed. "Rummy 500?" Everyone nodded and she dealt.

As they each rearranged their cards, Kayla asked, "Ruth, are you and Lance still planning on going up to Burlington?"

"Yeah, if we can get a ride. I told him we could just hitchhike, but he's not into that."

"I can bring you tomorrow."

"I don't want to put you out."

"You're not. I'm going to St. Albans. I'm first, right?" She picked a card from the deck, considered for a moment, then discarded the same card.

When it was his turn, Teague chose a card from the deck, decided on a course of action, and discarded.

"Teague, you're from Connecticut?" Lucy asked.

"I am."

"Cool. I'm originally from Meriden."

That wasn't his neck of the woods, but he asked politely, "How'd you end up here?"

"I fell in love with Matt's farm, and then I fell in love with Matt, so it worked out pretty well for both of us." She shifted her attention and asked, "Kayla, when do you go back to school?"

"Sunday." She played her cards.

Teague asked, "Where do you go?"

"Middlebury."

Happy that this was a topic he understood, he asked, "What are you studying?"

"Bio-chemical engineering. I'd love to be able to replace fossil fuels with something renewable, ya know?"

They played two more rounds before Kayla hit five-hundred. She shuffled the cards. "Rematch?"

Trying to be as polite as possible, Teague excused himself. "I've got an early day tomorrow."

Kayla grinned. "Next time, then."

He found Bailey sitting on a couch, next to a guy with long blonde dreadlocks, and thanked her for having him. She smiled, "Yeah, of course. You're welcome anytime."

As he followed the twisting road back to the house his mind wandered. He'd expected to feel totally out of place, and he had. But Cole's friends had gone out of their way to make him feel welcome. Lucy, who was from the same place he was. Kayla, who was going to college. Liam, who had greeted him like a friend.

He remembered the last time he'd seen Marlena, how she'd said she'd had to kiss asses to get them to come to her benefit. He knew, and so had she, that those people would expect Marlena to reciprocate at some point in the future. That's how the world worked.

Your world, Teague. But not Cole's.

He pulled into his driveway and stared at the house. It wasn't fancy, or unique. It was just a boring basic house, built on an unremarkable piece of land in the middle of nowhere. But as he shut off the ignition, made his way carefully up the snowy walk, he had the oddest feeling of coming home.

Chapter 10

The first day of March, Bailey woke to the sound of birds in the gutter above her bedroom window, the lyrics of "Scarlet Begonias" running through her head. It seemed appropriate; there was still a nip to the air, but the chill of winter was definitely losing its grip.

Rain didn't budge as she climbed out of bed. She wished she could stay with him but there was baking to do. She put coffee on first. She could manage on five hours of sleep, but three was really pushing it.

The night before had been worth it. Hangin' with her friends, listening to music, doing not much of anything. Seeing Teague, who came in sometimes to play cards with Kayla even though he always lost. Spending the night with Rain. She smiled to herself, remembering the feel of his arms around her.

Then, in the deep dark of very late night, he'd asked about Spring Tour. There hadn't been any pressure, he just needed to know her plans.

Leaving was so complicated. Making arrangements for someone to be at the shop, letting her mom know she wouldn't be there for Aria. And tour was almost a month. It was easier to stay home and take care of her life.

She turned the tape player on and stuck a bootleg in. As she put the first tray of cookies in the oven and started mixing muffin batter, she sang along, *"Ashes, ashes, all fall down."* She closed her eyes, remembering what it was like to hear "Throwing Stones" live. She was one of those kids who danced, and *god damn it* she wanted more than anything to shake her bones.

Then Jerry's guitar kicked in, and she knew she had to go.

She ran through the dates and venues in her head, considered the logistics of driving. She could easily do Landover and Hartford. After that was Canada. She'd skip that. Albany was less than two hours away, but she couldn't do the Knick. She'd already given Katelyn time off so she and Liam could go. She'd have to make a second set of arrangements if she wanted to do Nassau, and The Omni was way too far.

She'd settle for Landover and Hartford. Five shows, out of sixteen. It was better than nothing.

*** ***

Teague stood in the middle of the kitchen, a feeling of immense satisfaction in his chest. After weeks of stripping and sanding, removing hinges and handles, taping, priming and finally painting, the kitchen was a subdued shade of grey. The crisp, white trim popped. The freshly painted cabinets were sleek and modern. The appliances had been replaced and were now grey with black fronts.

All he needed was to replace the laminate table and vinyl uphol-stered chairs. He grabbed his jacket and headed into town.

He'd never bought furniture himself. He'd paid for it, when Marlena had decided to redecorate, but he hadn't chosen it. It was a surprisingly exciting idea, to choose what he wanted.

His first stop was Bailey's. There was just one person at the counter, waiting for their coffee. Teague read the menu board while he waited for his turn.

Bailey smiled when she saw him. "Hey, now."

"Hey." He smiled back. "I was wondering, what's the difference between Kona and Kenyan?"

She answered easily, "Kona's a nice, light roast. It's very mild and easy to drink. Kenyan coffee has a rich, deep flavor. It's more acidic, which some people consider bitter."

Surprised, he said, "Are you like the coffee equivalent to a sommelier?"

"I don't know what that means."

He smiled apologetically. "It's a wine expert."

She shrugged. "I'm not really an expert. I used to hang out in this coffee house on the Haight—"

"The hate?"

"The Haight-Ashbury? In San Francisco?"

He shook his head. "Okay. So you hung out at this coffee house."

"They had crazy shit there. Jamaican Blue Mountain and Tanzania Peaberry and just ridiculous stuff. Some of it's like thirty bucks a cup. So, ya know, when you're there every day, you just start to pick up on what's what."

Intrigued, he asked, "What makes a cup of coffee worth thirty dollars?"

She smiled, "In my opinion? Nothing. But that's what they charge for a cup of Kopi Luwak."

"What's that?"

"It's coffee made from beans that have been eaten and pooped out by a civet, which is like a cat."

"That's... interesting."

She laughed. "You could say that."

"Is it good?"

"No idea. I've never had it." She wrinkled her nose as she said, "I'm not really into drinking poop."

"Usually something I avoid as well." He was really curious, now, though. "Where do you even get that?"

"You order it. I could get it, if you want."

He shook his head. "I think I'm good. So, what's in my cup every day?"

"The house blend. It's a medium roast Arabica blend. Not too sweet, or too acidic. Enough body to satisfy, but not so much that you need to cut it with a knife."

He looked up at her menu board. "If I wanted to try something different, what would you recommend?"

"Depends what you're looking for."

He shifted his gaze back to her. "I have no idea how to answer that."

She crossed her arms, narrowed her eyes and considered him. "Do you drink beer?"

"I do."

"What's your favorite?"

"Guinness."

"Milk chocolate, semi-sweet or dark chocolate?"

He hesitated for just a moment, then said, "Dark."

"Why do you get a blueberry muffin every day?"

"What's that got to do with coffee?"

She said, "Guinness and dark chocolate are both bitter. Blueberry muffins are very sweet."

"Huh." He'd never given any of this that much thought. "I actually prefer cranberry orange, but you don't have them."

"Fair enough. You should probably try the Sumatra. Dark, full, and earthy." She laughed, the sound light and musical. "You look overwhelmed."

"Sorry. You're just kind of blowing my mind right now." He liked her laugh. He glanced back up at the boards. "I'll try the Sumatra."

She smiled. "Good choice."

Chapter 11

Bailey parked in the spot the attendant pointed to. She and Rain had slept late; the main lot at The Capitol Centre in Landover, Maryland, was full and they ended up in the grassy overflow lot.

Rain hopped out. "I'm gonna see who's around. I'll catch you up later?"

"Right on." Bailey climbed into the back, pulled a laundry basket from under the bed, and shifted clothes around until she found a blue flowered dress. She stripped her long sleeve sweatshirt off, pulled off the t-shirt underneath it, and slipped the dress on over her head. She considered for a minute keeping her jeans on, but it was unseasonably warm and she was already sweating.

She almost went barefoot— it was that nice out— but the main lot was asphalt and that meant glass. She slipped her Birkenstocks on, slung a purple and blue patchwork backpack over her shoulders and called softly to Delilah, "Come on, girl."

The aisle where she was parked was mostly yuppies. The few brothers and sisters there, sitting on blankets with handmade bead work or veggie bagels or whatever for sale, weren't people she knew. She smiled and nodded as she passed them but didn't stop to talk.

A couple guys, one with dreads tied back in a pony tail and one with wavy dark hair, walked past mumbling, "Doses, two for five, three for ten." She couldn't suppress a grin, knowing most people would assume it was a better deal to spend ten dollars without actually thinking about what the guys were saying. Not that it mattered to her personally. She never paid for LSD.

"Bailey! Hey now!" A sister in a patchwork dress, corduroys underneath and barefoot, hugged her.

Bailey hugged her back. "Hey, Melody. How's things?"

Melody squatted to pet Delilah. "Hey, girl." She scratched between her ears, and looked up at Bailey. "Fuckin' awesome. So glad to be here. We hooked up with a bus in Oakland and, man, it was a fuckin' crazy trip out. We musta got pulled over a dozen times, and we had fuckin' Quasar with us."

"Oh, shit."

"Right? Every freakin' time he chants that spell. You'd think after all these years he'd admit it doesn't make us invisible. We finally started telling the cops he was running a fever and was delirious. They all decided not to get too close, except in Ohio. They *tore* the bus apart, didn't find anything, then told us to bring Quasar to the hospital before he infected anyone else." Melody laughed. "Like crazy's contagious, right?" She gave Delilah one last pat, stood and asked, "Are you still in Vermont?"

"Yeah. You should stop in, if you're ever around."

"Right on."

Bailey continued the way she'd been going. Someone passed her wearing patchouli. Further down the row people were huddled together getting stoned, on kind buds from the smell of it. Somewhere there was a sage smudge burning. She inhaled, relishing the scents of the lot.

She paused at a display of t-shirts for sale. A girl, maybe four years old, her blonde hair in braids, came from behind the rack. With her semi-clean tie-dye and bare feet poking out from under a skirt that was too long she had the unmistakable look of a kid being raised on tour. She pulled her thumb out of her mouth to say, "Hey now, sistah."

Bailey smiled at the girl, tried to ignore the twinge of guilt she felt for leaving Aria at home. "How much are your shirts?"

"Ten each or two for fifteen."

Anywhere else hearing a kid that age quoting shirt prices would have been unheard of. On the lot it wasn't anything unusual. "Do you make them?"

"My mom does and I help."

Bailey nodded. She didn't buy anything unless it was hand-made. She chose a kid sized shirt with a line of dancing bears on it and started to pull out her wallet. But there was another shirt that caught her eye. It had what looked like the Dunkin' Donuts logo, but it said FUCKIN' GONUTS. That would be perfect for Teague. She gave the girl a twenty dollar bill and said, "Put the change towards your ticket tonight."

She took the money and disappeared into the van parked behind the racks of shirts.

Tucking the shirts into her backpack, Bailey continued down the row of cars. She hadn't told Teague she was leaving. It hadn't come up, and she hadn't wanted to bore him with talk of shows when she knew he wasn't into the Dead. But now it seemed rude and she wished she'd said something after all.

She'd crossed into the main lot. She headed for the coliseum, and the bank of pay phones she knew would be there. The line was predictably long, with at least twenty people waiting for a chance to call home. She didn't mind waiting, there was nowhere else she had to be.

She joined behind a kid who couldn't have been more than fifteen. He had the look, though. Sun-darkened skin, hair growing out from what had been a "respectable" length, and a tie-dye hanging from the waistband of his baggy jeans. He glanced at Delilah, then back up to Bailey. "Hey now."

"Hey now." He was tall and gangly, exactly the kind of guy she'd go for, if he'd been ten years older. She asked, "Did'ya just come from Oakland?"

"Yeah, you?"

"Nah. I couldn't make it out. Did you get in?"

"The second night. They did a killer 'Terrapin'."

"Nice." She'd always loved 'Terrapin'. "Are you in tonight?"

"Lookin' for a miracle." Delilah nosed him. He bent down to pet her. "What kind of dog is he?"

"She's a rottweiler. Her name's Delilah."

He cooed, "Hi, Delilah. Aren't you a beautiful girl." The phone line moved forward. The kid stood up, smiling. "I always wanted a dog, but my mom's allergic. I'm gonna buy a bus, and then I'm gonna get a dog."

That was the quintessential Deadhead dream— to buy a bus and turn it into a home on wheels. She doubted very much this kid would pull it off. It was very expensive, not just to buy and convert, but to run. She'd only been able to buy a van because she'd had a car to sell, and she and Jesse had hustled hard. Then again, anything was possible. Especially if he had someone at home sending him money.

The line moved forward again. The kid turned and said, "Bye, Delilah," before he walked to a just vacated phone.

"Nice to see you're making new friends." Bailey grinned down at the dog, who chose not to reply.

When it was her turn, she pulled her calling card from her wallet and went through the process of charging the call to her phone at home. Her mom's answering machine picked up and she left a quick message to let her know she'd made it to Maryland.

She almost walked away, but as she put the receiver back on the hook she changed her mind. Going through the whole process again, she dialed Cole's number. The phone on the other end rang and rang. Apparently Teague wasn't home, and didn't have an answering machine. Disappointed, she set the handset back on the hook and moved away from the phones. *Might as well go see who's around.*

She headed towards Shakedown. The main area, where most of the buses would be parked and people would congregate, was the best place to run into family. She scanned faces as she went, always looking for those she knew.

A guy, a bit taller than her, sandy blonde hair and a full beard, moving easily through the crowd, caught her eye. "Jesse!"

He was too far to hear her, and by the time she got to where he'd been he was long gone. Knowing she'd run into him eventually, she continued the way she'd been headed.

Chapter 12

Teague stopped short when he saw a stranger behind Bailey's counter.

The woman was probably about his mother's age. She wore her grey hair long and natural, and her face had a beauty that her age didn't diminish. "Good morning. What can I get you?"

He walked the rest of the way to the counter. "Coffee, please." Jiggling his keys in his pocket, he scanned the room. It seemed oddly empty.

"What kind of coffee would you like?"

"The house blend is fine. And a blueberry muffin, if you've got one."

She gave him a searching look, then asked, "Are you Cole's brother?" Surprised, he said, "I am."

"Bailey told me to keep an eye out for you, and make sure I saved you a muffin." She smiled, her eyes sparkling. "And she told me you look just like your brother." She held out her hand. "I'm Diana, Katelyn's mom."

"Teague. Nice to meet you."

He had his choice of tables. There was just one couple near the windows, and in the corner a kid with text books spread around him. Teague sat at his usual table and opened his paper. After a few minutes he realized he'd read the same line three times and still had no idea what it said. It was too quiet. It wasn't just Bailey that was missing. It was everyone he'd gotten used to seeing. *They must be at a Dead show.* It was the only thing that made sense.

There was no reason for him to stay, since Bailey wasn't around. Folding his paper, he started to get up just as Lucy walked in. She waved at she made her way to the counter. He settled back down to wait for her.

Cup in hand, she sat across from him. "Hey, Teague."

"Hey, Lucy." He grinned at having someone to talk to. "What brings you to town this morning?"

"We picked up a new customer, a restaurant doing local produce only. It's a great account, but they require everything to be delivered fresh every day and with Rain gone and the colleges on spring break I'm short staffed."

He offered, "I can help, if you need a hand."

"Thanks. I'll keep that in mind."

Curious, he asked, "Rain works for you and Matt?"

"When he's around."

"So between tours?"

"Eeehhhh, kind of." She wiggled her head, "He's not necessarily that predictable."

Thinking of how annoying it was when Cole called unexpectedly and needed to be picked up somewhere, he asked, "You're okay with that?"

"I don't have a lot of choice. He's Matt's brother." She smiled gently. "Honestly, though, when he's here he's great. He works hard, does everything we ask." She snorted. "And trust me, there's worse things he could be doing than going to see the Dead."

"Have you been?"

"To see the Dead? Yeah." Grinning, she said, "Pretty much everyone here does, as often as they can."

* * *

Teague changed into the junk clothes he'd bought specifically to wear while he worked on the house, filled a bucket with warm water and began saturating the next section of wallpaper. Stripping the walls was much harder, messier, and more time consuming than he'd imagined.

He considered calling Liam. The idea of paying someone else to do it was extremely tempting. But he remembered the pride he felt every time he stepped into the kitchen and knew he was going to do this himself, too.

The drip of the sponge each time he pulled it from the bucket was the only sound. There was no traffic, no dogs barking, no neighbors blaring music. He didn't usually mind the quiet, but this felt like more than silence.

This felt completely alone.

He dropped the sponge in the bucket and dried his hands on his jeans as he crossed to the shelves on the far side of the room. He pushed the power button on the stereo and jumped as music blasted from the speakers. He spun the volume dial, bringing it down to a tolerable level.

He recognized the song; it was one people sometimes sang to at Bailey's. He could picture them— Katelyn and Liam, Kayla, Rain— singing 'ashes ashes, all fall down' and dancing in the middle of the shop. It was just as easy to imagine Cole with them.

Guilt settled in his stomach.

Leaving the music on, he went back to stripping wallpaper. It was easy to believe Cole was a drug dealer and drug dealers belonged in jail. It was a lot harder when he thought of Cole as his brother, and impossible when he thought of Cole the way he'd been when they were young.

What he really wanted was to ask him, face to face, if he was actually dealing drugs. But he couldn't do that unless he was approved for visitation, and he hadn't even gotten an application.

Back in January, he'd given it a couple weeks. If he'd been in charge it would have been done right away, but he'd reminded himself that this was the government and 'right away' could mean anything. Then he'd figured Marlena would take her sweet time forwarding it, since she wasn't all that happy with him. When it hadn't come by early February he'd called her every day for a week. Not surprisingly, she hadn't answered or returned his calls.

At that point he'd called Bill, knowing lawyers had access to their clients, and asked him to have Cole resend the application. Then he'd waited again. Not knowing how often he saw Cole, or how long it would take, he'd given it plenty of time. But this was ridiculous.

He shut the stereo off, went to the kitchen, and dialed his mother's number in Florida. She answered on the second ring. "Hi, Mom."

"Teague. You have news?"

Pretending she'd continued with what would be a social norm, he said, "I'm doing great, thanks. The house is coming along. It's painstakingly slow and tedious, but I have nothing else to do at the moment so it's not a problem."

"What you really should do is go back to work."

Just the idea of that made him tense. *Not going to happen.* "Have you heard from Cole?"

"Isn't that why you're in Vermont?"

"Yeah, it is, but it's been months and I haven't gotten the application for visitation yet."

She ignored him and asked instead, "Have you tried to fix things with Marlena?"

This is not worth it. "Forget it. I'll just call the lawyer."

She snipped back, "That *is* what I'm paying him for, isn't it?"

90

"I'll be sure to remind him of that." He hung up before she could say anything more.

He found the ad in the yellow pages and dialed the office.

A cheerful sounding woman answered, "Law Offices of Whitney and Finkle. How can I help you?"

"Hi, this is Teague Gallagher. My brother, Cole, is one of your clients?"

"Hi, Teague. How are you?"

"Fine, thank you. I was wondering if Bill's available?"

"I'll see if he has a moment. Can you hold?"

"Sure. Thank you." He drummed his fingers on the kitchen table while he listened to elevator music.

"Teague?"

"Hi, Bill."

"Cynthia tells me you've got a question?"

"I haven't gotten an application for visitation. I was wondering if there was a problem I was unaware of."

There was silence for a moment, then Bill cleared his throat. "Teague, I'm sorry. I don't think Cole requested any visitors be put on his list."

Puzzled, he asked, "None?"

"Well, your parents are both in Florida right now, and your brothers are in Connecticut and California."

"I'm here, in Vermont."

Bill said, "He doesn't think you'll come."

"Why not?"

"He expected you to bail him out."

Of course he thought that. And instead, I left him there. He remembered the way Cole had avoided looking at him as he'd left the courtroom. *Damn it, I have to fix this.* Or at least make it as right as he could without bailing Cole out, because that was still out of the question.

"Is there some way I can contact him?"

"You can write to him."

Teague sat on hold again while Bill transferred him back to Cynthia. She gave him Cole's inmate number and instructions on how to address the envelope. "Make sure you keep the number. That's his for life."

Teague grunted. *No one should be stupid enough to go to jail twice.* "Thanks, Cynthia."

"No problem. Please don't hesitate to call if you need anything else."

All this time he'd been waiting, and Cole thought he wouldn't come. *I can't blame him.* He pulled the yellow legal pad he kept on the table towards him and wrote "Dear Cole," on the top line.

Dear Cole? What are you, writing a letter to Santa? He tore the paper off and wrote, "Cole,".

He had no idea what the hell was he supposed to say. *'Sorry I didn't bail you out but I don't trust you not to run'?* That wasn't going to win him any big brother awards.

Asking how he was doing was stupid. Telling him what he was up to felt like flaunting his freedom. He could apologize for not having taken the time to understand him for the last twenty-five years, but that was his problem, not Cole's.

Finally, he wrote that he hadn't received a visitor's application and Cole should have it sent to the house in Vermont. It wasn't great, but at least Cole would know he was there.

Chapter 13

The only sound in the dark room was Delilah licking herself. Sometimes that noise drove Bailey nuts, but at least it meant she wasn't completely alone. For the last week she'd spent her nights in packed hotel rooms and she missed the feeling of being surrounded by people.

There was just enough light from the digital clock on the nightstand that she could make out the pillow next to her, where Rain had spent so many nights recently. She hugged it, squeezed her eyes shut and inhaled the scent of pot and patchouli. The scent of Rain. If she'd asked, he'd have come home with her instead of continuing on to the next shows. She would never ask that of anyone, though.

Not even Jesse. *If you could even find him. Five shows, and you never talked to him once. The closest you got was seeing him the first day in Landover.* She didn't like to think he'd avoided her on purpose, but it wasn't easy to not run into someone for five entire days on the lot.

At five her alarm buzzed. "Come on, Delilah. Time to make the muffins."

She did her morning thing, took care of Delilah, and started baking. As she folded blueberries into the muffin batter, then spooned batter into the tins, she thought about Teague, and that he preferred cranberry orange.

She pulled her grandmother's cookbook from the shelf. By the time she'd inherited the collection of recipes, clipped from magazines or carefully transcribed onto index cards, every one already had chocolate thumbprints, or a smear of peanut butter, or a splatter of tomato sauce on it. She could practically feel her grandma beside her, telling her that was the mark of a good recipe.

There were a few muffin recipes, including one with a variation for cranberry orange. The timer rang and she swapped trays around, then lined up the ingredients for a second batch of muffins.

* * *

When Teague came in, he gave her a huge smile. "Hi, Bailey!"

She smiled easily as she greeted him. "Hey now."

"I'm, um, glad to have you back." His smile became awkward.

"I brought you something." She pulled the shirt she'd gotten for him out from under the counter and held it up.

A funny look crossed his face. "Fuckin' go nuts?"

She handed the shirt over the counter. "It made me think of you."

Although he looked unsure, he took the shirt. "Thank you."

She asked, "What are you drinking this morning?"

"Whatever you put in my cup."

"That's not something you should ever tell a Deadhead." Mischievously, she added, "You may end up with more than you bargained for."

"I just meant, whatever kind of coffee you give me is fine."

"I've got a Jamaican Blue Mountain blend, if you want to give it a try."

"Sounds great."

Unable to suppress a grin, she said, "I have something else for you, too." She set a muffin on the counter.

His eyebrows drew together as he picked it up and examined it.

"Bailey—" He looked slightly uncomfortable as he said, "You didn't have to do that."

She shrugged. "It's your favorite, right?"

He smiled a little. "Thank you."

* * *

Teague watched Bailey take care of customers as he finished eating. Her thoughtfulness had left him speechless. 'Thank you' had seemed so inadequate.

Once she'd taken care of everyone in line, she sat across from him. "How's the muffin?"

"Perfect." Her smile, the relaxed set of her shoulders, radiated happiness. He asked, "So, did you go on tour?"

"I don't tour anymore. I just did a few shows."

"That's not going on tour?"

"Not really. There are sixteen shows this spring, and I only did five."

That seemed like a lot of concerts to him. He asked, "Did you have a good time?"

"I did." She settled back. "So, what have you been up to?"

He snorted. "Stripping wallpaper. It sucks."

"Yeah, it does." She indicated the room around them. "This used to be a diner, and the whole place was done in wallpaper with roosters on it. I got everyone I knew to come help strip it, and it still took forever." Laughing, she added, "Although that might have had something to do with the fact that I paid them in beer and buds."

Still not comfortable with Bailey's off-handed way of talking about drugs, he said, "Well, it looks great now."

"It was worth it. Your house will be, too." She tipped her head a little, and said, "You know, people will help you, too. You just have to ask."

That wasn't something he was going to do. Aside from that he didn't want to ask for help, he wasn't going to pay in beer and buds. "It's okay. I don't mind doing it." Then he admitted, "And it's not like I have anything else to do anyway."

"Still haven't decided what you're going to do with your life?"

"No. I'm kind of just…" He'd been afraid to discuss this with anyone, knowing his family wouldn't understand. But Bailey was different. She waited patiently, her expression earnest. He said, "The thing is, I've spent so much time becoming a lawyer, then trying to be a good one, if I'm not going to be a lawyer anymore I don't really know what to do."

"Why don't you want to be a lawyer anymore?"

He sipped his coffee, thought about how to answer that. "I went into it for the wrong reasons in the first place."

She folded her hands on the table. "Why'd you choose it?"

He scanned her face. There was no sign of judgment, no malice. Just curiosity. He asked, "You want the whole story?"

"Yes."

"It's long."

"I've got time."

He'd never talked about this. He took a minute to figure out where to start, then said, "I was twelve when my parents got divorced, and I didn't really understand what had happened. I just knew that my dad had to move out. Then I heard my mom talking to her friends about how her lawyer had made sure she got everything she wanted, including both houses and the kids, and I got it into my head that it was the lawyer's fault we couldn't see my dad. I decided that I was going to be a lawyer, except I was going to help dads keep their kids instead of taking them away."

She smiled. "That's a great reason, Teague."

He shook his head. "It's not reality, though. First of all, my dad is not an innocent victim. He worked all the time. I think at first my mom didn't mind because she was living the lifestyle she'd always wanted. But he was *never* there. Not for holidays, not for school functions, not when there was an emergency. I will never forget, I broke my arm and she called him at work to ask him to come home. He refused, and she ended up having to drag all four of us to the emergency room. She was furious, screaming the whole way about how—" He stopped. He didn't want to admit to Bailey how bad it had been.

He continued, "I saw a tiny portion of my mom's side of the story. Nothing at all of my dad's side. I didn't understand that he was working to give her what she wanted, and she was never satisfied. That's something I've only come to understand as an adult," he smiled ruefully, "because I ended up in a relationship exactly like theirs. Lucky for me, I got out of it before it was too late. But not everyone does, and as a divorce attorney I saw both sides. Not everything, and not always the absolute truth, but I quickly came to understand that it's rarely as one sided as I'd thought."

He stared at his coffee, thinking for the first time in a while about what his life before Vermont had been like. "I specifically chose the firm I worked for because they were known for ruthlessly protecting the rights of their male clients. And once I began to understand that the men were as much, and sometimes more to blame, than the women I couldn't do it. It wasn't fair, and it wasn't right. So when Cole called me, said he needed help, I used it as an excuse to walk away from the life I'd come to hate."

Softly, she said, "I'm sorry that you had to go through all that."

"It's okay. I actually feel really lucky. Like I got the chance to hit the reset button before it was too late to start over." He raised his cup. "And as an added bonus, I now know the difference between

Kona and Kenyan."

A smile tugged at the corner of her lips. "That's Jamaican Blue Mountain."

He smiled in return. "And it's darn good."

* * *

Bailey sat at a table with a calculator and her checkbook. In high school she'd taken accounting in an attempt to get her required math credits without doing any actual math. It was the only class that had turned out to be useful in her adult life.

The mortgage was paid, the credit card was taken care of, and the checking balance was still in the positive. She'd never be rich, but she wasn't going without.

She glanced at the clock; it would be a while before Aria was out of school. The shop was empty and she had some time to herself. It would have been nice if Teague was still there. He'd left early saying he had work to do.

With nothing to occupy her mind she felt restless. *Because all your friends are on tour and you're home. And because you miss Teague.* She'd have liked to leave, to walk in the woods, or sit on a riverbank with her feet in the water. Instead, she gathered up the checkbook and the stack of bills she had to mail and brought them upstairs. She pulled her beading kit from its place on a shelf and went back down, quickly in case customers came in.

At the table by the front window, she opened the re-purposed tackle box. She lifted the top tray out and set it aside. The tray underneath held rows of tiny glass seed beads in plastic tubes, organized by color. She chose a tube of deep blue and one of silver and poured some of each onto a plastic dish. She threaded a needle and picked up the necklace she'd been working on. She began picking up beads one at

98

a time, weaving them together to form a straw-sized tube. Blue, blue, blue, silver, over and over.

The tape she had playing stopped. She left it, finding the silence soothing. The four-inch-long tube grew to five, then six inches. Two stripes of silver wrapped their way around the blue in a spiral. She had a lot more to do before it would be long enough. She added beads to the dish.

The bell on the door jingled and she looked up. A smile stole over her face as Teague came in, for the second time that day. "Hey now."

"Hey." He glanced around. "It's slow in here."

"This is pretty typical for early afternoon, especially with most family still on tour."

"Maybe I should always come in the afternoon."

More than happy to have him for company, she said, "You could."

He laughed, "No way could I hold out this long for my morning coffee." The smile lingering, he said, "Although afternoon coffee sounds great."

She set her beading on the table and got up. "What can I get you?"

"How about a large Sumatra."

By the time she made his drink he was sitting in the chair next to hers. She brought his coffee over and settled back down. "What brings you into town this afternoon?"

He sipped his coffee, then said, "I had to run to the hardware store. I'm painting the trim white in the entire house, so I needed new screws for the switch plates." He indicated her tray of beads. "What've you got going?"

"It's going to be a necklace." She picked it up and handed it to him.

He examined it closely for a moment before giving it back. "It's beautiful."

Heat rushed to her face at his compliment. "Thank you." She began adding beads again.

After watching for a few minutes he asked, "Can I try?"

She looked up questioningly. "You want to bead?"

"Yeah."

She handed him the necklace and watched as he chased a bead around the plate with the needle.

After a few attempts he said, "This is much harder than you make it look."

"I've had a lot of practice." She grinned. "You have to kind of press the needle on the side of the hole and it'll flip onto the end."

He handed it back. "I don't think I have the patience for this."

"It's not for everyone." She added a bead. "I like it, though. It's peaceful, almost like meditating. And I like seeing my ideas come to fruition."

"I hate that word."

"Fruition?" She raised an eyebrow in question.

"Yeah. See, I learned it from reading, so I didn't know how to pronounce it. One night at dinner I finally had the chance to use it, except I said fruit-tation. My brothers thought it was hysterical. They've worked it into conversation every chance they get for the last twenty years."

Surprised, she said, "I can't picture Cole teasing you."

"He didn't. He actually got mad at Shea and Callum for laughing at me. Even now when they say it he gets annoyed. He's always been..." He trailed off.

She smiled a little, thinking of how kind Cole was. "There was this one night, I didn't get into the show so I was just hanging out on the lot and this guy starts hitting on me. I tried telling him I wasn't interested, but he was following me, really harassing me, talking about all the things he wanted to do to me. It was dark and there weren't many people around and I got really freaked out. Then I ran into Cole. He slung his arm around me, kissed me, and loudly called me 'babe'. The guy got the hint. Then I felt stupid for being scared. But Cole," she smiled a little even though the memory made her miss Cole. "He just told me he'd always be there when I needed him."

Teague picked up his coffee cup, rotated it in his hands. "Bailey, he needs me now, and I let him down."

"What do you mean?"

"At his arraignment, when they brought him into the courtroom, he saw me. He looked relieved. He must have thought I was there to bail him out. But I couldn't. He'd have run and I'd have been responsible."

"I'm sure he knows that."

"It doesn't matter. When they took him back into custody he didn't even look at me."

"Teague—" She didn't know what to say.

"He's my little brother. I'm supposed to be there for him."

"You *are* here."

He set his cup down, harder than was necessary. "Being here's not enough. Do you have any idea what it feels like, to know you let down the people you love and not be able to do anything about it?"

Yeah, actually I do. That wasn't something she wanted to discuss with him, though. *And he's here. It's not his fault things are the way they are.* "You're doing as much as you can to help."

He shook his head. "What good is being a lawyer if I can't even get my own brother out of jail?"

She wished there was something she could say to help. *You know better than that. There's nothing you can say.*

His shoulders fell and he leaned back in his chair. "I'm sorry. I didn't mean to dump all that on you."

"It's okay. That's what I'm here for."

He searched her face, then said, "Thanks, Bailey."

She smiled softly. "Anytime."

Chapter 14

The moment she stepped into her apartment Bailey knew Jesse was there. There was a big external frame backpack leaning against the wall, dirty dishes on the coffee table, and the scent of pot lingering in the air. Ignoring the mess, she went to the bedroom, Delilah following. As soon as she opened the door Delilah bounded past and jumped on the bed.

Laughing, Jesse pulled the covers over his head. "Down dog!"

Standing against the door frame, arms folded across her chest, Bailey watched for a minute before calling the dog back. Jesse pushed the blankets down and turned to look at her, his long sandy-blonde hair in disarray around his thin face, pieces of it stuck to his beard.

Hurt, and happy at the same time, she said, "It's been a long time."

Sitting up, he said, "Yeah."

"What are you doing here?"

"I live here."

She clarified, "I figured you'd finish spring tour, at least, before you came back."

"I missed you." He held out a hand to her.

It had been months, she wasn't going to let him off that easy. When she didn't move, he got out of bed and came to her. He slipped his arms around her waist and kissed her.

She'd missed his touch, the way he kissed her, the familiar feel of his body against hers. Already she felt her resolve slipping. She tried to back away, determined to make him fight for forgiveness.

He let her go, hurt flashing across his face. "Bail."

"I looked for you in Landover. And Hartford."

He ran his hand up her arm. "You know how it is. The lot's a big place, it's easy to miss each other."

Her lips tightened into a thin line. She knew, but she also knew he'd have found her if he'd wanted to.

"Hey, speaking of Landover, remember that guy we met in Eugene? Nick? I ran into him." He reached behind himself and grabbed his jeans off the bed. He pulled a cassette tape from the pocket and held it out.

She glanced at it, folded her arms across her chest. *He only skipped Atlanta. It's not like he gave up a whole tour for me.*

"Bail, hey, babe, please."

You know how it is with him. You agreed to this. She took the tape. Hand written in black marker was her birthday, the previous fall. *He always knows exactly which shows I want.* She whispered, "They did 'Terrapin' that night. And that trippy 'Bird Song' with the flutes. That was such a good show."

She put the tape in the player she kept on top of her dresser. Her finger hovered over the play button. She knew if she pushed it music would fill the air, and memories would fill her head. Of dancing with him that night, and making love after the show. Of countless other shows, other nights, of years of history they shared. "You could have called."

"I know what it's like here for you. How hard you work, and that you take care of Aria, and I didn't want to bother you."

She stared down at the tape player. "Hearing that you're okay is never a bother." Struggling to speak, she said, "I was worried."

He moved behind her, wrapped his arms around her waist. "Baby,

103

I'm sorry I worried you." He whispered against her neck, "I'm so glad to be home."

No matter how long he was gone, what he did while he wasn't there, she could never refuse him when he came back. She pushed play.

* * *

Bailey was careful not to wake Jesse as she crawled out of bed. She dressed in the dark, called softly to Delilah and closed the door gently behind her.

As soon as she opened the shop she started looking for Teague. She knew he never came in until mid-morning, but every time the door opened she still hoped it was him.

When he came in just after ten she felt better. "Hey, Teague. How's things?"

"Good. I started stripping the ceiling in the living room yesterday afternoon." He grinned. "It makes a hell of a mess."

Picturing dripping wet wallpaper all over the floor, she said, "I'm sure it does."

He took his coffee and sat at his normal table to read his paper.

A while later Jesse came in from the back. He walked behind the counter and kissed Bailey. She smiled at him as he made himself a cup of coffee. Teague caught her eye. Her smile faltered.

Say something. "Hey, Teague, this is Jesse. Jesse, Teague, Cole's brother."

Jesse nodded, "Hey, bro."

Teague nodded back.

Jesse took a muffin out of the case. "Babe, when's the last time you changed the oil in the van?"

Bailey focused her attention on him. "Ummm…"

He kissed her and smiled, "I'll take care of it. And anything else it needs done. Do you need it today?"

Guilt for her anger the day before bloomed in her stomach. He'd always taken care of her. "Today's fine. I don't need to go anywhere."

He kissed her once more and went back upstairs, just as customers came in.

The steady stream of people kept Bailey busy. Usually she didn't mind, but she wanted to sit with Teague. By the time she had a break he was gone.

Trying to smother her disappointment, she set about cleaning up from the morning rush.

* * *

Teague was half way to Bennington before he realized he'd missed his turn, miles earlier. "You, Teague, are an idiot."

He began looking for a place to turn around. He'd been driving, lost in thought and mindlessly following the truck in front of him, a plumbing service truck with a picture of feet sticking out of a toilet bowl and a banner above saying, "In A Rush to Flush? Call Us!"

As he pulled into a parking lot, ignoring the sign warning against using it to turn around, his mind wandered back to Bailey's. There were other people behind the counter sometimes. Katelyn or Ann Marie, when they were working. And he'd seen Bailey kiss lots of guys— on the cheek. He'd never given it much thought. It seemed like everyone who hung out there hugged and kissed much more than he was used to.

It'd been obvious that Jesse was different. The way he'd seemed so at ease behind the counter, as if he belonged there. *He does. He's her boyfriend.*

But Bailey had stiffened the moment he'd come in, the way his mother did when his father walked into a room. And after Jesse'd kissed her, she'd looked right at Teague. *You've got enough going on. Bailey's none of your business. Just go home and strip wallpaper.*

He pulled onto the road, backtracking to his missed turn.

Chapter 15

Bailey knew, based on who was in the shop, that spring tour was over. Lance was kicking back on the couch talking to Ruthie, John and his new girlfriend were playing chess. Bailey greeted a couple who had paused to set frame packs on the floor by an empty table before making their way to the counter. "Where're you headed?"

The guy answered, "Going up to Glover."

"To Bread and Puppet?"

The girl nodded. "My sister's apprenticing, thought we'd go check it out."

"Right on." She got them each an organic tea and went on to the next group.

As she listened to their orders her eyes wandered down the line. Teague hadn't come in yet. *He'll be here, he's just late today.* It'd happened before, and it wasn't like she knew his schedule intimately. He could have a doctor's appointment, or a meeting with Cole's lawyer. There were a million logical explanations why he wasn't there. *He would have said something if it was about Cole.*

She filled orders, poured more cups of coffee. The steady stream of customers became a trickle, then died out altogether. She'd have another rush later in the afternoon, but for now things were quiet. And Teague still hadn't come in.

Maybe he really is going to come for afternoon coffee. She didn't quite believe that, though. He hadn't missed a morning in months.

Looking for distraction she decided to go upstairs and grab her beading kit. *What if he had an accident. Went off the road into the trees where no one can see him.*

She chided herself, *Damn it, Bailey, stop. He's fine.* She started up the stairs.

You weren't thinking about Peyton, were you. Or Dad. You didn't see that coming, did you?

It didn't matter that she knew she was being ridiculous. Her chest began to tighten. *He's alone. No one would know if something happened.* She tried to force her mind to stop. *He's young and healthy. Nothing's going to happen. But what if he something* did *happen.* Visions of Teague lying unconscious on Cole's kitchen floor flashed through her mind. *His house is so far away. It takes forever for an ambulance.*

As she touched the door knob at the top of the stairs she struggled to breathe, the weight on her chest becoming increasingly heavy even as she tried *not* to remember how long it took for an ambulance, once someone called for one.

You were right there when Dad died. You know damn well how fast it can happen. If something happened to Teague, it'd be too late, by the time anyone got there. She opened the door and stepped into her living room.

Jesse looked up from the couch and smiled. "Hey, babe." As their eyes met his smile faltered. He stood and came quickly to her. "Bail, hey, babe, breathe."

"I'm sorry." She wrapped her arms around him, held him close, as she always did when things went wrong. *He's here. Of course he is, because I need him.*

"It's okay." He ran his hand over her back, as he always had when she started to lose it.

She breathed him in, let the feel of his touch comfort her. *It's fine,*

Bailey. Teague's fine. He didn't have a heart attack. That doesn't happen to people his age. He's just late. Or something came up. Just breathe. She forced herself to take long, slow breaths. After a moment she stepped back.

"Do you want to talk about it?"

It'd been years since the last time she'd needed Jesse to talk her through a panic attack. Hell, it'd been years since she'd had one. "I just started thinking—" He'd expect it to be about her sister or her dad. She couldn't tell him she'd been thinking of Teague. "How things just... happen. When you least expect it."

He took her hands and held them. "Babe—"

Sage yelled up the stairs, cutting off whatever he was going to say. "Jesse! Bro, you coming?"

"Shit. Hold on, I'll tell him to forget it."

"No, it's fine." She could hear him coming up. "I'm fine. Go, do whatever you were going to do."

He glanced at the door, then back at her. "Are you sure?"

"Yeah, go."

He grabbed a backpack and slung one strap over his shoulder. Then Sage was coming through the door, already talking about meeting people at the music store. Jesse gave Bailey a quick kiss and they were gone.

She looked around at the mess he'd left. After one last deep breath, she began picking up the dishes he'd left on the coffee table. It annoyed her to leave them unwashed in the sink, but she had to get back downstairs in case someone came in.

It would be easier if she could have a second person there all the time, but she wasn't busy enough for that. Plus, she wasn't sure she wanted someone else there constantly. She liked her space.

She grabbed her beads and ran down the stairs, half-expecting to see Teague waiting at the counter. She immediately crushed disappointment when she stepped into a still empty room.

She'd barely started beading when Katelyn came in. "Hey, Bail."

"You're early."

Katelyn poured herself a cup of coffee. "Yeah. Liam's home with Mallory so I figured I'd come in and see what was going on here."

"Why's Liam home?"

Sitting across from her, Katelyn said, "He was out helping Teague this morning and it didn't take that long."

"What's he doing for Teague?"

"Teaching him how to spackle. Apparently Teague smacked a wall with a ladder."

Bailey looked up from her beads and asked, "How do you smack a wall with a ladder?"

"I think he swung it around." Giggling, she said, "All I can think of is *The Three Stooges*."

See that. A perfectly good explanation why he isn't here. Not wanting Katelyn to know how relieved she was that Teague was okay, she asked, "Did you ask your mom if you can hang out tonight?"

"Jeez, Bail. You make it sound like I'm in high school."

"I didn't mean it like that."

"I know. And I did, and she said yes. And now *I* sound like I'm in high school." She sipped her coffee, then said, "Sometimes I'm so jealous of you."

Slightly sarcastically, she said, "Because I didn't even finish high school?"

Katelyn smiled, "Yeah, partly. When you guys left, all four of you at once, it was the talk of the school. You were like legends."

Bailey snorted. "That's ridiculous."

"Not really. I mean, think about it. Everyone says they're going to do shit like that, but you guys actually did it." Softly, she added, "And what did I ever do? Get pregnant at sixteen, never go any further from home than two states over. Yeah, I'm jealous of you."

"Katelyn—" She didn't know what to say.

"It was my choice." She smiled a little. "And really, I wouldn't want it any other way. I love Mal, and Liam. And I was wondering—"

Bailey raised her eyebrows, "Yeah?"

"Can I have a couple days off in July? To go to Foxboro?"

Grinning, Bailey said, "Yeah. Of course. Do you have tickets?"

"Not yet." She squirmed. "I wanted to make sure I could go, first."

Feeling grateful for Katelyn always being part of her life, she said, "Today is a good day for a miracle. Or three."

Katelyn's jaw dropped. "I can't take tickets from you."

"Yes, you can. And you're going to. Because there's no one I'd rather miracle."

Humbly, Katelyn said, "Thank you, Bailey."

* * *

By the time Ellen picked up Aria and Bailey had finished cleaning up from dinner, the shop was full of family. She made her way slowly to the couches, stopping to greet each person she passed with a hug. Teague was way in the corner, playing cards with Lucy. She waved when their eyes met, but she wasn't headed in that direction.

There was an empty space on the couch, next to a guy she didn't know who was engaged in a conversation with Ruthie. She settled down and let the steady murmur of conversations flow over her. Occasionally one voice stood out for a moment as someone got excited, or laughter rippled through one of the groups scattered around the room. *This is perfect, exactly what I need.*

Lance broke into her thoughts. "Hey Bailey, you know Smack, right?"

She focused her attention on the guys next to her. "Yeah."

"Tell Thomas what he's like."

She shifted to be able to see them better. "He never shuts up. No one can stand it for more than five minutes before they smack him."

Thomas asked, "What's that got to do with dropping acid?"

She said, "That's how he got that way."

He cocked his head, looking skeptical. "Lots of people talk a lot."

Bailey shook her head. "No, brah. It's not like that. He never, ever stops. It's a steady stream of nonsense, even in his sleep."

"That sounds more like a mental disability. Something he was born with."

Lance said, "I'm telling you. He was mega-dosed."

Not caring to listen to the story of Smack, and how he'd wronged the wrong people, Bailey surveyed the room again. Matt and Lucy stood with their heads close, smoking a joint. Sage was by the back wall, his face alight with excitement as he talked to a woman Bailey didn't know.

And there was Kayla, her head barely at Teague's shoulder. That seemed such an odd relationship, Kayla who'd started taking chemistry to learn how to make LSD and Teague who was about as straight-laced as they came. Bailey wondered what would happen if Teague realized he played cards with the local acid supplier. As she watched, Kayla slid her arm around Teague's waist. She jerked her eyes away, back to the people immediately in front of her.

Rain was sitting on the opposite couch, leaning forward and talking to Jesse. It was something she'd seen hundreds, maybe thousands, of times. She'd known them both for more than twenty years, they were as close as it was possible to be. And that made her very uncomfortable.

It shouldn't have. Jesse knew she slept with other guys when he wasn't around. He wouldn't care that she'd hooked up with Rain. And Rain had known it was temporary. It was undoubtedly one of the reasons he'd done it. She just didn't want to be reminded that for months she'd slept with one of her best friends. *Katelyn warned you this would happen.*

She stood. Jesse and Rain glanced up as she walked between them. She ignored them as she made her way through the kitchen to the back door. She called softly, "Delilah." The rottie trotted over and followed her outside.

The cool night air felt good after the closeness of the people crowding her shop. She stood at the edge of her small patio and inhaled the scent of wet earth. Delilah splashed through a muddy puddle between piles of melting snow. Bailey could already picture the trail of footprints the dog would leave when they went back inside.

After a while she called Delilah and they went back in. The dog settled in the corner as Bailey scanned the room. Teague was still there, still with Kayla. Bailey remembered how uncomfortable he'd looked the first night he'd been there. There was no sign of that now.

She sat next to Jesse just as he took a hit off a fatty. He passed the joint to her. She pulled smoke into her lungs and held it as she passed it to Lance.

She leaned back, sinking into the couch. She closed her eyes, not caring who had their arm around who, and let her mind drift.

Chapter 16

Laughter broke the early morning quiet. It was just a few minutes before Bailey had to get up and most likely the people in her living room hadn't gone to bed yet. She gave Delilah's head a scratch. "Morning, girl."

She pushed the switch on the bedside lamp and blinked at the sudden brightness. Once her eyes adjusted, she stood, stretched and slipped a dress over her head. She ran a brush through her hair and shut the light back off.

Delilah was already waiting expectantly at the door. Bailey opened it and the dog trotted into the living room. Jesse glanced up as they came in. "Hey, Bail."

He sat on the floor, surrounded by tightly rolled clothes, blankets, and the few other things he carried with him. His wallet, his favorite bowl, a toothbrush and toothpaste, and his backpack. "Hey." She glanced at Sage and the girl he'd been hanging out with the night before, both in the middle of similar piles of things.

She slipped into the bathroom, glad for the excuse not to talk to anyone. She did her thing, then took a moment to steady herself. This wasn't the first time, or the last, that Jesse would leave.

As she stepped back into her living room she considered asking where they were going, but it didn't matter. She left them to their packing and went downstairs.

Once she'd let Delilah have a few minutes outside, Bailey brought out the big mixing bowl and set it on the kitchen counter. As she zested an orange, squeezed the juice into the bowl, her mind wandered. There had been a few people hanging out the night before who were on their way to a Rainbow Gathering. That wasn't something she had any real interest in. She loved the idea of a community where everyone was fed and cared for, and everyone was expected to contribute what they could. But she couldn't quite get past being expected to pray, even if it was called 'Oming'.

That's probably where Jesse's going. He'd probably think dealing the quirks of the Rainbow was better than being stuck in town.

* * *

Bailey tuned the radio to the local college station. All she wanted was to go upstairs, crawl into bed, and cry. Except her bed would smell like Jesse, so she'd have to change the sheets first. She mumbled, "Get your shit together, sistah."

She could sneak upstairs and smoke a joint. Not to get completely wasted, just to take the edge off.

That was a stupid thought. She had responsibilities.

As she turned to the back counter to pour coffee for a couple guys in Carhartt jackets she forced back tears. *You chose this life, Bail. Deal.* In the time it took to fill two cups she had her emotions under control. She handed out the orders, took payment. "Have a great day."

The one with the curly hair raised his cup. "You, too."

She watched the door, checked the clock, tried to keep herself busy. By the time Teague came in she felt like she was going to climb out of her skin. Seeing him, his smile lighting up his dark eyes, she felt calmer.

He was there, just like every day since January. She'd serve his coffee, wait for him to be situated, and go play cards. They'd talk, but not about anything. The weather. What the town council was doing. Whatever else he'd read in the paper.

Kayla's arm sliding around his waist flashed though her mind. She shoved the image away as he came up to the counter. "Hey now." She smiled.

He gave her a funny look. "Are you okay?"

She tried harder to smile. "Yeah. I'm fine." She turned to get his coffee. When she turned back the look of concern he gave her forced another crack in her facade. Her lower lip trembled as she handed him the cup.

Sounding worried, he asked, "Hey, Bailey, what's wrong?"

She shook her head. "Nothing."

He tightened his jaw as he gave her a disbelieving look. "Bailey."

A tear rolled down her face. "I'm sorry. It's just, Jesse left this morning. With Sage and that girl, to a Rainbow Gathering."

"I'm sorry."

"It's fine. I mean, he'll be back. I just..." She did *not* want to get into this, especially with Teague. "I just wish I could go with him." That was the thing. It wasn't that he was leaving, it was that *she* wasn't. Her throat closed and tears forced their way from the corners of her eyes.

The door opened. She and Teague both turned to see a group of women in designer jackets, hair teased and smiles lipstick perfect.

Teague's head snapped back to her. Softly, he said, "Go in back. I got this."

She tried to tell him no but he was already coming around the counter. "Teague—"

"Go, Bailey." His voice was so kind as he repeated, "I've got it."

She went. She had to. She couldn't greet customers while she was crying.

Crying, for Christ sake. Over Jesse leaving her behind. What the fuck was wrong with her? She never let this get to her. Not like this, anyway.

She stood in the kitchen and bit her knuckle, trying to hold back full-fledged sobs. She could hear Teague, taking orders. Jesus, he was doing a good job of it.

The tears came harder. *Jesse doesn't need me, Teague can do my job without any freaking training.*

Delilah came in and nuzzled her leg. "You love me, don't you girl." *I should just go upstairs, pack a bag and leave. Drive west, me and Delilah. We'd sit on the beach, like we used to, until...*

She knew she wouldn't do that. She had responsibilities, which was total bullshit. It wasn't her goddamn fault she was stuck there, taking care of her sister's kid. She'd given up her own life, and it wasn't *fair*.

Frustration coiled in her stomach, energy built. She had to get out. She yanked the back door and followed Delilah into the chill of spring in Vermont. Desperate to expel the darkness swirling inside her, she looked around. The remnants of last summer's flowers in their terra cotta pots sat on top of the brick wall that surrounded her patio. She grabbed one and threw it as hard as she could. *"Aaaaagggghhhh."*

The explosion of pottery and dirt was extremely satisfying. She grabbed another and threw it. Then another.

Drained, all the pots she'd had now in pieces, she sank to the ground and cried.

* * *

The cold bit into her butt. Delilah sat at the back door, whining.

When Bailey'd stepped outside energy had coursed through her. Now, she barely had enough to stand. She forced herself up, made her way across the patio and opened the door for the dog. She grabbed a trash bag, dust pan and broom and headed back outside. *You made that mess, go clean it.*

Cleaning up sucked. She did it anyway.

She put the dust pan and broom away, washed her hands, and went to stand in the doorway to the main room. Teague was at the counter, leafing through his newspaper, Delilah curled at his feet.

"Teague?" Her voice sounded scratchy, even to herself.

He turned around, a look of relief on his face. "Hey." He smiled a little.

"Thank you."

He waved her off. "No big. That's what friends are for."

For the first time that day she felt a real smile tug the corners of her lips. "Did you just say 'no big'?"

He laughed. "I did."

God, I'm glad he's here. She brushed a stray tear from her cheek. "Do you want to play cards?"

Chapter 17

Bailey glanced at the clock. It was nearly noon and Teague was still there. When Ann Marie came in to relieve her, she considered explaining that she had errands and thanking him for keeping her company. But she didn't want him to go. Instead, she asked, "Teague, I have to go out to Lucy's, to pick up supplies. Do you want to come with me?"

He looked surprised, but shrugged it off. "Sure."

"Cool." She led him and Delilah through the kitchen, out the back door, grabbing a jacket on the way. She smiled as she stepped outside. "It is absolutely beautiful out today."

"If you're an Eskimo." He zipped his parka, which he really didn't need.

Laughing, she unlocked the doors to her van. "It's not that bad." Delilah scrambled over the driver's seat, between the second-row captain's seats, and curled up on the bed. Bailey climbed in and leveled a look at Teague. "You coming?"

He hesitated. "Bailey, your van is orange. And it has curtains on the windows."

"Yeah." She started the engine. He didn't move. She leaned on the steering wheel and looked out the still open door. "Teague, just get in."

She had just about given up when he finally started moving. As soon as he was settled, she asked, "Is it really that bad?"

He glanced in the back. "You have a bed, in your van?"

"Doesn't everyone?" His look of sheer disbelief was perfect. She backed up, looking over her shoulder to hide her grin.

"Do you actually sleep in it?"

"Yeah. That's why I bought it." She pulled onto the road. "It's a thousand times better than sleeping in a car."

"Why would you sleep in a car?"

"Because you can't afford a hotel room."

Incredulously, he said, "You're serious."

"I am." She smiled, remembering her early days on tour. "It's not bad in the summer, especially when the venues let us camp in the lot. Everyone just slept outside. But in the winter, or in the city, it's not an option. And let me tell you, four people sleeping in a Chevy Vega sucks." She laughed, "Rain and Sage had a very close relationship our first tour."

* * *

What the hell am I supposed to say to that? Teague didn't know how to respond to a lot of the things Bailey and her friends said. They were so outside his experience he couldn't wrap his mind around them. Instead, he looked out the window.

He didn't usually get to look at the landscape, since he was driving. Being free to pay attention to his surroundings, he thought how odd it was up here. They'd pass a beautiful house, with fresh paint and a new Volvo in the driveway. Then the next house would have peeling paint, a swayback roof, and vines climbing up the chimney. The next would be a half-house-half-business. It could be anything; a gas station, an antique shop, an insurance agent. "Why do houses here have metal roofs?"

"Because snow slides off them. It keeps it from getting too heavy and collapsing the roof, and it prevents ice dams."

"What are ice dams?"

"It's when the snow melts off your roof and freezes in the gutters. You know you have them when there's icicles hanging from the house."

"Huh. And that's bad?"

"It means the snow melt is pooling and most likely seeping into your house. It's really bad." She asked, "Don't you get snow in Connecticut?"

"Yeah."

"You don't have ice dams?"

"We do, I just never thought about it." He shifted uncomfortably, feeling like he should have known that. "I lived in a condo. They have people who deal with that kind of thing."

"Huh." Bailey pulled into Lucy's. She told Delilah, "Stay, girl." She headed inside, straight to the counter, and addressed the girl standing there. "Hi, Sheila. Is Matt around?"

Sheila glanced into the back room. "Lucy? Is Matt around?"

Lucy came out front. "Hey, Bailey." She smiled at Teague. "Hi, Teague." She looked back to Bailey. "He's out in the greenhouse. Go ahead."

Teague followed, reluctantly. He remembered that Matt was doing something with hydroponics. And he remembered how open Bailey and her friends were about drugs. They'd passed joints right in front of him and talked about dropping acid the way other people talked about drinking cocktails. Trying not to sound like he was accusing her of being about to make a drug deal, he asked, "What are you getting here?"

"Plants." She opened the door into the greenhouse.

That doesn't exactly rule out pot. He followed her into the massive

121

structure anyway. The humid air inside smelled of warm earth. He unzipped his coat as he took in the rows of tables full of plants.

Bailey yelled, "Matt?"

His disembodied voice floated back, "Yeah?"

Teague tried to look at every plant as he followed Bailey down the aisle. The ones closest to the entrance were heavy with baseball sized tomatoes, the bright red contrasting beautifully against the green leaves. The next section was also tomatoes, but they were the size of golf balls and were still light green. After that was a section of the same kind of plants but with yellow flowers. He had no idea what the plants after that were.

Finally, Bailey stopped. "Hey now."

Matt smiled at her from over a row of plants. "Hey, Bailey. Teague. What's doin'?"

"Not much. I thought I'd stop in and see if you've got flowers yet."

He grinned. "Oh, baby, come see." He headed further into the greenhouse. When they got to a break in the row he cut through to join them. He hugged Bailey.

Then, to Teague's dismay, Matt hugged him before continuing in the direction he was heading. "Bails, you're gonna love this."

They followed him through a door at the end of the building. The drop in temperature as they stepped outside was nice, but then they entered another greenhouse. This time Teague was prepared for the heat, but he was struck full force by the scent of flowers.

The sheer number of plants was overwhelming. They grew on tables, in pots on the floor, hanging from the ceiling. Every color— vibrant reds, cheerful yellows, rich purple— splashed against a backdrop of green. Big heart shaped leaves in deep glossy green, tiny feathery sprays of bright Kelly green, tall spiky plants with white centers surrounded by light green. He rushed to catch up to Bailey.

Matt was telling her, "— as long as you keep the soil moist, they'll do fine."

"Will a globe work?"

"Should. What are you thinking for the trailers?"

She glanced around. "Creeping Jenny?"

"Right on. Do you have pots?"

Teague was sure he caught a sideways glance at him. She answered, "Last year I had plain terra cotta. I was thinking I'd like royal blue."

"I've got something. It'll be perfect with the yellows. How many?"

"Two. Four." She grinned. "Four. Can you do a couple scarlet begonias, too? In yellow pots?"

Matt said, "I think you missed your calling." They started back to the door.

Teague followed, feeling totally out of place.

Bailey asked, "How's your project coming?"

Matt turned back and wiggled his eyebrows at her. "You wanna see?"

"*Yeah*. Rain's been going on about it for months."

As he led them to a smaller greenhouse, he said, "You know, I could put something like this in the shop for you. Your windows are perfect. You could have fresh lettuce, every day."

"I don't serve salads."

"You could." He opened the door to the last greenhouse and they stepped into something that looked straight out of a sci-fi movie. A row of white pipes ran the length of the wall on one side, green plants sprouting from them every couple inches. He pointed, "That's romaine lettuce. Then further down is spinach."

In the middle was a triangular rack housing bigger pipes, and bigger plants. "Those are broccoli. And those," he pointed to a configuration of pipes that looked sort of like a tree, "are strawberries."

Bailey wandered through the building, looking at everything. "Can you grow carrots?"

"I can grow anything. It's a matter of the right size and shape container, and getting the nutrients right. I'm still experimenting."

"This is cool as shit, Matt."

He beamed. "Thanks."

* * *

Bailey carried a crate of supplies to the van and set it next to the one Teague had carried out for her. He'd been so quiet the whole trip, she worried something was wrong. Once they were on the way back to the shop, she said, "Matt's greenhouses are so freakin' cool. Sometimes I think I'd like to buy a house just to have greenhouses like that."

He turned towards her. "Bailey, that's what you'd need to grow pot."

She fought a smile. "Well, yeah. I mean, I was thinking how amazing it'd be to grow my own food. But if that's where you're going, I'll go with you."

"No, that's not what I meant."

"What'd you mean?"

"I mean, when you were telling me what it takes, I didn't really understand. But you were right. There's no way in hell Cole could pull off what Matt's got going."

She hadn't realized he was thinking of his brother. Much more seriously, she said, "No, I don't think so either."

He sounded very uncomfortable as he said, "Matt *is* doing it, though. And *Rain* helps."

She snuck a quick peek at him, then quickly turned her attention back to the road. "If you're thinking they're responsible for what was in those greenhouses," she shook her head. "Rain can't have done it for the same reason Cole couldn't have. After the east coast shows last fall he went west. He wasn't back here until after Cole was arrested. And Matt's not going to risk his farm. It's his whole life."

"You've gotta admit, it's convenient. Matt's got the knowledge, and he smokes pot."

She snorted. "That's your criteria? Everyone I know smokes pot, and nearly everyone knows how to grow plants. And if they really wanted to put the time into it, they'd figure out how to grow *pot*. Sage's been doing it since we were in middle school."

"Maybe it was Sage, then."

"No, Teague. I get it, that it makes sense that it was one of my friends, but it wasn't."

Desperation in his voice, he said, "How do you know?"

She took a deep breath, let it out slowly. "Because if it was, I'd know."

"You know everything that your friends do?"

They pulled into the lot behind the shop. She parked in her space and turned to him. "No, obviously I don't. But you've sat here at night, listened to everyone talk. They're not quiet about their drug habits."

He gave her a small smile. "I still can't quite get over that."

"Why?"

He shrugged. "I'm used to people talking about investment strategies or the trip they just took to Europe or whatever 'cause' they've decided to promote. Not how many doses it takes to trip for three days."

It was damn funny to hear him say that. "I'd guess the answer to that would be at least a dozen?"

"I'm not entirely sure. But according to Kayla, you eventually have to sleep so be warned that you'll have the most fucked up dreams ever."

Bailey laughed. "She *would* know that." She got out, walked around to the passenger side and opened the door. As she lifted one of the crates, Teague took the other. She pushed the van door closed with her elbow and started for the shop.

"Bailey, can I ask you a question?"

"Sure."

"Is acid really better than pot?"

Struggling to keep a straight face, she asked, "Why? Are you considering trying it?"

He went slightly pink. "No. It's just that something Kayla said had me curious."

The grin she'd been trying to suppress broke through. "The answer to that depends on you, personally." She set her crate on the ground so she could open the back door. "Kayla doesn't like pot because it gives her the munchies, so she spends the whole time she's high staring in to the refrigerator. LSD, though," she stopped, turned to face him. It was impossible to explain to someone who'd never done it what tripping was like. She shrugged. "You'd have to try it to get it."

He snorted. "That's not happening."

"If you change your mind, just to satisfy your curiosity, I can hook you up."

"That'd be a cold day in hell."

She gave him a wicked smile and tugged the sleeve of his jacket. "Good thing you've got a parka."

Chapter 18

In the middle of the afternoon the shop was empty. Bailey pulled a box off a shelf and settled at the table with Teague. "Do you want to play cribbage?"

He eyed the board, a simple piece of wood with rows of holes in an S shape. "You'll have to teach me."

"Sure. There's two parts to this. The play and the show." She shuffled cards and dealt. "You're going to discard two cards into the crib." She continued, explaining how to figure out what to keep then how to go about the 'play' portion. They played with open hands until Teague started to get the gist of the game.

After a while he asked, "How'd you learn this?"

"My dad taught me. He and my mom used to play all the time." She smiled, "In the beginning, I think he'd play me. The game would be so close, I knew if I'd just had one more hand, or if I'd done one thing different I'd have won. So I'd beg him for another game. I won probably one out of three. But after a little while I started winning more, and he started having to actually work to win, and by the time I was twelve we were evenly matched." She asked, "Are you ready to play for real?"

"Sure."

After a few games Bailey glanced at the clock. *Aria'll be here any minute.* Teague didn't know her niece, or any of what had led to her

127

being with Bailey every afternoon, and she wasn't sure she wanted to get into it. She thought about kicking him out, politely.

He counted his cards and pegged his score.

She didn't ask him to leave.

He dealt the next hand. She continued to play.

Then the door opened and Aria came running across the room, "Auntie Bailey! I got invited to a birthday party!"

Bailey turned in her seat as Aria came to a stop next to her and calmly said, "Aria, this is my friend Teague. Teague, this is Aria."

The little girl politely held out her hand to Teague. "It's nice to meet you."

He shook her hand. "It's nice to meet you too, Aria."

She looked back to Bailey. "So can I go? To the party?"

"We'll have to talk to Nannie."

"But it's on a Saturday, so I'll be with you."

Bailey saw the desperate look in her niece's eyes. "Most likely it's fine. But we still have to talk to Nannie."

Pouting, Aria said, "Okay." Then she asked, "Can I have a snack?"

"*May* I have a snack, *please*."

"*May* I have a snack, *please* Auntie Bailey?"

Bailey smiled at her. "Of course. Go start your homework, I'll bring it over."

Aria went to a table and started unpacking her backpack.

* * *

If Teague hadn't known their relationship, he'd have assumed Aria was Bailey's daughter. From her long, straight hair to her cute little nose, the family resemblance was unmistakable. Except that Aria had blue eyes. As Bailey settled back down, he said, "She looks just like you."

"Funny how that happens in families." She sounded sad.

He felt awkward, like he'd said something wrong. He didn't know what.

Aria called from the other side of the room, "Auntie Bailey? Could I have more milk?"

"*May* I have more, *please.*"

Aria gave her a resigned look. "May I have more, please?"

Bailey stood up. "Sure, baby."

Teague watched Aria as he waited for Bailey to come back. She was singing, although not loudly enough for him to hear the words. He realized he'd actually seen her before, on Saturdays. He'd never given much thought to any of the children in the shop, unless they were unruly. And Aria wasn't. Any time he'd seen her, she'd been sitting with Bailey's friends. *I probably just figured she belonged to one of them.*

Bailey sat down again and picked up her cards.

"Teague?"

He smiled self-consciously at getting caught spacing out. "Sorry." As he discarded into the crib he asked, "How old is Aria?"

"Six."

"She already has homework?"

"Crazy, isn't it? I don't think I had homework until at least fifth grade." Bailey played her first card. "Maybe third. But definitely not kindergarten."

He smiled as a long-ago memory surfaced. "When I was her age I used to assign myself homework."

Bailey's eyebrows went up. "Seriously?"

"I have two older brothers, and I wanted to do everything they did. If they were doing homework, I wanted to, too."

She smiled at him. "That's really cute."

"I'm pretty sure my brothers thought it was annoying."

"That's what siblings are for, right?"

He nodded. "Yeah, well, I also have a younger brother and I can tell you that he annoyed the crap out of me."

"I was the younger sibling, and I definitely annoyed my sister. Although she annoyed me, too. She used to tell people I was adopted, because she had blonde hair and blue eyes, and I obviously don't."

He played his card. "Me, Shea and Cole all look like my dad, but Callum looks like my mom. We teased him, too."

Aria called over, "Auntie Bailey, I'm done with my homework. I just have reading left."

"Put it in your backpack and put your dishes in the sink, please."

Aria did as she was told then skipped from the kitchen to the table where Teague and Bailey sat. "Can I play cards?"

"You don't want to watch *Ducktales*?" Bailey asked.

"Not today."

"You have to wait for Teague and I to finish our game."

"Okay. Can I move your pegs?"

"Yes. You remember how to move them?"

"Um hm. When can I play this?"

"You can be on my team right now. Come sit here, so you can see what I have in my hand." Aria scooted her chair around the table. "Don't tell Teague what my cards are, but see if you can find two numbers that add up to fifteen." While Aria looked at the cards, Bailey told Teague, "Go ahead."

He played his first card. "Nine."

Bailey pointed to a card and told Aria, "Put this one down with the numbers showing and say—" She whispered in Aria's ear.

Aria put the card down and triumphantly said, "Fifteen for two." She giggled and asked Bailey, "Did I do it right?"

"You sure did. Now move our peg two holes."

Teague was fascinated. His parents never would have allowed him to sit with them like this. Not that his dad was ever home, but his mom used to have friends over and all the kids knew it was death to interrupt them.

They finished the play and he counted his hand. "Fifteen two, fifteen four, and a pair for six. Aria, do you want to move my peg?"

"Yes!" She pulled the back peg and counted six holes from the front one. She turned to Bailey. "You count now, right?"

"I do. Can you tell me how many points I need to win?"

Aria touched each hole between Bailey's front peg and the end of the board as she counted out loud. "One, two, three," all the way to eleven.

"Let's see what I've got." She lay her cards down. "That's fifteen two, fifteen four," she indicated the starter card and continued, "Fifteen six, double runs for twelve and a pair for fourteen."

Aria jumped up. "We win!" She spun in a circle.

Bailey held her hand out and Teague shook it. "Good game."

Aria came around the table and held out her hand. He took it and she imitated her aunt, "Good game."

Her hand was tiny in his. Afraid to crush it, he shook gently. "Good game."

"Can we play Go Fish now? I'm good at that one." Aria pulled her chair back to the side of the table it had come from and climbed into it. She picked up the stack of cards and handed them to Teague. "Can you shuffle, please?" She gave Bailey a look, like '*See, I remembered my manners.*' Then she looked back to Teague. "I'm not good at that yet."

"Absolutely. Are you good at dealing?"

"Yup. I can do that."

He shuffled and handed her the cards. He caught Bailey's eye and smiled. "You don't have to teach me this one."

She tipped her chin down and gave him a wicked grin. "No, but you just agreed to play Go Fish with the six-year-old version of Kayla."

* * *

Their Go Fish game progressed very slowly. Bailey had to keep getting up to take care of customers. Finally, she said, "Just play without me." Usually when she had a steady stream of people coming through the door Aria entertained herself, often by talking to the adults who hung out there. But usually it was people from town.

It was interesting to see Teague talking to her. He looked so relaxed, and he smiled at least twice as much as he usually did. He shuffled, dealt, and played Go Fish as many times as Aria asked him to.

They were still at it when Katelyn came in. Bailey left her in charge and went to interrupt the current round of cards. "Who's winning?"

Teague made an obviously fake pained face. "Her. Again."

Bailey raised an eyebrow. "Really."

"I won every time." Aria put her hand next to her mouth, in an attempt to keep Teague from hearing what she said. "But I think he let me."

Bailey gave Teague a reprimanding look. "Teague, that's not fair."

He put his hands up. "I didn't, I swear. And I'm a lawyer, so you can believe everything I say."

Bailey couldn't help it. She grinned. "Okay. I hate to be the bearer of bad news, but the Go Fish marathon is going to have to continue another day."

"*Auntie Baileyyyy.*" Aria pouted.

"Sorry, sistah. It's dinner time."

Her pout turned to a sly grin. "Can Teague stay for dinner?"

Surprised at Aria's suggestion, because she'd never asked for anyone to stay before, she turned to stare at Teague. She couldn't think of any reason to say no. And now that Aria had said it, she really wanted to say yes. "Teague, would you like to stay for dinner?"

Teague looked as startled as Bailey had felt. "Aria, I don't think

Auntie Bailey was planning for a guest tonight."

"I wasn't, but," she really meant it as she continued, "I'd like it if you stayed. As long as it's not going to mess up your plans."

"I don't want to impose."

She waved him off. "You're not."

After a glance at Aria, Teague said, "Okay. Do you need me to go pick something up? I can run to the store and be back in twenty minutes, tops."

"You don't need to do that. I have plenty to share." She asked Aria, "What should we have?"

"Pancakes!" Aria beamed.

Bailey rolled her eyes. "You know how I feel about pancakes. How about veggie pasta?"

Aria thought about that. "Can we have ice cream after?"

Teague added, "Please?"

Narrowing her eyes at him, wondering if she'd been played, she finally said, "Okay. But only if you eat all your dinner."

Teague said, "Yes, Auntie," making Aria snicker.

* * *

The first thing Teague noticed when he stepped into Bailey's apartment was the lingering scent of incense, not quite hiding pot. He looked at Bailey; she didn't seem to notice anything as she set her shoes on a mat just inside the door. He took off his own shoes and followed her through the living room.

He'd expected something hippie-ish. Maybe tie-dyed curtains and peace signs. Instead, the cranberry couches, upholstered in fabric that looked soft and comfortable, went perfectly with the chocolate walls. Curtains in the same cranberry as the couches hung to the floor at the sides of huge windows.

Aria slipped her hand into his and lead him into a tiny kitchen, just big enough for a table and four chairs. The sunflowers on the wallpaper were a perfect match to the yellow of the cabinets, which was repeated in the flowers arranged in a vase at the center of the light oak table.

Aria said, "Everyone has to help."

He smiled. "Okay, what do you want me to do?"

"First you have to wash your hands."

Once they'd washed up, Teague asked, "Now what?"

Aria said, "We're going to make salad. I'm going to peel carrots and you can cut them." She got two carrots out of the fridge, the peeler out of the drawer, a cutting board from the dish drainer and put it all on the table for Teague.

Bailey put a pot of water on the stove to boil, then cut veggies for the sauce at the counter. "Aria, what do you want in the sauce?"

Confidently, she answered, "Broccoli, carrots, zucchini, and peppers."

"Teague, any requests?"

With a sinking feeling, he remembered he was in the land of tofu and bean sprouts. Too polite to ask for meatballs, he said, "Whatever you'd like is fine."

Aria handed him a small knife. "Here, you can use my knife. Auntie Bailey got it for me, so I could help her."

Teague took the knife from Aria, sat at the table and began chopping carrots as she directed. "This isn't hard."

Her face scrunching in question, Aria asked, "What isn't hard?"

"Making a salad."

Giggling, Aria said, "You've never made a salad?"

"I don't cook."

"Then how do you eat?"

Bailey answered, "With his mouth."

"*Auntie.*"

He smiled at Bailey's answer, and told Aria, "I have breakfast at Auntie Bailey's, then I get take-out every night."

Astounded, Aria said, "Really? Nannie and Auntie Bailey never get take-out. They cook every night."

Bailey caught his eye. She looked concerned, maybe. He smiled reassuringly. She turned her attention to her niece. "Aria, can you help me? The broccoli says it doesn't want to go into the sauce."

Matter-of-factly Aria said, "Broccoli can't talk."

"Yes, it can." Bailey held a floweret up to her ear and nodded like it was speaking to her. "It says jumping in is too scary."

Aria giggled. "Okay, Mr. Broccoli." She took the floweret from Bailey and held it over the pot. "All your friends are already in there. See Mrs. Carrot? And the Zucchini Twins?" She held the broccoli up to her own ear. "It'll be fine, I promise." Then she dropped the broccoli in.

Teague wasn't thrilled about the pasta, he wasn't that big into vegetables, but his mother had been very strict about manners. When Bailey served, he was determined to eat. With the first bite he realized it wasn't going to be a problem. He chewed slowly, relishing the slightly spicy, garlicky, tomato laden sauce. He knew when he had a piece of broccoli, or a carrot, but it wasn't gross. It was just different. "Bailey, this is good."

"You sound surprised."

He glanced at Aria. He couldn't say he'd been suspicious of Bailey's cooking. "It's very different than what I grew up on." He smiled a little. "I wasn't sure what to expect."

"Auntie Bailey makes the best veggie pasta, and burritos. Maybe tomorrow she'll make them for us. She learned to make them on the lot. That's where she used to live, before she lived here. Her and Jesse—"

"Aria," Bailey interrupted her, "did you have music today in school?"

The intentional redirection wasn't lost on Teague. He'd ask Bailey about it later. *Much later. Like, tomorrow.* Because this was nice, and he remembered vividly how upset she'd been when Jesse left, and he didn't want to ruin their night.

After dinner they stacked their plates in the sink. Bailey began setting everything out for ice cream and Aria asked, "Teague, wanna play Guess Who?"

He looked at Bailey. "Do you need help?"

She smiled softly. "I've got it."

He told Aria, "You'll have to teach me."

"'Kay." She set the game up and instructed him on how to play. He smiled when she said, "But you can't say the letters under the names, cuz that would be cheating."

* * *

For the second time in one day Bailey was about to have two separate parts of her life collide. She didn't *think* her mom would give much thought to Teague being there. Rain had been there recently, and sometimes Jesse was around.

Still, something about this felt different.

The moment Ellen stepped into the apartment Aria jumped up. "Nannie! This is Teague, He's Auntie Bailey's friend. He let me win at Go Fish, but I told him not to cheat at Guess Who. And I got invited to a birthday party! It's on a Saturday. Can I go? But Auntie Bailey says I gotta talk to you."

Ellen grinned. "One thing at a time, Aria." She looked at Teague. "Teague? It's nice to meet you. I'm Ellen, Aria's Nannie." She laughed, "And Bailey's mom."

He stood and held out his hand. "Nice to meet you."

Bailey told Aria, "Get your things together, please." To her mom, she said, "I can bring her to the birthday party, if it's okay with you. The invitation's in her bag."

Aria hugged Teague, then Bailey, then grabbed Ellen's hand. She dragged her to the door, saying, "See you tomorrow."

Bailey closed the door behind them and turned back to Teague.

He looked a little dazed as he said, "She has a lot of energy."

She was oddly conscious of being alone with Teague. "I'm sorry she put you on the spot, inviting you to dinner like that."

"It's fine." He waved it off.

"You didn't have to stay."

"I know."

She smiled a tiny bit. "I'm glad you did."

"Me, too." His voice was low, making him sound more serious than usual.

They stared at each other for an uncomfortable moment. She wanted to move closer, to sit and talk to him. But he wasn't like her other friends. He didn't share her history or her culture.

He cleared his throat. "Let me help you with the dishes." He took the bowls into the kitchen.

She followed. "You don't have to. I can do it."

"You fed me. I'm happy to help clean up." He turned on the water, squirted soap on the sponge, and began washing.

As she took the first dish, she said, "You probably shouldn't have let Aria order you around like that."

He glanced at her. "It was fun, to let her be in charge."

"Yeah, today. But you opened a door you can't close."

"Who says I want to?"

What the hell does that mean? And why is he looking at me like that? Maybe he doesn't mean Aria. Jesus, Bailey, what are you thinking? That just now, at the door— This makes no sense. She took the next dish. "So, do you want to come for burritos tomorrow night?"

He kept his eyes on the dish in his hands. "I don't want to impose."

"You're not."

He turned to her and their eyes met. "I'd love to come for burritos tomorrow night."

His gaze made her feel weird. She never felt like that, no matter who was looking at her. *What the hell is your problem?* She said, "Hey, Teague?"

"Yeah?"

"What are you gonna do when Cole gets out of jail and discovers you've pilfered his entire wardrobe?"

His cheeks reddened. He looked down at the Calvin and Hobbs shirt he hadn't given any thought to that morning and asked, "Is it that obvious?"

She laughed, feeling much better. "Yeah. It is."

Chapter 19

Teague purposely timed his second trip to Bailey's for mid-afternoon, when he knew she'd be slow. As he stepped up to the counter she yelled from the back, "Be right there."

He looked through the kitchen to the back door, open to the warm spring day. Bailey came in, wiping her hands. When she saw Teague she smiled, "Hey now. Coffee?"

"Sure. What'cha doing?"

"Painting." She poured his coffee and handed it to him.

He held up the bag he was carrying. Awkwardly, he said, "I wanted to replace the ice cream we ate last night."

"You don't have to do that."

He set the bag on the counter. "It's the least I can do."

"Auntie?" Aria called. She stuck her head in and saw Teague. "Teeeeague! I'm painting. Wanna come?"

"I'd love to." He looked to Bailey for permission.

"Come on back." She took the bag of ice cream and headed into the kitchen, the string of bells around her ankle tinkling softly with each step she took.

Teague made his way around the counter and to the back door. Ahead of him, Bailey crossed the patio, her purple paisley sun dress fluttering around her legs. She looked back to him and smiled.

He tripped over the threshold.

"You okay?"

Mortified, he tried to brush it off. "First day with new feet."

Her smile became more of a grin as she turned to Aria, standing at an easel with Delilah curled on the ground next to her. "Aria, did you need something?"

She glanced at Teague, then turned to her aunt. "May I please have another canvas?"

Bailey took a painting of blue and yellow butterflies off the easel and replaced it with a blank canvas.

Aria asked Teague, "What are you going to paint?"

Surprised, he said, "I'm just gonna watch you."

"You can paint, Teague. Right, Auntie?"

"Of course." Bailey took a half finished painting off the easel next to Aria and set a blank canvas on it.

He protested, "Painting's not really my thing."

"Auntie Bailey said you're painting your whole house."

Smiling, he said, "This isn't quite what she meant."

Aria turned back to her blank canvas. "What'd she mean?"

He looked to Bailey for help but she just said, "I have to put that ice cream away. If you can't find something, let me know." As she started back inside, she glanced over her shoulder at him. "This paint stains. You can borrow a shirt if you want."

He looked down at what he was wearing; a pale blue button down he'd chosen because he'd been sanding trim and it was messy. "No thanks, I'm okay in this." He looked at Aria, happily humming while she squeezed white paint into a mound on her palette. He asked her, "What're you doing?"

"Making light blue for the sky." She added a tiny drop of blue and started mixing. "You have'ta always start with the white and add a little bit of blue to it." She held up her fingers to show a little bit. In a very serious tone, she said, "Because if you do blue first you end up with a lotta paint. Auntie Bailey lets me use as much as I want, but she gets kinda mad if I waste it when I know better. Like one time, I tried to make purple, even though she told me you can't, and I used all the blue on accident."

"Why can't you make purple?"

"I don't know. It just comes out icky." She began putting her light blue paint at the top of the canvas. "She told me it was a *learning experience*, and now I knew for next time to use purple from the tube."

Fascinated by how different this was than his childhood, he asked, "Auntie Bailey taught you how to do this?"

"Um hm. She loves to paint. Nannie told me she wanted to be an artist when she was a kid."

Teague looked more closely at the painting Bailey had set aside. A fairy, her wings shimmering behind her, sat on a tree stump surrounded by flowers in shades of pink. Trees arched gracefully above her, trailing light purple blossoms from slender branches. A moss-covered path meandered past her into the forest. Even in its half-finished state, the skill of the artist was evident in the delicate features of the fairy, the use of shadow and highlights, and the varied textures of the flowers. "She's really good." He indicated the painting.

"That one's for my room. It's Fairy Princess Willa of the Woods and she's making all the flowers grow."

"Huh. Is that a book?"

Brushing paint onto her canvas, she said, "Kind of. It's a story Auntie Bailey tells me. We have a book to go with it, but it's not like a regular book." She looked at Teague, wonder on her face. "Fairies are real, you know. Sometimes we see them in the woods."

Teague raised an eyebrow, "Yeah?"

"Um hm." Going back to her painting, she said, "They just look like dragonflies when people see them. That's so no one catches them and hurts them."

"Did Auntie Bailey tell you that, too?"

"Um hm."

"Your auntie's pretty cool."

"She's the best!" Aria grinned. "Did you decide what you're gonna paint?"

Teague looked around for inspiration. Red Adirondack chairs and a small wooden table sat in one corner, facing yellow and red flowers in a bright blue pot in the opposite corner. There were pots bursting with yellow and purple blooms along the top of the back wall, and more hanging from Shepherd's hooks here and there. *Princess Willa of the Woods would be right at home here.* "I think I'll paint that flower pot right there." He pointed to a bright blue pot with a bunch of yellow flowers growing out of it.

"Remember, start with the sky. You can paint over top of it, but it's really hard to paint around the flowers if you do them first."

"Got it." He squirted white paint on the palette Bailey had left on the table next to the easel, added a touch of blue, and began mixing.

His mind wandered as he smeared paint on the canvas. *Aria talks about Bailey all the time, but she never mentions her mom. And Bailey's talked about her sister once? Maybe twice, in all the time I've known her. Although she never said anything about Aria, either.*

He watched Aria for a minute. She'd finished the sky and grass and was working on a pastel purple flower. "What are you going to do with your painting when you're done?"

"I don't know." She glanced at him. "You could have it, if you want."

He almost told her it wouldn't match his decor, then stopped himself. That was exactly the kind of thing his mother had said anytime he or his brothers had brought artwork, or any kind of project, home from school. Instead, he said, "I'd love that. Thank you."

Chapter 20

Much too late in the day for it to be called morning coffee, Teague took his first sip and turned from the counter. He stopped dead in his tracks. On the wall, where a Jimi Hendrix poster had been, was his painting, next to Aria's butterflies.

Horrified, he turned back to Bailey. She was looking at him with no expression whatsoever. "Bailey, what the hell is that?"

"I thought we could use some brighter art in here."

Whispering, but in a voice that was trying to yell, he said, "Jesus Christ! Take that down!"

Looking critically at the opposite wall, she said, "Why? Aria worked hard on it."

Red in the face, he said, "Not that one. The other one. For Christ's sake, it's horrible."

"I like it. It's vibrant, it really captures the feel of that afternoon. The bright sun, the yellow flowers, the electric blue pot. I feel like I can reach in and touch the petals. I would really like to keep it there." She paused, then added, "If you'd prefer, I won't tell anyone you did it."

Doubtfully, Teague said, "Yeah, but Aria will."

Bailey smiled softly. "She's proud of you."

"Shit. Whatever. Leave it up. I'll sign it if you want, nice and big."

He took his coffee to his usual table and tried to ignore the paintings.

This is probably the most embarrassing thing ever.

He was still stewing when Aria came in. She sat across from him, dropping her bag on the floor. "Hi, Teague."

"Hi, Aria."

Bailey asked from behind the counter, "Do you want a cookie, Aria?"

"Nah." She began to pull her homework from her bag.

*** ***

Something was wrong. Aria never did homework without being reminded. And she never refused cookies. Bailey set the catalog she'd been looking at on the counter and joined Aria and Teague. "Aria?"

She sat, slumped over the table. "I'm doing my homework."

"I see that. Do you want to tell me what's going on?"

She kept her eyes glued to her paper. "Nothing."

Bailey glanced at Teague, who shrugged. "I'm working on my coffee order, but if you need me you can come get me." She pushed her chair back.

"Auntie?"

"Yeah, baby."

She looked up, tears in her eyes. "We hadda do Mother's Day projects today."

Bailey's stomach turned.

"My teacher said I could do it for Nannie, and I wanted to, cuz I love her. But the other kids said it was 'sposta to be for my mom, and they wouldn't stop."

Bailey was equal parts heartbroken and furious. She forced herself to stay calm. "Sweetie, I'm so sorry." She gathered Aria into her arms and hugged her tight. "I'm sure they just didn't understand."

144

Aria looked up at her and said, "It's not fair."

Bailey choked back tears. "No, baby, it's not. It's not fair to you, or Nannie, or to your mom." The first tears rolled down her cheeks. She was vaguely aware of Teague getting up. When he handed her a napkin she tried to smile her thanks. She failed miserably.

Aria whispered against her chest, "Auntie? They said I couldn't love you and Nannie as much as they love their moms."

Bailey closed her eyes and held Aria. She rocked, as she had when Aria had been a baby. There was no way to make this right, nothing she could say to make it better. All she could do was hold her niece and give her as much love as she had.

*** ***

Teague didn't know what to do. He wasn't part of this, didn't belong there. *Hell, I don't even know what's going on, where Aria's mom is.* And this obviously wasn't the right time to ask.

He was sure Bailey didn't want him to see her cry. But he also didn't feel right leaving. So he sat there, trying to give them their space.

He looked around, just so he wasn't staring at them. His gaze landed on the paintings Bailey had hung. Now that the shock of seeing them there was past, he thought it was sweet that Bailey had hung Aria's painting. *Not so much mine. If Aria asked her to, though...*

He wondered if Aria had actually said she was proud of him. That seemed so backwards; it was supposed to be the adults who were proud of the children. *Like Mom and Dad were proud of us? They didn't even come to my law school graduation. Neither of them. Although it's not like it was just me. They didn't go to the dedication for Callum's first building, or the dinner when Shea got that award for Businessman of the Year.*

After a few minutes Aria sat up and asked, "Auntie Bailey? Could I have a cookie?" Her eyes glistening with tears, she added, "Please?"

Bailey wiped her eyes with the back of her hand. "Yeah. Of course." She held her for another moment, closing her eyes and kissing the top of her head before she let her go.

Aria slid back into her own chair and Bailey went to the kitchen.

Teague opened his newspaper and re-read an article he'd already discussed with Bailey because he didn't know what else to do.

"Teague?" Aria didn't look up.

"Yeah?"

Her voice soft, she asked, "After I do my homework will you play Hungry Hippos with me?"

His heart felt squeezed. "Sure."

*** ***

Bailey wiped down the back counter with disinfectant, listening to Teague and Aria playing Hungry Hippos. She wasn't sure who was more excited about it; Teague cheered for his hippo as passionately as Aria cheered for hers.

She set the cloth aside and leaned against the counter to watch them. Aria had been so right. It wasn't fair. None of it. She should have been playing games with her father, not Bailey's friends. And Bailey should have been with Jesse and her friends, at the Rainbow Gathering.

The round ended with Aria's pink hippo eating the last marble. Teague turned and looked at her. He smiled, his eyes alight with joy.

She smiled back, although what she felt was a confused swirl of things she couldn't figure out. *If you were at that Gathering you wouldn't be here, with Teague.*

When Katelyn came in, Bailey called Aria for dinner. She very purposely left it open. "Hey, anyone besides those hippos hungry?"

Aria said, "Come on, Teague. We gotta put this away. But we can play tomorrow." They put the game back in the box and Aria took his hand to lead him upstairs.

At the bottom of the stairs, Delilah bounded past, with Aria following. Teague stopped Bailey. "Let me buy dinner."

"It's fine. I have plenty."

"This is the third night this week I've eaten with you."

"And this is the third night this week I've told you it's fine." She smiled a little. "Can we please make it the last? You're welcome every night."

"Bailey—"

"Teague, I like having you here."

"You *guys*! Come *on*!" Aria called from half-way up the stairs.

Bailey brushed past him. "Come on, Teague."

*** ***

Teague glanced at Bailey as he handed her the first clean dish. He liked this time, after Aria had gone home and he and Bailey worked together to clean up from dinner. He worried, though, that Bailey was upset. She'd been quiet all night. He tried to think of something to say, some way to bring a smile to her face.

She stacked the dish in the cabinet. "Teague, I'm sorry you had to see that, with Aria, today."

He washed teriyaki sauce off a plate. "There's nothing to be sorry for."

They fell silent; clinking dishes, running water and Delilah chewing on a bone the only sounds.

As Teague started on the cups, Bailey said, "I just can't stand that there's nothing I can do. I mean, she's going to have to deal with this forever. It's not like my sister's going to magically come back to life."

Shit. No wonder they never talk about her. He handed Bailey the last cup and leaned back against the sink, his thumbs hooked in his pockets.

She set the cup in the cabinet and turned to face him, arms folded and her hip against the counter. "The thing is, I could call the school and tell them what happened, but all that's going to do is put more of a spotlight on Aria. They're going to call those kids down to the office, talk to them about how Aria doesn't have parents and that they need to be understanding of that. But kids don't know how to do that. Hell, *adults* don't know how to do that. They say all the wrong things, and you just end up feeling worse."

There was so much pain in her voice, he wished there was something he could do for her. But, like the people she was talking about, he didn't know what to say. "What should they say?"

"Nothing." She looked away. "When my dad died, the only people who got it right were Jesse and Rain." She looked back to Teague and smiled a little. "When they heard, they showed up at my house with a huge bag of Sage's homegrown. They sat with me for days, and never once tried to make it better."

Jeez, her sister and her dad? He asked the only thing he could think of, "How old were you when your dad died?"

"Seventeen." She sighed. "In some ways Aria's lucky. Peyton died when Aria was just a baby, so she doesn't have any memories of her mom. She never had to mourn her, she's never reminded of what she lost, she only knows me and my mom as parents."

"That has to be hard on you and your mom."

"I think the hardest thing is knowing my sister never had the chance to know her daughter, to be there when she took her first steps or for her first day of school. And it's going to be hard for Aria as she gets older. There's going to be more and more times like today, when she knows she's missing what most kids have."

He felt bad for asking, but he was too curious to let it go. "Where's her dad?"

"No idea. Peyton never told anyone who he was."

They stood in silence while he processed what she'd said. Finally, he said, "Aria's the reason you don't tour anymore."

"My mom needed help, and," she shrugged, "there's no one else."

"She's very lucky to have you."

*** ***

As soon as Teague was gone, Bailey opened the box she kept on top of the bookcase. She packed a bowl and sat on the floor with her back against the wall. She flicked the lighter, watched the flame dance in the darkness of the room.

Once she set the flame to the bowl, pulled the smoke into her lungs, the high would take her and the pain would lessen. Years ago she'd thought it would stop on its own, that she wouldn't wake up every day wanting her dad, wanting her sister. She knew now it never stopped. The void they'd left just became the background to everything else.

Jesse understood. He'd been there through the sharpness of new pain, had helped her find ways to soften the edges until it became tolerable pain. He understood, without needing an explanation, when there was a sudden resurgence.

Jesse's not here now, though. You needed him today, and he wasn't here. Teague was.

Delilah came over and lay next to her. Bailey absently stroked her head. "You like him, don't you. I know, I do, too." She let her head fall back against the wall. "It's kind of impossible not to."

She sat up, brought the bowl to her lips, touched the flame to the buds and inhaled.

Chapter 21

The painting was still there.

Teague decided if Aria wanted it up, so did he. When he got up to the counter he said, "Bailey? Can I get a tube of yellow paint and a brush?"

She laughed. "Well, it's not on my regular menu, but if that's really what you want."

He stared at her, feeling ridiculous. "Forget it."

"I'm sorry." More seriously, she said, "I can't leave right this second." She glanced at the people who had gotten in line behind him. "But you can go get whatever you need. The paint's in the closet, next to the bathroom. Upstairs."

* * *

Bailey was curious what Teague had in mind, but she couldn't give it much thought. With the nicer weather more people were out and about and she was busier than she'd been in a while. She saw him come back downstairs but as he walked through the room she had to turn her back to make coffees.

The next time she scanned the room a smile stole over her face. At the bottom of his painting, the yellow contrasting brightly against the deep red he'd used for the brick at the bottom of his painting,

Teague had painted "TEAGUE E. GALLAGHER '90."

A few minutes later he got in line. She couldn't stop smiling, thinking about him putting his name on his painting like that. When he got to the counter, she said, "There's a drum circle tonight at Katelyn and Liam's. D'ya wanna come?"

* * *

Teague had no idea what he was supposed to wear to a drum circle. *Because you don't even know what that it.* Accepting Bailey's invitation had been a knee-jerk reaction, and as he dug through the piles of Cole's shirts he almost wished he'd said no. His favorite shirt, the one with the dancing turtles on it, was dirty. Still not into wearing a tie-dye, he finally settled on a shirt with a skull on it, the brain cavity half red and half blue with a white lightning bolt separating them. *That's from the album with "Sugaree" on it.* He sang under his breath as he tied his shoes.

On his way through the living room he stopped and scanned Cole's music collection. Unsure if his brother had them in any sort of order, he was always careful to put the cassettes back in the spot he'd taken them from. *It'd be a lot more convenient if they were alphabetical. And if I knew the album titles.* He was starting to be able to remember, but there were dozens of Grateful Dead albums and some of the names were impossible. Like *Aoxomoxoa.* He didn't even know how to pronounce that, never mind remember it.

He found *Steal Your Face,* checked the time and grabbed his keys. He started the car and slid the tape into the player. It was right in the middle of 'Stella Blue'. He sang along as he drove, only half listening to the music. Bailey had given him directions, but they included things like 'turn left at the dancing bears' and he was afraid he'd miss one of the landmarks and not realize it until he was crossing the border into Canada.

Eventually, he pulled into the driveway of a very unremarkable L-shaped ranch. The house was grey with white trim and in the fading light he could just make out flowers along the front. He wondered if he had the right place, because it sure didn't scream 'hippie', but he figured it must be right because he parked next to a Chevy Cavalier with a bunch of Grateful Dead stickers on it.

The trees behind the house glowed with flickering orange light. *Jesus, that fire's gotta be huge.* He followed the sound of drums around back, to a huge bon fire surrounded by people sitting on the ground or on logs. He walked around the circle, looking at smiling faces in the firelight, until he saw Liam with his arm draped around Katelyn's shoulders. He squatted down. "Hey now."

They both smiled at him. Katelyn gave him a one-armed hug as she said, "Glad you made it. There's beer over there." She pointed towards the house. "Help yourself. If you need anything else feel free."

"Thanks." He looked around for Bailey. He didn't see her, but he did see Matt and Lucy, and there was an empty space next to Matt.

Lucy smiled as he sat down. "Hey, Teague."

"Hey now. Hey, Matt."

He nodded and started to pass a bowl.

"No, thanks. I don't smoke."

He passed it to the guy on the other side of Teague.

Teague looked at the faces he could see from where he sat. He recognized some from Bailey's. He didn't really know anyone, though. Although he'd spent quite a few of his nights at the coffee shop, he usually only talked to Kayla and Lucy, and whoever else wanted to play cards.

A guy he vaguely recognized paused on his way past and squatted next to him. "You're Cole's brother, aren't you?"

"Yeah, Teague."

"John." He held out his hand, and Teague shook it. "It sucks, what happened to him."

"It does. He goes to court on Monday, though, and hopefully his lawyer will be able to do something about it."

"Right on." John went to sit next to a woman a little ways away.

The reminder of why he was in Vermont in the first place didn't do much for the nerves that still rocked his stomach. He wished Bailey were there. Being with her always made him feel better.

Then she was next to him, making Matt move over so she had room. "Hey now." She handed him a beer.

"Thanks."

"My directions were okay?"

"Yeah, they were perfect." He told her, "I never would have found it on my own. And I have to admit, when you told me to look for the dancing bears I thought you were a little crazy." He laughed, "Then I saw the mailbox."

"Up here, landmarks are key."

Now that she was next to him, he began to relax and take in the scene. Smoke curled here and there from cigarettes, and from joints or bowls being passed constantly.

The air throbbed with the beat of drums, played by people scattered around the circle. There were guys and girls, with dreads or long hair flying wild as they moved to the music they created, some standing playing tall drums and some sitting with bongos between their knees. There was a guy in Teague's line of sight who had a drum tucked between his arm and side and each time he hit the drum head he squeezed his arm. It made sound almost like an amplified, elongated drip.

Here and there people danced. Sometimes someone would chant, sound with no words, and sometimes others joined in. Sometimes the sounds would die down to almost nothing. Then it would burst forth, the energy pulsing through Teague, becoming hypnotic in its intensity.

Matt got up and a girl in a flowing ankle-length skirt sat in his place. The smell of patchouli mixed with the tang of campfire and the unmistakably skunky scent of pot. Baily's voice blended with the drums as she talked to the girl next to her. On Teague's other side two people he didn't know talked about how magical the Yuba River was.

He sipped his beer, trying to ignore that Bailey's leg pressed against his. *Bro, what the hell? You can* not *be into Bailey. She's got a boyfriend.*

But when she turned to him and smiled, desire throbbed through him.

Chapter 22

Teague stumbled downstairs. He wanted a cup of coffee so wicked bad. Bleary-eyed, he opened the refrigerator door, grabbed the jug of orange juice, and chugged.

"Teague?"

He jerked around, nearly spit out a mouthful of juice before he managed to swallow. "Mom?" Shocked to see Priscilla sitting there, he asked, "What are you doing here?"

Her voice full of contempt, she asked, "What *are* you wearing?"

He looked down. He'd pulled on the jeans he'd worn the night before and nothing else. They were paint splattered and smelled like campfire. And pot. He put the cap on the orange juice and put it back in the refrigerator. He ran his fingers through his hair, trying to wake up. "I didn't know anyone was here."

"Well, thank god you're not *entertaining* dressed like that." He was well aware she expected everyone to be dressed 'appropriately' at all times, even sitting at home. Her navy pant suit, accented with a diamond broach on one lapel and a simple string of pearls at her throat, was typically impeccable. "I'd like coffee."

"I don't have any." She raised her eyebrows, making him feel like he had to explain himself. "I go to Bailey's every morning."

"Who is *Bailey*?"

"It's the coffee shop in town." He rubbed his hands over his face.

"I'll tell you what. Let me take a shower, get dressed, and then we can go out for breakfast."

He went upstairs before she could argue. As he showered, he tried to picture introducing his mother to Bailey, with her tie-dyes and the stud in her nose, attempting to explain that they were friends. *No way in hell I'm doing that to Bailey.*

He decided they'd go to the diner north of town. The coffee wasn't good, and it was bound to be packed on a Sunday morning, but he didn't know of any better option.

He grabbed a pair of tan slacks from the closet, threw on a pale pink Oxford, and went back into the bathroom. He picked up the tube of gel, remembered Bailey commenting on it when he'd first stopped using it. "Fuck it." He set the gel back down.

* * *

The diner wasn't as packed as Teague had expected and they were seated right away.

As they settled into the booth Priscilla looked around, her lips tightening in distaste, "This is *quaint.*"

Teague had eaten quite a few meals there and he barely noticed anymore that the benches were covered in brown vinyl or that the tables were showing wear after decades of use. "It's Vermont, Mom. What'd you expect?"

"I expect that the people here realize it's 1990, not 1960."

To his surprise, he felt the need to defend the diner. "The meatloaf is spectacular."

She raised her eyebrows. "I'll be sure to remember that, should I decide I'm craving *meatloaf.*"

He changed tracks. "So, Mom, I didn't know you were coming up."

"If you ever answered the phone you would have."

"I guess I've been busy." Not into having her ask what he'd been doing, he quickly added, "It's a lot more work than I'd realized to update the house."

"Why don't you *hire* someone?"

For a brief second he considered telling her they couldn't risk having anyone in the house, which *had* been true in the beginning, when the house had been littered with drug paraphernalia. Since then it had become something more. "It's satisfying, to work at something and be able to see the result."

"You must get that from your father." She waved her hand dismissively, gold and diamonds catching the light from the bare bulb fixture hanging overhead. "Should you decide to hire someone, Shirley just had the house in Warren done. She couldn't say enough about the designer. From what I saw today you could use the help."

"I'll keep that in mind." When the waitress came back he ordered eggs over easy and toast.

His mother stated, "Just coffee." Once the waitress left, Priscilla folded her hands on the table. "I'm sure Shirley can recommend a salon as well, unless you've decided it's time to go back to Connecticut, in which case you should make an appointment with *your* stylist."

This is how Cole must feel at home. Teague promised himself he'd never look at his brother, or anyone else, that way again. "I'm sure you didn't come up here to tell me I need a haircut."

"No. I'm here to reassure myself that you've got the situation with Cole under control."

"I hired the best lawyer I could find. He's doing what he can."

"What, exactly, is he doing? Aside from charging me a small fortune."

"I don't know, Mom. You'd have to ask him."

Her voice cold and tight, she said, "You're a lawyer, I'm asking you."

"I'm a divorce lawyer. I specialize in making people look bad, ruining their lives. I don't know anything about helping people like Cole."

His mother narrowed her eyes, kept them focused on Teague even as the waitress brought his breakfast.

He poked the eggs. All he wanted was to go home and strip wallpaper or something. "I've got Cole's lawyer's number at home. Although I'm sure he's not in the office on a Sunday."

"Considering Cole is due in court in less than twenty-four hours, I don't see that talking to him would make any difference." She stood. "I'm staying at the lodge in Stowe, should you need me. Otherwise, I'll see you in the morning."

* * *

Bailey was busy all morning. It wasn't until after lunch that she realized Teague hadn't come in. When she finally had a chance, she picked up the phone and dialed Cole's number.

The voice on the other end sounded suspicious. "Hello?"

"Teague?"

The tone changed instantly to friendly. "Hey, Bailey. What's up?"

"You didn't come in this morning. I wanted to make sure you'd gotten home okay last night."

"Yeah, I did. Thanks for inviting me."

She asked, "How come you didn't come in this morning?"

Teasingly, he said, "Why? Did you miss me?"

She didn't mind admitting, "Yeah, actually, I did."

There was a pause, then he said, "You'll never guess who was sitting in my kitchen this morning."

Not having a clue, she picked the most outrageous thing she could think of. "The Abominable Snowman?"

158

"Worse. My mother."

"Yeah?"

"She came up for Cole's court date tomorrow."

"Did you know she was coming?"

"No." He sighed. "She does what she wants, when she wants."

"Is it a good thing she's here?"

He made a derogatory noise. "Not particularly."

"I'm sorry."

"It's fine. I'm used to her."

He sounded so unhappy. Thinking she'd take his mind off it, she asked, "Do you want to come hang? Aria and I are going to play Candy Land."

"Honestly, I'm not really in the mood to be social."

She could respect that. Wanting to leave the door open for him, she said, "If you change your mind, we're here."

* * *

Teague set the receiver back on the hook. He paced the living room, lost in thought.

The next day he was most likely going to watch his brother be found guilty of possession with intent to sell. Unless something unforeseen happened, Cole would be sentenced to a minimum of fifteen years in prison. *If you were a criminal attorney maybe you could have done something about this. You should have done more anyway. Found some way to prove where he was, or found out who really set up that greenhouse.* A sharp bark of laughter escaped, echoed through the room. *This isn't a TV show. Lawyers don't hunt down the missing piece of evidence. They just spin what they're given to the advantage of their clients.*

That wasn't completely true. He was well aware that sometimes all a lawyer needed to turn a case was to ask the right question. As

159

far as he knew, Cole's lawyer had asked everything possible. And regardless of what his mom thought, Teague had done everything possible, too. There just wasn't anything he could actually *do*.

Desperate to drown out the noise in his head, he stopped in front of the shelves holding the stereo. He'd made his way through all the Dead albums in Cole's collection. Every one had songs he liked. And every one had songs he didn't like. *It's like dinner. You have to eat the vegetables if you want to have the ice cream.* He settled on *American Beauty*. The only song on the album he wasn't crazy about was 'Candyman', and he didn't actively dislike it, it just wasn't his favorite. Plus, it had 'Sugar Magnolia' on it, which always made him think of Bailey.

As the first notes of 'Box of Rain' filled the room he wondered what Bailey would think if she knew he was listening to the Dead. He smiled a little at the thought. *Surprised? Maybe. But maybe not. Everyone she knows is a Deadhead.*

He'd been surprised. When he's started listening, out of curiosity, he'd expected to dislike it as much as he disliked eating liver. Instead, he'd found that he was familiar with many of the songs. *From being at Bailey's. She's always got music playing.*

There was more to it than that, though. The Dead played rock, jazz, even country. And they did a lot of blues. He really dug that. And he appreciated that many of their songs told stories. They were usually kind of messed up, like Delia DeLyon who shot Stagger Lee in the balls, but that somehow made them more intriguing.

The image of Bailey behind the counter at the shop, smiling as she sang along to whatever was playing, flashed through his mind. *Bailey would never look at me the way my mother did this morning, no matter how long my hair gets. She wouldn't care if I cut it all off again, either.*

He shut the stereo off and went back to the kitchen. He pulled out the phone book, found 'Bailey's' in the Yellow Pages, and called her.

* * *

Teague used the back door, as he always did after hours.

Bailey smiled as he came in. "Hey now."

Just seeing her, he knew this had been the right choice. "Hey." He held up the bag of grinders he'd picked up. "I brought dinner."

"Cool. I've just gotta finish cleaning up."

He went around the counter to the seating area, where Aria was coloring at one of the tables. "Hey, girl."

She glanced up as he sat, swapped the purple crayon she'd been using for a red one, and said, "Hi, Teague."

"What are you doing here on a Sunday night?"

"Nannie's playing cards with her friends, so I get'ta stay with Auntie Bailey." She went back to coloring the paper in front of her.

He tried to look at what appeared to be an envelope. "What'cha got going there?"

"I'm writing a letter."

"To who?"

"The Boys."

"What boys?"

She kept her eyes on her paper, still writing. "The *Boys*, Teague. Jerry, Bobby, Phil, Brent. They have two drummers, you know. Mickey and Bill."

He stifled a smile as he realized she meant the Grateful Dead. "I did not know that, actually." He asked, "What are you writing to them?" He couldn't picture her writing the kind of star-struck love letters the girls he'd known in school used to write to David Cassidy or Donny Osmond.

"Summer tour's coming and I gotta get tickets to at least one show." She set the red crayon down and looked up. "Me and Auntie Bailey always mail order, and if you make the envelope really nice they make sure you win the lottery." She pushed the envelope over to him. The back was decorated with a rainbow and signed 'Aria Malloy'.

"That's beautiful." Curious, he asked, "Have you been to a lot of concerts?"

"Um hm." Her face lit up. "Wanna see my ticket stubs?"

"Sure."

She stood up, walked a few steps, and turned back. "Come on."

He stood to follow her. "Where are we going?"

"Upstairs."

As Aria skipped past the counter, she told Bailey, "I'm gonna show Teague my ticket stubs." She continued towards the stairs.

Teague stopped, though, and asked Bailey, "Is that okay? For me to go up with her?"

Bailey glanced in the direction of the stairs, made sure Aria was out of earshot. Concern showing on her face, she asked, "Are you okay?"

Knowing she cared made everything else fade into the background. "I am."

She scanned his face, then nodded. "You better go. Aria'll be looking for you."

By the time he walked into Bailey's apartment Aria was sitting on the floor with a photo album on the coffee table in front of her. "I'll be there in a second."

Not looking up, she said, "'Kay."

As he put the bag of grinders from Sal's in the fridge, he glanced around the yellow kitchen. He remembered the first time he'd been there, how he'd thought it needed to be updated. Now, looking at the flowered wallpaper, the white counter top with the avocado green squiggles running through the laminate, he felt warmth in his chest. The meals he'd eaten in this kitchen were easily the best of his life. And it had nothing to do with the food.

"Teague?" Aria called from the living room.

"Coming." In the living room he settled next to Aria on the floor.

She opened the cover of the book. "You don't need tickets when you're a baby, so I don't have them for all the shows I've been to."

The first page had four ticket stubs. Aria pointed to the last one, which had a skeleton printed in black ink with silver glitter in it. "This one was one of my favorite shows ever. Me and my best friend, Mallory, went to that one together. And they played 'Scarlet Begonias' into 'Fire on the Mountain.'"

He read the ticket, saw the date was April 2, 1987. "You remember that?"

"Yeah." She turned the page. "If you can't remember, you can just look at Dupree's. See? They always put the set lists in."

The yellow paper on the next page had a list of dates, venues and songs. April 2, 1987 was starred in blue pen. So were the other two shows at the Centrum in Worcester, and both shows at the Hartford Civic Center. "You were at all these?" He pointed to the stars.

"Um hm. That was before I had to go to school."

They continued turning pages. "You've been to a lot of concerts."

"Auntie Bailey's been to way more." She closed the album, brought it back to the book shelf, and came back with a second one.

Teague opened the cover of the second album. There were pages and pages of ticket stubs. Some were printed on colored paper, although most were on white. Many were the kind he was used to, with the Ticketmaster logo watermarked on them and the event information printed over it. A lot of them had pictures printed on them. An Egyptian eye, a bear, the logo from the *Steal Your Face* album. He scanned them as he turned the pages, saw names of states from California to Connecticut and everything in between.

The first pages, with tickets dated from 1982, had set lists scrawled on scraps of paper with them. After a while the hand written lists were replaced with copies of Dupree's Diamond News. The newsletters were as varied as the tickets. Some were yellow, some blue, and some were on white paper but the ink was colored.

He was nearing the end of the book when the door opened and Bailey came in. "How's it going in here?"

Aria said, "Good. I'm just showing Teague your book."

Delilah nosed her way past Bailey and lay next to Teague. He rubbed her side, making her nub of a tail thump against the floor. The feeling he'd had in the kitchen earlier, of being home, came back so strongly it hurt. *That's ridiculous. This isn't your home.*

But as Bailey sat on the edge of the couch, next to Aria, he couldn't shake the feeling that this was right.

"Aria, that was that show last summer where it poured. Remember?" She pointed to one of the tickets. It was crumpled and the words smeared. It looked like it'd been through the laundry. "Jerry sang that Tennessee Jed was going to wind up *wet,* and he was *laughing* while he sang."

"I remember. That guy kept talking about lightning and saying it was dangerous and everyone was cheering."

Bailey snorted. "Like a little weather's gonna stop us." She turned the pages, towards the front. "It rained at this one, too. And Katelyn and Liam were there."

"Oh, yeah. Because Nannie and Diana came and worked at the shop so we could all go together."

Sounding surprised, Bailey said, "You remember that? You were like four."

"I remember when we went to Hartford, too. And there was that big circle and everyone was saying 'ommmm.'"

Smiling, Bailey asked, "Yeah, but do you remember what they played?"

"No." Aria crossed her arms and pouted a little. "I was three. How am I supposed to remember that?"

"I'll give you a pass on that one." She closed the book. "Why don't you put that away and go pick up the things you left downstairs. Then please wash up for dinner."

"'Kay." She took the book and skipped to the bookshelf.

Bailey led Teague into the kitchen and handed him a stack of plates. As he set them on the table, he asked, "How many shows have you been to?"

"I don't know. I've never counted." She began pulling grinders from the bag. "The two years I was on tour I went to almost every show. I probably made it into fifty. Since I came home I go to like ten or fifteen a year. That's—" She paused, then said, "It's gotta be at least a hundred and thirty?"

"Do you remember every one?"

"Maybe." She smiled a little as she carefully tore the tape holding the paper on the first grinder. "After a while things get confused, unless there's something that really stood out. Like when they bust out a 'Dark Star', or the show last year where it was pouring, or the crowd got crazy and crashed the gates."

He set napkins next to the plates. "I have never understood gate crashers."

She set half a ham grinder on Aria's plate. "For some people it's the only way they can see the show."

"Why don't they just buy tickets?"

She filled cups with water. "Lots of reasons. When I first started going you could buy tickets the day of the show. But now, shows sell out. And, honestly, a lot of people go hoping for a miracle." He looked at her quizzically. She said, "That's when someone gives you a ticket for free."

Surprised that anyone would do that, he asked, "Does that happen often?"

"All the time."

It would never have dawned on him to go to a concert without a ticket. "Do you go without having tickets?"

She shook her head. "Not anymore. Back when I started I didn't care if I got shut out. The next best thing to being at a Dead show is being on the lot. But with Aria, it's different." She glanced towards the living room, then turned back to him. Quietly, she said, "Don't tell her, because she loves to decorate envelopes, but I actually use Ticketmaster now. Mail order is cool, but if I order over the phone it's a guarantee that I'll get the tickets I want."

He smiled. "Your secret's safe with me."

Chapter 23

Teague wasn't sure what he was more unhappy about— having to dress up for the second day in a row, putting gel in his hair for the first time in months, or that his mother was going to be there. He sipped the coffee he'd picked up at Rich's Citgo. *Definitely the worst part about today is the coffee.* Even the styrofoam cup was distasteful.

His mood was slightly improved by seeing his mother sitting stiffly on the hard wooden bench outside the courtroom, like any other normal person. *Being a first-class bitch doesn't win you favors in criminal court.* He sat next to her. "Mom."

"The lawyer is late."

"Court starts at ten, and chances are he's with Cole."

She scanned the other people waiting for the session to begin, then repositioned her hands over her purse. "Can you believe there are people in *jeans.* You'd think they'd come to court dressed appropriately."

"Maybe that's all they have."

"Jeans are for construction workers, not respectable adults." She made an exasperated sound. "Although, considering that they're here, they obviously *aren't* respectable."

"You're here."

"Not by choice."

Teague turned and gaped at her. "Do you really think anyone is here by *choice?*"

"If they didn't want to be here, they wouldn't have broken the law."

He sat back and tried to ignore her. He watched people come in and get in line to check in, then sit on the bench or stand in small groups talking.

"Apparently the clothing stores here are in line with that diner."

Completely confused, he asked, *"What?"*

She sniffed. "That man is wearing *brown polyester*. That was in style when people were still eating *meatloaf*."

Nice, Mom. You managed a dig at a stranger and your son at the same time. He tried drowning her out by concentrating on listening to a couple guys swapping stories of what had landed them in court. One had gotten caught riding dirt bikes on private property, the other was there for simple possession. Neither was looking at time.

"Teague, Mrs. Gallagher." Bill greeted them.

"It's *Ms.* Wesley." Priscilla stood to greet Cole's lawyer.

Bill bowed his head. "My apologies." He led them off to the side, to relative privacy.

Anxiously, Teague asked, "How is he?"

"Hanging in there. He keeps his head down and does as he's asked. That looks good for him, and it could help with a shorter sentence." He looked back and forth between Teague and Priscilla. "I just want you both to know what to expect today. I've put together as much evidence as I can find showing Cole wasn't here for extended periods of time last year. Unfortunately, it's a lot harder to prove where someone was than where they weren't. He's prepared—"

Teague stopped listening. *Something... there's something there.* He walked away as his mom began explaining how important it was to her, personally, that Bill find a way to free Cole. He paced, trying to grasp that *something* just at the edge of his brain. *We can't prove where he was because he uses cash. He travels by car, so there's no plane tickets.*

Who the hell drives that... Tickets!

Bill was making his way past the desk where defendants were checking in, at the far end of the room. Teague almost ran, "Bill!"

He turned. So did everyone else in the room. Teague didn't care.

Bill came back, met him in the middle of the room. "What's wrong?"

"Tickets."

"Sorry?"

"Deadheads keep their ticket stubs. If we can find Cole's, we can prove where he was."

"A ticket stub isn't going to have a name on it."

Sure he was onto something, he said, "If he ordered tickets, there'd be a record of it and we could match them."

"Even if he ordered them, there's no way to prove he used them himself." He shook his head. "I'm sorry, Teague."

*** ***

Teague picked up his coffee cup and rotated it in his hands. Bailey sat across from him, patiently waiting. After spending the entire day with his mother, he couldn't help thinking Priscilla would have a field day with Bailey. *Who pierces their nose? That's disgusting. It looks like her wardrobe came from the Salvation Army— in Woodstock. If she did something with her hair she'd be so much prettier.* He recoiled at that thought. Bailey was beautiful just the way she was.

Finally, he met her eyes. "He looks awful. Pale, thinner." He thought about how Cole had looked and added, "He looks stressed."

Concerned, she asked, "So, what happened?"

"Nothing. His lawyer asked for a continuance. They set another date for his hearing."

"Are you going to be able to see him soon?"

"No." Guilt ate at him. "Bailey, I don't deserve to see him."

"Teague, you do."

He traced triangles on the table. It was important to him that she understood. "The last time I saw him, before all of this, was at Christmas. He called me a few days before, said he'd made it as far as Wallingford and could I come get him. He was hitchhiking, it was snowing. I left work in the middle of the day to get him. He was cold, wet, and hadn't had a shower in days. I brought him back to my house, let him get cleaned up, lent him dry clothes, fed him."

Smiling a little, she said, "That was very kind."

He shook his head. "No, it wasn't. I only brought him home because I didn't have a choice. I made him shower and gave him clothes because I didn't want him sitting on my furniture."

Reassuringly, she said, "Hitchhiking hippies are filthy."

"You don't get it. It wasn't about him being dirty. It was about him being *him*. I didn't want him there at all. I never knew what to say to him, or what kind of crazy shit he was going to talk about. It was uncomfortable. As soon as I could get a hold of our oldest brother, Shea, I brought Cole to his house."

"We're uncomfortable with people who are unlike us. I'm willing to bet Cole was just as uncomfortable at your house as you were to have him there."

"But he's my *brother*."

Gently, she said, "Teague, Cole came back here after Christmas. There wasn't much family around, so he and I spent a bunch of time together. Whatever happened, he wasn't upset."

"He should have been." He pulled his wallet from his pocket, played with it as he talked. "He'd asked me, in the car after I picked him up, what I wanted for Christmas. I didn't want anything. I can just buy something if I want it. He can't afford the kinds of things I'd have considered appropriate anyway. I told him my family was there, and that was enough. It was a lie, really. Just something to say so he didn't buy me anything."

He paused, wanting to make sure he got it right. "But he listened. I don't know how else to explain it." He opened his wallet and took out a black and white picture of four boys with identical smiles, ranging in age from six to sixteen, their arms around each other's bare shoulders. He slid the picture across the table and pointed to each face. "That's Shea, Callum, me and Cole."

She picked it up, carefully touching just the bottom corner, and examined it. A smile touching her lips, she handed it back. "It's a beautiful picture."

"That's the last time I can remember Cole smiling like that. Or any of us. It was taken here, in Vermont. The summer before my mom served my dad with divorce papers. When I opened it on Christmas, saw what it was, all I could think of was that my mom had brought us to Vermont that year specifically so she could tell the judge that she needed the house because it was part of our childhood. It wasn't true, that was the only time we ever went there. But if I'd been her lawyer, that's what I'd have said.

"But that's not what Cole saw. For him, this was the best trip we'd ever taken. When he looked at this picture, he saw the four of us, having the time of our lives. I know, because he talked about it for years." He tucked the picture back into his wallet and looked straight at Bailey. "I had the chance to do the right thing. To be there for my brother, and I didn't. Not just at Christmas, but every time he showed up. And now, he's stuck in jail because I can't get him out, and he won't even allow me to visit him."

*** ***

Bailey wondered how she'd feel if she were Cole. *I wouldn't want to see Teague either.* She knew what it felt like to be treated like shit.

But the Teague sitting in front of her wasn't the same person who had first come into her shop in January, and the defeated tone in his voice pulled at her heart strings. *He came up here to help Cole and he never left. There's gotta be a reason for that.* For a while she'd thought it was because he was trying to figure out what to do with his life. Now, though, she suspected it was guilt.

She wished there was something she could do to help, but as long as Cole was in jail and Teague couldn't see him, she didn't see any way for this to get better.

She thought about asking if he wanted to play cards. Night after night, for years, she'd sat with Jesse or her mom playing cards, not talking about how much she hurt. Maybe it hadn't made her feel better, but it gave her something to focus on besides what she'd lost.

None of them had known what else to do. It had always been her dad who was the master at understanding exactly what people needed. *He'd have done something to show me life was still worth living.*

Inspired, she said, "Hey, do you want to go to Quechee with me tomorrow?"

Looking totally confused at the sudden change in topic, Teague asked, "What's Quechee?"

"It's a town. There's a river and a gorge, it's cool. Will you come?"

"Yeah, sure."

He didn't sound enthusiastic, but she smiled anyway. "Cool. I'll pick you up at ten."

"I can meet you here."

"Your house is on the way."

"I have to come here anyway."

Nearly laughing as she suddenly understood his issue, she said, "Teague, I'll bring you coffee."

Chapter 24

Bailey rang the doorbell and stepped back to wait. She was about to ring again when the door opened.

"Hey now." Teague grinned.

She returned his smile. "I brought coffee."

"Thanks." He took the cup she held out and stepped aside. "Come in, I'll be ready in a minute."

"Teague," she breathed his name, putting her hand to her heart as she scanned the room. "This is beautiful." The dark blue walls could have been too dark, even with the bright white trim, but the big windows at both the front and back of the living room let in plenty of light. White couches and accent furniture brightened the room even more. Even the weird red stove seemed to fit in this room. She turned her attention back to Teague, who was sitting on the couch putting sneakers on. "I pictured you as more of a grey guy."

"Honestly, so did I. But then I went to buy the paint, and this just seemed right." He stood up. "Ready?"

As he followed her out to the van she said, "My mom wants to know if you can come for dinner on Sunday."

"I didn't realize we at the 'bringing the guy home to meet the parents' stage of our relationship already."

She stopped in her tracks. She hadn't thought of it that way at all. Wanting to make sure they understood each other, she explained,

"Aria talks about you all the time. My mom wants to get to know you better and she says she's too tired after work to have a proper conversation."

He turned. Still smiling, he said, "Ah, I see. Well, since it's for Aria, I'll definitely make room in my schedule."

* * *

Teague tried to hide how relieved he was to be out of the van. It wasn't that it was orange, or that it had curtains in the windows and Grateful Dead stickers all over it. It was that Bailey drove the winding mountain roads much faster than he was comfortable with. While she took Delilah to the side of the Quechee Gorge Visitors Center parking lot to go to the bathroom, he stood on solid ground and thanked God they'd made it there alive.

Bailey came back and asked, "You okay?"

Too quickly, he answered, "Yeah, fine. Why?"

"You look a little green."

Not wanting to tell her it was her driving, he said, "I'm just not used to the roads here."

She raised her eyebrows skeptically but didn't say anything. She led him onto the bridge, along a narrow strip of concrete at the edge of the road. Teague looked over the metal railing into emptiness. Far below, the river ran straight and fast, churning in a frothing white line. On one side, dark green pine trees blocked the view of the river bank. On the other, the bright green of early summer leaves ended far enough back that Teague could see the steep V of rock holding the river in place.

Any calm that had returned to his stomach since he'd gotten out of the van was gone. Each time a car crossed the bridge, wind buffeted their backs and the road beneath their feet vibrated. The railing seemed wholly inadequate. "How far do you think it is to the bottom?"

"It's 168 feet." She turned to him. "Want to go down there?"

"That drop would kill you."

She smiled. "There's a path, Teague. Through the woods." She brushed past him, going back the way they'd come.

He followed her into the trees and made his way down a steep path, constantly watching for roots and rocks that jutted up here and there. As he glanced up to see Bailey and Delilah far ahead his toe caught a root and he lurched forward. Grabbing a tree, glad he was behind Bailey and she couldn't see his clumsiness, he righted himself.

At the river's edge they paused to watch the water flow over and around rocks, shooting through the channel in a thick wave. "How deep is the water?"

Looking into the clear mountain river, Bailey said, "I have no idea. I've never tried to go in here. The current is so strong, it'd pull you under those rocks and you'd never get out."

"I thought water was only this blue in the Caribbean."

Shrugging, she said, "There's a lot of places that have blue green water."

As she led him further into the woods, Teague caught glimpses of the river through the trees. Eventually Bailey turned down an offshoot of the main path and they were again on the river bank, although it wasn't like any 'river bank' he'd ever pictured. Layers of grey rock had somehow been upended, the broken edges had been worn down over time so that the twenty feet between Teague and the water, although far from flat, was walkable.

Making his way carefully over the uneven ground, he tried to take in everything around him. Flowers, yellow and purple heads on slender stems, had taken hold in crevices, looking impossibly like they were growing out of the rock. Birds flitted from tree to tree and dragonflies buzzed by small pools of water trapped in depressions in the rocks. *Aria's fairies in disguise.* He smiled when a butterfly landed on Delilah as she drank from one of the pools.

Bailey sat on the edge of the water, slipped her shoes off, and hung her feet in. He sat next to her, pulling off his shoes and rolling the bottoms of his jeans up before putting his feet in as well. The sun warmed him, a pleasant contrast to the icy mountain water running over his feet.

He snuck a look at Bailey. She'd leaned back, supporting herself with her arms. Her face was tipped towards the sky, eyes closed, and a tiny smile played at the corners of her lips. Her hair hung behind her, long and straight. He had the most insane desire to run his fingers through it, to see if it was as soft as it looked. He noticed that her hair wrap was gone. He wasn't sure if he liked that or not. He remembered when he'd first met her he'd hated it, but it seemed like such a part of her, having it gone seemed wrong.

She opened her eyes and turned to him. Embarrassed at being caught staring, he said, "This place is beautiful."

She smiled sweetly. "It's always been one of my favorite places. See how the rocks are layered, and they're tilted up?"

It had been impossible not to notice. "Yeah."

"It was caused by an ice sheet that cut through the bedrock and forced it up. But my dad used to tell us a giant had been walking by and saw this piece of rock. He thought it was a cookie, so he picked it up and broke it in half. He bit one half, realized it was a rock, and dropped it back to the ground. It landed with the broken side up, which is why the layers are vertical instead of horizontal. Then, he spit out the part he'd bitten, which is how the water got here."

"Your dad told you the river was giant spit?"

She laughed, the sound soft and clear. "Yeah."

"And you still put your feet in it?"

"I guess I never thought of it quite that way." She pulled her feet from the water and wrapped her arms around her knees. "He was always telling us stories like that. He'd take us hiking and have me convinced the mushrooms were actually houses and if I was quiet enough I'd see the brownies who lived in them. And I was probably twelve before I stopped believing that dragonflies are actually fairies in disguise. They ruled their woodland kingdom from their capital city, which I thought was in the lake at Woodford."

"Is that where Princess Willa of the Woods lives?"

Surprise flickered over her face. "How'd you know that?"

Hoping he hadn't made a mistake, he said, "Aria told me. She believes it, too. Well, about the dragonflies, anyway. She didn't mention the lake."

"My sister would be furious at me for filling her daughter's head with bullshit." She slipped her feet back in the water. "She outgrew make believe much quicker than I did."

"Was she older than you?"

"By just over a year."

"Wow. That's close."

She smiled sadly. "My parents thought if they had kids close together they'd automatically be best friends."

"Were you?"

She picked up a rock and turned it over in her hands. "When we were small we were. I think probably because we didn't have anyone else to play with. But as we got older," she fell silent for a moment before finishing, "I think it would have been better if we'd been further apart."

The pain in her voice was so obvious, he wished he could take her hand, to let her know he cared. Or pull her into a hug and hold her until it went away. Anything to ease the sorrow.

Chapter 25

After dinner Aria colored while Teague helped Bailey wash the dishes. She only half-listened as Aria talked about the new kid in her class. "Nannie gave me two cookies today in my snack, so I shared with Bryce."

"That was very kind of you, Aria." Bailey gave her an encouraging smile over her shoulder.

"His cubby's next to mine. Mrs. Ellis put a sticker on it so he'd know where his place was. It's a bear, 'cause Bryce starts with b and so does bear. He said in his old school they didn't have cubbies, they had lockers." She looked up from the picture she was coloring. "What's lockers?"

Teague answered, "They're like cubbies, but they have doors on them that lock."

"Did you have lockers, Teague?"

"In junior high and high school."

"Did you have a sticker of a tiger on yours?"

Bailey tried to hide a smile as he gave her a puzzled look. "No. We didn't have stickers on our lockers."

"So how'd you know which one was yours?"

"They had numbers on them."

"Oh." Aria didn't sound impressed. "Was yours ten?"

Looking even more puzzled, he said, "I don't remember what

numbers I had, but I don't think I had ten."

Bailey whispered, "Tiger, ten and Teague all start with t."

A smile spread over his face. He asked, "Aria, what's the sticker on your cubby?"

"A aardvark." She added, "It's a funny animal. They eat *ants*."

"Sounds yummy." Smiling bigger, he said, "Maybe Auntie will make ants for dinner tomorrow night."

Aria's face fell. "Tomorrow's Friday. I don't come on Fridays." Sounding hopeful, she asked, "Auntie Bailey, can you make them on Saturday instead?"

Struggling not to laugh, she turned around. "Sweetie, that's not really something I'm going to cook."

"Why not?"

She started thinking if there was something she could cook that they could pretend were ants.

Teague saved her the trouble of trying to figure it out. "Aria, ants starts with 'a' also." He sat at the table next to her. "Aria Aardvark ate ants after accomplishing artwork."

She giggled.

He said, "Teague the tiger tickled the tadpole." He tickled Aria, making her shriek. After a moment he stopped and they both settled back into the chairs, still laughing a little.

"I'm not a tadpole."

"No, but Aria doesn't start with t."

"Okay, do b, for Auntie Bailey."

"Bailey," He looked at her, his expression sobering. The smallest smile tugged at the corners of his lips. "Bailey bakes beaucoup bagels."

"What's boo coo?"

He said, "It's French for a lot."

"Auntie Bailey doesn't bake bagels *at all*. Plus, you forgot her animal."

He was still looking at her. It made her heart pound. Why the hell did it make her feel like that? Why the hell was he *looking* at her like that?

He said, "Buffalo Bailey baked birthday bananas."

Aria burst out laughing. "Teague, Auntie Bailey *hates* bananas."

He glanced at Aria for a second, then turned back to Bailey and said, "Butterfly Bailey's my best buddy."

He's serious. He thinks I'm his best buddy. Not up to figuring out how she felt about that, she asked, "Okay, who wants icky ice cream?"

"What's icky ice cream?" Aria asked.

"All ice cream's icky." Bailey got the carton from the freezer anyway. As she scooped she listened to Aria and Teague still making up sentences with all the same letter. She wished there was a grown-up version of putting a sticker on a cubby. Teague was, in effect, the new kid. And she wanted him to know this was his place.

Is that really what you want? For Teague to be here? She stopped scooping and stared at the container of ice cream. *You're being stupid. He said buddy, which isn't anything more than a friend. Any look you think he's giving you is in your mind.*

"Bailey?"

She jumped, knocking a bowl off the counter. It hit the floor and shattered, spraying glass and ice cream everywhere. "*Shit!*"

"Stay still." Teague was already up. "There's glass right near your foot. I'm going to get shoes. Aria, stay in that chair."

Tears spilled over, ran down her cheeks. "Aria, baby, I'm so sorry." She twisted, keeping her feet still so she didn't step on glass. "That was one of the bowls you made."

"It's okay, Auntie." Her voice quivered as she said, "We could glue it."

Teague came back and grabbed a handful of paper towels. He picked up a chunk of bowl and showed it to Bailey. She knew there was no way they were gluing it. Quietly, she said, "Can you please put the pieces in the sink?"

He did as she asked, then wiped up the ice cream. "I think you can move now."

She went straight to Aria, picked her up and snuggled her. "I'm so sorry."

Aria wrapped her legs around Bailey's waist and buried her face in her shoulder. Her voice muffled, she said, "It's okay. It was a accident."

"I don't think we can glue it."

Aria pulled away a little. "Can we make a new one?"

Resilient kid. "Yeah." She smiled through her tears, "That's a great idea."

"Tomorrow?"

"I'll ask Nannie if I can take you."

She looked over Bailey's shoulder. "Teague, you're gonna come, right?"

Before Bailey had a chance to remind Aria that Teague had his own life, he said, "Absolutely."

"Auntie?"

"Hmm?"

"Can you make the ants?"

The laughter that bubbled up felt so good. "I'll see what I can do."

*** ***

Bailey wandered around her mom's living room while she waited for Aria to finish changing into play clothes. It was probably a good thing she was taking her; she could hear frustration in her mom's voice. *She shouldn't still be taking care of little kids. She should be relaxing, working on her garden, reading.*

And Dad should be with her. She ran her fingers down the length of the bookshelf, thinking of when her dad had built it. She'd been with him the day he'd bought the paint; she remembered he'd said the deep red was period correct for their old farmhouse. *And he took me for ice cream. Just like always.*

She pushed that thought away. She scanned the titles in a row of books. Her mom had everything from *The Hobbit* to *Gone with the Wind* to cookbooks and gardening manuals.

Her eyes landed on the baby names book she'd used back in school, for the project she'd had to do, and she remembered when she'd first met Teague. He hadn't known what his name meant. She pulled the battered book off the shelf. It fell open to the first "B" page, the spine worn from being opened to that spot repeatedly. She'd circled her own name, and her sister's, years ago. Neither of them had particularly good meanings.

She didn't look, but she knew Aria was listed, too. Peyton had drawn a heart in the margin next to it, although she wouldn't have needed the book to know an aria was a solo in an opera.

Bailey flipped about three-quarters of the way through the book, then went page by page until she found the 'T' section. She followed down the columns until she found it. Teague's name had a nice meaning, although she wasn't sure 'poet' fit him.

*** ***

The pottery shop had a dusty scent Bailey found somewhat unpleasant. She assumed it had something to do with the rows of pottery waiting to be glazed.

Aria asked, "Auntie Bailey, what are you going to make?"

"A coffee cup." She chose a nice, big one.

Teague laughed. "Obviously."

182

She smiled at his teasing. "What about you?"

"I'm thinking an ice cream bowl."

Sarcastically, she said, "Obviously."

He grinned as he reached for a bowl big enough for a gallon of ice cream.

Aria giggled, "Teague, you'll get a stomach ache if you eat that much ice cream."

"Maybe I'll share it with you and Auntie Bailey." He changed direction and picked up a much smaller bowl, though.

Bailey handed Aria the same kind of bowl Teague had chosen. As they settled at a work table, she asked, "Teague, have you ever glazed pottery?"

"Nope."

Aria explained, "You gotta make sure you don't put it on too thick, cuz it'll bubble. And you can't tell what color it is until after they cook it, so you have to go by the sample on the container." Looking embarrassed, she said, "The one that goes on light purple comes out dark blue."

"It's a good thing I have you here to teach me."

Aria beamed.

Bailey picked up a brush and dipped it in the jar that looked like light purple glaze. "The vase you made for Nannie turned out beautiful." She carefully spread a layer of glaze over the mug, picturing bold blue containers and bright yellow flowers.

"It just wasn't what I thought it would be." Aria began applying glaze to her bowl in big splotches.

Teague said, "Sometimes those are the best kind of things. The unexpected ones."

Bailey smiled a tiny bit, thinking how nice this unexpected thing was turning out to be.

Chapter 26

Teague was nervous as he navigated the winding back road, following the directions Bailey had given him to her mom's. He'd been joking about bringing the new guy home to meet the parents, but that was exactly what he felt like.

He'd asked Bailey a dozen times what to bring and she'd insisted that he didn't need to bring anything. But he couldn't show up empty handed. In his old life he'd have picked up a bottle of good wine. After a lot of thought he decided to bring ice cream and toppings.

The white farmhouse looked like something from a postcard, complete with a porch with two rocking chairs. He got out of the car as Aria ran out to the driveway, Delilah close on her heels. "TEEEEAAAGUE!!!"

He scooped her up and swung her around. "Hey, girl!" He held her and rubbed noses. Then he put her down and tickled her until she shrieked laughter. He petted Delilah, got the grocery bag out of the car and let Aria lead him towards the side door.

She asked, "Is that ice cream?"

"Of course."

She burst through the door. "Nannie, Teague brought ice cream!"

Ellen turned from the counter. "Hi, Teague."

"Hi, Ellen. Thank you for inviting me." He smiled nervously as handed her the bag.

Taking the bag, she said, "Aria, go get Auntie and tell her Teague is here please."

"Okay, Nannie." She scampered off.

Teague said, "I hope Bailey's not too mad that I brought ice cream. I almost didn't, because I know she doesn't approve, but it's Aria's favorite."

As Ellen put the carton in the freezer, she said, "I have no idea why she's so dead set against it. We've never been opposed to desserts here."

Standing in the cozy kitchen, with its red and white plaid curtains, worn wood table and chairs, and Aria's artwork pinned to a cork board, he knew it had been a much better choice than wine would've been. "She calls it 'icky ice cream.'"

Ellen laughed. "Sounds about right."

Fishing for something else to talk about, he pointed to a framed painting of a rainbow arching over a flower, hanging between the windows. "This must be Aria's work."

"It is. She loves to paint."

He pointed to a painting hanging above the table. "This is Bailey's." Having seen a few of her pieces, he knew without having to ask.

"It is." She crossed her arms lightly over her chest. "She did that when she was in high school."

The depth of the painting took his breath away. Velvety soft petals adorned dainty purple flowers, held aloft by slender green stems. Rocks, their once jagged edges worn smooth with time, nestled vertically to the river's edge. Blue-green water rushed past the fairy sitting on the riverbank. It brought back the memory of the sun on his skin, the cold mountain water tugging at his feet. "This is," he paused to frame his thoughts. "It captures exactly what it feels like to sit on the bank at Quechee."

Sounding surprised, Ellen asked, "You've been to Quechee?"

"Bailey and I went a couple days ago."

Then Aria was back, with Bailey in tow. "Hey, Teague." Bailey smiled at him.

He loved that particular smile; it made her eyes light up. He'd give up ice cream forever just to see that smile. "Hey, Bailey."

"My directions were okay?"

"They were. Thank you." She looked so pretty in a summer dress, her hair flowing over her tanned shoulders. *You're staring.* He couldn't stop, though. All he wanted was to push her hair back and kiss her bare skin.

"Nannie, I'm *starving.* Teague's here. Can we eat now?"

"Did you wash your hands?" Ellen asked.

"Yes. That's what took me so long."

Glad for the distraction, Teague turned to Ellen. "What can I do to help?"

"I thought we'd eat outside, the weather's so nice." She handed a stack of plates to Bailey, glasses to Teague, and a bundle of silverware to Aria. "You can all go set the table."

"Come on, Teague, I'll show you where to go." Aria skipped out ahead of everyone else.

Teague and Bailey shared a smile as they followed. On the patio at the back of the house, Teague set out the glasses Ellen had given him and looked around. "This is beautiful, Bailey."

"My mom has always had a knack for gardening." Flowers in all colors bloomed in planters set around the flagstone patio, in the surrounding garden, and along a path leading to a shed. Trees provided shade over a hammock, and Teague could easily see a young Bailey curled up with a book in one of the Adirondack chairs tucked into a corner under a vine covered pergola.

Ellen came out, carrying a huge salad. "I hope you're hungry." She smiled, "I think I overestimated."

"Nannie said she didn't know what you liked, so I told her you like salad." Aria beamed, "She made the kind with grilled steak and beets. Wait till you try it. Nannie's the best cook."

Bailey raised an eyebrow at her niece.

Aria amended quickly, "I mean, besides Auntie Bailey." Except then she looked back at her grandmother and said, "They're both the best."

Teague squatted next to her and said, "I think you should stop while you're ahead."

Her expression softening, Bailey said, "Aria, sit. And give Teague his space, please."

She sat, but she couldn't stay quiet. Teague didn't care that she dominated the conversation. By now he was familiar with the names of the children in her class, the things she did at recess, and what she was learning in school. He still loved listening to her.

* * *

After dinner Aria brought Teague to the back yard to show him her swing set while Bailey cleared the table. On her second trip into the house she paused at the sink and looked out the window at Teague. A smile spread over his face at whatever Aria said. It looked good on him.

Ellen said, "He's cute."

Bailey jumped, she hadn't heard her mother come in. Trying to hide her surprise at being caught watching Teague, she mumbled, "I guess."

Ellen asked, "You don't like him?"

"I like him. But not like that." She scraped plates, avoiding her mother's knowing smile. "I think it's good for Aria to have a guy to look up to. Someone who's not..." She trailed off, not sure how to finish without insulting her own friends.

"It's good for you, too."

She understood exactly what her mother was saying and it made her very uncomfortable. "We're just friends." Picking up the next plate and scraping it into the trash, she said, "Guys like that don't pay attention to girls like me."

"Sure looks like he's paying attention to you."

"What exactly does that mean?"

"He's here."

Bailey paused, a plate half-way into the dishwasher. "He's here for Aria." She dropped the plate into the slot.

Ellen gave all her attention to moving leftover salad into a plastic container. After a moment she asked, "You took him to Quechee?"

"I did." Wondering how her mom had known that, she looked quizzically at her.

She held her daughter's gaze. "I didn't think you went there anymore."

Softly, Bailey said, "It was the first time I've gone since Dad…" Her eyes flickered to a spot on the floor, between the island and the back counter. She wiped a tear, hoping her mom didn't notice.

"I'm glad you did. And that you took Teague." She smiled. "He's—"

Dancing through the door, still dragging Teague, Aria sang, "I scream, you scream, we all scream for ice cream!" She stopped dancing and asked, "Can I have ice cream now?"

Bailey narrowed her eyes at Teague. "Who said we have ice cream?"

"Teague brought it. He brought whipped cream in a can, too. I ate all my dinner." She gave what Bailey knew Aria thought was her most winning smile.

Crossing her arms over her chest, pretending she was really considering her answer, Bailey said, "I guess, since Teague brought it."

Aria grinned. "Yeah!"

Ellen started towards the cabinet where she kept the bowls.

"Mom, sit. We've got this." Bailey got bowls and set them on the island in the center of the room while her mom went to sit at the table.

Teague picked Aria up and set her on his hip so she could pull the ice cream from the freezer. "I want a lot," she told her aunt.

Now eye to eye with the little girl, Bailey gave her a skeptical look. "You get what you get and you don't get upset."

"Auntie, come on. It's special cuz Teague's here." She squeezed her arms around his neck.

"Yeah, Bailey. It's special." Teague grinned devilishly.

Caving to the pressure, Bailey scooped ice cream. "You can deal with it when she has a stomach ache, Teague."

Still holding Aria on his hip, he said, "I will. Because she won't." Then he whispered to Aria, "You won't, will you?"

Aria assured him, "No. I won't."

After dessert, Aria asked Teague, "Will you play Go Fish with me? Please?"

"As long as Auntie Bailey plays, too."

Glancing at her mom, Bailey said, "I've gotta do the dishes."

Ellen waved her off. "Go, play."

Heat rippled through Bailey when her eyes met Teague's. *What the hell?* She forced herself to respond, "I'll find the cards."

In the living room, she searched through a drawer.

Behind her, Teague asked Aria, "Is this you?"

Bailey glanced over her shoulder to see him pointing at a picture on top of the bookshelf.

Aria answered, "Yup. And that's Delilah. You know her. And that's her brother, Samson. He got hit by a car."

"Oh, I'm so sorry."

Bailey quickly turned back to the drawer. She picked up a box, shook the cards out and started counting.

"It's okay. He's in heaven, with my mom and my grandpa. That's my mom." Bailey didn't turn around but she knew Aria must be pointing to the big picture on the wall, the one from Peyton's graduation. She braced for Teague to say something about how beautiful Peyton had been. Everyone always did.

Not giving him a chance, Aria continued, "She died when I was a baby. And next to her is my grandpa. I never knew him cuz he died before I was born. And the girl next to Nannie, the one with the grumpy face, is Auntie Bailey." Aria snickered. Bailey knew that for some reason she found it ridiculously amusing that Bailey had been irritable that day. "Nannie says Auntie was a peach back then, that's why she was making that face."

Teague said, "I'm sure Auntie Bailey was just having a rough day. It happens to all of us."

She turned to see him looking at her. When their eyes met he smiled a little. She held out the box in her hand. "I found cards."

* * *

Bailey walked Teague out to his car.

He paused by the driver's door. "Bailey, thank you for having me here tonight. I had a really good time."

"Me, too." She shuffled her feet, waited to see if he'd say more. It sort of seemed like he was going to. *This is the part in the movies where the guy kisses the girl.* But Teague didn't. Instead, he opened his car door.

Then he turned back. "Bail?"

"Yeah?" *Yes!*

"Cole's got court tomorrow. My mom's not coming. She says it's too stressful for her. And my dad," he shrugged. "He never comes for anything. Callum and Shea both have to work and they can't just fly to Vermont, so it'll just be me. I was wondering if you'd come with me."

Hoping the disappointment didn't show, she nodded. *See that? He didn't kiss you. Mom's completely wrong. And you're an idiot for even thinking it. Guys like Teague don't pay attention to girls like me.* "Yeah. Of course. Do you want me to meet you at your house?"

"I'll pick you up. It's on the way to the courthouse, and—" He grinned, "I have to come in for coffee anyway."

She watched his car until he rounded a bend and the trees blocked the tail lights.

Chapter 27

The rustling of the pink button-down shirt Bailey had borrowed from her mom was unbelievably loud as she wiggled in her seat. She glanced around the courtroom, hoping no one else had noticed. *It wasn't that loud. And other people are moving.* That didn't calm her nerves, though. The bailiff had already removed two people who'd ignored his warning to stop whispering. *They can't kick you out for moving.*

But maybe they could. She glanced at Teague, noticed the tight set of his jaw. *He's nervous, too.* She considered taking his hand, just to let him know she was there. *Yeah, great idea. Because you're not confused enough already?*

She turned her attention back to the front of the room. The judge was telling the current defendant that he had six months to pay the fine he'd been given. She'd missed what his crime was. It was impossible to keep track, they went through cases so fast. In the last couple hours there'd been at least thirty people called up for everything from reckless driving to DUIs to domestic violence. Most of them just said they weren't guilty and were given a new date. A few had a lawyer with them. Most of those had charges either dropped or their punishment drastically reduced.

It was a huge relief when the judge finally called for a recess. Bailey stood and stretched before joining the line of people streaming from the room. Teague asked, "Do you want lunch?"

"Not really. This is all making me feel sick." She stood at the window, watched cars on the street below.

Teague went to the vending machine at the end of the hall and came back with a bag of M&M's, a package of cheese crackers and two bottles of water.

Bailey accepted a water. "Teague? Do you think all those people are really innocent?"

"No."

"How come they say they are?"

He chewed his cracker, sipped water, and answered, "They have to if they want a chance to talk. If they plead guilty the judge will just assign the harshest possible punishment and move on."

"Oh." She played with the bottle of water. "I felt bad for the old people who were dumpster diving."

"Me, too."

"They had a good point. If K-Mart's just throwing that stuff out, there's no reason why they can't use it." He didn't say anything so she continued, "I've done that, you know. Not clothes, but food. McDonald's and Dunkin' Donuts both put whatever they have left at the end of the night in bags next to their dumpsters. There were nights I'd have gone hungry, if I hadn't known that. But I didn't know it was illegal."

"If they bagged it, and put it where you could easily get it, maybe it wasn't." He leaned against the wall and turned his water bottle in his hands. He moved away from the window to stand in front of the suite directory next to the courtroom doors. He sat on the bench and drummed his fingers on the seat next to him.

Finally, she sat next to him and asked, "Are you okay?"

"Yeah." He looked up the hallway. "Usually your lawyer comes to tell you what to expect, but I haven't seen ours."

"Is that bad?"

"It probably doesn't mean anything. He's got to talk to the prosecutor and prep Cole, so maybe he just hasn't had a chance to get out here."

After that they sat in silence until the doors opened for the afternoon session. It was immediately apparent that this was different. The morning's crimes seemed petty compared to assault with a deadly weapon, child pornography, and third-degree larceny. The judge took longer with each case, asking for information and details from the defendant and the lawyers. Instead of being given community service or fines, people received years in jail.

When the bailiff led Cole in Bailey whispered to Teague, "Why's he handcuffed like that?"

The bailiff gave her a dirty look. She mouthed, "Sorry," and tried to sink lower in her seat as Cole took his place next to his lawyer.

The attorney to the right stood. "Good afternoon, Your Honor. Henry Jackman for the State, in regards to State versus Cole Gallagher. That's G-A-L-L-A-G-H-E-R, case number 19421995. Pursuant to a plea agreement, the State is willing to accept a plea of guilty to the charges of possession of less than an ounce of marijuana, a misdemeanor which carries a sentence of up to five years. Mr. Gallagher has been in the custody of the State for just shy of seven months and has been a model citizen. As part of the agreement, the State is willing to release him with time served."

Holy shit! Teague was still clenching his jaw, though, and her sudden optimism waned. *He must know something I don't.* She missed what they said, but started listening again when Cole's lawyer, Bill, stood up.

"Good morning, Judge McGregor. William Whitney, on behalf of Cole Gallagher."

"Is that your understanding as well?"

"Yes, it is, sir."

Pulling his glasses down and peering at Bill, Judge McGregor said, "You've discussed the agreement and all implications in full with your client?"

"I have."

"And you're confident that this is in his best interests?"

"I am."

He shifted his gaze slightly left. "Mr. Gallagher, please stand and raise your right hand."

Cole swore the tell the truth and answered a lot of questions about who he was. Bailey flinched a little when he said he didn't have a high school diploma. That wasn't something anyone wanted to admit. But he affirmed that he was able to read and write, and he understood everything that was happening.

The judge shuffled papers on his desk. "Will counsel please approach the bench." Both lawyers went to talk to the judge.

While they talked, too quietly for anyone in the audience to hear, Bailey lost all hope. *If the lawyers were in agreement that Cole should go free, the whole thing should be over.*

Mr. Whitney didn't look upset on his way back to the table, though. He whispered to Cole, whose shoulders relaxed a bit.

The judge asked Cole to tell him what had happened on New Year's Day.

Cole stood. "I was walking home from Bailey's and —"

The judge interrupted, "Who is Bailey?"

"It's a coffee shop."

"Continue."

"So, it was wicked cold, but no one was going out my way so I had to walk. Bailey would've let me stay—"

"I thought Bailey's was a coffee shop."

"It is, but Bailey owns it."

Does he know I'm here? What if they call me to say something? Bailey's stomach tightened. *I should have stayed home.*

The judge nodded. "Continue."

"Bailey would've let me stay at her place, but I wanted to go home."

"Why didn't you drive?" The judge asked.

"I don't have a car." The judge made a note, then motioned for Cole to continue. "So, I'm like half-way home when this car pulls up next to me and I'm thinking someone's gonna give me a ride. But then the cops get out and start asking me what I'm doing and saying they don't believe me because you'd have to be stupid or on drugs to be out walking in the freezing cold. And the next thing I know they're handcuffing me, dumping my backpack out on the ground, saying they know why I'm out there. Then they wouldn't let me call anyone, so I didn't have a lawyer the first time I was in court."

"The report from the arresting officers' states that they believed you were illegally growing marijuana in the abandoned greenhouse on the property you were arrested on."

"Your Honor, I was on the road. Not on the property."

"The report also claims you were argumentative."

Cole hung his head. "Yes, Your Honor. I felt they were harassing me because I have long hair."

The judge looked him over. "Mr. Whitney tells me, and Mr. Jackman confirms, that the police collected evidence proving you were not in Vermont beginning July the second and ending November the fourth of last year. Please state for the court where you were during that time."

Bailey's heart pounded so hard she could hear it. Admitting you were a Deadhead was not likely to win favor in the eyes of the law.

"I was following the Grateful Dead."

Please don't ask what he does. Please, please. If asked, he'd have to either lie under oath, or say he sold acid. And sometimes pot or shrooms. But mostly acid.

"You realize, Mr. Gallagher, that the followers of the Grateful Dead have a reputation for possessing and distributing illegal drugs."

"Yes, Your Honor."

Bailey thought she almost saw a smile on Judge McGregor's face. *Is that even possible?* She'd have to ask Teague.

"Mr. Gallagher, you understand that I have the power to deny the recommendation of the prosecutor and try you on the original felony charges of possession with intent to sell."

"Yes, Your Honor."

"And yet you admit freely that you associate with a group of people known to take and sell illegal drugs?"

"Yes, Your Honor."

He nodded. "By entering a plea of guilty you understand that you will forever have a criminal record. Should you be arrested again, for any crime in this or any other state, you will be tried as a repeat offender."

"I understand."

"Cole Gallagher, I accept your plea of guilty to one misdemeanor charge of possession." He looked at Cole over the rim of his glasses. "I don't want to see you in my courtroom again."

Cole sounded relieved as he said, "No, Your Honor."

* * *

Teague paced while he and Bailey waited in the hallway. He'd heard the judge release Cole, but it felt unreal. He wanted to see his brother. To get in the car with him and drive away.

"Teague, I don't understand what happened." Bailey looked up from the bench.

Pulled from his thoughts, he stopped pacing. "What do you mean?"

"They just let him go? After all the stuff that cops said in the newspaper?"

Taking a seat next to her, he said, "Bill and the prosecutor made a deal."

A line formed between her eyes. "Because of new evidence?"

"That's what they said."

"How come they didn't tell the judge what the evidence was?"

He shrugged. "They didn't need to, because they'd already worked out a deal."

"I'm sorry. I don't understand any of this."

He smiled a little at her confusion. "Most of what happens in a criminal trial is done between the defense attorney and the prosecutor before they go into court. So what you saw today was just them telling the judge what they'd worked out, and him approving it."

"When Cole admitted that he knew Deadheads do drugs it looked like the judge smiled."

"Yeah, I saw that."

"Why?"

"My best guess? The judge has a personal interest in something having to do with that. Maybe he appreciates when suspects tell the truth, or he has a kid who's a Deadhead."

"How did Cole know to say that?"

"Bill made sure Cole knew what he'd be asked, and exactly how to answer it."

The line between her eyes deepened. "How'd he know the judge would ask that?"

"Because he works in this court all the time. He knows the judges and their quirks. That's one of the reasons I hired someone from here, rather than petitioning to be allowed to represent Cole myself. It's entirely possible that if Cole had lied, the judge would have refused the plea deal."

"I thought you didn't know about criminal law."

"I don't, really. But I am a lawyer, and a lot of the things we do are the same."

"Cole's really lucky to have you."

He wasn't sure he agreed. Or at least, he didn't think he'd done anything other than hiring someone who knew what they were doing. He didn't want to argue, though. Instead, he settled back against the wall, glad of Bailey's company. Next to her, he felt calmer. *I need to do something to thank her. Not just for today, but for everything. I never would have made it through this without her.* He had no idea what, though.

Bill and Cole came down the hall from the holding area. Bill smiled at Teague and Bailey. "Nice to see you."

Bailey hugged Cole. He held her tight as he said, "Hey, sistah."

"I'm so happy to see you." She kissed his cheek.

Cole nodded acknowledgment to Teague. "Never thought I'd be happy to see you."

Bill said, "You should be. He got me thinking about ticket stubs, and that's the reason you're walking out today."

Keeping an arm around Bailey, Cole started for the elevator. "Can we go, before they change their minds?"

Teague lagged behind Bailey and Cole on the way to the car. It had been a shock to see her kiss his cheek, the way he hugged her, that they walked together towards the parking garage. *You're such a dumbass. Of course she kissed his cheek. They're friends. She told you they'd spent a bunch of time together.* He stopped walking, a new thought occurring to him. She'd never said anything about it, but he was pretty sure Bailey and Rain had had a thing before spring tour. It was possible she and Cole— *Brah, don't even go there.*

At the car Cole took the front seat. Teague would've preferred to have Bailey next to him, but he couldn't think of any way to say so without either offending Cole or giving Bailey the wrong idea. *Which is what? That's what you want, isn't it? But it's not what she wants. She's here as your friend, and Cole's friend.*

Cole turned in the seat and asked Bailey, "What's up with that shirt?" He gave her a dubious look. "It looks like something Teague would wear."

Bailey pulled at the shirt. "Is it bad?"

"Wicked bad." He settled into the seat. "Can we go to like McDonald's or something? Jail food sucks."

Teague started the car. "Anything you want."

Bailey asked, "Can you drop me off at the shop first? I've got shit to do before Aria gets there."

Teague glanced at her in the rear-view mirror. "Sure."

All the way to Bailey's, Cole played with the radio. "Man, I miss this so much." He sang along, the windows down, his long hair billowing in the breeze.

Sometimes Bailey joined in. No matter how hard he tried to tell himself he was being ridiculous, it made Teague jealous to hear them singing together.

When he got into town he stopped in front of the shop. Bailey grinned, "Cole, behave."

He winked. "Never."

She rolled her eyes and asked Teague, "Are you coming back?"

"As soon as I go change."

"'Kay. See you." She headed into the shop and he pulled away.

Cole asked, "So what's up with you and Bailey?"

"Nothing."

Giving Teague a knowing grin, he said, "Jesse's not around, huh?"

"What's that supposed to mean?"

He shrugged. "Jesse doesn't ask what she does when he's not

around."

"We're *friends*, Cole."

Throwing his hands up in mock defense, he said, "Just asking."

They lapsed into silence. Teague felt like he should say something. *What the fuck are you going to say? How was prison? Glad to have you back? I'm sorry I treated you like shit last time I saw you?*

There was one thing he could ask. "What ticket stubs was Bill talking about?"

"From all the shows I did last year. They were in my backpack, which," he added bitterly, "the cops still have."

"Bill said he couldn't use your ticket stubs because there's no way to prove it was actually you who used them."

"I guess it was because the police already had them in evidence, and there wouldn't have been a reason for me to be carrying around someone else's ticket stubs."

"And the prosecutor was willing to accept that?"

"Bill said he didn't have to prove I was innocent, just that there was a possibility I wasn't guilty. And he said if the prosecutor wouldn't budge he'd petition for a jury trial. Something about convincing twelve people, all who live around here and probably know at least one Deadhead."

"You waived your right to a jury."

"He said you can change your mind as long as it's before the trial starts."

If Teague had learned that, he'd forgotten it. *And that's why you hire a criminal lawyer. And why you're not one.* "I gotta tell you, man, whatever Bill did, he did it right."

Cole gave him a skeptical look. "And all this time I thought you wanted me in jail."

Guilt twisted in his stomach. "I'm sorry, Cole. I was an asshole."

Cole cranked the volume on the radio, ending all possibility of further conversation.

At McDonald's Teague pulled into a parking space. As he opened the door Cole said, "What the fuck, dude. Can't we go through the drive-thru?"

"I don't eat in the car."

Cole stared open mouthed for a moment, then said, "Forget it. I'll eat at home."

"Are you sure?"

"Bro, I'm not going inside in *this*." He pointed at his prison clothes.

He had to admit, now that Cole had pointed it out, he wasn't too keen on being seen in public with him dressed like that. "Why are you in prison clothes, anyway?"

"Because that's what inmates wear."

He eyed him for a moment before saying, "Shouldn't you wear a suit to court?"

"Brah, your lawyer has to petition for that, and someone has to bring it to court for you. Did Bill ask you to bring a suit?" When Teague didn't respond, Cole continued, "Anyway, they only do that for murderers and shit. Drug dealers aren't any big deal."

Christ, I don't know much more about this than Bailey. "We can go through the drive-thru just this once." As he pulled into the lane he asked, "Why didn't they give you back what you were wearing when you were arrested?"

"Why didn't you bring me a change of clothes?"

"I didn't know I had to."

Cole shook his head. "And Mom always said you were the smart one."

He has a right to be angry with me. "I'm sorry. I didn't know you were going to be released today, and I honestly thought when you were they'd give you back your clothes." Embarrassed, he said, "That's what happens in the movies."

"Yeah, because movies aren't real."

"I didn't know, Cole. I've never done this."

"Aren't you a lawyer?"

Beginning to get frustrated, he said, "I don't do this. I'd never set foot in criminal court before January."

Cole sighed. "My clothes wouldn't be at the courthouse, they'd be at the prison. But even if I'd been released from prison I wouldn't have my shit. It didn't make sense to leave it sitting there for fifteen years, so had it shipped home."

"I didn't get anything."

"I don't live with you."

"I've been here since January, though."

Cole narrowed his eyes. "My clothes went to Connecticut, because that's my legal address. Why have you been here since January?"

Not into explaining the disastrous state of his life, he asked, "What do you want to eat?"

"A Big Mac and fries. And an apple pie. Two pies. And make the fries a large."

Once they'd gotten Cole's order and were on the way home Cole asked, "You're not here to make sure I stay out of trouble, are you?"

"Nope. Feel free to get in any trouble you want."

Cole looked at him suspiciously. "Where's Mom?"

"No fuckin' clue." He was perfectly happy to not know where his mother was, as long as it meant he didn't have to deal with her.

"So, you're staying at the house. Here. In Vermont."

"I am."

"And you've been here since January?"

"I have."

Cole ate a few more fries. "Don't you have work? And Marlena?"

Keeping his eyes on the road, Teague said, "I quit and we broke up."

"Huh."

They lapsed into silence. Teague hadn't known how to talk to Cole before, now it was even worse. He was relieved when they pulled into the driveway.

While Teague locked the car, Cole ran up the steps to the porch and yanked the door. "Dude. What the fuck?"

Teague followed, "It's locked."

"Why?"

Ignoring what he considered a ridiculous question, he unlocked the door.

Cole stopped immediately inside and looked around the living room. "Holy shit. It's clean. And *blue*."

"I thought it could use some updating." Teague's chest swelled with pride as he took in the room.

"Where's all my shit?"

"Your clothes are washed and folded, on the bed in the small bedroom. All the other things," the pipe he'd found on the coffee table all those months ago flashed through his mind, "are in your room."

"You've been in my room?"

"Just to clean."

Staring at him, Cole said, "You cleaned *my room*?"

"Not really." All the work he'd done sounded really bad all of a sudden. "I just got rid of whatever food there was."

Turning away, Cole began to wander through the room, eventually stopping at the shelves where the stereo sat. He ran his fingers over his tape collection.

Very conscious of the fact that he'd been through all Cole's tapes, Teague said, "I made sure I put everything back where it came from."

"You listened to my *tapes*?" He turned, his eyes narrowed accusingly as he looked at his brother. "Did you sleep in my bed, too?"

Teague had always thought of the house as belonging to their mother. This was the first time it occurred to him that their mother owned it, but it was Cole's *home*. And he'd invaded it. He lied. "I mean, I had to move things, to paint. But I put it all back."

"What are you going to do now?"

"I'm working on painting the bathroom down here, then I'm going to start on the bedrooms."

Cole's face scrunched up and incredulously he said, "You're staying here? Like, *living here?* In this house?"

He thought that over for a second, then nodded slightly. "Yeah, I guess I am. As long as it's okay with you."

Cole stared at him long enough that it was uncomfortable. "Whatever." He went upstairs, leaving Teague standing in the middle of the living room.

He mumbled, "That went well."

He went to his own room, antsy to get back to Bailey's. It was a relief to wash the gel out of his hair, and to put on normal clothes. Clothes were going to be somewhat of an issue, since most of what he usually wore belonged to Cole. Maybe Bailey would go shopping with him. He'd managed to buy jeans and new shoes, but he had no idea where to get shirts. He slipped his 'Fuckin GoNuts' shirt on, stuck his feet in his Birkenstocks and went down to the living room.

Cole passed him on his way to the front door.

"Where are you going?"

With his hand on the door knob, Cole looked back at him. "I thought you weren't here to keep tabs on me."

"I'm not."

"Put the key back. Or leave the door unlocked." He raised his eyebrows. "No one's gonna break in out here."

Teague waited until whoever picked Cole up was out of the driveway before he, too, left.

Chapter 28

Despite having every window in the house open Teague woke covered in sweat. On his way through the living room he mumbled to Cole, "Why the hell isn't this place air conditioned?"

He grunted but didn't reply. Teague wasn't surprised. In the days since Cole had come home their conversations had mainly consisted of Teague asking Cole if he needed anything and Cole saying he was fine. It wasn't the kind of relationship he wanted with his brother, but it was better than nothing.

Teague pulled the orange juice from the fridge, took a swig, looked back into the living room and asked, "What are—" The phone rang, interrupting him. He turned away from Cole and answered, "Hello?"

"Hey, Teague."

He smiled, "Hey, Bailey."

"We're going swimming. Do you want to come?"

"Yes. Definitely. I had no idea how hot it got up here."

"I'll pick you up in half an hour." She added, "With coffee in hand."

Bailey, bearing coffee, was an idea he could definitely get behind. Even better, "Iced coffee?"

* * *

Bailey signaled for Delilah to sit when Teague opened the door. "Iced coffee was a killer idea." She handed him a cup. "I put it on the menu and Ann Marie had sold seven cups by the time I left."

He bent down to pet Delilah. "Cool." He smiled up at her, "Or should I say n-ice."

That was so corny, she had to smile. "Are you ready?"

He stood up, rubbed the back of his neck, looking sheepish. "I have a slight issue."

She looked past him, to Cole sitting on the couch. "No issue. Cole can come, too." She hoped he would. She'd barely seen him since he'd been home. "Cole? Do you want to come?"

He looked at Teague, then back to her. "Where are you going?"

"Althea Falls."

"There's always a million people there."

"It shouldn't be too bad. It's a weekday. And we're picking up Aria, and meeting Katelyn and Liam, so Bolton and Triple Buckets are both out."

His eyes shifted to Teague again. "I think I'm just gonna hang here."

"Right on." She asked Teague, "Ready?"

"I don't have a bathing suit."

"You can wear whatever you have for shorts. It's just a swimming hole. I'm going in this." She indicated her shorts and tank top.

He shook his head. "I don't have shorts. At all. When I came up here in January I wasn't expecting to stay."

"You can wear cut-offs."

"Cut-offs?" He raised his eyebrows.

"You know, you just take jeans and cut them?" He was giving her such a weird look, she said, "If you don't have something you can cut, we can go back to the shop and check the donation box."

His brow creased. "That's…" He shook his head a little. "I'll cut a pair of my jeans." He stepped aside, "Come in. I guess it's gonna be a few minutes before we leave."

Teague headed for the kitchen. Delilah went straight to Cole. He rubbed her head when she put it in his lap. Bailey sat next to him and asked, "Are you sure you don't want to come?"

"Yeah. Sage wanted me to go up to Burlington with him anyway."

She felt the color drain from her face. "Do you really think that's a good idea?"

He smiled a little. "His mom bought some antique chairs and he's going to pick them up for her. I told him I'd give him a hand."

Relieved that they weren't doing anything that could land him back in jail, she said, "I better go see what your brother's doing." A smile snuck across her face. "Apparently he's never made cut-offs?"

Cole snorted. "I can't believe he's going to."

Teague came back, holding a pair of heavy, black-handled scissors. "Want to help me destroy my wardrobe?"

"Sure." She followed him upstairs, to the room at the far end of the hall. It was exactly what she'd expected from him. No piles of clothes on the floor, no papers or pocket contents strewn across the top of the dark wood dresser. The pale blue bedspread and throw pillows were hotel-perfect. A light breeze, enough to make the matching blue curtains flutter but not enough to actually cool anything, circulated from a box fan propped in one window.

He turned back to her. "I'm going to paint up here, but I wanted to finish downstairs first."

This close, she could really appreciate the depth of his eyes. "It's cool. I mean, you just sleep here, right?"

There was a pause before he said, "Pretty much."

Jesus, Bailey. You're asking about what he does in bed? Her heart beat harder.

She jerked her eyes from his and stepped into the room. Trying to find something else to say, she noticed the bed posts. "Did you know pineapples are a sign of welcome?"

Giving her an amused smile, he said, "I did not. I just figured the person who chose the bed had terrible taste."

Her face went red. She could feel it. "It's like a traditional... southern... hospitality... thing." *Shut up. Just... shut up. Now.*

"Huh." He went past her to the dresser and pulled open the bottom drawer. "How'd you know that?"

"My dad was into antiques."

He chose a pair of jeans and laid them on the bed. "Where should I cut?"

She indicated a spot and he started cutting.

She stood in the middle of the room, feeling ridiculous. Like some middle school girl who didn't know how to talk to a boy. Which was ridiculous in itself. She talked to guys all the time. She talked to *Teague* all the time.

He held up the newly made shorts. "Good?"

"I think so."

"Be right out." He took the shorts into the bathroom.

She stood at the window, picking at the frayed edges of her own cut-offs, while she waited for him to change. *What the hell is the matter with you? Thinking about Teague's eyes. And his bed.*

"Not much to look at." He came to stand next to her.

"I like it. Nothing to see but trees." A smile touched her lips, "I lived in a place like this once, between tours. There were probably twenty other people living in the house, plus there were two buses in the driveway. And there was a guy who lived in a tepee out back. I scored a mattress in the living room."

"That sounds... interesting."

"It was. There was always something going on, always family in and out."

He stepped back so she could see his shorts. "How do they look?"

She turned from the window. He stood there in a white t-shirt

209

with a row of dancing bears across the front and newly made, yet-to-be-frayed cut-offs. His hair, which he'd tucked behind his ears, fell in waves to his collar and he wore Birkenstocks. She smiled, "Perfect."

* * *

Teague tried not to watch Bailey, or the road. And definitely not the speedometer. It wasn't as bad as when she'd driven to Quechee, but he still wasn't comfortable. "Bailey, I could have driven."

She waved him off. "You wouldn't know how to get there."

Aria piped up from the back, "Teague, Auntie Bailey knows how to get everywhere. She could even get all the way to California, right Auntie Bailey? She's been there a lotta times."

He turned in his seat so he could see Aria. "Have you been there?"

"No. But when me and Mallory—"

"Mallory and I." Bailey corrected.

Aria rolled her eyes. "When *Mallory and I* grow up we're gonna go. We're gonna live at Greyhound Rock, and smoke a joint on the Haight."

"Aria!" Bailey scolded her.

Her brow creased. "What? That's what Jesse always says."

Bailey sighed audibly. "Just because Jesse says something doesn't mean you can."

"Yeah, but—"

"No 'yeah, buts,' Miss. Jesse *swears*, too, and *you* know *you're* not supposed to."

Teague tried to redirect them both. "Aria, have you been to the place Auntie Bailey's taking us now?"

She perked up. "A ton of times." She launched into a description of waterfalls.

He let Aria talk, which she did until Bailey pulled into a dirt turn-off and they climbed out. Aria stood next to the van watching Delilah sniff the ground while Bailey shrugged on a backpack and handed a second backpack to Teague.

A car pulled up behind them and Katelyn got out from the passenger side. "Bail, this was the best idea." She turned to open the back door. A shaggy black and white dog jumped out, followed by a girl about Aria's age. Katelyn called, "Mal, wait!" but she was already running to Aria. Sighing, she said, "Mallory, keep an eye on Daisy, please."

The girls hugged and immediately started talking. In a whirlwind of movement, they were all headed down a barely visible path through the woods.

Teague asked Bailey. "Who's the other girl?"

"Mallory? She's Katelyn and Liam's daughter."

He stopped dead in his tracks. Bailey stopped, too. He said, "How old were they when they had her? Twelve?"

"Sixteen, actually." Bailey turned back to the trail and started walking again.

Teague hurried to catch up. Before he could wrap his mind around Katelyn and Liam being parents, they stepped from the closeness of the trees into bright sun.

As his eyes adjusted he saw that the woods opened to a clearing at the edge of a river. From the end of the trail a flat rock sloped gently to a circular pool, held in by a sheer cliff on the opposite side. The pool was filled by a river which ran down a series of rock ledges, like giant steps. It emptied over a waterfall at the other end and disappeared into the woods beyond.

Apparently Bailey was right about it being a weekday. There was no one else there.

"Teague!" Aria ran towards him. "Come on!" She grabbed his hand. "We got a frog! You gotta come see it! Liam will only let us keep it a minute, so we gotta be quick."

* * *

Bailey set her backpack down next to Katelyn's. "Mallory got tall."

Katelyn glanced to where the girls were looking at something Liam was holding. "I can't believe she just finished kindergarten."

"Aria's stoked that they're in the same class next year."

"Right?" Katelyn sat to untie her sneakers. "I heard their teacher's really good, too."

Leaving their shoes with the backpacks, they walked to the upper end of the pool and sat on the edge with their feet in the water. Bailey asked, "Are you going swimming?"

"Not if I can help it. I have my period."

"That sucks."

"Better than being pregnant."

"True." Bailey was careful about that. She'd been lax about birth control when she was younger and had just always been lucky. Since she'd started taking care of Aria, she took it very seriously. She wasn't interested in having someone who relied on her a hundred percent.

She watched as Aria took Teague's hand and pulled him towards the water. When she was knee-deep she turned and splashed him. Bailey would have scolded her for splashing. Teague, though, splashed her back. Bailey braced for Aria to cry. Instead, she laughed.

Katelyn said, "He's good with Aria."

"Yeah. He is."

"Bail? I'm not trying to pry, but, is he going to Pittsburgh with you?"

Puzzled, she said, "No. Why?"

"Mal and Aria were talking about what shows they were doing and Aria—" She stopped, as if she was reconsidering. Then she said, "Aria told Mallory that Teague was going. With you. I didn't say anything, but I was surprised, because I didn't think you guys were serious."

That Katelyn thought her and Teague were *anything* was unnerving. She looked back to where he was lifting Aria, then dunking her into the water. He'd taken his shirt off and water droplets glistened on his bare skin. The muscles in his arms and down his back rippled as he lifted Aria again. "We're not. We're just friends."

At that moment, he turned. He caught her eye and smiled before Aria called his attention again.

"You sure about that?" Katelyn asked.

* * *

Aria jumped off a rock into Teague's waiting arms. The momentum forced his arms down, then as he pulled her back up and out of the water she shrieked, "Again!"

"I need a break." She wasn't heavy, but she'd probably jumped fifty times and his arms were getting tired. He slogged back to shore and deposited her on the rock. "Let's go have a drink."

She ran ahead of him to where Katelyn, Liam and Mallory were sitting on a blanket. The moment she got to them, she sprawled next to Mallory.

Teague found a bottle of water in his backpack, looked back to the river as he took a swig. Bailey was sitting at the upper end of the pool, her face tipped up to the sun and her eyes closed. The sun touched her, highlighting her bare shoulders. God he loved tank tops. He got a second bottle of water and brought it to her.

As he sat down she opened her eyes. "Hey."

"Hey." He handed her the water. "It's gorgeous here."

She returned his smile. "Glad you like it."

"What were you and Cole talking about buckets?"

"There's a lot of places to swim in Vermont. Triple Buckets is amazing, especially for cliff jumping. But it's not family friendly."

213

She looked out over the water. "I can take you some time, if you want to go."

What he wanted was to tell her he'd happily go anywhere with her. Instead, he said, "That sounds cool."

"You mean n-ice?" He raised his eyebrows in question and she laughed. "They're mountain streams. They're freezing."

"Colder than this?"

"Probably. The pools are deeper than here."

"This water actually feels pretty freakin' good."

"Do you want to go in?"

"If you do."

She slid off the rock into the water. He watched as she swam towards the middle, then flipped to her back. She didn't seem to notice that her purple and blue paisley tank top, so light and airy while she'd been dry, now clung to her curves. She kicked lazily through the water. "Are you coming?"

He inched off the ledge, dropped in next to her. The water was so clear he could see all the way to the bottom of the river. He tried to stand, only to find it was much deeper than it looked.

Bailey laughed as he floundered. "Teague, it's like ten feet deep."

"Thanks for the warning." He splashed at her.

She laughed again and splashed back. "Sorry. I didn't realize you needed one." She swam towards the other end of the pool.

He followed, swimming until suddenly there were rocks under his feet. He stood, an arms' length from Bailey.

She tipped her chin down and smiled.

His heart hammered in his chest. He moved closer, started to reach for her. Her smile faltered as she took a step towards him.

"Daisy! Damn it! Give that—" Katelyn yelled as the dog jumped into the water with what looked like a shirt in her mouth. Delilah hit the water a split second after her.

Bailey went after Daisy, yelling at her own dog, "Delilah! Go lay down!"

Teague grabbed Daisy as she swam past but she wiggled out of his grip. "Sorry!"

Katelyn waved an exasperated hand. "Forget it. She'll bring it back when she's ready." She went back to where Liam sat with the girls on the blanket.

Bailey hauled Delilah from the river as Daisy swam to the edge and trotted back to Katelyn on her own.

Teague followed slowly. *It's better this way. Kissing Bailey? Probably not the best idea. Especially in front of Aria.* He couldn't help feeling disappointed, though.

* * *

Teague lifted a sleeping Aria gently from the back seat and followed Bailey.

Half-way to the house Aria mumbled, "Teague? Will you tuck me in?"

"Yeah, of course."

Bailey held the door for them, her heart swelling at the sight of Aria's arms clasped tightly around Teague's neck. As he went past her, Aria said, "Night, Auntie. Teague's gonna tuck me in."

Ellen came in from the living room. "Did you have fun?"

"Mmmm hmmm. Night, Nannie." She snuggled her face deeper into Teague's neck.

"Hi, Ellen." He asked Aria, "Where's your room?"

She pointed towards the living room. "Through there, up the stairs."

Once he was gone, Bailey turned to her mom. Nervously, she said, "Mom? I was wondering if you'd mind if Teague came with Aria and I to Pittsburgh." Her face felt hot and she added, "If you're not okay with it, you can say no. I haven't asked him yet."

"Why would think it wouldn't be okay?"

"We're staying in hotels, and he's a guy, and I wasn't sure how you'd feel about it."

"I'd be more concerned with how Jesse feels."

She rushed to clarify, "It's not like that. We're just friends."

Ellen asked, "How does Teague feel about that?"

"I'm sure he feels fine about it." It was really annoying that everyone seemed to think she was sleeping with Teague. Even her own mother.

After a moment Ellen said, "I think Aria would love it if Teague went with you."

Relieved, Bailey smiled. "Cool."

* * *

Bailey ran a thousand versions of one question through her mind.

She still wasn't sure how to ask, even as she pulled into Teague's driveway. Lights spilled from the downstairs windows forming rectangles on the porch, but in the van it was dark. If he said no, he wouldn't be able to see the disappointment on her face. It was perfect. "Teague?"

He turned to her.

Crickets chirped. Or maybe those were June bugs. She didn't really know. "I, um, had a really good time today."

Even in the dark she knew he smiled. "I did, too."

"I was wondering…" Her chest felt tight. "Aria and I are going to Pittsburgh, to see a show." She swallowed, sure he was going to say no. "Do you want to come? With us?"

He didn't answer immediately.

She added, "I know it's not really your thing. I just thought…" She wished she could see his face. "Forget it. It was stupid." She laughed nervously.

"I'd love to."

"You would?"

"Yeah." He moved in his seat. "Yeah, I would. Is it too late for me to get a ticket?"

For a moment she couldn't quite process that he'd said yes. Excitement soared through her. *Teague's going to a show!* Trying to sound nonchalant, she said, "No worries. I have extras."

Chapter 29

Teague stood in the middle of his living room and assessed the painting now hanging on the back wall. He'd chosen that spot because he'd see Aria's work every time he stepped through the front door, but there was no denying the pastel purple flowers in their soft pink pot clashed horribly with the dark blue he'd used on the walls.

"New plan." He carefully took the painting down and carried it to the kitchen. There was an expanse of open wall above the table, a spot he could look at every night while he ate dinner. *Except you never eat here anymore.*

A smile crept over his face as he thought of Bailey and Aria. *Maybe I can have them here for dinner.* He got the tools from the living room and began measuring to make sure he put the nail in the exact center of the wall. *Except you don't cook. So what are you going to do? Serve take-out on paper plates? Not an option.*

He marked the spot with his fingernail, grabbed the hammer and put a nail in the wall. *You could take them out. Someplace nice. Not Sal's, that's too boring.* Visions of dinners at five-star restaurants with Marlena flashed though his mind. He snorted, trying to picture Bailey in place of his ex. *No way in hell.*

The painting hung, he stepped back. He'd been considering repainting the kitchen to a color with more personality, but with the neutral grey wall behind it Aria's artwork popped. "Perfect."

And now, for coffee. He smiled. *And to see Bailey.* He grabbed his keys from the table by the front door. As soon as he started the car the cassette in the deck whirred. When he'd bought his car he'd been annoyed that Marlena had insisted on a tape deck instead of upgrading to a CD player, because *she* hadn't replaced her tapes yet. Now he was glad, because Cole had a huge tape collection, but not a single CD.

"Terrapin Station" started. Embarrassment lingered at the back of his mind, knowing he'd been wearing a shirt with the dancing turtles from the cover of this album for months without realizing it. *No one else knows you didn't know.*

He parked in the lot behind Bailey's, next to a Jeep with a line of dancing bear stickers across the back window. Once he'd have ignored the bears. Now he knew he was parked next to a Deadhead.

The shop was full of people. Katelyn was taking orders and Bailey was filling them. Katelyn smiled and greeted Teague. "Hey now."

"Hey. It's busy today."

"It's summer." She shrugged, as if that explained everything.

Bailey turned from the back counter and handed him a mug, handle first. "Hey, Teague."

He took the mug. *This is from when we did pottery.* He remembered Bailey had used light purple— the color Aria said turned deep blue. "You made this."

She tipped her chin down a little and smiled a tiny bit. "I thought you should have your own mug. Here."

He turned it, saw his name in yellow on the front. The warmth that spread through his chest, the feeling of being accepted, was overwhelming. "Thank you, Bailey." That seemed entirely inadequate for such a perfect gift, but it was all he could manage. He had the horrible feeling that if he tried to say more he'd get choked up, and that wasn't something he was willing to risk. Especially not in front of Katelyn. He took his coffee and started towards an empty table, then noticed Ellen and Aria and changed course.

"Hi, Teague!" Aria grinned up at him.

Ellen smiled, indicated the empty chair across from her. "Would you like to join us?" As he sat, she said, "We were just talking about you."

Surprised, he said, "All good, I hope."

Aria beamed, "I was telling Nannie how I taught you to paint."

"Aria's a very good teacher. And she's a very good artist."

"She takes after her aunt." There was a touch of sadness in Ellen's voice. "Aria told me this was your first time painting?"

"My brother, Callum, was the artist in our family."

"It's funny how kids get pigeonholed like that. In my family I was 'the practical one.'" She made air quotes. "And I'm afraid I continued the habit with my own kids. Bailey was always the artist, and Peyton was the performer."

Aria asked, "What were you, Teague?"

"I was the smart one." He smiled crookedly, feeling the need to come clean. "Between me and you, though, I'm not smart. I just decided on what I wanted, and I worked really hard until I got it."

"I'm smart." Aria looked from Ellen to Teague. "I can count all the way to a hundred! Wanna hear?"

Ellen stopped her. "I'm sure Teague would love to hear you count to a hundred, but you and I have shopping to do."

He smiled, "Maybe tomorrow you can count for me."

"'Kay. See you later." She hugged him.

Sunday mornings were always busy and he knew it would be hours until Bailey was free. Some days he stayed there and waited. Read the paper or hung out with whoever else was around. This day, though, he had an idea. He was going to figure out a way to show Bailey that he appreciated her being part of his life.

* * *

It was midafternoon by the time Teague carried bags of groceries into the kitchen. He'd helped Bailey and Aria cook, but making an entire meal himself was a completely different thing. Unsure of how hard it was going to be, he'd chosen a recipe labeled 'easy' in the cookbook. "You are an embarrassment to the word 'man'. You don't even know how to grill a steak."

"You talk to yourself often?" Cole opened the refrigerator and drank directly from the milk jug.

"Didn't realize you were here."

"I'm leaving, actually."

Still hoping things would get better, he said, "I'm going to cook Chicken Piccata, if you're interested in dinner."

"I'm *leaving*. Summer tour starts on Wednesday. It's a long way to Kansas."

"Oh." After an uncomfortable moment, he said, "Do you need anything? Money, or a ride, or…"

"I'm good." He stuck the jug back in the fridge and left the kitchen.

Teague was still emptying bags of groceries when a car pulled into the driveway. He watched out the window as Cole threw his backpack in Sage's car and climbed in after it. It was kind of stupid, since he and Cole hadn't spent any time together, but suddenly Teague felt very alone.

Call Bailey. No, that's stupid. You have no freaking idea how to cook this chicken. He read over the recipe, decided it was too much of a risk to try to feed her. *Ask her to teach you.*

Really liking that idea, he dialed the shop. "Bailey's, Katelyn speaking."

"Hey, Katelyn, it's Teague. Is Bailey there?"

"I'm sorry, Teague. She's not around. I can leave her a message?"

Disappointment shot through him. "Nah. I'll see her tomorrow."

He hung up the phone and stared at the package of breasts on the counter. "Well, at least if this comes out like shit no one will know but me."

Resigned to eating alone, he put on Terrapin Station before going back to the chicken.

Chapter 30

It was quiet in the shop, with most of the people Bailey knew gone for summer tour. She'd have liked to have been on tour, too, but spending time with Teague made up for it. And they were going to at least one show, in Pittsburgh. *As soon as Aria gets here.*

She sipped her coffee and surveyed the chess board while she waited for Teague to make his next move. He picked up a knight, grinned, and said, "This is probably a terrible move." He set the piece back on the chess board.

She considered what he'd chosen to do. "Not as bad as some you've made."

"I have a good teacher."

The smile he gave her made her feel all mushy. *She really liked that for the last few days he hadn't shaved. He didn't have a full-on beard yet, but it was getting there.* She wanted to reach out, take his face in her hands and run her fingers over it. *What the fuck, Bail? That's Teague. Your friend. You really wanna go messing with that?* The thought of Rain talking to Jesse flashed through her mind. *Yeah, because you're stupid. Keep your freaking hands to yourself.*

"Bail, it's your turn."

Jerked back to reality, she felt her face get hot. "Sorry." She looked at the chess board. *At Althea, though. The way he looked at me. And he's here, going to a show.*

The back door opened and Aria came running in. "Auntie Bailey! I'm here. We can go." She turned to Teague. "You packed your toothbrush, right?"

He grabbed her in a bear hug. "Hey, girl."

She giggled as he tickled her. "Hey, Teague. Do you got your toothbrush?"

"Of course. I packed everything you told me to."

Bailey listened to Teague and Aria. *You are a fucking idiot. He's not going to Pittsburgh for you. He's here for Aria.*

Aria turned to Bailey. "So can we leave now?"

Ellen came in looking harassed and set a backpack on the couch next to Bailey. "Sorry we're late. We were half way here when she realized she forgot her blanket."

Bailey raised an eyebrow at Aria. "Don't I get a hug?"

She leapt into her arms. "Hi, Auntie."

"Hi, Sweetie." Bailey looked at her mom. "Did you write down the number for your hotel?"

"I put it in the front pocket of Aria's bag."

"I'll call and let you know when we get back."

"I'll be in seminars every day, but you can leave a message with the front desk. And they changed my flight home, so I'll be back on Wednesday night. I hope that's okay."

"Of course."

Ellen asked Aria, "Can I have a kiss goodbye?"

She sprang from Bailey's lap and nearly tackled her grandmother. "Bye, Nannie. Be good till I get back."

Ellen smiled, "I will." She squeezed her granddaughter once more and kissed her cheek. "I love you."

"I love you, too."

Ellen said, "You guys have fun."

Bailey started putting the chess pieces away. "Aria, can you take

Teague upstairs and get Delilah, please?"

"'Kay." She grabbed his hand and pulled him towards the door as she called over her shoulder, "Bye, Nannie."

* * *

Bailey pulled her hair into a ponytail and rolled the window all the way down. She glanced back at Aria, who had her feet resting on Delilah. "Ready?"

"Ready!"

She looked over at Teague. "Ready?"

"Ready."

Her heart skipped a beat at his easy smile. She smiled back before pushing the play button on the tape deck. The first notes of "Goin' Down The Road Feeling Bad" filled the van. Joy bubbled up, threatened to explode in her chest. She sang, the words coming easily.

* * *

The tall, green mountains gave way to lower, green foothills. Small towns were replaced by larger towns, the spaces between them becoming less, and soon Teague recognized the roads and skyline.

Just over the Connecticut border Bailey turned the music down. "We're going to Pittsburgh. I basically know how to get there, but I don't want to miss anything. Can you map the route?"

"Sure." He pulled the atlas out. The next time he looked up they were coming into Hartford. "Man, I almost forgot how ugly this place is."

Snickering, Bailey scolded him, "Teague! That's not nice."

"No, but it is true." Glancing at the cluster of cement and glass buildings surrounding the road, the ribbons of asphalt curving over and around, the never-ending stream of cars making their way to wherever, he realized how much he'd come to love Vermont. "I mean, you gotta admit that where we live is pretty amazing."

Aria interrupted, "Auntie Bailey, can we have McDonald's?"

Bailey answered off-handedly, "Yeah, baby. As soon as I find one."

Teague checked the exit number on the next sign. "The next McDonald's is off Exit 32."

Curiously, Aria asked, "How'd you know that?"

"I used to live here."

Aria looked at the buildings, the tons of cars everywhere, and said, "I'm glad you don't anymore."

Grinning at her honesty, Teague agreed, "Me, too."

* * *

Teague stared at the road in front of the van. Pennsylvania was much bigger than he'd realized. It felt like they'd crossed the border from New York ages ago. He turned to look at Bailey, her face lit by the dash lights. She had such a beautiful profile, especially her lips. She seemed to be smiling all the time, even now when all she was doing was driving.

As he watched, her eyes closed, a bit longer than a blink. She sat straighter, rolled the window down. "Bail, you okay?"

She glanced at him, then quickly turned back to the road. "Yeah. Why?"

"You've been driving for hours."

"I'm fine." She rolled the window up a little.

* * *

The road rolled on ahead, seemingly endless. Bailey felt herself start to drift. Grudgingly, she admitted, "Teague, we need to find a hotel."

"We don't have reservations?"

"No." She glanced at him. "How would we do that?"

"Call the hotel and tell them the day you're arriving."

Completely at a loss, she said, "How would I know which hotel to call?"

"You pick one that's in the area you're going to."

"How would I know that?"

He swiveled in his seat and stared at her. "I thought we were going to Pittsburgh."

"We are. But... forget it. I have to concentrate on the road. Can you watch the signs?"

As they came near the next exit he said, "The Hideaway Hotel is off this exit."

Bailey snorted. "I'm not that tired. How about a Motel 6 or a Super 8?"

A few exits later there was a sign listing five hotels. She took the exit. In between a McDonald's and a steakhouse was a Ramada.

"How about that?" Teague asked.

Bailey scanned the building as she sat at a red light. "No. It needs to have doors that open to the parking lot."

His eyebrows drawing together, he asked, "Why?"

"Because we have a dog." She drove past a strip mall and a dry cleaners before she pulled into a no-name motel with a sign advertising HBO in all the rooms.

Once the van was parked, he told her, "Stay here. I'll take care of this."

"Just don't tell them about Delilah." Bailey leaned back in her seat and closed her eyes.

* * *

This was not the kind of place Teague would have gotten a room. Ever. But he could see that Bailey was exhausted, and Aria was asleep sitting up. For one night, it would do. He dinged the bell on the counter and waited.

The guy who came out looked about as old as the motel, his red flannel shirt and jeans only slightly newer.

"I need a room, please."

"Just you?"

He hesitated for a second. Maybe he should get two rooms. But something stopped him and instead he said, "No, I've got my wife and daughter in the car."

The guy looked him up and down, not hiding it. "That'll be thirty-five for the room and a hundred for the key deposit."

Shocked, he said, "The key deposit is more than twice the cost of the room?"

Pulling a registration form from under the counter, he said, "Just wanna make sure we get our keys back."

Teague grunted. He filled out the form the guy handed him, pausing for a moment to look at the van through the front windows. He didn't know Bailey's license plate number. He finished and handed the form back.

"I'll just need some ID. And payment, of course."

He pulled out his driver's license and his American Express.

The clerk looked at his ID, turned it around and looked at the back, held it up to the light. "Huh." He looked at Teague, squinted at the license in his hand, looked back at Teague. "That's an interesting name. French?"

"Irish."

"How do you pronounce that?"

Just wanting to get Bailey and Aria into bed, he said, "Like league, with a T."

"Huh." He went back to looking at Teague's ID. "Where'd you say you were from?"

"Connecticut."

After looking at the form, then out at the van, then back to Teague's ID, he finally picked up the American Express card and examined it. Without looking at Teague, he said, "The van's from Vermont."

Teague had the sudden feeling something was wrong. "Yeah, that's my wife's."

Wrinkles of doubt formed on the clerk's forehead. "You're from Connecticut and your wife's from Vermont?"

His tired mind trying to work out a way to cover his lie, he said, "I'm from Connecticut, but I live in Vermont now."

"Your license says Connecticut."

"I guess I really should get that changed."

Giving Teague a distrustful look, the clerk handed him his ID and the credit card back. "Cash only."

Teague took the cards back and leveled a look at the guy. "There's a sign right behind you that says American Express."

"Just remembered, rented my last room an hour ago."

They stood, staring at each other. When the door opened, they both turned as Bailey stuck her head in. "Teague? Is everything okay?"

"Yeah, hon, it's fine. Stay with Aria, I'll be right out." He smiled what he hoped was a reassuring smile.

As she went back out the guy said, "I'll tell you what. You pay cash for the room and I'll waive the key deposit."

Not about to argue, Teague exchanged cash for a key.

Back in the van, Bailey asked, "Why'd you call me hon?"

"I lied and said you were my wife." Scratching his head, Teague told her, "Bailey, I didn't think that guy was gonna give us a room.

He kept looking at my license, like he didn't believe it was me."

"You do look different than you did a few months ago."

"He wouldn't take my credit card. I had to pay with cash."

She gave him a knowing grin. "Welcome to my world. Wait until you try to order dinner."

"Why?"

"Usually they make us pay first."

"That makes no sense at all."

She started the van. "Where's our room? I'm tired."

Chapter 31

Teague stared at the red and blue skull sticker on the car in front of them. The car inched forward. Bailey followed. The barest breeze came through the open window, not enough to relieve the stifling heat in the van. He wished they'd taken his car. *No way in hell you'd have talked Bailey into that.*

Aria asked, "Auntie Bailey, can I come sit with you?"

"No, baby. You've gotta stay buckled."

"I can sit on Teague's lap and he can buckle us both."

"You have to stay in your seat until we park."

"But we're barely moving."

"Aria, please." She leaned forward, her face tight with concentration. "Stop kicking my seat."

Hoping to distract Aria, Teague asked her, "What's your favorite song?"

She pouted, but answered, "I don't know. 'Sugar Mag Sunshine Daydream'?"

Bailey smiled a little. "Right on. Ya think they'll do that tonight?"

"I hope so."

He asked, "What else do you want to hear?"

Aria put a finger to her lips, thinking. "'Cosmic Charlie.'"

Bailey said, "You know they never play that."

"Why not?"

"They just don't. They haven't played it since 1976. What about 'The Wheel', and 'Uncle John's Band'?"

"Maybe they'll do 'Touch of Grey'." Aria giggled.

Bailey said, "Funny. And maybe they'll just do drums all night and you won't get to sing, Miss Aria."

Aria asked, "Teague, what do you want to hear?"

He said the first thing that popped into his head. "'The Monkey and the Engineer'?"

Bailey turned and stared at him. "'The Monkey and the Engineer'?"

Nervous that he'd said something stupid, he asked, "Do they not play that anymore?"

"Not in a long time." She tipped her head and asked curiously, "Where'd you even hear that?"

"Cole has a lot of tapes. From the store, though. Not like yours."

"Huh." She turned back to the road, moved forward a car length. "See if I have Radio City Music Hall, October 31 in the tape box."

He fished the box of tapes out from under his seat, opened the lid and read hand written labels. There were dozens of tapes, each with a place and a date, but not that one. "I don't see it."

She asked, "What other songs do you like?"

He didn't want to say anything stupid again. He thought about what everyone sang to at the coffee shop. "I like 'Sugaree'. And 'Scarlet Begonias'. And the one about ashes?"

Grinning, Bailey said, "That's called 'Throwing Stones'. It's a great song."

Aria said, "I like 'Fire on the Mountain'. They did that when I went last summer. Remember? Not at Foxboro, though."

"That was at JFK. I'm pretty sure we've got that tape, if you want to hear it."

"Yes!" She bounced in her seat, as much as the seatbelt would allow.

Teague found the one labeled 'JFK 1989', slid it into the tape player and pushed the play button. The sound of a crowd, cheering and whistles, erupted from the speakers. Then "Hell In a Bucket" started and Teague watched, fascinated, as Bailey relaxed behind the wheel. By the end of the first verse she was sitting back, smiling, nodding her head in time to the music.

* * *

Bailey stood next to the van and stretched, relieved to be parked and out from behind the wheel. It was wicked hot and all she wanted was a cold beer. She opened the side door. "Aria, put your shoes on, please."

Crossing her arms, Aria said, "I don't wanna wear shoes."

"You can't go barefoot here."

"Why not?"

Digging in a bag, looking for Delilah's leash, Bailey said, "This is an asphalt lot. You know the rules."

Even though she started looking for her shoes, Aria still argued. "Jesse doesn't wear shoes."

Bailey glanced at Teague. It didn't seem like he was paying attention. She pulled the leash from the bag and quietly said, "Jesse's an adult and he can do whatever he wants. *You* are six and if I bring you home with cuts or burns on your feet Nannie will never let me take you to a show again."

Aria put her shoes on and climbed out. She spun, making her sun dress flair around her. She asked Teague, "What are you gonna sell?"

Bailey said, "Teague's just going to hang with us today." She handed Aria a small patchwork backpack and a display of beaded jewelry, locked all the doors of the van and clipped the leash to Delilah's collar. They started walking down the aisle between rows of cars.

Aria told Teague, "It's okay not to have anything to sell. Jesse never does, either. But he can spange really good and he makes a ton of money. Like enough to get a room all the time."

Shocked, Bailey asked, "What makes you think Jesse spanges?"

Aria shrugged. "He never has anything to sell."

"There's nothing wrong with someone needing help and asking for spare change. But that's not what Jesse does."

"What does he do?"

Idiot! You should have let that go. Telling Aria what Jesse, and most of her friends, actually did was out of the question. Her mind working quickly, she said, "He works, and saves money, just like Teague, so they don't have to sell things at shows. They can just go and have fun."

"But at home you work." Puzzled, Aria asked, "Why can't you save money and just have fun?"

Very conscious of Teague staring at her, she said, "Because I like to sell bead work." She forced a smile. "Are you hungry?"

"Nah, not yet." Aria skipped ahead, Bailey, Teague and Delilah following.

Teague spoke quietly, "Bailey, if you need money, all you have to do is ask."

"No, it's not like that." She held her own display of jewelry and made eye contact with people sitting behind their cars as she passed. "I really like doing bead work, and if I'm here I might as well sell it." She glanced at Teague, "But I don't have to, if I don't want to. It's not like we're gonna starve if I don't."

* * *

Teague recognized "Hell In A Bucket" playing from a dark green Ford Maverick, noticed two pairs of feet sticking out the open car door as he passed it. Two women coming the other way stopped for a moment and sang along with the chorus before continuing the way they'd been headed, their long dresses fluttering around their bare feet. A guy dragging a cooler on a skateboard stopped to sell beer to a group of people sitting on the trunk of a gold Buick Century. *Who sells beer in a parking lot?*

Back in Vermont it had been easy to get swept up in Bailey, in her world. What he hadn't understood was that her world was much, much bigger than a coffee shop in a small city in Vermont. And he knew next to nothing about it.

As they made their way down the aisle a woman sitting in a lawn chair behind a shiny silver Volvo called Aria and Bailey over to look at what they were selling. Bailey handed Delilah's leash to Teague. "Can you hold her for a second?"

The woman wore a bright, obviously brand new, tie-dye and her bangs were teased into a huge pouf. She asked Aria, "Did you make this?" as she fingered a piece of shell held onto a satin cord by a band of tightly woven beads.

"I did the bead work. It's abalone, from Greyhound Rock in Santa Cruz. Right, Auntie Bailey?"

"That's right, Aria."

Teague saw the woman's eyes widen a bit and knew she was interested. She asked Aria, "Have you been to Santa Cruz?"

Aria answered, "No. Auntie Bailey used to live there, when all she did was tour, and I'm gonna, too, when I grow up."

The woman's eyes darted to Bailey, then back to Aria. "Where do you live?"

"Vermont. This one," she pointed to a necklace with a deep red square of rock about the size of a small olive, "is from there. It's a garnet. Auntie Bailey took me to the," she paused and screwed her lips up. "I forgot. What's it called?"

Bailey said, "Quarry."

Aria grinned. "The quarry, where they used to mine them and I found it there."

The woman asked, "Are you going to see the concert tonight?"

"Um hm! It'll be my fifteenth show." She grinned, "That I remember, anyway."

The woman pulled her purse from under her chair and began digging in it. Without looking up, she asked, "How much for the shell?"

Bailey laid her hand on Aria's shoulder and said, "Twenty."

Aria looked up questioningly, but didn't say anything.

The woman began counting bills. "And the garnet?"

"Fifty."

"I'll take them both."

She smiled as she handed Aria the money. Aria tucked it into her backpack, took the two necklaces off her board and gave them to the woman. "Thank you, sister."

"Have fun tonight."

Aria spun in a circle, then cheerfully said, "I will!" She skipped down the aisle.

Teague waited until they were a ways away, then asked Bailey, "Did you raise the price on those?"

"What do you mean?"

He gave her a stern look.

She shrugged. "She could afford it."

Disapprovingly, he said, "Bailey."

"Teague, she paid for the story. She's going to go into work tomorrow and tell all her friends how she went to see the Dead and she bought this necklace off an actual hippie child who mined the garnet herself, and how the abalone came from a real Deadhead, who got it from the beach in Santa Cruz."

Stunned, he asked, "Did you teach Aria to say those things?"

"No." She looked up at him, her expression hurt. "That's what really happened."

"You took Aria to a garnet quarry?"

"Yeah. It's cool as shit. We can go when we get back, if you want."

"Auntie?" Aria called.

Teague hung back, feeling bad for accusing Bailey of lying. He watched as she walked to where Aria was standing, in front of a woman with long blonde hair pulled back in a ponytail, cooking on a Coleman stove next to handmade cardboard sign proclaiming, 'What the fuck, it's only a buck!' Her shirt, a tie-dye with a picture of bears driving a purple convertible, was most definitely not new and the car she was set up behind was covered with bumper stickers saying things like, 'Who are the Dead and why are they following me?'. Teague thought if someone were to peel all the stickers off the car might fall apart.

Aria asked, "Can I get a grilled cheese?"

"Yeah, of course. Teague? Do you want one?" She turned to him and smiled.

"Sure." *Damn, that smile.* He'd have said yes to anything she'd asked.

Bailey pulled out her wallet and told the woman, "Four, please."

"Four dollars." The woman smiled softly at Aria as she handed her a sandwich. "Are you in tonight, little sister?"

Aria smiled back. "Yup. Are you?"

"Not yet."

Confidently, Aria said, "You'll get in."

Bailey gave the woman a ten and took the rest of the sandwiches, but not the change the woman began counting out.

They sat on a curb to eat. Next to Teague, Aria fed Delilah pieces of grilled cheese. On his other side, Bailey leaned back and tipped her face to the sun. He loved the way she looked with she sat like that, like she was one with the world around her.

A guy dropped down next to Bailey. "Hey, sistah!"

She opened her eyes and sat up. "Tony?" She gave him a huge hug. "What are you doing here?" Sitting back and grinning, she said, "This is waaaay east of the Rockies."

"No doubt." He smiled, "I hitched a ride with these cats, and next thing I was in Kansas. I figured, what the fuck, I'll do summer tour!"

"Brah, I didn't think I'd ever see you again."

"No shit, right! How've you been?"

"Still kickin'. You?"

They talked for a few minutes, then he said, "Hey, I gotta go. There's this dude. See ya, Bailey!" and he walked away.

Teague asked, "Someone you know?"

"Yeah." She looked around him to Aria. "Ready?"

She didn't talk to him as they made their way through throngs of people. She couldn't have even if she wanted to, because Aria chattered constantly.

"Teague, this is Shakedown. That's where all the buses park. And where everyone hangs out. I mean, not *everyone,* a lotta people just sit by their cars, but it's kinda like Main Street. That's what you said, right Auntie Bailey? So if you're looking for someone, or you need a miracle it's a good place to go." She pointed at a green bus with a wide purple stripe down the side. "Auntie! That's Tobias' bus!"

"Let's go say hi." Bailey led the way to what used to be a school bus, stuck her head in the doorway, and called, "Laurel?"

A woman's head, a blue and green scarf tied around her dark dreads, came into view at the top of the stairs. "Hey, Bailey."

Bailey looped Delilah's leash over the mirror on the side of the bus and stepped in, Aria following and Teague bringing up the rear. The woman hugged Bailey, then Aria.

A little blonde boy stood up from the bed at the back of the bus. "Hey, Aria. Wanna see the crystals I got from Bear?"

She slipped past Laurel. At the far end of the bus she climbed up to sit next to Tobias, looking at what he had spread out on the bed.

Laurel said, "Teague, right?"

He held out his hand. "Yes."

"I've seen you at Bailey's." She smiled as she shook his hand, "And I know Cole. He's around, somewhere. We saw him in Kentucky. This tour's a bitch. Only one night in each city, spread out all over the place. I almost wish we'd skipped it." She turned to Bailey. "I'm surprised to see you here. I thought you stayed closer to home with Aria."

"Usually I do, but I owed her a show and this was the only one that worked with everyone's schedules. What's doing around here?"

Teague wished he could ask Laurel about Cole, but she and Bailey were talking and he didn't want to interrupt. *Do you really want to get into your family shit with a stranger, anyway?* Trying to distract himself, he looked around. The bus was full of colors; woven Mexican blankets in various shades of blue were laid across the bed, the windows were covered with scarves in red and orange, and above the stove were cabinets completely covered in stickers with dancing bears or rainbows or skeletons.

His attention was brought back by Bailey standing up. "Safe travels."

"Right on." Laurel hugged Bailey, then to his surprise she hugged Teague. He hugged her back.

Outside, he indicated the other buses parked in the row and asked Bailey, "So all these buses are like that?"

"Sort of. Laurel's bus is really nice. Some just have the seats pulled out and mattresses on the floor." She smiled, "Those are killer. They're just a big party all the time. I was on one for a while that this guy, Sean, had. It was crazy." She took Aria's hand and moved down the aisle.

* * *

Bailey filled a bowl with dog food and one with water and set them on the ground next to the van. She tied a rope to the door handle, attached the other end to Delilah's collar. "Be good." She patted the dog, who scooted under the van, out of the sun.

"Everyone ready?" she asked brightly.

"You're just going to leave Delilah?" Teague asked.

"Yeah."

"Aren't you worried, leaving her? That someone's going to do something to her? Or take her?"

Flatly, she said, "No. Absolutely not. No one here would ever do anything like that. She's safer on the lot than she would be anywhere else in the world."

To her relief, he didn't push it. Explaining would mean reliving losing Delilah's brother Samson, and she wasn't into that.

As they headed towards the stadium anticipation began to build in her chest. Aria danced, weaving between people. That was easily her favorite thing about bringing her niece to shows— seeing her dance. Near the entrance there were people everywhere with their finger up, chanting or yelling, or singing, 'I need a Miracle' or 'Just one'. A lot of people held cardboard signs, decorated with flowers or bears or Steal Your Faces. Bailey told Aria, "Pick who you want to miracle."

Aria looked around. "Can I pick someone I know?"

"Of course. Do you see someone?"

"No, I was just asking." She continued to look at the people they passed. "Brother or sister?"

"Either. Whoever you want."

Aria grabbed Bailey's hand and pointed to a young woman sitting on the sidewalk. She had flowers braided into her hair and she wasn't yelling. Aria never picked the ones who yelled. "Her."

Bailey handed Aria a ticket. They walked over to her together, then a few feet away Bailey stopped and let Aria go by herself.

The little girl held out the ticket. "Come to the show, sistah."

Sheer joy shone from her face as she hugged Aria. "Thank you."

* * *

Teague sat next to Aria and listened as Bailey distracted her from having to wait while Crosby, Stills and Nash exited the stage. "What letter does terrapin start with?"

Aria answered immediately, "T."

"Do you think they'll do a 'Terrapin' tonight?"

"I hope so."

"What else starts with t?"

"Teague!" She looked up at him and grinned hugely.

He smiled reflexively. So did Bailey, as she met his eyes. She continued, "Can you think of something else?"

"Auntie Bailey!" The crowd erupted into cheers as Aria jumped out of her seat and pointed at the stage. "Teal starts with t! Bobby's shirt is teal!" Aria yelled as she jumped up and down, pointing.

Bailey agreed, "It sure is."

Teague looked across the stadium to the stage, saw the guy in the really short tan shorts and teal polo shirt. He filed away in his brain that that was Bobby. Next to him was Jerry. After spending months with Bailey and her friends, there was no way to not know who he was— the guy with the bushy grey hair and beard, in the black t-shirt, wearing aviator sunglasses. Neither of them looked the part of 'rock star'.

None of the guys on stage did. The keyboardist had on a short-sleeved button down which was completely at odds with his lumber-jack beard. The bassist reminded Teague of his eighth-grade science teacher with his lanky build and wire rimmed glasses, although he'd never seen a science teacher wear gym shorts and crew socks with sneakers. One of the drummers looked like somebody's grandfather, right down to his Hawaiian shirt, and the other wore a tie-dyed tank top but was clean shaven and still managed to look respectable. Despite their lack of 'boy band' appeal, every available seat was taken and the entire floor was packed with fans. Teague figured there had to be at least fifty-thousand people in the stadium.

Jerry picked out a few notes, talked to the keyboardist, adjusted the guitar strap over his chest. There were other cords, soft drums, the general sound of musicians tuning. Then the crowd burst into cheers as tuning morphed into "Touch of Grey".

Teague could hear Bailey, singing every word as she danced. And it wasn't just Bailey. It was Aria, the people behind him, next to him. And when the chorus began, it was *everyone*. The entire stadium erupted, sound pouring over him from all directions as fifty-thousand voices joined in, vowing to get by, to survive.

Aria danced in front of her seat. There was no way she could see the stage, she was way too short. Teague stooped down and picked her up, set her on his shoulders.

She yelled over the music, "No, no! I gotta dance!"

He put her back down and she immediately went back to dancing. Bailey smiled as she sang, as she moved her feet back and forth, swinging her arms slightly in time to the music.

With no break between, the song changed. Bobby sang about Moses riding a quasar and left-handed monkey wrenches. The words began to slip from Teague's lips, his voice disappearing into the air to join all the others.

* * *

Bailey held Aria's hand as they made their way back to their seats during the break. She asked, "What'd you think of the first set?"

Aria settled into her seat. "It was okay. I like 'Touch of Grey,'" she smiled mischievously, "even though I know you don't."

"That's fine. You're allowed your own opinion. For instance, I happen to love Brussels sprouts, even though hardly anyone else does."

"Auntie Bailey, that's not music."

"It could be. Maybe there's a band out there right now, practicing in their garage, just waiting to burst onto the scene." Loving the way Aria looked at her like she was crazy, she continued, "Their lead singer's name is Franz, and he just booked their first show at the bar down the street. You know the one, *The Pumpernickel Pub*? While he was waiting to talk to the manager he looked at their menu board and the special of the day was Brussels sprouts, so when the manager asked what the name of their band was he said the first thing that popped into his head. Brussels Sprouts."

Teague slid into his seat. "Do you want some pretzel?" He held up a big stadium pretzel.

"Thanks, Teague." Aria took the piece of pretzel he tore off for her. "That's way better than Brussels sprouts."

He gave her a puzzled look. "Well, I do actually like Brussels sprouts, especially with bacon, but I don't think they serve them at the concession stand." He broke off another piece, the twisty middle part, and handed it to Bailey.

As she took it she wondered if he knew the middle was her favorite part. She took a bite, tried to sneak a look at him as she chewed. He was watching something, the people around them? She wasn't sure.

The house lights went out, plunging them into darkness. Everyone began cheering.

A few notes of guitar were quickly drowned out by drums, deep and distinctive. Then, a bit of cymbals. Stage lights shone on Bill and Mickey as they beat out the intro to "Samson and Delilah". Then guitar joined back in and the rest of the stage lit up.

Bailey grabbed Aria and set her on her hip. Aria wrapped her arms around Bailey's neck and sang. She could feel the tears, hers on her cheeks and Aria's on her shoulder, but she didn't care. She loved Delilah, had loved Samson, too. Despite that she missed him terribly, "Samson and Delilah" was and always would be one of her favorite songs. She let the music fill her, drown out every other thought in her head as she sang, as she moved to the beat.

Aria squirmed. Bailey set her down, took her hands and danced. They sang to each other, "If I had my way!"

* * *

Bailey put Aria on her shoulders. Her biggest fear was that they'd get separated. It wasn't just that her niece was tiny compared to most of the people making their way out en mass out. It was that those people were stoned, tripping, flying higher than a kite on adrenaline.

Aria reached for Teague's hand. "Don't lose us."

Bailey felt high even though she hadn't taken anything. *I don't want to lose him either.* "Teague, they did 'Throwin' Stones'."

Aria said, "And you got a 'Terrapin' at your first show ever!" She put her head against the top of Bailey's and yawned.

They let the crowd carry them out of the stadium, into the parking lot. There, finally, the stream of people began to break up as they headed different directions. Bailey heard drums, knew on Shakedown there'd be a party in progress. If she didn't have Aria, she'd have headed that way.

Instead, she took a moment to orient herself and began to make her way to the van.

By the time they got there Aria was snoring. She unlocked the back doors and carefully laid Aria on the bed. She muttered a little but didn't wake up. As quietly as she could, Bailey pulled a blanket out and handed it to Teague. "Can you put this out, please, so we can sit. If we try to leave now we'll just have to wait in traffic."

He had the blanket spread out on the ground in front of the van by the time she came around with Delilah. They sat together, Bailey between Teague and the dog.

"She's still asleep?" Teague indicated the van, and Aria.

"Um hm. She's always been able to sleep anywhere."

Teague was very close. Close enough that if she wanted to she could touch him.

"Bailey?"

She turned to him, his profile lit by the street light two rows over. "Hm?"

"Thank you, for bringing me here. It's been really cool."

There was a flutter in her stomach, a feeling she immediately understood. She wasn't sure what to do with that. Teague confused her. And she confused herself. So she did nothing.

Chapter 32

Bailey lay as still as possible. She could feel Aria breathing next to her, hear Teague in the other bed and Delilah on the floor, all sound asleep.

They'd driven until she hadn't been able to go any farther before they'd found a room. She should have been out cold as soon as her head hit the pillow. But she couldn't shut her brain off. All she could think about was Teague.

The way he'd looked at her, during the show and later when they'd been waiting to leave, had made her feel tingly. It wasn't the first time she'd noticed it, it was just becoming harder to ignore.

She opened her eyes. If she concentrated she could just make out the darker shape of Teague against the emptiness of the room behind him. She wondered what would happen if she crawled into his bed. Imagined him wrapping his arms around her, holding her tight while they drifted off to sleep together.

That was stupid. So stupid. She rolled over and put her arm around Aria. Teague might let her into his bed for a while, but someday he was going to wake up and remember who he was. Realize what he was giving up by hanging out in some hippie coffee shop all day instead of working and having a real life.

And when that happened, no matter what kind of looks he'd been giving her, he'd leave.

Just like Jesse does. And Dad. Except Dad didn't leave you on purpose. Tears sprang to her eyes. *Think of something else. Teague. No, no no. Not Teague. The hammock, in Mom's back yard. The warm sun, a light breeze.* She stayed perfectly still, imagining the soft rocking of the hammock.

Delilah whimpered. *You miss Samson, too, don't you.* The dogs had always slept curled next to each other. Bailey reached down and rubbed Delilah's head. Hanging her arm over the bed felt even more like the hammock in her mom's yard. *Concentrate on the sun. The way Teague looks when he smiles. Damn it, no. The hammock.*

Delilah's tail thumped. *Dreaming, probably.* She fixated on the feel of the dog's fur under her fingers and finally felt her mind begin to drift. *Yes! Sleep!* Her mind jerked awake. *No! Don't think about falling asleep, that keeps you up. In the hammock, Delilah next to you, the sun, the breeze. The sun, the... Teague next to you... in the hammock...* The thump of Delilah's tail seemed to match the swaying of the hammock. *Samson would have loved Teague, too. Concentrate on the hammock... the breeze... the...*

It was impossible to concentrate, especially with Samson butting his head against her leg. "What's the matter, boy? You want to go out?"

She opened the kitchen door, shivered at the blast of cold air. "Go if you're going." Samson stayed where he was, staring at the blanket of snow on the deck. Bailey laughed, "Afraid of a little snow? I should have named you..." The feeling that something wasn't quite right stopped her from continuing.

Her dad teased, "You talk to that dog like he's a person."

"He is." Unable to put her finger on what was wrong, she went back to peeling carrots. This was her favorite time of day, before Mom and Peyton got home, when she and Dad cooked dinner together. They were having baked chicken with all the trimmings, Mom's favorite.

247

Dad was always thinking about Mom, always trying to make sure she was happy.

She asked, "Do you think this is enough carrots?"

Teague glanced over. "Aria loves carrots. Especially when you glaze them."

Unease wormed into her stomach. *Teague isn't supposed to be here.* She peeled another carrot. *But he is, and that's all that matters.*

He sang "Brown Eyed Girl" as he cut potatoes. Bailey smiled to see him use the knife as a microphone to sing the sha-la-la parts.

The sense of unease grew. Teague didn't sing when he cooked. He didn't sing at all. *That was Dad.* A cold ball of fear formed in her stomach. *We were making chicken that night.*

Teague raised his eyes to meet hers, the smile making the brown sparkle. "Bail—" His face went slack and he fell to the floor.

Bailey screamed, "Teague!" She ran to him, knowing already it was too late. She shook him, tears running down her face, making fat wet blotches as they landed on his flannel shirt. "No! Teague, stay with me. Oh God, please, please. Not again."

"He's dead."

She jerked around. "Peyton. Thank god you're here. Save him, *please.*"

Peyton stood on the other side of the kitchen, arms crossed, wearing the grey angora sweater Grandma had gotten her for Christmas, looking just as beautiful, just as put together, as Bailey remembered. "I can't do that."

"You can. You said you knew what to do. You said if you'd been here, instead of me... You said you knew how to save him!"

"Sorry, little sistah, this one's all on you."

Desperately, she begged, "Peyton! Help me, please! He's dying!" She looked back down at Teague, his face frozen in death, his tongue black and his eyes staring at nothing. It was too awful, too much.

It's a dream! Wake up!

Desperate to escape the nightmare, she clawed towards consciousness. Her heart hammered in her chest as she struggled to breathe.

Teague's voice was tinted with fear as he mumbled, "Bailey, it's okay. I'm here. I'm right here. It was just a dream. I've got you. I'm not going anywhere."

She shook with terror. *It was just a dream. He's alive. He's fine.* With her face pressed against the warmth of his chest, she breathed in his scent. *Cedarwood. He smells like cedar.* It was a good, comfortable smell.

He rocked her, his arms clasped tightly around her, until she stopped shaking. After a while he shifted position. Panic welled in her chest, "Don't let me go."

"I won't. I'm right here. We're just going to lie down. I can't keep my eyes open."

She lay next to him, relieved that he kept his arms around her. The dark silence of the hotel room bore down on her. She pressed against his side and concentrated on the sound of his heart, beating loud and strong, as she tried to quell the horror of the dream. She mumbled, "Don't leave me."

Hardly even a whisper, he answered, "I won't."

Chapter 33

Bailey eased out of bed, crossed to the bathroom as quietly as she could. Alone, she stared at herself in the mirror. *How are you going to explain to Teague what happened last night?*

She closed her eyes, tried to sort out what she felt. She'd seen that scene played out more times than she could count— over and over until she'd screamed for it to stop. And every time Jesse had held her, soothed her until she could get herself under control. Or until he'd packed a bowl, one handed so he didn't have to let her go, and she'd gotten blissfully stoned.

Except it hadn't been a dream, it had been a memory. And it hadn't been Teague on the floor, it'd been her dad.

Somehow, the dream had been worse. "What did you get yourself into." She opened her eyes. *You deserve this. You knew better than to let your guard down. Friends leave, too. They die, too. Just because you're not sleeping with him won't make it any less painful.*

"Bailey?" Teague knocked softly, "You okay?"

She opened the door. He looked half asleep, his hair a mess and his eyes not fully open. Relief flooded through her. *God, you're so stupid.* She forced a smile and whispered, "Yeah, I'm fine."

He searched her face, then said, "I'm gonna go see if there's coffee in the lobby."

* * *

The hills were familiar, which was good because Aria was getting restless. "Auntie Bailey, how come we couldn't go to the next show?"

They'd been over this, but she repeated it anyway. "Because Katelyn's going and I don't have anyone to cover me at the shop."

"When can I go again?"

"I don't know. I'll have to look at the schedule." She felt bad, but she couldn't change things. "It's a lot harder now, because you can't miss school."

"How much longer till we get home?"

"Another hour."

"I'm hungry."

"We can stop at McDonald's when we get home." Bailey snuck a quick peek at her niece. She was curled up in the seat, one hand resting on Delilah's side.

"Can we stop at a rest area?"

"There isn't one between here and home. Besides, if we stop it'll just make it take longer to get there."

"Could you tell me a story?"

She'd been driving for hours, she didn't have it in her to make something up. She suggested something she knew by heart. "*The Lorax?*"

"No. I wanna hear about Samson and Delilah."

She didn't know the Bible well, but she could probably remember enough of the song to get through. "Samson was the strongest man on Earth."

Aria stopped her. "No, I mean our Samson and Delilah. When you found them."

She felt her lips tighten into something close to a frown. Samson hadn't been gone long enough for her to be able to talk easily about him, and she didn't like telling stories that included Jesse when she was with Teague.

Just avoid mentioning him. "We'd been at Joshua Tree, camping, just before the Vegas shows. We left very early in the morning because we wanted to drive as far as possible before it got too hot. We made it to Blythe by breakfast. We ate, got gas, and everyone went to the bathroom. By the time we got on the road again it was already sweltering. And I don't mean hot like we have at home. I mean the air is so hot it feels like when you open the oven door and stick your face in. Everyone else wanted to get a hotel room and wait for it to get dark, but we were only a few hours from Vegas and I thought it made more sense to get a room there."

"Who was with you?"

So much for leaving Jesse out. "Me, Jesse, this sister named Meg and her boyfriend Banyan."

Aria interrupted, "That's a funny name."

"Well, it's not really his name. Anyway,"

"What's his real name?"

"I don't know. I never asked."

"Why not?"

"Because it's rude."

"What's it mean?"

"To be rude?"

Aria sighed. "No, Auntie. His name."

"Banyan? It's a kind of tree."

"Why'd you call him that?"

"I did because that's how I was introduced to him. But I think it got started because banyan trees have lots of skinny roots that grow up next to the trunk, and Banyan had lots of skinny dreads that kind of looked like that."

"You know a lotta people with funny names."

Bailey smiled a little. "That's because a lot of hippies take names that describe them, better than the names their parents gave them."

"Is your real name Bailey?"

"It is. And it's Auntie Bailey to you. So, anyway, after we left Blythe we drove for a while then everyone had to pee again. You know how that is, right? When we're traveling with a bunch of people and someone has to pee." Bailey watched Aria in the rear-view mirror as she nodded. "I pulled into a rest area. Out there the rest areas aren't like they are here. There's no buildings, no bathrooms or vending machines. They're just a place to park for a little while, and usually they have a barrel of water in case your radiator is overheating.

"I climbed over the guardrail to pee. The sand was so hot I could feel it through my shoes. As soon as I was done I started back to the van, but something moved by the water barrel. It scared the shit out of me. I figured it was a snake or something. But then it whined, just loud enough that I could hear it, and I noticed there was a rope tied to the guardrail.

"There were three puppies, huddling in the tiny spot of shade from the barrel. A girl and two boys. They were overheated, dehydrated and starving. One was barely breathing. We untied them and gave them some water. We didn't have anything they could eat." She felt the tears start but she kept talking. "The one who was the worst off didn't drink. We were still discussing what to do, if we should go back to Blythe or continue on to Vegas, when I knew it was too late."

She took a minute, let herself feel sadness over the one she couldn't save. When she was ready, she continued, "When we got to Vegas we took a room in the first hotel we found. By then all that mattered was air conditioning, and finding a store that sold puppy formula. I sat all night with the two that were left, sure they were going to die, too. But they were fighters.

"The whole time we were there I never left the hotel room. I skipped going to the lot, missed the shows, and I didn't care. By the time we left, the puppies were running around, chasing each other, yipping when they saw food coming. I named the boy Samson, because he was strong. And of course his sister had to be Delilah."

She glanced in the mirror. Aria was asleep, her hand still on Delilah's side. The dog slept, too. Bailey glanced at Teague.

He gave her a sad, sweet smile. "Bailey, I'm sorry about Samson."

She was glad she was driving and couldn't really look at him. If she'd been able to she'd have broken down in tears. "He lived a good life, and he died instantly. If there was pain, it was brief. That's all a dog can ask for."

* * *

Bailey parked in her space behind the shop. Delilah bounded out as soon as she opened the door and headed to the grassy area at the edge of the parking lot.

Aria stretched and mumbled, "We didn't stop at McDonald's."

"Sorry, baby. You were sleeping." Bailey pulled Aria's backpack out from under the bed and handed it to her. "We can order pizza."

Aria took the backpack and climbed out of the van. "Can Teague stay?"

"If he wants to." She caught his eye, tried to read his expression. They hadn't talked much on the ride home, and neither of them had mentioned the night before. She had no idea how he felt about it. *Hell, I'm not sure how I feel about it.*

"You're gonna stay, right?" Aria took his hand.

He smiled down at her. "I'd love to."

"Aria, can you please get Delilah and wait by the door?" Bailey reached for her own bag, giving Aria a minute to move out of earshot. "You don't have to stay, if you have things to do."

Teague picked up his backpack and slung it over his shoulder. "The only thing I have to do is eat pizza. Unless," he looked unsure as he said, "you were just being polite because Aria wanted me to stay."

She took in his tousled hair, the way his clothes were rumpled from the long drive, the nervousness in his expression. She didn't want him to go. Softly, she said, "It's not just Aria who'd like it if you stayed."

They held each other's gaze, too long for it to be an accident.

"Auntie? I gotta pee."

The moment broken, Teague turned to his car, popped the trunk and dropped his bag in. Bailey got her bag and locked the van. On the way to the building, she said, "Teague, can you do me a favor? I want to check on the shop. Can you take Aria upstairs? I'll just be a minute."

"Take your time. If you want, I'll order the pizza."

"Yeah?"

"Sure. What do you like on it?"

"Everything except anchovies."

He followed Aria upstairs, calling Delilah with him. Bailey headed to the front of the shop.

There was a young couple talking quietly in the corner. The only other person in the shop was Katelyn. She was sitting at a table reading a book. "Hey, Bailey! How was your trip?"

"Good. How was everything here?"

"Ann Marie was busy in the mornings. It's been pretty quiet for my shifts. Everything's in the safe."

"Thanks, Katelyn."

"No problem." A glint in her eye, she asked, "How'd it go with Teague?"

Bailey tried to answer nonchalantly. "Fine. He had a great first show. Well, the second set, anyway." She wasn't sure she was

255

convincing, though, because Katelyn gave her a knowing look.

"So you dropped him off at home?"

"He left his car here."

"So he's on his way home?"

Feeling very uncomfortable, she said, "No. He took Aria upstairs. We haven't eaten, so he's staying for dinner."

Katelyn nodded. "He eats here most nights, doesn't he?"

"I guess. Aria likes him to stay."

"Aria does, huh?"

Deciding she didn't want to continue the conversation, she said, "I'm gonna go unpack before the pizza gets here."

Katelyn gave her a huge grin. "Okay."

At the top of the stairs she paused. She could hear Teague and Aria talking. She tried to hear what they were saying, but they were too quiet. After a minute she opened the door to see them sitting on the couch, a book spread across their laps.

They both looked up. Teague smiled as he said, "Pizza'll be here in about ten minutes."

Her heart pounding, Bailey said, "Cool."

* * *

Teague knew he should go. It was late, Bailey was curled up at the other end of the couch, yawning, and Aria definitely should have been in bed already.

But Aria looked at him with those big blue eyes and asked, "Will you read it again?"

He couldn't bring himself to get up. Instead, he flipped the book back to the first page. Aria giggled as he tried to wrap his tongue around the impossibleness of Dr. Seuss's *Fox In Socks*. After the last page he closed the book. At some point Bailey had fallen asleep. He told Aria, "Go brush your teeth."

"I'm not tired."

"I know, but Auntie Bailey is. And I have to go home, so you have to go to bed."

"Will you come back tomorrow?"

"Of course. Now brush your teeth."

As soon as she was gone, he gently touched Bailey's shoulder. "Bail, it's late. Go get in bed."

Bailey whispered, "You can stay if you want."

Sudden desire pounded through him. That was *exactly* what he wanted. Especially after the night before, and waking up in the morning with her against him. He'd lay as still as possible, trying imprint on his memory the feel of her as she slept against his side. He raised his fingers to touch her hair, "Bail-"

Then Aria was back. He dropped his hand. Staying in the same hotel room, comforting Bailey when she'd had a nightmare, was one thing. Staying over at Bailey's place, with Aria there, was something completely different.

He scooped Aria up. "You get in bed and let Auntie sleep, okay?"

"'Kay." She kissed his cheek and hugged him.

He put her down and watched until she was in the bedroom. Then he knelt next to Bailey. "Aria's in bed. I'll lock up behind me. Are you good?"

She opened her eyes and smiled softly. "Yeah. I'm good."

It took everything in him to leave her. He paused at the door, turned back one last time. Bailey was still curled up on the couch.

It wasn't the right time to stay. No matter how much he wanted to.

Chapter 34

The morning rush was in full swing when Teague got to the shop. Still, Bailey took the time to talk to him as she made his coffee. "You're here early."

"Yeah, I had this pressing appointment first thing this morning, so, here I am."

Seeming truly curious, she asked, "What appointment?"

"It's with the most beautiful girl." He smiled, "I met her a while back, at this hippie coffee shop, and I haven't been the same since."

"She must be pretty special."

God, he loved those eyes. He could spend all day staring into them. "She is."

Bailey tipped her chin down and looked up at him.

The door opened, the bell above it reminding Teague that there was a line of people behind him. "Where's Aria this morning?"

"Upstairs getting dressed. She should be down in a minute."

He was half way through his first coffee when Aria came down. He grabbed her and tickled her. "Hey, girl. Shouldn't you be in school?"

Between squeals of laughter, she said, "It's summer."

"Then you should be in summer school."

"There's no such thing!" She squirmed, trying to get away from his tickling.

Laughing, Teague let her go.

"Can we play Operation?"

"Sure." He dug the game out and set it up.

Delilah wandered in and sat next to his feet. He petted her while Aria took her first turn.

She took a card, picked up the tweezers and examined the little plastic piece she was supposed to remove. Her tongue snuck out the corner of her mouth as she concentrated.

He told her, "Be careful. The funny bone's tough."

She hit the side of the slot, making the red bulb on the board light up and the buzzer buzz.

Delilah lifted her head at the sound.

Teague considered letting Aria try again, but that seemed like it wouldn't be teaching her the right life lesson. Instead, he chose a card and picked up the tweezers. He easily grabbed the elastic and pulled it from the "patient's" leg. He paid himself for the successful surgery and chose another card. This time he was supposed to pull the butterfly from the stomach. He glanced at Bailey, still serving a line of customers. *Beautiful Butterfly Bailey. Christ, she puts butterflies in my stomach. You're so lame, bro. Never, ever say that out loud.*

Turning back to the board, he decided he'd lose on purpose. He messed with the butterfly, then hit the edge. "Aw, darn." He handed the tweezers to Aria and rubbed Delilah's head. She'd flinched at the buzzer; he figured she probably didn't like this particular game.

After a few more turns Teague started thinking he really didn't like this game, either. Neither he or Aria seemed able to pull the stupid pieces from the holes and every time the game buzzed Delilah jumped.

This sucks. Maybe Bailey would let me take Aria swimming? Except you have no idea how to get back to that place. Maybe Bailey'd tell you. He nearly laughed out loud at that thought. Bailey never told him anything she didn't absolutely have to. *What else do kids like?*

Someplace I know.

After three more rounds of failed attempts at 'surgery' he said, "Aria, I need another cup of coffee."

"Can I practice? I won't keep anything."

"Sure." He went up to the counter and waited until Bailey had a moment. Then he asked, "Bailey? It's so nice out. Can I take Aria to the playground? Let her run around for a while?"

"I can't impose on you like that."

Shaking his head, he said, "You're not." He looked back at Aria, hunched over the game while she waited for him to come back. "I can take care of lunch, and I'll pick up something for dinner on my way back, too, so you don't have to cook."

She searched his face for a moment, then called, "Aria, come here, please." Aria skipped to the counter. "Teague has graciously offered to take you to the playground."

"Yeah!" She grabbed his hand and started towards the door.

"Hey! I'm not done with you." Aria turned back. "You listen to him the same way you'd listen to me."

"Okay, okay." Beaming, Aria pulled Teague from the shop.

Bailey called after them, "And no ice cream, you two."

Teague glanced back and smiled devilishly, wondering how she'd known he was thinking that.

* * *

Teague pushed Aria on the swing, sending her above his head.

"Higher!"

He pushed her again. "Last time, girl. Auntie Bailey's gonna think we forgot about her." He sat on the swing next to her to wait for her to lose momentum.

She brought her feet forward, then back.

"Hey, no pumping."

She giggled, but she didn't pump again. The swing slowed until she was only going a few feet off the ground. "Teague?" She moved her head so she could keep him in her sights. "Do your feet itch?"

Completely at a loss, he said, "No."

"Good."

He struggled with a smile, wondering what she was talking about. "Do yours?"

"No. I don't get itchy feet." She dragged her feet in the dirt to stop the swing, wrapped her arms around the chains and looked at him earnestly. "Do you think yours will?"

"Ummm… I don't really know. I mean, I guess they *could* itch." Despite his best efforts, he laughed.

Aria frowned. "It's not funny."

"I'm sorry." As seriously as possible, he asked, "Why are you so worried about my feet?"

"Because I don't want you to go away." She made the swing move a little. "Like Jesse."

Jesse's name felt like a punch in the stomach. The memory of Bailey's tear-streaked face the day he'd left flashed through Teague's mind. He reached for the chain and made Aria's swing stop. "Aria, I'm not going anywhere."

She held his gaze for a moment, then jumped off the swing. "We better go or Auntie Bailey's gonna think we forgot her."

"And we better pick up something for dinner." *Something good, because Bailey and Aria freaking deserve someone to treat them right.*

"Ice cream?" Aria smiled up at him.

Teague snorted. "You know I'll be in trouble with your aunt if I take you for ice cream. How about grinders."

"I guess." She climbed into the front seat of his car and buckled. "You don't sound thrilled."

Aria watched out the window as he pulled onto the street. "I like ice cream better."

"Me, too." He asked, "If you could pick dinner, something besides ice cream, what would it be?"

"Lasagna."

"I think they make that at Sal's."

She turned to him, her expression quizzical. "Why don't you just make it?"

He'd managed a fairly decent Chicken Piccata, but his attempt at pork chops had been a disaster. Deciding he wasn't ready to cook for Bailey, he said, "I don't cook, remember?"

"Just look it up. In a cookbook. That's what Auntie Bailey does."

The car behind him honked. He went through the intersection. Paying attention to where he was driving, he said, "I can make Chicken Piccata."

"What's that?"

"Chicken with lemon sauce and capers."

Aria wrinkled her nose. "I don't think I like capers. Anyway, Auntie Bailey says the only way to get good at something is to practice. And plus, if it comes out bad we'll just order pizza."

"We had pizza last night."

"That's what we always do when something doesn't come out good."

"Does Auntie Bailey have to order pizza often?"

"Only once in a while."

He thought it over. *Lasagna can't be that hard.* "You help Auntie Bailey cook, right?"

"Um hm. Nannie, too."

"Have you ever made lasagna?"

"Yeah, sometimes. Nannie lets me do the noodle layers."

By the time he pulled into Bailey's he'd made a decision. Instead of going into the shop he led Aria across the green. He didn't have a cookbook with him, but he knew exactly where to get one.

* * *

"Hey, Bailey, can we use your kitchen?" Teague juggled shopping bags as he came through the door.

"Sure. What are you making?"

Aria grinned, "You'll see." She led Teague upstairs.

In Bailey's kitchen, Teague carefully read the recipe again. He already knew what to do, since he'd read the recipe about ten times in the grocery store, but he didn't want to mess it up. "Okay, I'm going to cook the pasta and brown the hamburg. You can grate the cheese and mix the ricotta." He got the grater and gave it to Aria.

As she started on the mozzarella, she asked, "Are you going to make bread?"

"I guess we should have picked up a loaf. Maybe once we get this in the oven we'll run back out to the store."

"Can't you just make it?"

He smiled at her confidence in his questionable culinary skills. "I'm sure I could, but tonight we're going to figure out lasagna. Next time we'll work on bread."

"Auntie Bailey makes beer bread a lot. I help, it's really easy."

"Let's get this going, then we'll see what we can do."

Once he had water on and the beef browning, he marked the lasagna page in the cookbook and turned to the bread section. He looked at each recipe, page by page.

Aria stood next to him and looked at the pictures. Pointing at cinnamon rolls, she said, "Those look good."

"Yeah, they do. So do those." Teague showed her bagels. "I used to live near this place that made the best bagels. I tried to get your aunt to make them for me once, but she said she didn't have time."

"Why don't you make them?" Aria looked at him, innocent curiosity in her eyes.

"Aria, seriously, one thing at a time." He found Italian bread and read the recipe. "Definitely no homemade Italian bread tonight, girl. This says it takes four hours. I'm thinking that dinner at nine o'clock tonight isn't a great idea." He continued looking. "I don't see a recipe for beer bread. I'll tell you what. Tonight, we'll run back to the store, then next time we'll make the bread from scratch before we start the lasagna."

"Okay. Your water's boiling."

* * *

Aria jumped up from the couch as soon as Bailey opened the door. "Hi, Auntie Bailey! Are you hungry?"

Smiling at her niece's enthusiasm, she said, "Starving." Aria ran to the kitchen. Bailey waited for Teague. "It smells amazing in here."

He set the book he'd been reading to Aria on the coffee table. "Let's hope it tastes good."

In the kitchen, Bailey asked, "What is all this?" The table was formally set for three, complete with a candle in the center.

Aria beamed. "We made a restaurant. Sit down and I'll be your waitress."

Bailey sat and Aria handed her a menu. Bailey's chest constricted, seeing the painstaking effort Aria had put into writing out what they were eating. "What's caprese salad?"

"It's tomatoes and cheese. That's what's in the bowls." She pointed to a bowl set on top of a plate at each place. "Teague said he used to eat it all the time in Connecticut. And the bottom plate's not for food. It's called a," she glanced at Teague.

"Charger." He unfolded a paper napkin and set it across his lap.

"Charger," she repeated. "After we eat our salad course we have the main course. That's the lasagna. And the plate for that goes on top of charger, too." Leaning closer to Bailey, Aria whispered, "I told Teague you wouldn't wanna wash extra dishes but he said he'd do it. So I let him use two plates insteada one."

Trying not to smile, because Aria was taking this so seriously and Bailey didn't want her to think she was laughing at her, she said, "Fancy."

"Teague said his mom made them always have a proper table."

The smile Bailey'd been fighting broke through as she watched Teague stab a tomato. It was impossible to reconcile him now, with his hair tucked behind his ears, a full beard, and wearing a blue and green tie-dye shirt, with the Teague who had first walked into her coffee shop. Or to picture him sitting at a formal dinner.

Once they'd finished their salads Teague handed Aria plates of lasagna. She carefully set them at each place before adding thick slices of Italian bread to yet another plate. Trying not to giggle, she asked Bailey, "Can I get you anything else?"

"No, thank you." Bailey struggled with love so big it threatened to make her cry. She took a bite of lasagna. "This is so good." She grinned at Aria and Teague. "I was expecting take-out. This is way better."

As soon as he was done eating, Teague started the dishes.

"You cooked, I can clean." Bailey started to stand.

"Bailey, sit and relax. I've got this."

"Are you sure?" She felt so bad, letting him do all the work.

"Yeah. I'm sure. Plus, I promised Aria I'd do the dishes." He winked at Aria. "And I always keep my promises."

Bailey stared at his back as he washed dishes, watched his shoulders rippling under his t-shirt, noticed the comfortable way he worked in her kitchen.

Aria asked Bailey, "Will you play Connect Four with me?"

Tearing her eyes from Teague, she nodded. "I'd love to."

* * *

Bailey listened to Aria's slow, deep breathing. She wished like crazy that she could sleep, too.

She rolled over and stared into the dark.

Other than when Jesse was home, or the rare occasion she had Aria overnight, she slept alone most of the time. It didn't usually bother her, and if it did she brought someone home for a night or two. The closest she'd come to having anyone share her bed regularly had been Rain.

Even if Aria wasn't there, and Rain had been around, she wouldn't have invited him home.

She carefully eased out of bed, tiptoed across the floor and as quietly as possible opened the door. She stood in the doorway for a minute, to make sure Aria was still sound asleep. When she was sure, she shut the door.

In the near dark of her living room she made her way to the bookshelf between the front windows. As she opened the wooden box she kept there moonlight glinted off the abalone inlay that covered the top. She moved the pile of grocery and gas receipts she'd shoved in there when Aria had been about four, knowing if she opened the box receipts weren't something she'd be curious enough about to explore.

Bailey packed her favorite bowl, the soapstone one that her friend Calvin had made for her years before. The flicker of the lighter was bright in the darkness, the familiar feel of the smoke filling her lungs was welcome. She held her breath, puffed out her cheeks as she held on as long as possible, and finally coughed hard.

There was no one to pass the bowl to. She took another hit.

She sank down to the floor, put her head on the sill of the open window. A soft breeze ruffled the curtains, stirred her hair. She closed her eyes and concentrated on the buzz in her brain.

Chapter 35

It was easier for Bailey to ignore that she wasn't on tour when she was working. The people who came in weren't family, they were just people from town. No one mentioned venues or set lists.

She played the radio, tuned to the college station. They played a lot of Violent Femmes and Sex Pistols. They never played The Dead.

There was nothing to remind her of the life she was missing out on.

Aria came down earlier than usual. She rubbed her eyes as she came behind the counter. "Auntie, where's Teague?"

"He didn't come in yet. Do you want a muffin?"

"When's he gonna be here?"

She signaled for Aria to wait while she took the next person in line. Turning to the back counter to make the coffees, she answered, "I don't know. He doesn't have a set schedule."

She pouted. "When is Mallory gonna be back?"

"In a few days, but you'll already be at the Cape with Nannie." Needing to distract Aria, she said, "I haven't fed Delilah yet. Can you please take care of it?" She turned to give the coffees to the woman waiting at the counter.

She glanced at the door as someone came in, but it wasn't Teague. Disappointment and relief mingled. The night before, sitting alone in the dark, she'd realized being with him was the only time she felt whole.

She'd handled it by smoking another bowl.

* * *

The drive into town seemed to take longer than normal. When Teague finally pulled into the parking lot his usual space was taken. He ended up parking in the commuter lot two streets away. He grabbed the paper bag from the seat next to him, thanked god it was summer, and walked two blocks to Bailey's.

It was quiet in the shop, other than the background music. Bailey looked up as soon as he stepped through the door. The smile that spread over her face made him feel warm. "Hey, Bailey."

"Hey."

He set the bag on the counter and said the only thing he could think of. "Can I have a coffee?"

As she got it, she said, "Aria's been looking for you all day."

"I promised her we'd go to the playground again."

"She mentioned that." Bailey handed him his mug. "Usually she spends part of the day with Mallory, so it's pretty boring for her when they're gone."

"Where is she?"

"Upstairs. I told her she could watch TV until you got here."

Surprised, he said, "You have a TV?"

She laughed. "Doesn't everyone?"

"Yeah. I just never saw one."

"I keep it hidden. You'll see when you go up."

He sipped his coffee, took a minute to enjoy the bitterness. After he swallowed, he asked, "Did you have breakfast?"

"A while ago." She grinned crookedly. "You've gotta get up pretty early if you're going to have breakfast with me."

"I guess this'll have to count as lunch." He opened the bag he'd set on the counter. "What do you like on your bagels?"

"Cream cheese, cucumbers, sprouts and raisins."

He stopped with his hand half in the bag and stared at her. "Really?"

She shrugged. "Yeah. Why?"

"I just never…" That was weird, but he didn't want to offend her. "I have butter or cream cheese."

"Plain is fine."

He pulled a not quite round and fatter on one side bagel from the bag and handed it to her.

As she took it she asked, "What's this?"

"A bagel."

She smiled. "I can see that. I meant, why are you giving me a bagel?"

He grinned. "Try it."

She took a bite, chewed, and swallowed, her eyes getting big as she did. "Oh my god, Teague. This is killer. Where did you get it?"

"I made it."

Her jaw dropped. "You made this?"

"Do you like it?"

"Uh huh." She took another bite. "I didn't know you could do that."

"I didn't either. I never did before."

"Are you serious?"

"Yeah. This is my second batch. I wanted to make sure the first time wasn't a fluke."

"Teague, you could sell these."

"Yeah? Like on the lot?" He liked that idea.

"If you wanted to. I meant here, though."

Really glad that she liked them, he grinned. "Are you offering me a job?"

She stared at him for a long moment, like she was thinking. Finally, she asked, "Do you need one?"

"No. But I'd be happy to make bagels for you. Shit, Bailey, you won't even let me pay for my coffee. It's the least I can do." He loved the idea of being able to give back to her.

"I'll tell you what. I'll buy whatever ingredients you need and you can use the kitchen here, because in order for me to sell them they have to be made in a commercial kitchen, but I can't let you do this for free."

"There's no way I could take money from you."

"We'll see how you feel about that at five in the morning."

"Five in the morning?"

Grinning slyly, Bailey said, "Yeah. That's what time I start baking."

* * *

At five-thirty the next morning a bleary-eyed Teague stumbled into the kitchen at Bailey's shop to find her singing to the radio, muffins already in the oven and working on cookies. She smiled as he came in. "Hey, Teague. You're late. I thought you'd changed your mind."

Somewhat regretting this, he grunted. "Coffee."

"As soon as I get these in the oven. This is my space," she indicated the counter against the wall. "You can use the prep table," she pointed at the stainless-steel island in the center of the room, "and I'll be out of here by six-thirty, so you can have the whole kitchen to yourself."

"Thanks." He took a couple minutes to familiarize himself with where everything was. Concentrating on what he was doing, afraid to make a mistake in front of Bailey, he ignored her completely.

* * *

Taking his fourth cup of coffee to the couches in the back, Teague sat down for the first time that day. He leaned back and closed his tired eyes, wondering how Bailey did this every day. Five-fucking-o'clock in the morning. Even when he'd been a lawyer he hadn't been in the office until seven.

* * *

"Teague, Teague, Teague! Are we gonna go to the park? You promised." Aria stood in front of Teague, smiling her winningest smile.

Teague opened his eyes, mortified to realize he'd been asleep. He sat up, trying to hide it. "Hey, girl. Where'd you come from?"

"Upstairs. Are we gonna go?"

"Yeah, of course." He rubbed his hands over his face, wiping the sleep out of his eyes. "Let me just finish my coffee." He picked up his mug and took a sip.

It was ice cold.

He got up, intending to see if Bailey would give him a refill. He hadn't taken a single step and she was there, handing him a cup. "I made your coffee to go." Their eyes locked.

And held.

The moment seemed to stretch forever as Teague stared into Bailey's hazel eyes. He struggled to pin a name to what he felt; gratitude for the coffee, relief that she didn't bust his balls about falling asleep, or something else entirely.

Taking the cup, he knew it was something else entirely. "Thank you."

A smile lighting her eyes, Bailey said, "You're welcome. If you wanted to pick up something for dinner on your way back…" She trailed off.

That was an invitation, and he accepted immediately. "Sure. What would you like?"

"Whatever you get is fine."

Her tone was too serious. He broke the mood on purpose. "Ice cream it is, then."

Aria cheered. "Yeah!!!" She grabbed Teague's waist. "You're the best!"

He picked her up and they rubbed noses.

"Teague." Bailey's reproving tone couldn't quite hide the amusement in her voice.

He put Aria back down. "Don't worry, we'll get something Bailey-approved." Pretending to whisper behind his hand, he said to Aria, "And ice cream."

Bailey rolled her eyes. "I have to go back to work. You two behave."

"We will," Aria said as she took Teague's hand and started to lead him to the front door.

"Or not." Teague grinned back at Bailey.

Chapter 36

Teague listened to Bailey read *Willa of the Woods* to Aria. He turned the water on just enough to rinse the soap from the plate, but not enough that the sound drowned out Bailey's voice. Willa was on her way to a magical place she'd been to long ago, where the music never stopped, and Teague wanted to hear if she found her way back there. It was important, because she needed the music to keep her magic strong. Finished with the dishes, he stood in the kitchen doorway. From where he was he could see the pages of the book.

He'd thought Bailey was reading, but there were no words with the pictures.

Fascinated, he walked around the couch and sat next to Aria. She kept her eyes glued to the drawings in what Teague now saw was a sketch book. Bailey, though, glanced at him. He smiled and she looked back to the book, her expression unreadable.

Aria turned the page to a drawing of a river. Teague was startled to realize it was Queeche.

Bailey continued, "The princess was sure she was going the right way. She continued through the woods, following the trail past stately trees and clusters of wild flowers, until she came to a fork in the path. She stood for a while, unsure of which way to go. Then she thought she heard music from the left."

She turned the page to a picture of a path winding through close woods. "The trail narrowed. The branches of the trees met overhead, blocking the sky. Willa began to doubt herself. She didn't remember this part of the woods." Her voice took on an ominous tone. "It was dark, and she was alone, and the way the wind moved through the trees made it sound like someone, or *something*, was following her."

She turned the page. The next picture was of a fallen tree, covered with moss. There were clumps of orange mushrooms here and there. Teague remembered Bailey telling him her dad said mushrooms were fairy houses.

"Now she was sure she'd never been this way. She turned, deciding to go back. But as she did a fox stepped out from the trees. *'Hello, Willa.'* The fox sauntered closer. *'It's been a long time.'* Willa breathed a sigh of relief. She knew this fox; they'd heard the music together. She smiled, *'Hello, Fox. Will you come with me? I'm looking for the music.'* He backed away. *'I'd love to, but I was on my way to the other side of the wood. I heard there's a gathering there.'*"

Teague liked the way Bailey lowered her voice for the fox, and used a sing-song tone for Willa. He could see why Aria was so enchanted. He was, too.

As Bailey turned the page there was a knock on her door and Ellen came in.

Aria jumped up. "Nannie!" She ran to her grandmother and hugged her.

Bailey closed the book and slipped it on a shelf as she greeted her mom.

* * *

Bailey wished she'd been able to talk Aria into a regular book instead of Willa. She made a mental note to hide it as soon as Teague left. She was mortified that he'd heard that night's story. *At least he didn't hear where you were going with it. Because you're an idiot, and you can't stop thinking about him.* She asked her mom, "How was your trip?"

"Productive. I'm glad to be home, though."

Ellen looked tired. Bailey said, "Aria, Nannie had a long flight and I'm sure she wants to go home. Can you please go get your bag?"

"'Kay, Auntie." She skipped to Bailey's bedroom.

Ellen asked, "Teague, how was your first show?"

He smiled, "I had a great time."

Then Aria was back. "Teague, are you gonna be here tomorrow?"

"You know it." He picked her up, rubbed noses, hugged her tight and set her back down. "Be good for Nannie."

"I will. Bye, Auntie Bailey. I'll see you tomorrow." She gave Bailey a hug and a kiss. Then she was dragging Ellen out the door.

In the sudden quiet Bailey was very aware that she and Teague were alone.

It was the first time in over a week and, despite that they'd spent countless hours with each other, she didn't quite know what to do.

"I should-" he started.

"Do you want-" she laughed as they spoke over each other.

"I should probably go." He stuck his hands in his pockets. "Five o'clock comes pretty early."

Disappointed that he was leaving, she nodded. "Yeah, it does."

They stared at each other.

"Teague?"

"Yeah?"

She wanted to ask him to stay. *He just said he's going to go. Maybe he doesn't want to.* Instead, she said, "Thanks for all your help with Aria. I really appreciate it."

"I'm happy to. She's a blast."

"So I'll see you tomorrow?"

"Bright and early." He smiled a little.

276

"'Kay."

He went to the door and opened it.

She tried to think of something else to say, but nothing seemed right.

He turned back, smiled once, and was gone.

She stood there, staring at the closed door, for far too long.

Chapter 37

Scooping cookie dough didn't take enough concentration to keep Bailey from thinking about Teague thanking her for bringing him to Pittsburgh. Or how he'd looked at her the day they'd gone swimming. Or how when he left each night she didn't want him to go.

For a while she'd been sure that his increased presence had been for Aria. But that didn't hold water. He stayed every night now, whether Aria was with her or not. And he'd been there every day for a week, at 5:30 in the morning, making bagels.

As she turned to slide the tray into the oven, he glanced up. An involuntary smile slipped over her face, seeing him covered in flour. *Now or never, Bail.* Nerves screaming, she forced her voice to be casual. "Hey, Teague?"

"Yeah?"

"Do you think there's a way you can pre-make bagels?"

He looked up at her questioningly. "You don't want them fresh every morning?"

"No, that's not what I meant. I mean, like, I make cookie dough and freeze it raw so that when I'm not around whoever's covering for me can just pop the frozen dough in the oven instead of having to make everything from scratch in the morning."

His brow creased. "I don't think I can freeze the dough raw."

"What about if you made the bagels, and just didn't do the last part.

What if you froze them after boiling them?"

"I have no idea. I can try it today, if you want."

Ask him. "If it works, can you make a whole bunch?"

He narrowed his eyes. "Planning to get rid of me?"

His joking helped ease her nerves. "No, actually, I'm planning to catch the last part of summer tour, and I thought maybe you might want to come with me." *God, please don't say no.* Hands sweaty, she added, "My mom's taking Aria and Delilah, so it'll be… quieter."

There was no hesitation at all. "How many bagels do you think we need?"

"We'll be gone for like two weeks, and we probably need two dozen a day."

His jaw dropped. "That's a freakin lot of bagels."

"I can just take them off the menu while we're gone."

He eyed her for a minute, then said, "I'll figure it out."

She turned back to her cookie dough, a grin stealing over her face.

* * *

Bailey began pulling clothes out of the dresser.

This was easier than packing for spring tour, when there was always the possibility of anything from sunny with highs in the 80's to a blizzard. In the summer, it was most likely going to be hot and dry, or hot and wet. She grabbed an ankle length skirt with a blue flower pattern on it and a faded red paisley sun dress. She added her favorite overalls, with a stripe of purple corduroy running down the outside of each leg, just in case it got cold at night. Then she changed her mind and swapped those for regular jeans, in case she wanted to wear them under a dress. Next went a 'Terrapin Station' shirt that had been left in her car by a sister she'd been friends with on her first tour but hadn't seen since, and a tie-dye that had been given to her by this guy she'd known in Santa Cruz.

She began to pull out a blue and green 'Eyes of the World' shirt, then stopped. That was Jesse's.

Memories suddenly crowded her head. Jesse coming towards her on the lot, smiling to see her. Jesse sitting in a coffee shop on the Haight, at a drum circle in the desert, right here in her bedroom.

She absolutely did *not* want to think about him right then.

She crammed the shirt back in the drawer and instead threw a Summer Tour '87 shirt into her bag.

* * *

It was late afternoon by the time Bailey rang Teague's doorbell. He opened the door wearing just jeans, hung low on his hips. Her stomach did a strange little flip thing. "Hey."

"Hey." He stood to the side to let her in.

There were clothes scattered all over the living room. She walked past him into the disarray. "Is Cole back?"

Laughing, Teague said, "No. I'm just having an issue."

"What's your issue?" She moved a shirt so she could sit on the couch.

He shut the door and came to stand in the middle of the living room. "I have no idea what to bring."

"Whatever you have is fine." When he didn't move she said, "Just throw a bunch of shirts and a couple pairs of shorts in a bag. Bring a pair of jeans in case it's cold."

"Okay, I'll bring the blue oxford, the beige button down, and two pairs of black slacks."

"Perfect." She picked up the t-shirt that was lying next to her and threw it at him.

He caught it and looked at it. "You think Cole'll notice if I steal his clothes?"

"Do you care?"

After a moment of hesitation, he said, "Nope," and slipped the shirt she'd thrown at him over his head.

* * *

Teague had been staring at the bit of road lit by Bailey's headlights for what felt like hours. Without Aria, the drive was much quieter.

"Teague, do you want to put a tape in?"

"Sure. Which one?"

"Any one you want."

When he'd gone through Bailey's tapes before it had always been to find something specific she'd asked for. He had no idea what to pick. These weren't studio albums, where everyone knew what the band had recorded and released. Each one was unique. He pulled a tape out and read the hand written set list for it. He slipped it back in, chose another. Then another.

"Are you looking for something specific?"

"I don't know. I just want to pick something good."

"They're all good." She glanced at him for a second. "Is there a particular song you want?"

He shifted so he could see her face. "'Cosmic Charlie'?"

"They haven't played that since 1976. I don't have it on tape. Not here, anyway." She glanced at him. "You've been spending too much time with Aria."

He grinned, then said, "How about 'Sugar Mag Sunshine Daydream'?"

"Mmmmm.... Merriweather, June 20, 1983."

He started reading labels. "How'd you know they played that *that* day?"

"I was there."

"And you remember that, specifically, they played that combination of songs?"

"Yeah."

Disbelievingly, he said, "How? That was seven years ago."

"At a place called *Merriweather*, it was *pouring* rain. Lightening, mud slides, the entire lot was flooded by the time the show got out. And all anyone could talk about after was this kick-ass super fast 'Sugar Mag', then as they go into 'Sunshine Daydream' Bobby makes some crazy comment about how aborigines think the dream world is real and this is all a dream. Of course I remember. It was perfect."

He found that tape, read the jacket. *Damn, 'Sugar Mag' into 'Sunshine Daydream'. She was right.* Curious how well she actually knew each show, he read, "October 18, 1989, The Spectrum."

"What about it?"

"What'd they play?"

She grinned, "They did this trippy 'Bird Song' with flutes that night. And in the second set there was a 'China Rider'. And they did 'Terrapin'."

"How can you remember that? Seriously."

"That one's easy. It was my birthday. I got a fourth-row miracle."

Hoping this time he didn't randomly pick some other show that happened to be a special date, he read, "August 1, 1982." Figuring that was a long time ago, and not really fair to give her just a date, he added, "It says 'OK Zoo'."

She laughed, "I thought you were going to give me hard one. They opened with 'Jack Straw', then did 'They Love Each Other'. There was a 'Tennessee Jed' and 'Me and My Uncle'."

"You were there?"

"I was."

He asked, "Were you at every show you have a tape of?"

"Most of them."

"Do you have a tape of every show you were at?"

"No." She shook her head. "I've been to way more shows than that."

He thought it over, then said, "You know what they played because you listen to the tapes."

"I know because this is what Deadheads do. It's no different than a kid who memorizes baseball stats. Except instead of collecting cards, we collect ticket stubs."

"Bail, I have no idea what I'm looking at. Can you pick something?"

After a moment, she said, "Halloween at Radio City Music Hall. Part One." He found the tape and put it in the player and she said, "Fast forward for like ten seconds."

He counted to ten and pushed play. It was in the middle of a song he'd never heard.

"This isn't a Dead tune. I don't think I've ever heard it any other time."

"Should I fast forward more?"

"No, just wait."

When that song ended a man's voice said they were going to do a song about tragedy narrowly averted, then someone said, "'The Monkey and the Engineer.'" Teague turned to see Bailey grinning as she drove. And when the song started, she sang every word.

Chapter 38

The single line of cars inched their way through corn fields. Eventually they turned, one by one, onto a dirt road. Teague expected Bailey to be stressed, as she'd been when they were waiting to get into the lot in Pittsburgh. Instead, she looked totally happy.

She followed the parking guys' directions as they flagged her into a space on the grass, next to a baby blue Cadillac Eldorado. She locked the doors of the van, taking nothing but a little cross-body purse, and asked, "Ready?"

"You're not going to sell anything?"

She smiled as she headed down the row, an anklet of silver bells jingling slightly as she moved. "I'm thinkin' I just wanna hang today."

Everything had a much more laid-back feel than at Three Rivers, although Teague couldn't put his finger on exactly what was different. People sat on blankets laid out on the grass and sold food, or clothes, or handmade jewelry. Yuppies chilled in lawn chairs, drinking beer kept cold in styrofoam coolers. Sometimes there were groups of people with guitars and drums and instruments he couldn't name, playing their rendition of Dead songs, or their own songs. There were circles of people playing hacky sack.

Bailey paused to watch a guy in a knitted hat throw a red and yellow center stick in the air and deftly catch it with the black sticks he held, juggle the stick a few times, and throw it again.

She said, "Aria always wants to try that."

"It looks hard."

"It is."

Curiously, he asked, "Where do you get those?"

"Devil Sticks? Someone will have them for sale."

"Maybe we can get Aria a set."

"I always tell her no. I'm afraid she'll use them in my mom's house and break something."

Teague considered that. "What if I keep them, and only let her use them with me?"

"Sure, if you want."

A little further on she bought two stickers, skulls with a lightning bolts through them, from a guy in a beat-up green Chevy van. She held them up to Teague. "Your first Steal Your Face." She slid them into her purse as she said, "When we get home we'll put one on each of our cars, so we match."

He'd never considered putting a sticker of any kind on his car, but he knew as soon as they got back to Vermont he was going to. "What's a Steal Your Face? Besides the name of an album."

"It's the skull with the lightning bolt through it." She drifted, meandering in the same direction they'd been going. "Some people say it means the band's playing so hot they stole your face, or you're trippin hard, but really it was a logo they put on their equipment in the early days so they could find their shit when it got mixed in with other bands' shit."

He asked, "How'd you know that?"

"Because a while ago I knew a guy…" She trailed off.

He was glad she stopped. He really didn't want to hear about other guys.

She stopped in front of a teenage-ish girl sitting on a pink comforter behind a yellow Ford Granada, a display of jewelry in front of her.

There were crystals wrapped in wire and hung from satin cord, big glass beads strung on leather, and polished stones in nets made of tiny seed beads. Bailey looked them over carefully, chose a leather strip with a long blue bead held in the center by intricate knots on each side. She pulled the pin securing the piece to the board, held the anklet up so Teague could see the way the sunlight shone through the glass bead, and motioned for him to sit in the grass next to her.

She held it around his ankle for a moment. "That'll fit." She asked the girl, "Where are you from, Sister?"

She smiled softly. "Connecticut, originally."

"How long have you been on tour?"

"Since spring last year."

"Are you in tonight?"

"Not yet. Are you?"

"Hoping for a miracle." Bailey held the anklet out. "How much for this?"

"Five."

She gave her a ten. "Put the change towards your ticket."

The girl slipped the bill into her pocket. "Right on."

Bailey tied the piece of leather around Teague's ankle. The way her fingers brushed his skin sent spikes of heat deep into him. As they started down the aisle again, he asked, "We don't have tickets for tonight?"

"Yeah, we do."

"Why'd you tell her we didn't?"

She shrugged. "It's not cool to rub it in."

"Huh." He asked, "Why don't you take your change?"

"Because I've been very fortunate. I can afford to spread the wealth." She raised an eyebrow. "You're full of questions today."

"Sorry. I'll stop."

"It's okay. You can ask anything you want."

286

"Why do you call everyone 'brother' and 'sister'?"

"Because we're all brothers and sisters."

"At home you call the women 'sistah'."

She smiled. "Those are my friends."

He mulled that over for a minute. "So it's a more familiar term?"

"Yeah, I guess." A few rows later she pulled him towards a group of people sitting between a brown pickup truck with a bashed in rear bumper and a light green VW van with the top pushed up. As she squatted down everyone turned. Brief looks of panic turning instantly to smiles of recognition on half the faces.

One of the women said, "Hey, Bailey!" and everyone scooted around to make room for her and Teague to sit.

She hugged the woman, and the guy she sat next to. "Hey, Feather, Caleb. This is Teague."

"Hey, bro." Caleb nodded.

"What's shaking?" Feather asked.

"Not much."

Teague listened as Bailey and Feather talked about where they'd been, about the shows so far this tour and who else was around. Bailey asked about a bunch of people specifically, some Feather said were there and some she hadn't seen. He noticed she didn't ask about Jesse.

He'd wondered on and off if they'd run into Bailey's boyfriend, had no idea what would happen if they did. Most likely he'd just pretend he was there with Bailey as a friend.

For a while he'd thought that was true, that Bailey hung out with him because there was no one else around, or because Aria asked for him to stay. It had happened so slowly, it had been easy enough to ignore that his feelings towards her had changed.

It wasn't so easy now. She glanced his way often, smiled every time their eyes met. And every time his gut clenched pleasantly.

Caleb pulled out a bowl and Bailey packed it. After her hit, she reached around Teague to hand it to the girl next to him. As he watched the bowl make its way around the circle he thought it was fascinating that everyone was so nonchalant about getting high. *You'd think you'd be used to that by now.* But he wasn't.

Someone down the way yelled, "Six up!"

Everyone scattered. Teague followed Bailey as she walked between cars, away from the aisle they'd been in. As they joined the stream of people walking towards the main stretch, Teague asked her quietly, "What just happened?"

"The cops are coming." She looked up at him, her eyes bloodshot. "Never trust a guy in a baseball hat."

"Why?"

Her smile wasn't quite what it normally was. "They're undercover DEA. That's how they tell each other apart. Everyone knows that. Now you do, too."

He wondered if that was true. It seemed kind of stupid. If everyone knew, they weren't undercover. He looked around for guys in baseball hats anyway.

Bailey went on, "I mean, guys with dreads can be DEA. I seen this sister get dragged off by a guy I knew once. Man, it sucked hard core. But, ya know, everyone knows they gotta be careful no matter what. Never let anyone take your picture, either. The feds, they got a file on everyone here. They *know* who's doing what. I always worried about Jesse, until I saw him coming down the aisle. Maybe he's in jail…" She trailed off.

Teague realized she was really high. It was weird, almost like this wasn't Bailey.

He wondered how long it would take to wear off.

"Hey, look. Burritos." She wandered over to a couple sitting on the ground behind a brown van and bought a burrito wrapped in tin foil. She peeled the foil down, took a bite, then held it out to Teague. "Want some?"

"No, thank you." He felt a little sick to his stomach.

Still eating her burrito, Bailey weaved between people. Teague stayed with her, not just because they were there together, but because there were a lot more people here and he was worried about her. She smiled at everyone, stopped to talk to random people, and bought a brownie.

When they came to a line of trees, she sat down. "Man, it's so nice to just sit, don't you think?"

"Yeah." He didn't know what else to say.

* * *

Bailey began to make her way back towards the van. Aria wasn't there to need a nap, and she didn't have to get Delilah settled, but she needed her shoes. She kept an eye out, as always, for people she knew and for people she felt like she should avoid. It was so ingrained in her, she did it anytime she was on the lot.

"Hey, babe." Sage came from somewhere, joining her and Teague. "Teague."

She hugged him, "Hey now."

Teague nodded. "Hey, Sage."

Sage draped his arm over Bailey's shoulders and they continued the way she'd been going. He spoke softly, "Can you hook me up? I've got a bit, but there's these kids looking for a sheet."

She glanced at him, worried. Selling a single hit of acid to a stranger was nerve wracking. Selling a whole sheet was terrifying. "What kind of kids?"

"College kids."

"You're sure they're okay?"

"Yeah, and they're willing to go five a hit."

She didn't like that, either. Anyone willing to pay that much made the hairs on the back of her neck prickle. "You're *sure* they're not setting you up?"

"I'm tellin' you, they're cool. They're paying *ten bucks* for *one hit* where they're from. They stand to make a killing."

Keeping her purse between her and Sage, she unbuttoned it and pulled out a baggie. Very careful not to change her pace or do anything to draw attention, she slipped a sheet from the bag and passed it to Sage. She didn't look at the folded bills he gave her as she slid them and the baggie back into her purse.

He kissed her head, "Thanks."

"Be careful."

"Always." Then he was gone, joining the people headed the other direction.

Teague asked quietly, "What just happened?"

Not wanting to freak him out, she asked, "What?"

"With Sage."

She glanced over her shoulder. He was long gone, lost in the crowd. "Nothing. Oh, look at those." She stopped at a white van with tie-dyes hung from a rope strung between the open back doors.

Teague had struggled to pack, eventually ending up with some of Cole's clothes. She thought he deserved his own shit, and not just one 'Fuckin GoNuts' shirt. She chose a red and orange tie-dye with the Cheshire cat on it. The colors would go nicely with his dark hair. She pulled it off the line and handed it to him. "Do you like this?"

He was looking skeptically at her, but he said, "Yeah, it's killer."

It was funny as hell to hear Teague say 'killer'. She turned to the guy sitting on the bumper of the van. "How much?"

"Ten."

Bailey pulled out her wallet but Teague beat her to it. He smiled as he handed the guy money and said, "Thank you."

Back at the van, she hid what she didn't want to take into the show. Most of the time security made everyone throw out whatever contraband they tried to sneak in, and it sucked to lose it. But occasionally they'd arrest someone, if they had more than what could be considered for personal use, or if they fought back. Bailey wasn't about to fight anyone, and she wasn't taking more than she thought was reasonable.

The crowd was thicker in front of the amphitheater, so many with their finger up or holding a sign, looking for a miracle. She told Teague, "We've got two extras. Do you see anyone in particular you want to give them to?"

After a minute he said, "Her." He indicated a woman with wavy brown hair and freckles. She was smiling, sitting on the curb with her finger up. Bailey gave her a ticket.

"Thank you, kind sister." She stood and hugged her "Enjoy the show." She drifted away to get in line.

"One more." She looked at faces, read signs, waiting for something to catch her attention.

"Bail," Teague pointed to Rain, his finger held above his head.

It'd been a while since she'd seen him and her heart soared as he hugged her. She kissed his cheek. "Hey now."

"Hey, sistah." He squeezed her harder.

She squeezed him back. "Damn it's good to see you."

He let her go and turned to Teague. "Hey, brah. Nice to see you finally made a show." He hugged Teague, too. "Are you in tonight?"

"We are."

There was no question who their last ticket was going to. Bailey asked, "You wanna come?"

"Hell, yeah!" She handed him the ticket. He picked her up and spun her around.

Laughing, she kept one arm around Rain and slipped her other arm around Teague. "Let's go!"

Once they'd gotten through the gates, she started looking for a place to sit. This was her favorite kind of venue; reserved seating in front of the stage, surrounded by a bowl of open grass for general admission. She didn't care where she was in relation to the stage, didn't care if she found family or not. All she cared about was that she had space, and she was with Teague and Rain.

As they passed a crowd of people a sister with long black dreads stepped toward them. Rain let go of Bailey and slung his arm over the girl's shoulders. She had a voice that resonated, like Janis Joplin. "Hey, Babe. You got in." She kissed Rain soundly on the mouth.

He grinned. "'Course I did." He glanced around. "Do you know Bailey and Teague?"

She reached across Rain, keeping one arm around his back. "I'm Amy."

Bailey shook Amy's hand, already loving that Rain was with someone. "Let's find a spot." As they continued walking, she asked, "Who else's with you guys?"

Rain said, "No one else from home."

"We're on Sean's bus," Amy answered.

"Is it still insane?"

"Hell yeah." She rolled her eyes. "But the people I was with before I met up with Rain didn't have room for anyone else, and Sean did."

Rain asked, "Who's with you guys?"

"Just me and Teague."

"Are you taking riders?"

She grinned, hoping Rain and Amy would join them. "Are you looking for a ride?"

"Could be."

"If you are, let me know. We're camped on the farm."

"Right on. Us, too."

Eventually they chose a spot in the Phil Zone. Once Bailey was settled on the grass, Teague on one side of her and Rain on the other, she glanced around. Security here was lax, but it never hurt to check. Satisfied, she pulled a baggie from her purse.

"Rain." She nudged him, showed him.

He nodded. She pulled off two little squares of paper. Rain took one and gave the other to Amy.

Bailey turned to Teague. Quietly, she said, "Do you want to trip with me?"

He whispered, "Is that acid?"

"Yeah." She tore off two hits. She slipped one under her tongue and held the one out to Teague.

"Bailey, are you crazy?"

"No. Why?"

"We're in the middle of a concert."

"Yeah? And?"

* * *

Teague stared in disbelief at Bailey. She'd just dropped acid in front of him, like it was nothing. "People do crazy shit on acid. Jump out of windows and shit."

Her expression softened. "There's thousands of people here who aren't going to let anyone do anything that stupid."

He stared at her, tried to reconcile her calm demeanor with the things he'd heard about LSD. Then he thought about how the afternoon had been, with her stoned and him sitting there watching. How he'd wished he'd taken a hit when he'd had the chance. How, if he was honest, he'd been curious for a while.

He took the piece of paper from her. It had a tiny picture of Cookie

Monster on it. He remembered what'd happened earlier with Sage. He'd been sure they'd done something, although he hadn't been able to see what. "Where'd you get this?"

"Kayla. See the cookie monster? That's hers, because of the time she accidentally dosed everyone."

Momentarily distracted, he asked, "How do you accidentally dose everyone?"

"She laid sheets and thought she washed the bowl she'd used, but she forgot. Well, she didn't really forget. More like, she wasn't careful and ended up spending the rest of the day talking to flowers in the field next to the house." She grinned as she continued, "Anyway, then the next day she made cookies in the same bowl. Everyone who ate them tripped their balls off."

He pictured tiny Kayla, who he'd spent countless hours playing cards with. Incredulously, he said, "Kayla makes acid?"

"Yeah." Bailey raised her eyebrows. "She's a chemistry major, remember?"

"I thought that was so she could save the world."

Bailey laughed. "That's just what she tells her parents so they'll pay for her to go to school."

He examined the paper. "You brought this from home?"

"Yeah." She slipped her hand into his. "If you don't want to, it's cool."

He put the tab under his tongue. Bailey grinned and squeezed his hand. He concentrated on her, on the calm that she radiated, and wondered how long it took for LSD to kick in. It wasn't instant, since he didn't feel any different. The people next to him were talking about how they'd broken down on the way to Orchard Park and ended up missing the show, and how some kind brother had let them use his tools to replace their water pump. After a while, he asked Bailey, "How long does it take to work?"

"Probably twenty minutes or so."

"How long does it last?"

"Depends. Five or six hours. Maybe more."

He tried to do the math in his head. They'd come through the gate at six-ish, so it would hit him at like six-thirty. "How long does a show last?"

"Three hours?"

He started counting. *Six-thirty, seven-thirty, eight...* When he got to fourteen-thirty he stopped, unsure of what he'd been counting or why it mattered.

He looked at Bailey, her face lit by the late afternoon sun. He loved the way the green of her eyes mingled with the brown. It was fascinating, how they swirled so her eyes were nearly all green. The brown flowed back, making patterns like pouring milk into coffee. "Where does the green go, when the brown flows in?"

"What?"

"I mean, it has to go somewhere." He watched her eyes as they changed, as the colors danced. Then it was right there, and he understood. "I see. It's just that the green was behind the brown. But they're turning, so now the brown is behind the green."

"Teague, you're tripping."

He had to tell her, to make her understand how amazing this was. "Bailey, you're beautiful. Your eyes, you, yooouuuu, yyyyooouuuuuu aaarrrrreeee beeeaaauuutifuuuuullll."

* * *

Bailey felt the first hints of LSD kick in. The way the light around Teague seemed to glow, that the colors everywhere were brighter. She paid attention, waiting to see what would unfold.

The band came on stage, began tuning. Tuning became "Help On

The Way". She stood, pulling Teague up with her, and began to dance, keeping his hand in hers. "Help" morphed into "Slipknot!". By the time "Franklin's Tower" ended the colors on the flags around the stage were swirling together, twisting to the rhythm of the music. She knew they weren't supposed to do that, that it was in her mind, but if was so fascinating she didn't care.

Teague squeezed her hand, reminding her that their fingers were intertwined. She looked down at her hand, holding his. Electricity ran between them, red and orange and warm and tingly. It flowed from him and rippled over her. She traced her finger over his hand, watched the glow as it swirled, then settled back like it had never been disrupted.

Letting go of him, she danced, watched as her hands left trails of color swirling though the air.

* * *

Sound was everywhere, pulsing in his ears, pushing pleasantly against Teague's skin. He closed his eyes to let it flow over him, into him. It danced in the dark behind is eyelids, purple and blue and green, then streaks of yellow, twisting, breaking apart, coming back together.

He needed to pay attention. He sank to the ground, lay back on the cool grass, and concentrated on the patterns. The red drums exploded through the blue guitar, swirling into a perfect purple background for the yellow of the words. Songs changed, each with their own colors, and Teague watched them.

And then the laughter began.

* * *

Bailey sat in the grass with her eyes closed and rocked back and forth.

The drums beat in her ears against electronic pings accenting the wah-wah-wah of notes held and distorted. She let it wash over her, fill her, carry her away.

Then the laughter started, quietly, then louder and louder from the stage, from everywhere around her. She held her hands over her ears, desperate to make it stop. *It's just the acid. Just the acid. Not real.*

She reached for Teague's hand, felt nothing but grass next to her. Panic exploded into her mind. She opened her eyes, turned her head, forcefully ignoring the jeering faces surrounding her. The laughter filled her head, taunting her, *"He's gone. Because they all leave you. They all do. Hahahahaaaaa..."*

Her eyes landed on Teague. He was there, solid, and not laughing. She reached for him, desperate to make the laughter stop. He took her hand, held it firmly and his steady presence anchored her to sanity as the laughter came again. *You're tripping, that's all. He's here. Right here.*

* * *

The world around Bailey shimmered, but she'd peaked long enough ago that if she concentrated she could see reality, for a moment at least. The crowd swept them out into the night and they were separated from Rain and Amy. That was okay, it was Teague she had to take care of.

She took his hand. If she didn't hold tight he'd get lost and she couldn't let that happen. She'd dosed him, knowing full well he'd be gone all night. She was responsible for him.

She tried to focus, to hold onto one important thought: she had to find her van. She wandered through the crowd, keeping Teague with her. She was looking for something. Something important. "Egg rolls." She stopped under a battery powered flood light. "Can I have one?"

The guy with the spatula grinned, like the Cheshire cat. Bailey knew it was the acid, but she changed her mind anyway. "No Cheshire cat egg rolls." She drifted away.

Her van. She was looking for her van.

It was in the lot on the other side of the trees. She remembered, there was a path. She followed the stream of people headed away from the amphitheater.

* * *

Teague lay in the grass next to the van and stared at the sky. "Bail."

She didn't answer.

"Bail."

"Yeah?"

"Do you hear it?"

"What?"

"The stars." He watched as the points of light swayed in time to the beat. *Stars aren't supposed to move. Are they?* He shook his head and they stopped. The pounding of drums echoed in his ears. "You hear it?"

"Shhh." She took his hand. "Just be."

The stars danced in time to the beat of the drums.

Chapter 39

Teague woke up alone in the back of Bailey's van, no idea how he'd gotten there. The night before was one fucked up swirl of shit that didn't make sense.

He opened the door to find Bailey sitting outside the tent they'd pitched, because they hadn't intended to sleep in the van. He crawled out and sat next to her. "Hey."

She smiled at him. "Hey."

"What'cha doing?"

"Enjoying the morning." She looked out across the tents, cars and campers dotting the gently rolling hills. Fog hung over the makeshift campground, an oasis offered by a sympathetic farmer to the tens of thousands of Deadheads descending on a small Indiana town without the capacity to house them all. "I've always thought fog was magical."

"Maybe there's fairies hiding out there."

"Maybe."

"I think I might have seen fairies last night. Dancing a few feet in front of us."

A grin spread over her face. "Oh yeah?"

"Maybe." He cleared his throat. "The most fucked up thing, though, was they were *laughing*."

She turned, a perplexed look on her face. "Laughing?"

"Yeah."

"Huh."

In the quiet that followed he was very aware of her hand next to his. She'd taken his hand, kept it in hers, the night before. He moved, just a fraction of an inch, and touched her fingers. She turned her hand to meet his, sending heat surging up his arm, into his veins.

* * *

Bailey's insides fluttered, the heat of Teague's touch reaching into the deepest part of her. She squeezed his hand. For a moment she was disappointed when he let go. Then he touched her hair, gently slid his fingers through the long strands.

She reached for him, let her fingers tangle in his dark curls. The tiniest smile touched her lips and her stomach roiled with nerves as he leaned towards her. She felt like a teenager again, giddy over the idea of her first kiss. His lips touched hers, soft and warm.

Overwhelming desire to be closer to him surged through her. She tasted his lip, pulled it into her mouth. *More, more, god more.* She slipped her hand around the back of his neck, let her eyes close and melted into the kiss.

He moved back first. She opened her eyes to see him looking at her. *Teague, say something. Please. Was this okay? Or did I just fuck up big time.*

He brushed his fingertips along her cheek, down her neck, and across her shoulder. *Thank god.* She shivered, goosebumps breaking out on her arms.

Looking suddenly worried, he asked, "Are you cold?"

She whispered, "No." Scared of how strong her response to him was, she said, "Teague? I need coffee."

He slipped his hand to the back of her neck and pulled her to him. Barely a whisper, he said, "In a minute."

Her eyes slid closed as his lips met hers. Her pulse beat like the ocean in her ears, roaring through her veins, drowning her in need.

* * *

Teague traced his fingers over the softness of Bailey's shoulder. *She's perfect. Absolutely perfect.* He let his forehead rest against hers, brought his hands to rest on her shoulders. "You take my breath away." It would have been so easy to keep going. To climb into the tent, to make love to her right then. "Your eyes are fascinating, the way the brown and green meet." He moved away a little, so he could see them better.

Her serious expression slipped away, replaced by a grin. "I think you mentioned that last night."

The memory of the way the colors in her eyes had moved, changed, danced, struggled to the surface. He grasped at it. "I remember that." Heat rising to his face, he said, "It was…"

"Trippy."

"Yeah." He loved the way she said it, wanted her to say it again. "I never understood before exactly what the word meant."

"I bet you do now."

Her smile made him feel tight inside, like his chest was being squeezed.

She touched his face, just for a moment. "Coffee."

"Coffee." He smiled.

* * *

Bailey sat on the grass next to the van. While she waited for water to heat she used a screwdriver to punch holes in the bottom of a newly emptied Maxwell House can. She lined the can with a paper coffee filter, balanced it on top of an empty Snapple bottle, and added coffee grounds.

Teague settled next to her. "What'cha doing?"

"Making coffee."

He raised an eyebrow. "Looks like a complicated way to make coffee."

"You know how you always forget something when you go on vacation?"

"Yeah."

"I forgot the coffee pot and the cups." She carefully poured hot water over the grounds.

"We could go get coffee."

"We could. But every place in town is going to be overrun right now. This'll be a hundred times quicker." She handed him a bowl of oatmeal. "Hungry?"

He took the bowl. "I can barely cook with a full kitchen, and here you are making breakfast with a single propane burner."

"You are an amazing cook. Your lasagna is killer." She reset the makeshift coffee maker on a second bottle. "And no one makes better bagels."

Amy sat next to her. "That's fuckin' cool as shit."

"Hi, Amy. Coffee?"

"Hell yeah." She took the bottle Bailey handed her. "Rain said you own a coffee shop?"

Bailey made a third bottle then set the pan back on the propane burner and added more water. "I do."

"You should sell coffee on the lot. It's just about the only thing you can't get."

Teague said, "We could get a bus and do Bailey's on location." Grinning, he said, "We could call it Bailey's Breakfast Bus. Your coffee, my bagels, we'll make a killing."

Laughing at his enthusiasm, Bailey said, "Teague Gallagher, you really drank the Kool-Aid, didn't you."

Still smiling, he shrugged. "I guess I did."

Rain dropped down next to Teague. "Hey, Bail. You setting up shop?"

"Apparently Teague and I are buying a bus."

"Cool. Looking for riders?"

"Didn't we have this conversation last night?"

Rain nodded, "Yeah, we did. That's why I'm sitting here. Were you serious?"

Bailey handed him a bottle of coffee. "Rain, do you even have to ask?"

He glanced at Teague. "Don't wanna step on any toes."

Teague paused, a spoonful of oatmeal halfway to his mouth. "No toes here."

"Right on." Rain sipped his coffee. "Damn, Bail. You really should sell this."

* * *

Teague scanned the labels on the tapes in Bailey's collection. They still didn't mean anything to him, although he knew they meant something to her. He chose one at random, slid it into the tape deck and hit play.

There was no preamble to the electric guitars; the tape was half way through. From the seat behind him, Rain said, "'CC Rider'."

Teague didn't know the song, so he didn't join in with Bailey, Rain and Amy as they sang along. When the next song started, though, Teague instantly recognized the guitar intro to 'Bird Song'.

Bailey sang along, "Do do do do do do."

Amy said, "Did you know this is about Janis Joplin?"

303

Bailey swayed to the music. "Yeah. It's one of my absolute favorites."

Rain leaned forward. "Did you know 'He's Gone' is about Mickey's dad? He stole a whole shit load of money from the band when he was their manager and disappeared."

"Really?" Bailey glanced back at him. "I always thought it was about Pigpen."

"Bail, Pigpen died in 1973. They've been playing 'He's Gone' since 1972."

She snorted. "What the hell do you want from me? In 1972 I was seven years old."

Teague watched out the window, half-listened to the conversation in the van. There hadn't been any question, for him, about Rain and Amy joining them. Now, unable to join in their conversation, he almost wished it was still just him and Bailey.

As soon as Bailey was parked Rain and Amy headed out into the lot. Teague waited for Bailey to lock up.

She came around the back of the van, slipped her hand into his. "Ready?"

That something so small could feel so huge was unnerving. He pulled her to him, wrapped his arms around her and held her close. She looked into his eyes, her expression serene as she slid her arms around his waist. He kissed her, smiling a little as he did. She smiled back and any doubts he'd had disappeared. He said, "Now I'm ready."

They made their way towards the main entrance of the venue, where people would be hanging out.

"Are you hungry?" She pulled him towards a guy selling veggie stir-fry.

"Sure." He paid for two plates and they sat on a curb. As they ate he watched the people around them, hanging out in groups or walking by. "Bailey?"

"Hmm?"

"Those kids over there." He nodded in the direction he was looking. "Are they family?"

"Looks like it."

The guys' jeans hung low on their thin hips. One had on a shirt with a skull wearing a crown of roses, the other had a tie-dye hanging from the back of his waistband. There were two girls, one in a flowered dress and the other in cut offs and a Steal Your Face t-shirt. All four were barefoot, scruffy, their hair long. One of the girls had dreads. They were smiling in the easy way he'd come to associate with Bailey. And not one of them looked old enough to drive. He asked, "How old do you think they are?"

"I don't know. Fifteen, sixteen, maybe?"

"They look like they've been on tour forever."

"They probably have been."

"Do you know them?"

Raising an incredulous eyebrow, she said, "Even when I was here every day I didn't know everyone."

"How many people are there on tour?"

She shrugged. "No idea. There's more in the summer, when colleges are out."

"So you think those are college kids, here for the summer?"

"No." She eyed them critically. "They're doing tour, full time."

"You can tell the difference just by looking at them?"

"Yeah." She smiled serenely. "Their clothes, the way they stand, that they're talking to each other but they're all keeping an eye out, too."

Curious, he asked, "How old were you when you started touring?"

"Seventeen."

Sure he'd misunderstood something, somewhere, he asked, "You drove cross country when you were seventeen?"

"Um hm. A few times."

Shocked, he asked, "Your mom let you do that?"

"She didn't have a choice." She set her plate aside and leaned her arms on her knees.

Mulling that over, he asked, "What about school?"

"What about it?"

"How'd you go to school, if you were following the Dead?"

"I didn't. I dropped out."

Shocked, he stared at her. She didn't strike him as a high school dropout. "That's... So, do you have your GED or something?"

"Nope. Don't need it for what I do."

It had never crossed Teague's mind to go against expectations so blatantly. *Whose expectations are those? Yours? Society? Your parents?*

Bailey stood up. "Ready?"

Distracted, he took her hand and let her lead him thought the lot. *All those years you never understood why Cole wouldn't conform. He smiled like Bailey. He didn't give a shit about expectations. But you. Did everything 'right' and your life fucking sucked. Bailey's made you smile more in the last six months than you've smiled in the last thirty-two years.*

"Bailey?" He jerked her to a stop, looked into her questioning eyes. "Do you regret it?"

Her expression became puzzled. "What?"

"Going on tour instead of finishing school?"

Pain crossed her face, like the time he'd accidentally brought up her sister before he'd understood about Peyton. "Sometimes things aren't meant to be." She shrugged. "So you take what you have while you have it."

She started to walk away, obviously upset. *Fix this, you idiot.* He pulled her back, held her against him with one arm around her back. He touched her cheek, ran his thumb over the softness of her skin. "Bail, I'm sorry."

The smile she gave him was forced. "Nothing to be sorry for."

He searched her face for some hint of what this was about. *No goddam clue.* "I didn't mean to upset you. I was thinking about how much of my life I've wasted doing things I hated because I was supposed to, and how you always seem so content."

She sighed. "Teague, things aren't always what they seem. I loved tour, and I don't regret going. But that doesn't mean I don't sometimes wish I'd taken a different road."

He seized the opportunity, hoping he was saying the right thing. "I'm so glad you didn't." Leaning forward, he kissed her softly before putting his forehead against hers. "Because if you had, I wouldn't have met you." He'd known before that he wanted her, but the feeling that filled him now was so strong, he thought he might burst. "And Bailey, I am so glad I met you."

In the middle of the lot, people walking by all around them, he wrapped his arms around her and kissed her.

Her arms slid around his waist, tightened to keep him close. She whispered against his lips, "Me, too."

* * *

Teague let Bailey decide where to go. The only thing that mattered to him was that he was with her.

"Bailey! Hey, Bailey!" The shout came from behind.

Teague turned with Bailey to see Cole coming towards them, holding hands with a girl with long strawberry-blonde hair.

Bailey let go of Teague's hand and hugged Cole.

Not sure how his brother felt about the unexpected meeting, Teague said, "Hey, Cole."

Cole looked from Bailey to Teague before he said, "Shasta, this is Bailey. And *Teague.*"

Teague caught the dubious tone when Cole said his name. Shasta, though, either didn't hear it or didn't care because she hugged Teague. "Hey now."

He hugged her back.

She hugged Bailey, too. "Bailey, it's so cool to finally meet you. Everyone talks about you all the time."

Bailey smiled. Teague noticed her cheeks tinted slightly pink. She pointed at the backpacks both Cole and Shasta were carrying. "I thought you were with Sage."

Cole said, "Sage hooked up with this chick. And she's," he gave a lopsided smile, "a little overwhelming. And you know how it is to find someone to take two riders, especially mid tour."

Bailey nodded. "Sure do." She glanced at Teague.

He smiled, unsure of the proper response in this situation.

Cole said, "We ended up hitchhiking from New York. We missed yesterday because we got stuck in the middle of nowhere, and finally got a ride in this morning with some lady on her way to see her grandchildren in Colorado."

Bailey asked, "Are you going to Chicago?"

"Planning to."

"Where are you going after that?"

Cole took Shasta's hand. "We were thinkin' we'd go back to Vermont for a while."

Teague didn't miss the quick glance Cole threw his way. Or the one Bailey gave him. He nodded to her, hoping she'd understand that he wanted her to invite Cole to join them.

She said, "We've got room, if you guys want to ride with us."

Cole looked at Shasta, who looked relieved. He nodded, although he didn't look as happy as she did. "Yeah, right on."

"Come on, we're parked right over there." As Bailey led them back to the van she said, "We hooked up with Rain and Amy, too."

"Cool." Cole grinned. "The more the merrier."

* * *

Bailey closed her eyes and danced. Her hair swung around her, tickling her arms. Sweat trickled down her back. The story of how Jack Straw hunted his buddy down flew from her lips. Then the final line, sharing the women and the wine, died out and in the space after Bailey let herself be still while she waited to hear what would be next.

"They Love Each Other" was followed by "Desolation Row", and she danced.

Then came "Row Jimmy", slow and sweet, and she swayed to the music.

Teague's touch, his hands on her hips, the feel of him behind her, brought her momentarily back. Then, as he swayed with her, slid his arms around her, she leaned back into him. *Rock the baby,* she sang in her head, *sweet you roll.* She held his arms tight to her. *This is so sweet.*

The song ended, but still Teague held her.

She mumbled, "I've never danced with anyone before."

He kissed her neck. "Never?"

"Unless you count Aria."

"Not the same thing."

"No. It's not." *Not even close.*

"Picasso Moon" started and she grinned as she took his hands and began to move them through the air in time to the music.

"Ninja hands."

She let go and turned towards him. "What?"

"Ninja hands." He moved his hands the way she'd done.

She grinned at the appropriateness of the term, and at the smile on Teague's face as he danced like a hippie.

* * *

The sound of people partying, laughter and loud voices, drifted through the walls of the tent. Too beat to party, Bailey lay on top of the sleeping bags she'd zipped together so they'd be big enough for both her and Teague. It was hot, even in the middle of the night, and she wished they were sleeping out in the open.

She curled up against Teague, ignoring that they were both sweaty. He mumbled, "I love the last song they did tonight, before the encore. The one about the Cadillac."

She trailed her fingers along his side, let herself enjoy the way his skin felt. "'Not Fade Away'."

"Yeah. I love the way the audience sings. They just go on and on, and the band's not even on the stage anymore, but the audience keeps going."

"No doubt, it's wicked cool."

"Bailey, you're beautiful when you dance."

She knew he'd watched her but it made her feel self-conscious for him to say it.

He shifted, wrapped his arms more tightly around her. "You're beautiful all the time."

Being told she was beautiful wasn't something she was used to and she had no idea what to say. She closed her eyes and let herself drift to sleep in his arms.

Chapter 40

Fitting six people and all their stuff in Bailey's van wasn't easy. Teague worked at piling four big frame backpacks in the back while Rain and Bailey mapped out their route and Cole, Shasta, and Amy went to see if anyone knew about the next venue.

Satisfied that everything was stowed in the best possible way, Teague shut the door and joined Bailey just as everyone else came back.

"No one knows anything. They've never heard of the World Music Theater or Tinley Park." Cole grabbed a bottle of water from the back seat and drank before passing the bottle to Shasta.

Bailey folded the atlas so the page they needed was open. "We've got tonight off. I'm thinkin' we go up there and see what there is."

Teague said, "I need coffee."

Bailey grinned. "Sorry, brah, you're gonna have to live with whatever shit they serve at the nearest gas station."

He smiled as he wrapped his arms around her and kissed her forehead. "I'm telling you, next tour we're doing Bailey's Breakfast Bus."

Cole looked from Teague to Bailey. Curtly, he said, "Ready?" He got in the van and moved all the way to the back of the bed.

Shasta began to follow Cole, but paused and told Bailey, "Thanks, ya know, for inviting us to ride with you."

"I'm happy to have you." She let go of Teague and gave Shasta a quick hug before she went around to the driver's side.

Teague climbed into the passenger seat and looked back at Cole, forcefully rearranging the pillows on Bailey's bed. As he turned around and settled into the seat, he remembered Cole commenting on Bailey being with Teague the day Cole'd gotten out of jail. *I didn't just show up with Bailey, who was his friend. I hijacked his house, and now I'm going to shows. Can't really blame him for being mad.*

Cole'd made another comment that day that stuck in Teague's mind. *Something about Bailey and Jesse, and what she did when he wasn't around.* He tried to look at her without being obvious. Her face was serious, all her concentration on driving. *Is this, me, just a diversion for her? It's been, what, seven months since we met? And Jesse was home for like a week?*

He glanced back, to where Rain had his head in Amy's lap. They smiled as they talked, the kind of smile people who totally get each other share. Teague was sure Bailey and Rain had had a thing, and it had ended when Jesse came back. *She does what she wants, and when he shows up it's like nothing happened. What the fuck kind of shit is that? And you knew this before, and you, what— ignored it?*

As soon as Bailey pulled into line at the gas station Cole got up. "I'm going to the bathroom." Everyone else followed him as he climbed out.

Alone with Bailey, Teague thought about asking her what was going on. *Bail, hey, this thing between me and you. What's gonna happen when Jesse shows up? Yeah, that's exactly what you want to ask her. But what the fuck are you going to do? For all you know, he could be at the next show, and then what? You gonna pretend you and his girlfriend are just friends?*

When she was one car away from a pump he said, "I'll pay, if you want to pump."

She smiled, "Right on."

Inside the gas station Teague went straight for the coffee machines, nodding to all the other Deadheads hanging around. He poured a coffee for himself and one for Bailey. He sipped his drink before he even made it to the counter.

"You know you gotta pay for that, right?" The woman behind the counter glared at him.

Not in the mood to be nice, he said, "Yeah. Twenty on pump two." He dropped cash on the counter. He immediately felt guilty for being short. "The coffee's really good. Thank you."

The woman's scowl lessened.

He smiled, "Have a great day."

She smiled just a little. "You, too."

Look at that. You weren't an asshole and you made that woman smile. He made his way back to the van. *Bailey has always made you smile, too. Even when you were an asshole.*

"Hey, Teague."

He stopped at the sound of his name and turned to see Feather. "Hey now. How's things?"

"Excellent." She gave him a hug and kissed his cheek.

He kissed her cheek in return, hugged her as much as was possible with a cup in each hand. "You on your way to Tinley Park?"

"For sure."

He noticed Bailey pulling away from the pump. "I'll catch you up later."

"Safe travels." She smiled serenely as she walked away.

He made it half way to the van before he was stopped again, by a guy he recognized from home but didn't know by name. "Brah, did'ya get in last night?"

Teague nodded. Remembering what the people around him had talked about the night before, he said, "Yeah, fucking killer 'China

Doll', right?"

"No doubt."

By the time he made it to where Bailey had parked, she was gone and the van was empty. Teague settled into the passenger seat, surveyed the scene and sipped his coffee. *Seriously never knew there were so many Deadheads. This is insane.* He smiled a little. *And I'm one of them.*

Bailey came back smiling triumphantly. "I found someone selling muffins! They didn't have cranberry, so I got you blueberry."

Despite his misgivings about their relationship, he couldn't help noticing the way the sun caught the highlights in her hair, that her skin was a warm brown and the freckles across her nose had popped after the last few days spent outside. *She's beautiful. And she's not mine.*

"Hey, are you okay?" She set the muffins on the dashboard and took both his hands.

There was no good way to answer that. "Bail…" *What are you going to say? You want her.*

She let go of him, put her hands on his face and kissed him. "Teague?" she sounded worried.

He pulled her close, to stand between his legs, and kissed her. Her lips parted and he tasted her, gently at first but when she reciprocated he wrapped his arms tightly around her and kissed her deeply.

She held him close. *Brah, what the fuck are you doing? This girl, she's on loan to you.* He couldn't bring himself to care. He was surrounded by her presence, by coffee and sandalwood and the scent that was *Bailey*. And he let himself believe, because he wanted to, and because it was so easy to do when she was in his arms, that he could have her.

* * *

314

In the parking lot of the only grocery store in Tinley Park, Bailey stowed the groceries she'd bought in the back of the van. Finished, she stood in front of Teague. "What's going on?"

His brow creased slightly. "Nothing. Why?"

She tipped her head, examined him for a moment. "You've been quiet all day, and you have that 'Teague's thinking about something' look."

He smiled a little. "I have a look?"

"Yeah, you do." She ran her hand over his arm. "I just want to make sure whatever you're thinking about's good."

He looked over her shoulder for a moment, then refocused on her. "I was just thinking how unreal it is that I'm here."

She turned to lean her back against him, looking out at the mass of hippies milling around the parking lot. "I think we all feel like that at first."

Her heart pounded in her chest as he slipped his arms around her. His breath was hot on her neck, his beard tickling her shoulder as he leaned forward and spoke softly, "I'm really glad I'm here with you."

She was glad to be there with him, too. But it scared her, to realize this had gone way beyond being friends. *Didn't you want that, though? That's why you asked him to come in the first place. But you didn't realize, did you, that you were going to feel like this about him.*

"Bailey?"

"Hmm?"

"Do you think people can change?"

She turned in his arms, looked into his deep brown eyes. "Yeah, I do."

He took her face in his hands and kissed her gently, their eyes remaining locked on each other.

"I'd tell you two to get a room, but there aren't any." Cole opened the side door and sat on the floor of the van.

Keeping his eyes on Bailey, Teague said, "Hi, Cole."

Cole continued, "I ran into Harvard and he said the hotels are all booked."

Rain leaned against the side of the van. "There's only two campgrounds and they're both full."

Bailey asked, "Where's everyone staying?"

"Apollo and Samantha are leaving their bus right where it is." Cole pointed to a school bus, now painted with a sun and stars on a background of blue, parked at the other side of the parking lot. "Everyone else I talked to says they don't know. Probably in their cars, wherever they can find a place to park."

Shasta said, "Maybe we can score floor space."

Bailey shook her head doubtfully. "For six of us?"

Rain said, "We can just stay here."

Bailey thought that over. "I don't think we can all sleep in the van. There's no way we're fitting all six of us in the bed. The seats don't go back, like they did in the Vega, and there's not enough space on the floor."

"Me and Amy can sleep here." Rain pointed to the strip of grass in front of the van.

"Brah, it's two feet from a main street. No fucking way." Amy looked at him like he was insane.

Bailey thought about what they'd passed recently. As far as she could remember, there was basically nothing. Fields, houses, a strip mall. Some of the flattest landscape she'd ever seen. "We can go back to the last rest area we passed. At least there'll be a bathroom and we can pitch a tent."

Disbelievingly, Teague said, "You're going to pitch a tent in a rest area?"

She looked at each of her friends. "Anyone have a better idea?"

* * *

Teague could not wrap his mind around what was happening. It was worse than camping illegally in a rest area.

On the way back to the highway they'd seen a long line of cars at the edge of a field, and people laying out sleeping bags in the grass. Bailey had pulled over and talked to some of the people, none of whom had actual permission to be there. After a short discussion, much too short in Teague's opinion, it was decided that being within sight of the World Music Theater was a much better idea than driving who knew how far to a rest area.

Quietly, Teague said, "Bail, we're going to just sleep on the ground?"

"Yeah." She started to pull a sleeping bag off the bed.

"What if it rains?"

"If you're worried about it, me and you will sleep in the van."

"This is trespassing."

She left the sleeping bag where it was and looked at the cars behind them as more and more joined the line. "If someone asks us to leave, we'll leave. No big."

"There's gotta be a hotel somewhere."

She took his hands and held them. "This is fine. I swear."

He knew he was defeated. Even if he could talk Bailey into some other option, he'd never be able to convince the others. "Okay."

Rain called from a few feet away, where everyone else sat in a circle. "Bail?" He held up a bowl.

"Be right there." She turned back to Teague and searched his face.

He wondered what she was thinking. *Probably that I'm being a yuppie. Or that she wants to go smoke that bowl.* "Go." He indicated their friends.

She still hesitated. Then she squeezed his hands, smiled slightly, and turned away. He watched her walk through the grass and sit between Amy and Cole.

The easy way they sat together, the smiles and hugs they shared, sent a jolt of jealousy through him. He'd never had that kind of comfortable friendship with anyone. And he wanted it.

Before he could change his mind, he shut the van door and walked quickly to the group. Squatting next to Bailey, he said, "Hey. Can I join you?"

She looked at him curiously as she scooted closer to Cole. Amy nudged Rain, making room for Teague to join their circle.

Rain took the first hit and handed the glass pipe to Amy, who passed it to Teague. His hands shook slightly as he brought it to his lips, as he watched smoke curl up through the stem. He pulled it into his lungs, held it there as he passed to Bailey.

This was nothing like acid, which had crept up on him, slowly skewing his perceptions. This was quick. By the time he'd coughed out the hit he was already having trouble concentrating. When the pipe came around a second time he took another hit without hesitation.

He lay back in the grass. Next to him, Amy and Rain were talking about something, their voices low and slow. Cole and Shasta left, not that it mattered. In the field insects buzzed loudly. A light breeze whispered across his skin and through the flowers growing at the side of the road. He closed his eyes and let his mind float.

The soft rustle of Bailey lying in the grass next to him pulled him back. Her warm hand as she twined her fingers with his seemed like it had always been meant to be there.

He opened his eyes and turned his head so he could see her. "Bail."

She was smiling, her eyes half closed. "Yeah?"

Sunlight touched her face, and he touched where the sun shone. Her skin was so soft. Slowly, he trailed his fingers down her cheek, her neck, her throat. He touched her breast through her shirt. A thought tugged at his brain, *not supposed to do that.* He didn't know why, though, so he continued. The fabric of her shirt was so delicate, he could feel her nipple harden through it.

Her nipple wasn't the only thing to get hard.

A bird flew overhead, catching his attention. He rolled to his back and watched the row of blackbirds on the power lines above, chirping noisily as they shuffled positions. If he tipped his head back a little he could see Bailey's van, glowing orange in the late afternoon light. They'd gotten groceries before they'd come out here.

He stood, made his way to the van. He dug though the boxes Bailey had carefully packed in a bin under the bed until he found a bag of gorp. "Good old raisins and peanuts." He laughed at himself as he sat in the doorway and started picking out the raisins.

* * *

Bailey lay next to Teague on the bed in the back of her van, listening to the steady rhythm of him breathing. She remembered how it'd felt when he'd touched her breast. The heat from his fingers, the pleasant throbbing that had rippled through her.

She rolled to her side so she could see him. He was staring at the roof. She touched his face, ran her fingers over his beard.

He shifted, moved to his side. "Hi."

"You were." She couldn't help smiling.

He grinned in return. "Yeah, I was." He moved, pushing her gently to her back and propping himself on an elbow next to her. He touched her cheek, ran his fingers down her neck, as he'd done earlier.

She gasped as he slid his hand over her breast, shuddered as he cupped it. Her eyes closed as she tipped her head back. His breath was hot on her skin as he kissed her neck, his beard ticked as he kissed across her collarbone. She ran a hand over his shoulders, felt the way the muscles rippled as he moved.

He whispered against her throat, "Bailey, you're so beautiful. My beautiful Butterfly Bailey."

Her heart hammered in her chest. *Do I have condoms? I don't think so. Does he? Do we need one? My last period was—* She began counting days.

The side door opened. Teague jerked away, turned to the door.

Cole raised an eyebrow. "Sorry." He shut the door.

Teague moved, sat up with his back against the side of the van. He sighed. "Guess I should have checked the doors."

"One of the hazards of having riders."

His head dropped back, against the wall.

She sat up next to him and took his hand. "Teague?"

"Yeah?"

This had been bothering her for a while, but it hadn't been something she was comfortable bringing up. She didn't think she could continue to ignore it, though. "What's going on with you and Cole?"

"I don't know." He leaned forward, elbows on his knees and his head in his hands. "It's not like we were close before, but now..." He shrugged. "I'm pretty sure he'd prefer if I wasn't here."

The pain in his voice was so sharp, she pulled him to her and wrapped her arms around him. Slowly, he relaxed against her as the tension left him. Finally, she moved back and looked him in the eye. She wanted to tell him that as long as they were alive, there was hope. That was too close to home, though, and she couldn't bring herself to say it out loud.

Instead, she said, "I'm sorry, Teague." Guilt surged as she realized the predicament they were currently in was her fault. "I should have talked to you before I invited them to join us."

"I'm glad you asked them." He sighed. "I've let Cole down enough times. I want to be there for him as much as I can be."

"I don't want either of you to be uncomfortable, though."

"It's okay. We live in the same house and manage to basically avoid each other, I'm sure we can make it a few days on tour together."

* * *

Cole and Shasta sat on their sleeping bags a few feet from the van. Bailey made her way over to them and sat in the grass next to Cole.

"Hey."

He nodded.

Softly, she asked, "Cole, what's going on with you and Teague?"

Shasta said, "I'm going to see if I can bum a cigarette."

"No, you can stay." Cole reached for her as she stood.

She smiled. "I'll be back."

Bailey sat cross-legged, facing Cole. When he didn't say anything, she asked, "So, what's the deal?"

He squinted at her. "I should be asking you that."

She glanced at Teague, practicing Devil Sticks with a couple guys from a few cars away. Not willing to analyze her own feelings, or be distracted from the issue at hand, she said firmly, "Cole."

"What?"

"Come on."

Anger tinting his words, he said, "He left me there for six months. *Six months.* Then he shows up with you? Like all of a sudden he's family? What the fuck, Bail. He's the most uptight asshole. This, whatever the hell he's doing, is some sort of, I don't know, mid-life crisis or something."

She sighed. "I get that. When I first met him, he totally was a dick."

"Yeah, he was. He was supposed to bail me out, not leave me there to rot."

"You know he couldn't."

"Bullshit. He's got plenty of money."

"You know you'd have run, and it isn't fair to expect Teague to be responsible for that."

He stared hard at her. "Teague thinks hippies are all drug dealing losers and they belong in jail."

"People change."

"Maybe, but he's been a dick his whole life."

She didn't doubt that was true, but she also knew all Teague had needed was the chance to be himself. "When you called him, he dropped everything to go to Vermont. He lost his job, his girlfriend, pretty much his whole life, over it. Because you needed him."

"He didn't fucking *do* anything."

"I know, because I sat there with him every day, saw how frustrated he was that he couldn't do more, saw how much it hurt him that he couldn't see you."

Bitterly he said, "I'm sure. Because he was always so happy to see me before."

"Cole, give him a chance."

"Fuck that."

She picked a piece of grass, watched the glossy green blade as she tied it in a knot while she thought about how to help Cole and Teague bridge the gap between them. Finally, she said, "My sister and I didn't speak for over two years before she died. Neither of us could see past our own pain, to what the other was going through." She looked up, fighting the sadness she always felt when she thought of Peyton. "You and Teague have something we didn't."

Quietly, he asked, "What?"

"Time to make it better." She stood, smiled as much as she could manage before she went to join Teague.

322

Chapter 41

"Bailey."

She tried to ignore Teague.

"Bail. Come on." He shook her insistently. "Bailey. Get up."

The panicked tone in his voice penetrated her sleepy brain. "What?"

"They're towing cars. Bail, come on. We gotta go *now*."

Yellow lights flashed from the far end of the field, illuminating the chaotic scene of everyone who had parked on the side of the street for the night trying to leave before anyone could stop them. Dragging her sleeping bag, Bailey ran for the van. Everyone else was already inside, jostling for seats. Bailey added her sleeping bag to the pile on the floor, shut the door behind her and got in the driver's seat. Fully awake, she asked, "Ready?"

"Yeah, go." Teague sat in the passenger's seat and buckled his seatbelt.

As she pulled away from the curb, left the flashing lights behind, she asked, "Any ideas what to do now?"

Rain said, "I'm not really down with risking that again. Why don't we see if we can find a hotel, even if we have to drive closer to Chicago."

"Bail, were there pay phones somewhere?" Teague asked.

"Yeah, back at the grocery store I think." She pulled a U-turn and headed back the way they'd come.

* * *

Relief washed over Teague as he hung up. He tucked his credit card into his wallet and shoved his wallet in his back pocket before he turned to Bailey and said, "We're good. I got a suite. Two queen beds and a pull-out couch."

"I thought all the rooms were booked."

He smiled a little. "One of the benefits of being a lawyer with an American Express Gold Card."

She took his hand and started back to the van. "What do I owe you?"

"Don't worry about it. I've got it."

"I can't let you pay for my room."

He stopped her, pulled her to face him. "Yes, you can. And you're going to." He ran his hand down her hair. "Bailey, I want to."

She searched his face for a long moment then nodded. "Okay. But we have to figure out what everyone else's share is."

"What do you mean?"

"Usually it's ten each for a bed and five for floor space, but if the room was really expensive we can charge them more."

"I'm not charging anyone."

"They expect it." She smiled a little. "That's one reason they didn't mind sleeping outside."

Adamant, he said, "No. This is my contribution to," he made a circular motion to indicate everything around them, "this."

Softly, she said, "I'm sure everyone will appreciate it."

Chapter 42

Teague watched as Bailey pulled her freshly washed hair over her shoulder and began working a brush through the ends. When she caught him looking at her, their eyes meeting in her reflection in the mirror, she smiled.

He went to her, took the brush from her hand. She kept her eyes on his reflection as he began to work through the snarls. He couldn't return her gaze, though. He had to concentrate on not pulling too hard. Slowly, the knots let loose and eventually he could run the brush from the top of her head all the way to the ends in one smooth motion along each section of hair.

He handed her the brush. She dropped it on the bag next to her feet, then took his hand, pulled his arm around her and whispered, "Thank you."

Teague wrapped his other arm around her and held her close. She closed her eyes and leaned back into him, bringing her hands up to hold his arms. Loving having her so close, he kissed the top of her head.

Bailey turned in his arms, brought her hands to his face and studied him for a moment, her lips curved just slightly in a tiny smile. Then she stood on her toes and kissed him.

Her lips were soft against his. So was the skin of her back as his hands found their way to the top of her shorts. She wrapped her arms around him tightly, bringing him hard against her as she pulled his lip into her mouth. Heat exploded, surged through his veins as he tasted her in return.

The bathroom door opened and he pulled back immediately.

Cole looked at them, shaking his head as he went past.

Embarrassment replaced all the passion Teague had felt just a second before. He'd gotten so caught up in the moment, in Bailey, he'd ignored that with four other people sharing the room there was no privacy.

Bailey kissed him lightly. Her voice just loud enough for him to hear, she said, "We could sleep in the van, if you want to be alone."

He looked in the mirror, at his brother and their friends in the room behind him. He was determined to make up his previous shortcomings to Cole. And he wanted, very much, to be part of this life. To be able to share stories when he ran into people he knew, to be accepted as one of them. "No, it's fine." Then, to prove it, he kissed her again.

She smiled as their lips met, and as she let go and turned away. "We should probably get going. It's almost eleven."

Cole shoved clothes into his backpack. "Hey, Bailey, remember those dudes in Santa Cruz? We always had to sneak out of every hotel we stayed in with them, because they tie-dyed all the sheets. What the fuck were their names?"

"Derek and Ethan." She folded her arms and looked at Cole.

"They make the fuckin' best shirts."

Rain was on his hands and knees, looking for a shoe. "Why do you think they always put Lima beans in the soup at St. Bubbles?"

Amy asked, "Who named the soup kitchen St. Bubbles?"

"I think it's really St. Francis," Rain said. "No idea where St. Bubbles came from."

Cole zipped his backpack and said, "Remember, Bailey, we used to go early so we could take a shower?" Then he laughed. "Oh, wait. You weren't allowed to shower there."

"Why?" Amy looked curiously at Bailey.

"Cuz her and Jesse—"

"Cole." She gave him a stern look.

"What?"

She glanced at Teague.

Cole followed her gaze. "Oh, yeah, sorry."

Teague didn't care that Cole was harassing him, but he did care that he was using Bailey to do it. There was nothing he could do right then without making a scene, other than distracting everyone. He asked, "Is everyone okay with staying here tonight?"

Rain had found his shoe and he lay back on the bed with his hands behind his head. "I'm thinking after last night we should if we can."

Amy straddled him, leaned down to kiss him before sitting back up. "I am definitely all for a bed and a shower."

"I'll go take care of it." Teague stuck his shoes on, grabbed a clean shirt from his bag, and pulled it over his head.

Cole looked critically at Teague. "Teague, where'd you get that shirt?"

Bailey grabbed Teague's hand. "Come on, it's almost eleven." She pulled him into the hallway. As soon as the door was closed, she said, "You should probably see if Rain will lend you a shirt or two. Until you have enough of your own."

* * *

Traffic had been at a complete standstill for so long that Bailey's leg shook on the brake pedal. They could see the exit, it was about seven cars in front of them. They just couldn't get to it. Finally, she shut the van off and looked at Teague. "Well, this sucks."

Cole leaned between the front seats. "What do you think's going on?"

"No idea." Bailey looked down the line of cars, none of which were moving.

"Let me out, I'll go see." Rain opened the door and stepped onto the highway.

"I'm coming, too." Cole jumped out after Rain, followed by Amy and Shasta.

Bailey told them, "Don't go too far, just in case we start moving."

"No worries, we'll find you." Rain closed the side door, leaving Bailey and Teague alone.

After a minute, Teague asked, "Bailey?"

"Hmm?"

"You've known Cole a long time."

She glanced at Teague. "Yeah."

"How'd you meet him?"

Shrugging, she said, "I don't know. When you've been around a while you start to just know everyone else who's around, too. Especially back when I started touring. There were a lot less people."

He was looking down, like he didn't want to meet her gaze. "Did you and Cole ever…" He turned to her, leaving the rest of the question unspoken.

"No. Cole and I are just friends."

"Like you and Rain?"

"No. Not like me and Rain." She didn't like where this was going. *It's inevitable. He was around then.* "Cole and I really are just friends. Rain and I," she looked forward, at a Honda CRX with the row of dancing bears across the back. "We have a long history."

"Longer than you and Cole?"

"A bit." She smiled a little and said, "The first time I met Rain, there was this boy who pulled my pigtails and made me cry. Rain punched him in the face and told him if he ever touched me again he'd kill him."

"Nice."

She smiled at his sarcasm. "We were five, Teague."

Both his eyebrows went up. "You've known him since you were five?"

"I have. He's always been one of my best friends, always looking out for me. After he punched Jesse in the face that day, it took about ten years for anyone to so much as look at me again. When Jesse wanted to ask me out, he asked Rain's permission first." As soon as she'd said it, she wondered why she'd brought up Jesse. *Again. You can't hide from this forever, anyway. Seriously, what are you going to do when you do finally run into him? Or when he comes home?*

"So, should I have asked Rain's permission before I kissed you?"

She liked the nervous way he asked, and the funny way it made her feel. *Take what you have while you can. For all you know, Jesse may never even show up again.* She looked at Teague, at the sincere concern in his eyes. *This is what you want and you know it.* "I think you've got his blessing."

The side door opened and Rain, Amy, Cole and Shasta piled back in. Rain leaned between the front seats and said, "They're not opening the lot until five."

"What?" Bailey stared at him in disbelief.

"That's what I heard."

She put her head down on the steering wheel and moaned, "What the hell? If they're not opening the lot until five, we're going to have to sit here for hours."

Rain said, "We're lucky. We're at least in sight of the exit. There's cars backed up behind us as far as I can see, in both directions."

Bailey looked at the cars in front of her. "How come the people in front of us don't just go someplace else? At least get off the freaking.

exit ramp."

"They can't. The buses are all lined up to get into the lot and no one can get past them. We're just gonna have to wait." Rain sank back into a seat.

"Why are they not opening the lot?" Bailey asked no one in particular.

Amy said, "Supposedly they're trying to control the scene."

"By making us sit on the highway?" Bailey snorted. "That's more likely to cause a riot than control anything."

Cole said, "Bail, turn the radio on."

"No way, brah. I'm not risking a dead battery when we can finally get off the highway."

"Oh, yeah, good point." He started rummaging around in his bag.

A minute later Amy held a bowl out to Bailey. She shook her head. "Pass."

Amy shifted to Teague. He shook his head, too. "I'm good." She swiveled in the seat and passed it to Cole for a second round.

* * *

By the time the parking attendant flagged Bailey into a space she didn't care that it was in the mud, that the gates were already open, or that the sky was swirling with crazy clouds. She wanted out, she wanted a beer, and she wanted something to eat that wasn't whatever they could find in the van.

It wasn't looking promising. It was so late, people who would have normally been selling grilled cheese or veggie burritos were already headed into the show. Worse, they'd already seen two separate sets of cops making people open every beer in their coolers and dump them on the ground. Forcing Deadheads to destroy their own livelihood was, in Bailey's opinion, the cruelest form of cracking down on vending.

She stretched, trying to work out the stress. Teague came up behind her and massaged her shoulders. "You okay?"

She leaned on the hood of the van. "Yeah. I just need something to eat, and a beer."

"You want me to see if I can find you something?"

"Not if it means you're going to stop what you're doing."

Rain came over to her. "I'm gonna see if I can score tickets. If I get in, where are you going?"

"The Phil zone, probably."

"Right on." He started to walk away.

From a few rows away someone yelled, "Six up!" The shout was repeated down the rows.

A guy in cargo shorts and no shirt, with short dark hair and a Steal Your Face tattoo on his shoulder, came running down the aisle. The two guys chasing him had the unmistakable look of plainclothes police, in their blue polos and khaki shorts.

Rain yelled, "Six up!" as he stepped casually into the space between the fleeing Head and the pursuers.

One of the cops pushed him unceremoniously out of the way just as the guy ducked between two VW campers.

Bailey lunged forward, grabbed Rain to keep him from falling. "You okay?"

"Did he get away?"

"I think so." She hugged him and whispered in his ear, "Be really careful here, please."

"I'm already not digging the vibe." He hugged her back. "I'm just gonna lay low."

She stepped back. "I'll see you inside?"

"Yeah." He turned to Amy. "Ready?"

Cole and Shasta were still in the van, digging through their backpacks. Bailey climbed in and quietly said, "Hey, don't trust anyone."

Cole crammed a baggie in his pocket and said, "I got it, Bail. Don't worry."

"I'm serious, Cole." She glanced at Teague, who was still watching where the cops had gone. "Please."

"I just got out of jail. I have no intention of going back."

Shasta said, "We're just going to sell necklaces." She pulled a stick from her bag, showed Bailey wire wrapped stones, each hanging from hemp twine looped over the stick.

Still not completely trusting Cole but unable to do anything about it, Bailey said, "Okay." She almost backed out of the van, then instead asked, "Do you guys have tickets for tonight?"

Cole said, "Yeah, we're good."

Bailey smiled. "Cool. I'll see you inside."

*　*　*

Bailey sat in the grass, which was really more mud, then stood back up, too antsy to sit still. Everyone they'd run into was talking about the scene, all saying be careful. There were people all over the lot with big video cameras on their shoulders, looking very official. And instead of regular security guards, the venue was being watched over by actual police. They wore polo shirts instead of uniforms, but the guns at their hips marked them as clear as day. Getting through security had been so sketchy she'd almost ditched the joint she'd carefully pushed into the very bottom of her purse, just to avoid any possibility of problems.

Teague stood next to her, near the front of the general admission area. "Do you think they'll do 'China Cat'?"

She continually scanned the faces around her as she answered, "I hope so. Maybe 'Sugar Mag Sunshine Daydream.'"

The first notes started, Bobby tuning. And with it, the strangest echo.

Teague looked down at Bailey, suddenly concerned. "Did you dose me?"

She shook her head. "No." She looked around, wondering what the fuck that was.

"Please tell me you hear that, Bailey."

"Yeah, I do." She made a face, "Maybe they've got the soundboard wrong."

But it wasn't the soundboard. The band made adjustments, obviously not happy with the sound either. After minutes of fiddling, "Touch of Grey" started and the echo reverberated over the crowd.

Bailey mumbled, "I hate this fucking song." And suddenly it felt like everything in the world was wrong.

All she wanted was to be home, playing cards in the shop with Teague, where she didn't have to figure out where to sleep with six people, or ignore the looks from Rain and Cole every time she was near Teague, or worry about where Rain and Cole *were*. Those cops trying to look friendly were really freaking her out. She sat on the ground, put her head on her knees.

Teague sat next to her and rubbed her back. "Hey, are you okay?"

She squeezed her eyes tight shut. "This place is a fucking nightmare."

"Hey, Bail, it's okay."

"No, it's not. Rain should be here. And Cole. Especially Cole. He said he had tickets. So where the hell are they?"

"There's still a shitload of people coming in. Maybe they're just not through security yet."

She couldn't hold it together. Tears sprang to her eyes. "Or maybe they got busted." She looked up. "What *is* that echo?"

He stood, pulling her with him. "You usually stay further back, don't you?"

"Yeah."

"Come on, maybe Cole and Rain just can't find us." He led her through the crowd, going carefully up the muddy slope.

As they got further up the echo faded. Then, as they finally got to the edge of the crowd, she saw Feather and Caleb. She hugged them each. "Hey, have you seen Rain and Amy? Or Cole and Shasta?"

Feather nodded, "Yeah, Cole and Shasta are that way." She pointed towards the gates.

The tightness in Bailey's chest loosened a little. "Thanks." Needing to see Cole for herself, she pulled Teague behind her in the direction Feather had pointed.

When she saw him, she ran to him and hugged him tightly. "Damn it, Cole, don't ever scare me like that again."

"Like what?"

Instead of explaining, she stepped back and asked, "Where's Rain? And Amy?"

Shasta said, "We haven't seen them."

Bailey's chest started to tighten again.

Cole assured her, "He's fine, Bail. He knows what he's doing."

She nodded. *He's fine, he's always fine. He just didn't get in. When you get back to the van, they'll be there waiting. Like always. Don't panic.* She was, though. She could feel the fear building, squeezing her lungs, rolling in the pit of her stomach. *You're being stupid. Just stop.*

The people around them sang the chorus, but Bailey didn't join in. Then from just behind them there was a huge eruption of cheers as a flood of people began pouring over the fence and running into the crowd. And coming towards them, weaving around other Heads trying to get out of the way of each other and the police who were beginning to respond to the melee, were Rain and Amy.

"Come on!" Rain grabbed Bailey's hand and pulled her.

She glanced around to make sure Teague was following. Next to him, a cop grabbed Cole.

"*What the fuck!*" Cole struggled as the cop tried to drag him towards the front gates. "*I have a ticket! I have a fucking ticket!*"

Bailey yanked her hand out of Rain's and reversed direction just as Teague shouted, "Six up!" Then he was running, slamming into the cop, yelling, "Run!"

The cop's grip on Cole slipped and he twisted, freeing himself. He was instantly swallowed by the crowd. Bailey watched in horror as the cop turned towards Teague. But Teague, too, disappeared into the sea of tie-dyes.

Bailey turned and sauntered off. *Don't run. They chase you when you run.* She'd taken a dozen steps when Rain slipped his arm around her.

Quietly, he asked, "What the fuck just happened?"

Fighting panic, she said, "I don't know! Are they okay?"

"I think so. But that cop looked *pissed.*"

Bailey almost turned around, but she knew better. Instead, she led Rain and Amy back towards the general area she and Teague had chosen when they'd first gotten there. "Where's Shasta?"

Amy said, "She went the other direction."

They got away. They all got away. The sense of dread Bailey had been fighting all night was stronger than ever. She concentrated on breathing, on not losing her shit in front of Rain and Amy.

* * *

Teague wove between people. "*Cole!*" He yelled, glanced around as he ducked between two girls spinning. Cole was nowhere in sight. "Damn it." He moved in the direction of the spot where he and Bailey had waited for everyone else before the show had started.

The hand on his back scared the shit out of him. He jerked around, intending to run again.

"Brah, that was fucking insane!" Cole continued the way Teague had been headed.

"Jesus Christ, Cole, am I happy to see you." Relieved that Cole had gotten away, he said, "We gotta find Bailey. She's gotta be freaking out."

"I'll catch you up. I gotta find Shasta first."

"I'll come with you." He followed Cole as he changed direction.

"I thought you said you weren't here to keep an eye on me."

"I'm not."

"Then why are you following me?"

He was pretty sure telling his brother it was to protect him was a bad idea. Instead, he said, "Because if I come back without you Bailey will never speak to me again."

* * *

Bailey stood with her back to the stage, watching for Teague or Cole. She ignored the annoying echo and the cheers from the crowd. It had been way too long. Either Teague hadn't figured out where to look for her, or something had happened. *If something happened it's your fault. You brought him here. You're responsible for him.*

"Friend of the Devil" started. A girl in a purple prairie dress spun. As she moved a space opened behind her and there was Teague, stepping around the girl and in the process spilling a little of the beer he was carrying. Cole and Shasta were right behind him, and all three of them looked perfectly happy.

She was relieved and furious at the same time. "You asshole!" She grabbed Teague and hugged him.

"You're gonna spill your beer." He passed the cup, and the pretzel he had in his other hand, off to Cole before returning her hug.

"*Do not ever* do anything like that again!"

He grinned as he looked down at her. "Jeez, Rain saves some total stranger and he gets hugged for it. I save Cole and you yell at me?"

"*Yes!* Because you *assaulted* a police officer." She buried her face against his chest to hide the tears of relief she couldn't stop. "And I was worried sick."

"I'm sorry. I didn't mean to make you worry." He held her tight, kissed the top of her head. "I got you a pretzel. And a beer."

He brought me food. And beer. Suddenly extremely grateful for him, she said squeezed him tight. "Thank you."

* * *

Teague listened to the trilling of the keyboards, the softness of Jerry's voice, the constant beat of the drums. He liked the bass, in this song it felt like the deep beats kept the rest together.

More than that, he liked the dreamy look on Bailey's face. He pulled her to him, held her close and swayed with her. She sang softly. *She knows every word. To every song.*

As he ran his fingers over her arm, he mumbled, "You've got goose bumps."

"It's the music."

He closed his eyes, felt Bailey in his arms and the music coursing through him. *This is so right.*

The song ended and she stopped swaying. She opened her eyes, a smile lingering on her lips as she muttered, "'Bird Song', Teague." She sat on the ground, ignoring the mud. The band left the stage for the set break.

He sat next to her, wrapped his arm around her back. She leaned into him. Around them people moved, sprawling on the ground, going for a bathroom break or to buy a beer or talk to friends. He ignored the constant motion, instead concentrating on her body against his.

He needed to know she was okay. He'd seen the sheer panic on her face when she couldn't find Cole and Rain. Had felt it in the way she trembled, heard it in the rising pitch of her voice. He'd have done anything in that moment to fix things for her.

And he'd seen her, through the crowd, looking for him with the same fear in her eyes. Had seen the relief when she'd finally seen him. *I'd do it all again, just to see that look.*

"I'm gonna go see if I can get a beer." Rain asked, "Anyone want anything?"

Cole stood. "Yeah, brah, I'm in." He turned back. "Teague?"

"Hell yeah." He joined his brother and Rain as they made their way through the crowd.

* * *

Teague wanted a shower so freakin bad. It'd rained during the second set, which hadn't deterred anyone from dancing, and everyone was covered in mud. He and Bailey stopped to buy another shirt so he could stop stealing Cole's clothes, and they got a burrito to share. By the time they got back to the van they found Cole and Shasta sitting on the ground with two people Teague didn't know.

Bailey did, though. She squatted down next to them and hugged them each. "Hey now, Harvard. Hey, Kelly." She glanced behind herself, "This is Teague."

Teague sat next to Bailey and shook hands with Harvard and Kelly.

Cole said, "Bail, we got floor space, right? They slept in their car last night."

She looked at Teague. "Do we?"

Without any hesitation, he said, "Yeah, of course."

Just as Bailey finished giving them directions to their hotel, Rain and Amy showed up. "Kelly, Harvard, fuckin' cool." Rain hugged them each and sat down. "Where are guys staying?"

"With Bailey, now. How about you?"

Rain smiled, "With Bailey and Teague."

After a few minutes, Harvard and Kelly left and everyone else got in the van. It was so late, it didn't take long to get out of the parking lot.

Getting into their room was another thing entirely.

Teague looked around in awe. It was like the lot had been transplanted into their hotel. Guys played hacky sack in the hallway, people had their doors propped open and music spilled out, there were Deadheads everywhere.

Bailey surveyed the scene, laughing. "Looks like we're not the only ones who decided a bed's the place to be."

Harvard and Kelly showed up a while later with four other people in tow. Bailey collected five dollars from each of them, and from a bunch of random people who were looking for a place to sleep. By the time she closed the door there wasn't any space left. There was even someone sleeping in the bathtub.

Chapter 43

The morning after the last show the parking lot of the hotel was insanity. Dozens of Deadheads had stuff spread all over the ground as people separated their belongings from their friend's if they were going different ways, or tried to fit their new rider's belongings into their cars. Tour was over and there was a mass exodus as people headed to wherever they went in between.

Bailey, Teague, Cole, Shasta, Rain, and Amy repacked Bailey's van and started east. Bailey drove until she was too tired, then Teague took over.

"Bailey, I can drive, too." Rain said.

Raising one eyebrow, she said, "Teague's got it."

"Come on, you know I can drive."

Laughing, she said, "Yeah, I remember your driving. That's why Teague's behind the wheel and you're not."

Amy asked, "He's that bad?"

"Actually, he's a good driver. As long as he can figure out if he's supposed to take the high road or the low road."

Incredulously, Rain said, "Jesus, Bailey, that was like ten years ago."

"Yeah, Rain, that's why you haven't driven in like ten years."

"You drop one hit of acid, one time, and no one ever lets you forget about it."

Bailey snickered, "One hit, one time?"

Teague asked, "How the hell did you even get the key in the ignition?"

Rain grinned, "I started driving before it hit me."

Teague scratched his head. "Huh."

Cole said, "See, Teague, acid doesn't hit you quick, like pot. It kinda sneaks up on you."

Bailey told Cole, "He knows. He's got experience with Cookie Monster."

"What the fuck, Bailey!" Teague looked at her in utter shock.

"What?"

"Anything else you want to tell the world about me?"

"I'm sorry. I didn't think it was a secret."

He just shook his head.

Trying to mollify him, she said, "Teague, first off, Rain and Amy tripped with us that night." Grinning, she added, "And if I'm not mistaken you smoked some pretty gnarly kind buds, like, *this morning*."

Cole leaned between the front seats. "Hey, does Mom know what you're up to?"

"Hell no! And I swear to god, Cole, that if you tell her I'll kick your fuckin' ass."

"Bailey, didn't you explain to him that hippies are non-violent?"

"I don't get involved in domestic disputes." She grinned at Cole's teasing.

* * *

Bailey dropped Rain and Amy off at Matt and Lucy's, then drove to Teague and Cole's. Cole grabbed his pack, handed Shasta hers, and hugged Bailey. "Thanks for the ride, Bailey."

"Any time." She turned to Teague, leaned against the van and folded her arms. Teague stood in front of her. She asked, "What are your plans for tonight?"

He pushed her hair back behind her ear, ran his hand down her neck, and kissed her. "I thought I'd take a shower, maybe throw in a load of laundry. Then I'm planning to go get a cup of coffee." His smile grew. "I haven't had a decent cup of coffee in two weeks."

Bailey clasped her hands behind his back, keeping him against her. "That sounds like a pretty good plan. I have to go pick up Delilah, then I'm thinking I could use a cup of coffee myself. And maybe get pizza delivered after."

"Sounds excellent." He wrapped his arms around her, held her close. He didn't want to let her go.

She whispered, "Teague..."

"Go. Get Delilah, see Aria. I'll see you in a little while." He kissed her gently.

She stepped back, ran her finger across her lips. Suddenly her serious expression was replaced by a grin. "Later, brah."

Teague grinned, "See ya, sistah."

He stood in the driveway and watched the van until it was out of sight.

* * *

Bailey fed her last pizza crust to Delilah and leaned back into the couch. She'd picked the softest, squishiest couch she could find for her apartment, and she absolutely loved it. "Ya know, I love going to shows, being on the lot and all, but there's something about kickin' back on your own couch."

Teague swallowed a bite of pizza. "This is a pretty great couch."

Bailey grinned. "Thanks."

"Ya know what I like best about it? You can actually sit on it."

Bailey raised an eyebrow. "Isn't that what couches are for?"

Teague snorted. "That depends on who you ask. If you're talking to my mother or my ex-girlfriend, they're intended to show you have impeccable taste in home decor."

"That's..." It took Bailey a second to think of a word that wasn't rude. "Interesting."

"If I ever have a place of my own, I'm not going to have a single room that I don't use, or furniture you can't sit on, and I'm never going to take my shoes off."

"Never? Not even to go to bed?"

He grinned, "Nope. Not even then."

Laughing, she said, "I'm thinking you may change your mind when you have to wash your sheets every day."

"Most likely I won't make it that far. I'm thinking it's more like it'll be when I have to take a shower." He ate his last bite of pizza, followed Bailey's lead and gave the crust to Delilah, put his plate down and sat back with his fingers laced behind his head. "That was pretty decent, but nowhere near as good as that pizza we had in Chicago."

"That wasn't the pizza that was good, it was the pot."

Smiling, Teague said, "Yeah, that too."

"So you like it, do you?" She smiled knowingly.

He didn't answer right away. "I do." He turned towards her, then continued, "Kayla told me once that she likes acid better than pot, and at the time I thought she was nuts. But I actually agree. Pot makes me feel out of it, and it's nice but I kind of feel like I'm missing what's going on. Like everything has the same importance, whether it's you talking or a faucet dripping, and I can't sort it out."

Bailey nodded. "That's a good way to explain it."

"But acid is completely different. It's like, what you see is kind of based on the real world. Your brain doesn't create things from nothing, but things are so distorted. It's fascinating." Teague thought

343

back to the night he'd dropped acid with Bailey. "When we tripped, I saw you as an angel."

She snickered. "You were definitely tripping. I'm no angel."

"You were so beautiful." He moved his hand to her face, ran his thumb across her cheek. "You still are."

Bailey's heart quickened as shivers of pleasure surged through her. She shook her head, though, and denied his words. "I'm not. I'm just me."

He moved closer. As his lips met hers, she closed her eyes. She wanted to feel him, just him, and nothing else. She ran her hand up his arm, tangled her fingers in the back of his hair.

He pulled back and she opened her eyes. He put his forehead against hers and whispered, "It's so quiet with just the two of us."

"That's what I always have the hardest time with when I get home. I miss having people around."

"It's nice, though, to be alone with you."

"Not worrying about anyone opening the door. Not having to listen to other people having sex."

The smile that touched his lips was cute. "Yeah, that wasn't too much fun."

She took his face in her hands. He kept his beard short, not like most of the guys she knew. It was soft under her fingers. She leaned into another kiss, mumbled against his lips, "You have the most beautiful eyes." She ran her hands down his sides, pulled at his t-shirt. *I'm going to have sex with Teague. Holy shit.*

Suddenly the reality of it hit her hard. This was Teague, who had become so much a part of her life she couldn't imagine a day without him. Teague, who was always there, listening to her, making sure she was safe and fed and not too tired to drive. The wave of love that crashed over her as she looked into his eyes stopped her breath. *Oh my god, oh mygod ohmygod... I love Teague.*

Panicking, she stood up. *That can't be. Fuck!* She went to the bookcase and opened the box she kept on top of it, desperate to take the edge off the raw emotion raging through her. She pulled out her favorite bowl and started to pack it. Her hands shook. *Breathe, Bailey. In two seconds you'll be fine.*

She felt him come up behind her and purposely ignored him. Even when he put his hand on her hip, she kept her eyes on what she was doing.

"Bailey." Gently, he made her turn to him. He ran a hand over her hair. "What's going on?"

Forcing a smile, she said, "Nothing."

He ran his fingers over her cheek. "Bail." He put his hand over hers, closed his fingers around the bowl she'd so carefully packed. "Don't, please."

She looked up questioningly.

"I don't want you to float away."

"I just need..." She couldn't explain that she needed to take the edge off her feelings.

"If you're not okay with this, with us, if this isn't what you want, tell me."

The hurt in his eyes tore at her heart. And she *was* okay with this, and it *was* what she wanted. It was just really, *really* scary. "I'm just nervous."

He wrapped his arms around her and pulled her close. "Then we'll take a step back, until you're not nervous anymore."

Damn it, that's never going to happen. Because I love *you. And I* can't *love you.* The pressure of his arms holding her, the warmth of his body, the sound of his heart beating, all comforted her. *God, I want him.* She slipped her arms around his waist, found the bottom of his shirt and traced her fingers over his bare skin.

He took the bowl from her and set it back in the box before slipping

345

his arms around her. When he pressed his lips against hers, pushed his body to hers, her head swam. This, the way he held her, the way he kissed her, was sweet, and gentle. She let herself fall into it, feel every place they touched, acknowledge that he was hard against her, and that she wanted him.

When she pulled at his shirt, he helped her take it off. When he touched her side, the tips of his fingers finding bare skin, she shivered.

"You've got goose bumps."

Her eyes half-closed, she mumbled, "Mmm hmmm."

"There's no music this time."

"It's you."

He bent down, pulled her shirt up, and kissed her hip. She gasped. She could feel his smile against her as he continued to kiss along the top of her shorts until he got to the center. Then he moved her shirt up further and kissed a line to her breast. She ran her fingers through his hair, and pulled him back up. He brought her shirt up, over her head, and dropped it next to his.

She took his hand and led him to her room. She didn't want their first time to be on the floor. She closed the door behind her, keeping Delilah out. He stood in front of her, stared into her eyes for what felt like an eternity. Then he kissed her.

Her knees buckled. She wrapped her arms around his neck to keep from falling, and as he held her tighter she kissed him back. Barely able to breathe, she moved to the bed and lay down, her feet hanging off the side as she tried to kick off her shoes.

He sat next to her and laid a hand just above her knee. She stopped moving her feet and lay very still, the shock of pleasure from his touch overtaking her. As he slid his hand down her leg, she closed her eyes. He trailed his fingers to the back of her knee and she shivered. When his lips touched the soft skin, already sensitive from his fingers, she gasped.

He ran his hand down her calf, slowly trailing his fingertips over her ankle. The bells she wore jingled. He carefully undid the clasp and let them fall to the floor. Then he gently pulled her shoe off.

Bailey sighed. As fucked up as it was, this was the most erotic thing she'd ever felt. By the time he had her second shoe off, she was moaning softly. Then, his hands were gone.

Opening her eyes, she saw that he was pulling his jeans off. She felt a twinge of disappointment; she wanted to take his jeans off. But then he knelt between her feet and she didn't care how his pants got off, as long as they were off.

She could mess with buttons and zippers next time. This time, she just wanted to feel him in her.

Her eyes rolled back and she arched with desire as he kissed her inner thigh. Her shorts rubbed against her, in an annoyingly exciting way. She started to unbutton them, but Teague placed his hands over hers and stopped her. "I got this."

He undid the top of her shorts. She heard the zipper click, just a few notches. Then, his lips were pressing against her skin. His beard felt prickly, but she liked it. Rocking her hips against him, she reached to touch him, ran her fingers through his curls. He pulled the zipper a little further, kissed lower, then even lower.

Bailey moaned, "Teague, please." She felt his lips move, knew he was smiling. Practically begging, she said, "This isn't funny."

He spoke against her, the warm rush of his breath making her writhe with need, "Relax, Bailey."

She tried. He pulled her shorts off and she knew she would finally be satisfied. But instead of taking her, he kissed her hip. His fingers found her breast and barely touched the side. She reached for him, grabbed him and tried to pull him over her.

Ignoring her attempts to get him closer, he kissed inch by inch up her side, until he reached her breast. He sucked the soft swell, the pull of it searing through her core. "Teague, Teague, oh god…"

He continued up her chest, kissed the hollow of her throat, up her neck. He kissed her collarbone on one side, while trailing his fingers across the other. Finally, he kissed her mouth.

She met him, pulling him to her, sinking her fingers into his hair, thrusting her tongue to tangle with his. When he moaned in response, the vibration tingling Bailey's lips, she pleaded, "Now, Teague."

He wrapped his arms around her and held her tight as he sank into her warmth. His face buried against her neck, he moaned.

Having him inside her was relief. For a moment. But as he began to move, to push deeper, to slide out, to push into her again, she felt the need growing even more. Her insides began to tremble, to squeeze as he pushed. Tighter and tighter, she wrapped herself around him.

Her muscles relaxed, then tightened again, longer this time, stronger, making him push harder.

Over and over, she felt him inside her, touching the deepest part of her, and the clenching grew stronger, lasted longer, the times between shorter and shorter.

His arms tightened around her. He groaned, strained against her, pushed deeper, as his body was wracked with his orgasm.

His throbbing, forcing into her against her own need, pushed her into oblivion. She cried out as she tightened against him uncontrollably, over and over she arched, wanting more, grabbing his ass and pulling him into her, as their cries mingled in each other's ears.

Teague moved off Bailey, lay next to her, bringing her to rest on his chest. Their ragged breathing echoed in her ears. She ran her hand down his side, hoping to calm him. He inhaled sharply, trembled under her touch. "Do you need more?"

He trailed his fingers gently up and down her back. His voice was almost inaudible. "I want more, but," Bailey could hear his smile, "it's gonna have to wait."

She closed her eyes and let herself feel the throbbing of the orgasm still pulsing in her. She rocked her hips, making it stronger.

"Do *you* want more?"

The concern in his voice was beautiful. She kissed his stomach, making him tremble again. She sighed, "Later." She smiled, "I don't think I can take more right now."

She settled against him, noticing vaguely that it had gotten dark. Her last coherent thought as she drifted to sleep was that she was glad she didn't have to get up and turn out the lights.

Chapter 44

Bailey pulled the blanket tighter, warding off the sudden chill when Teague rolled over to snooze the alarm clock.

"Five o'clock is ridiculously early." He settled back down and held her tightly against him.

"Mmmm. Yeah."

"You shoulda opened a bar instead of a coffee shop."

She snorted, "Bars don't sell bagels."

He smiled. "I could learn how to make hot wings."

Reluctantly, she pulled away from him and sat on the edge of the bed. "I really do have to get up. I never took Delilah out last night."

Teague propped himself up on an elbow and watched her. "I'm gonna have to run home to shower and change."

Bailey turned back to him. "Why?"

"I don't have clean clothes here." He gave her a wicked grin. "I wasn't planning on staying last night."

"You can shower here. Shirts are in the third drawer, take whatever you want. I'm sure your pants are fine." As she talked, she pulled a shirt from the drawer then grabbed her shorts off the floor and put them on. She leaned down and kissed Teague. "I mean, unless you really want to go home."

He pulled her back into bed. "Nah. I think I'm good." He kissed her, making her smile.

She didn't let him keep her there, though.

In the coffee shop kitchen, Bailey hunted through a box of bootleg tapes. She really thought that allowing anyone who wanted to, to record concerts was just about the coolest thing the Dead did.

She stopped, her fingers on a tape. She read the words, written in black marker, and memories flooded unbidden into her mind. All the good she'd felt that morning was suddenly gone. She picked up the tape and held it.

Jesse hadn't been back in months. He hadn't called, written, nothing. He hadn't tried to see her at any of the shows she'd been at over the summer.

She turned to the trash can and started to throw the tape in. But at the last second she stopped. This was her first show. It was special, whether Jesse had been there or not.

Opening a drawer, not caring which one, she shoved the tape to the back, behind boxes of plastic wrap and aluminum foil. Then she jammed a tape into the player and cranked the volume.

When Teague came in, he turned it down. He came up behind her and kissed her neck as he slid his arms around her waist.

"Mmmm." Bailey closed her eyes and let herself feel Teague. This was exactly what she needed. After a minute, she said, "There's coffee."

Letting her go, Teague moved to the other counter. "I'll get us both a cup, once I have the first batch of dough rising."

Giving him a Bailey smile, she said, "I am so looking forward to it."

Smiling back, he asked, "What are you listening to?"

Bailey answered off-handedly, "Metallica," then began to sing along. She liked having Teague there. Just his presence in the room felt good and for the first time since she'd gotten to the kitchen she felt at peace.

Raising an eyebrow at her, he started pulling out what he needed to bake. After a few minutes, he asked incredulously, "You know all the lyrics?"

"Yeah. Why?"

"I'm just surprised, I guess, that you listen to this."

She laughed. "You have no idea how many Deadheads have Metallica tattoos under those tie-dyes."

"Bailey, you continually surprise me."

Laughing again, she went back to baking.

* * *

Ellen dropped Aria off on her way to work. The little girl tackled Teague as soon as she saw him. He picked her up, swung her around, and hugged her. "Hey, girl."

She giggled as his beard tickled her. "I missed you."

"I missed you, too. They did 'China Cat Sunflower'. I wished you were there with me. Next time maybe we can go together and we can dance." To her delight, he waltzed around the room.

He put Aria down and she asked, "What are we gonna do today?"

"Do you want to paint?"

"Sure."

Teague led her to the closet where he knew Bailey kept her art supplies.

* * *

Family had started making their way back and there were too many people around for Bailey to be able to leave for lunch. She had grinders delivered and sat at a table with Aria and Teague. It was so cute to hear Teague talking about whatever little kid things Aria wanted to discuss. She'd heard very serious conversations about why cartoon characters could run so fast, how grown-ups knew which roads to take to get places, and the best way to catch a frog.

"Maybe Saturday we can go for a hike and try to catch a frog?" Teague glanced at Bailey for approval.

"Sure. We can see if Katelyn, Liam and Mallory can come, too."

"Yeah!" Aria bounced in her seat.

Finished with her lunch, Bailey wrapped her leftovers and ran upstairs to put them away. The dishes from the night before were washed and stacked neatly in the rack to dry. *Teague must have done that.* It made her smile, that he cared.

Back downstairs, she switched from tapes to the radio. She was really in the mood for variety.

Rain and Amy had come in and were sitting on the couch surrounded by people Bailey didn't know. She stopped to hug them both.

"Your new employee is pretty good," Rain said, pointing to Teague who was behind the counter listening to an older woman give her order.

"Yeah, he's not bad." Bailey went to the front and leaned on the counter. Using her best laid-back super-slow voice, she said, "Hey, bro, I need a decent coffee. Not that shit they serve at that gas station up the street."

Teague crossed his arms. "Well, now, I'm going to need cash for that. Before I pour it."

Struggling not to smile, Bailey said, "Come on, kind hippie rainbow brother brah. Hook a sistah up."

"I think you might be more comfortable at that place in town. Where all the other hippies get their coffee."

Bailey scrunched her nose up, grinning. "Yeah, I think you might be right. I'll just mosey on up there, leave all you lawyers to your thing."

Teague raised an eyebrow. "All us lawyers, huh? How many of us are there?"

"Around here? Just one. And that's more than enough." She laughed, "Now get out. I've got work to do, and I think you've got coloring waiting for you." She pointed to where Aria was laying out crayons.

Teague came out from behind the counter, mumbling, "This is quite a promotion. Hot shot Connecticut lawyer to unpaid nanny." But when his eyes met Bailey's, she could see he was happy. And when he paused to kiss her gently on the forehead, she was happy, too.

Late in the afternoon Bailey made coffee, half listening to the radio. After a set of commercials the DJ started talking. Everyone in the place went silent as he repeated what he'd said.

"Brent Mydland, keyboardist of the Grateful Dead, has died, apparently of an accidental drug overdose. Our thoughts and prayers go out to his family." The stunned silence in the coffee shop was deafening.

Someone muttered, "Oh shit."

That broke the silence. Suddenly there was talking, crying, people getting up and moving around. Bailey looked at Teague, tears in her eyes.

Her chest was too tight. She could barely breathe. *No, God, no. It has to be a mistake.* "Oh god. Oh my god." She started crying. Then Teague had her. He wrapped his arms around her, held her tight, calmed her down.

Her tears slowed and Teague led her to the couches, sat with her next to Rain. Everything was a blur, the faces, the voices, the people around her. She heard the door open and really didn't give a shit. Whoever it was could make their own damn coffee.

"Bailey, I gotta go take care of customers. Are you okay, here, with Rain?" Teague looked at her, concern in his beautiful eyes.

She swallowed, nodded. "Yeah." As he stood, she grabbed his hand and smiled weakly. "Teague? Thanks."

He left her, to handle what she couldn't.

* * *

Teague sat next to Bailey, the conversation swirling around them all about Brent. People talked about where they'd seen shows, when Brent had been especially amazing, and what trials and tribulations he'd been through. There was a lot of talk about summer tour, and especially Tinley Park and how his playing had been there.

It seemed impossible that many of the people in the room had seen him just days earlier, and now he was gone.

The door opened and Teague felt tension spring from nowhere, a ripple that started at the front of the shop and moved back to him. He looked to see who could have caused it.

And there was Jesse.

* * *

For a split second Bailey thought it must be a dream. Jesse was standing in the doorway.

But she knew it had to be real, she never dreamed of Jesse anymore. She got up and walked to him, so relieved that he was there. Having him with her would make it easier to bear the pain, just as it had when her father had died. And when she'd lost her sister.

Jesse had been there, had helped her deal, every time her world had collapsed. Of course he'd be there now.

He held his arms out and she fell into them. She mumbled against his chest, "Did you hear?"

"Yeah. Shit, Bailey, what's going to happen?" He choked back tears.

"I don't know." They stood in the middle of the shop, holding each other.

* * *

The pounding in Teague's ears was loud enough to drown out all other sounds.

He walked out the back door.

Clenching his fists, trying to get the rising anger under control, he knew he was done hanging out. If he stayed there for one more second, had to watch that fucker touching Bailey, and her letting him, he'd lose it. There was no way in hell he was going to do that in front of all his friends.

He yanked the door of his BMW open and got in. As he drove home, he thought he really hated this car. *Hated* it and everything it represented. His old life, working to please his mother and his ex-girlfriend, knowing nothing he did was ever going to be good enough.

He stepped through the front door of the house he shared with Cole and his anger doubled. There dishes piled on the table, pizza boxes stacked on the floor, and his brother was oblivious to it. Cole sat on the couch, doing bong hits with Shasta.

This was all Cole's fault. If he hadn't gotten himself arrested Teague would still be in Connecticut, still be a divorce lawyer. Would probably still be with Marlena, and everything would still make sense.

All he had now was a closet full of ratty clothes, a car he hated driving, and the most fucked up relationship imaginable.

Cole slurred, "Hey, man. What'r you doin' here?"

"I live here."

"Thought you'd be with Bailey."

Anger surged through his veins, his brain exploded with it. He hated Cole, hated this house, this life, every-fucking-thing. He picked up a ladder-back chair, one that should have been in the kitchen, and threw it as hard as he could at the front window. The chair and window both smashed to pieces all over the front porch with an earsplitting crash.

Then he turned and walked upstairs.

He paced back and forth in his room. Throwing the chair had been good, but it hadn't been enough.

This had nothing to do with Cole or this house. Nothing to do with his car or his lack of a future.

It had to do with Jesse.

Teague was there every goddamn day. He respected Bailey, he helped her when she needed it, kept her company when she was lonely, listened when she talked. And that fucker walked in and she went straight to him. Jesse didn't give a *flying fuck* about her. If he did, he wouldn't leave her for months at a time. He'd be there every fucking day.

Teague punched the wall.

Pain shot up his arm.

It felt good. He hit it again.

And again.

And again.

When he'd beat his anger out, he slumped on the floor. There was nothing to replace the anger, just tired, hurt emptiness.

He took a shower, washed the blood off his hand and the smell of hippies out of his hair. When he was done he lay in bed, felt the throbbing pain of his bruised and battered hand, and thought about what he's just done. And why.

It wasn't about Jesse.

It was that he was completely and totally in love with Bailey.

* * *

Teague didn't get up to make the bagels. Instead, when he did finally get up, he went downstairs and grabbed his car keys. He drove to the gas station and bought a shitty cup of coffee just for the caffeine. Then he went into town.

He parked on the street, refusing to even use Bailey's parking lot. He went to the head shop first, figuring it was a good place to start.

He was greeted by Sage. "Hey, Teague."

"Hey, Sage. What're you doing here?"

"Working off a debt. What can I do ya for?"

"Is Rain around?"

"Not here. Try Bailey's. Everyone's there."

"Yeah, thanks." He started to walk out, then noticed a Snodgrass pipe on display. He was gonna need something, he might as well have the best. Besides, the red and orange ripples inside the glass appealed to him. He pointed to it. "Can I get that?"

The surprise on Sage's face turned quickly to a grin. "Yeah, brah. You want me to wrap it?"

"Na, I'll just take it." He paid Sage, not even flinching at the triple digit price tag, and slipped the pipe into his pocket.

"You know how to use that?"

He gave Sage a nod. "Yeah, man, I got it."

He had no intention of going to Bailey's. Instead he went to the record store, then the comic book shop. He finally had to acknowledge that if Rain was in town he probably was at Bailey's.

Heading back to his car, he decided he'd just get a goddamn bottle of something and go home.

As he pulled out of the parking space, he saw exactly what he wanted; Rain and Amy walking down the street. He stopped and rolled down his window. "Hey, Rain. You got a minute?"

"For sure. What's up?" He leaned on the side of the car.

Teague didn't even flinch. He didn't care anymore if the paint got scratched. "You have kind?"

"Yeah, how much?"

Teague really had no idea. He said something that sounded good. "A quarter?"

Rain glanced around, then back to Teague. "For you I do."

* * *

Sitting alone on his bed, Teague packed his new pipe, lit it, watched the smoke fill the stem as he inhaled. That was the coolest thing about glass pipes. He held his breath as long as he could, then coughed like he was gonna die.

As his mind drifted away he smiled. This was niiiiicccceee.

He took another hit.

Fuck Bailey. He was better off without her.

Chapter 45

Bailey lay in bed, very early morning just starting to brighten the room. She looked at the wall. It was easier than looking at anything else. The weight in her chest was so heavy she wasn't sure she'd be able to get up.

She could feel Jesse, on the other side of the bed. It irked her that he'd come in so late, had woken her up, and now he got to sleep in. She knew, without having to get out of bed, that there were dirty dishes laying around. And he smelled like cigarettes.

The smell of pot, of patchouli, of coffee, were good smells. The smell of Teague was a good smell. The stench of cigarettes was not.

The hope that Teague would be there in a little while to make bagels finally got her up. She ran a brush through her hair, called to Delilah, and went downstairs. She ignored the mess Jesse had left. She'd clean it later. Shit, she might as well wait anyway, and do Jesse's breakfast and lunch dishes as the same time.

As she put the second tray of cookies in the oven she glanced nervously out the back door. It appeared that Teague wasn't coming—for the second day.

* * *

Aria asked Bailey for about the thousandth time that morning, "Is

Teague coming today?"

Bailey normally had oceans of patience with Aria. Not today. She was upset about Brent. She was dealing with Jesse. She had no idea where Teague was.

He'd disappeared without so much as a goodbye and hadn't come back. She'd tried calling his house but Cole said he wasn't there. *Of course he's not going to talk to you. Jesse's back.* She went back over the last time Teague had been there, could feel his fingers twined with hers, the simple act showing her he was there. *Why the hell did you leave him? He was there for you. He always has been.*

She couldn't bring herself to tell Aria why Teague had left, or why he hadn't come back. "I don't know, Aria. Please, can you go color?" She wanted to cry. Close the shop, crawl into bed and feel sorry for herself. Just when she'd thought things were perfect everything had fallen apart.

When Ann Marie came in for her shift, Bailey took Aria up to her apartment and fed her dinner. She tried to do it like she always did, to have fun and joke around, but her heart wasn't in it. It didn't help that Jesse was there, sitting on the couch doing nothing.

She was relieved when her mother came to get Aria. As soon as they left, Bailey told Jesse that she was going out. He didn't even ask where, or who with. He just kissed her goodbye.

Bailey drove to Teague's. She wanted to see for herself that he wasn't there.

The first thing she saw was that his car was in the driveway. The next was that there was a huge piece of plywood nailed over the front window and there was a broken chair surrounded by glass on the front porch.

Stepping carefully over the glass, she knocked once, walked in the front door and stopped dead in her tracks. Teague was sitting on the couch taking a hit from a bong. "Teague?"

He coughed, then grinned. "Heeeeyyyy, Baaaileyyyy."

"What the hell are you doing?"

"Bong hits. Want some?"

"No!" She picked up a baggie from the coffee table. The tiny bit at the bottom was enough for her to see this wasn't shwag. "Where did you get that?"

"Cole left it here. I'd'a got my bowl, but man, it's all the fuckin' way upstairs."

Stunned, she said, "The pot, Teague. Where'd you get the pot?"

He laughed, "Oh, yeah, that. Rain. Fuckin red hairs and everything."

His eyes were completely bloodshot and he was grinning a stupid stoned smile. Anger simmered; this wasn't Teague. The Teague she knew would never sit home, alone, high as a kite. That was not the same thing as sitting around with your friends, sharing. That was hanging out. This was getting high for the sake of getting high.

Teague slurred, "Right on. You and Jesse, fuckin' killer."

Bailey felt tears well up, guilt replacing the anger. Because that made sense, in the worst kind of way.

Teague set the lighter to the bowl, pulled smoke up the chamber. Bailey turned and walked out.

* * *

Teague's alarm clock went off at five.

Although his mind was clear, or more likely because his mind was clear, he felt like shit.

He was no better than Jesse.

Actually, he was worse.

Everyone knew what Jesse was like, but Teague expected better of himself.

He'd walked out on Bailey, had just left, and hadn't been back.

It didn't matter that she'd gone to Jesse. Teague didn't expect anything different. If he was honest with himself, he'd always known he and Bailey could never be.

But they were friends, and he'd turned his back on her.

And she'd come looking for him.

He got up, dressed, and drove to Bailey's. The back door was propped open and he noticed immediately that the kitchen was silent. He stood against the door frame, watched her working at the counter. "Bailey."

Slowly, she turned towards him. Her eyes were red rimmed and swollen. Knowing she'd been crying made him feel even worse. "Bailey, I'm sorry."

Her voice soft, she asked, "For what?"

"I promised you I'd make bagels, and help with Aria, and I haven't. I shouldn't have left like you like that."

"It's okay. Everyone leaves me. I'm used to it."

Anger boiled. She wasn't crying over him; that fucker had done it again. "Jesse left?"

"No." Bailey's shoulders slumped. "He's here." She looked at him pleadingly, "Are you, um, I…"

Teague grappled with what to do. What he really wanted to do was go upstairs and beat the living shit out of Jesse. Not for any other reason than that he was fucking with Bailey.

That wasn't gonna happen, though. He'd never hit another person, and he wasn't about to start. Especially not with Jesse. He wasn't worth the effort it would take or the trouble it would cause.

"Teague?"

Seething, but determined to keep his word, he said, "Yeah, I'm here to make bagels." He turned his back on Bailey and reached for the flour.

* * *

Everything was different.

Bailey could feel Teague's presence in the kitchen, but she couldn't talk to him. She wanted to, to try to make it better, but everything she thought of seemed wrong to say. It didn't help that he was silent. She hoped that once the baking was done, after the morning rush and before Aria got there, they'd have time to talk. And maybe by then she'd think of something to say.

There was so much going on and she needed him.

She never got the chance, though. As soon as he brought the second batch of bagels out to her, he left.

* * *

Teague wandered from the kitchen to the living room, then to stand on the front porch, then back to the kitchen. He couldn't understand how anyone could not do anything all day. It had been different when he was hanging out with Bailey, but just being home alone sucked.

He sat on the couch, the TV playing something he wasn't paying attention to, and stared at the plywood he'd nailed over the window. He thought he should probably call Liam and see if he'd come help him fix it.

He thought he should probably fix the holes he'd punched in his bedroom wall, too. Although that was something he knew how to do now. He smiled a little; it was pretty fucking amazing that Attorney Teague Gallagher knew how to spackle.

He called Liam and left a message on his machine. Then he dragged the tub of joint compound from the basement up to his room.

* * *

Teague brought two beers out to the porch while Liam finished putting his tools away. "Thanks for this, man. I owe you."

Liam laughed. "Wait till you get my bill. You owe me, all right."

Sitting in one of the two chairs he'd bought for the porch, Teague cracked one beer, and set the other on the floor for Liam. "Whatever you charge, it was worth it."

"I'll take that beer and call it even." He came and sat in the other chair, popped the top on his beer and took a swig.

"Not this time, bro. I'm paying you for the window and your time."

Instead of arguing, Liam asked, "Are you coming to Bailey's tonight?"

Teague rocked his chair back on two legs. "Nope."

"Ya know, you can still hang."

Teague leaned forward and his chair thumped down. "Yeah, I know. But I don't want trouble. I may punch Jesse in the face if I see him."

Liam smiled. "I won't stop you. Pretty sure no one else will, either."

Teague snorted. "I thought hippies were non-violent."

"All I'm sayin's I've watched Jesse fuck with Bailey for years."

Gazing out into the woods, Teague said, "That's Bailey's choice."

Liam shifted, "Dude, look, Katelyn told me to get you there. If I don't she's gonna be pissed."

"Why?"

"She's worried about you. You know how women get."

Teague knew he was looking at another long night alone, and suddenly the invitation was a lot more appealing. "Yeah, whatever. I'll be there."

"Right on." Liam finished his beer and left.

Teague went inside and got another beer. He sat on the porch and drank it slowly, contemplating not moving from that spot. He had a case of Sam Adams in the fridge, he could easily stay there all night. He looked out at the trees, watched a bat swoop after something too small for Teague to see.

What he really should do was pack his shit, or at least whatever he could find that was salvageable, and go back to Connecticut. He was out of work, and out of practice, but he could get back into the swing of things easy enough. Maybe he'd open his own firm. The Law Office of Teague E. Gallagher.

That was probably his only option. If he tried to get a job in another firm they'd want to know what he'd been doing for the last eight months, and why he'd left his previous firm. He wasn't into answering either of those questions. But if he opened his own practice, he could start slow. Wills, real estate deals, uncontested divorce. *You could go into criminal law. Maybe actually help people instead of just getting them the best deal you can work.*

Abruptly, he got up, grabbed his car keys and drove into town.

The whole way he wondered why the hell he was torturing himself. Being in the kitchen with Bailey, when they were both busy working, was bad enough. But purposely going to hang out? Knowing that he'd have to see her with Jesse? That was intentionally stupid.

Yeah, he deserved every damn thing he got.

The room was packed and he saw people he knew as soon as he walked in. Matt and Lucy, Lance and Ruth, and of course Bailey and Jesse. He nodded to Bailey; she acknowledged him with a tight smile.

His first stop was to grab a beer. Then he went to talk to Katelyn.

Hugging him, she said, "Teague, I'm so glad you came. We've missed you."

He kissed her cheek, surprised at how good her greeting made him feel. "I've missed you, too."

"Liam said your new window looks fantastic."

Teague felt a flush of embarrassment. "Liam's really good at what he does." Purposely changing the subject, he asked, "How's Mallory doing?"

Katelyn grinned at the mention of her daughter. "She's good. We got a letter from her first-grade teacher and started doing some school shopping, so all of a sudden she's nervous. But she'll be in the same class as Aria, so that's cool."

Teague's heart ached. Aria must have gotten a letter from the teacher, too. He hadn't known; he hadn't seen her since the day Jesse had showed up. Jesus, he missed her. Instead of acknowledging that, he said, "I still can't get over what the kids have to do in school. I remember playing Simon Says and taking naps when I was their age."

Katelyn smiled, "It is pretty incredible. Mallory's already reading actual books! I mean, not like 'The Odyssey' or anything, but Dick and Jane stuff."

Grasping for something to talk about that wasn't going to hurt, Teague asked, "Did you like 'The Odyssey'?"

Leaning comfortably on the counter, Katelyn and Teague discussed, in depth, their take on Homer's works.

They were still at it when Kayla came up next to Teague. "Hey, Teague. It's been way too long."

"Hi, Kayla." He kissed her cheek. "How's things?"

"Good." She put her arm around his waist. "What'cha been up to?"

Teague looked down at Kayla, at her long blonde hair, the way her lips curved into a seductive smile. He answered, "Nothing, really. Just hanging out."

She led him to a corner, grabbing each of them a beer on the way. "I heard you decided to redecorate your room."

Raising an eyebrow at her phrasing, he said, "You could say that."

Kayla took his hand and carefully examined it. The scabs were nasty, but the bruises were beginning to fade. They'd gone from angry black-purple to purple with a more greenish tint. She gently kissed the back of his hand. "It's a good thing you didn't break anything."

Teague's eyes unwillingly flickered to Jesse for just a second. *Too bad.* "Yeah."

"I heard your new window looks amazing, though."

He narrowed his eyes slightly. "Is there anything you don't know?"

Laughing, Kayla shrugged. "If there was, I wouldn't know."

Teague smiled, "That's so true."

"So, last year I had this wicked cool professor. He had this theory about the whole universe being just a toy for giants in another world. Like a Lego set, kind of."

Teague listened as she explained this entire theory. He didn't care much what she was saying, and he got the feeling she was just talking to talk, but he was more than happy to have a reason to give her all his attention. And not to have to come up with a topic of conversation.

His mind wandered. He remembered so many days, sitting here with Bailey, quietly enjoying coffee. Or just being together. They'd never needed to fill the air with so many words.

Realizing Kayla had asked him a question, he tried to recall what she'd said. "It's an interesting theory."

Kayla looked at him speculatively. She started telling him some other thing about relativity, but there was no way in hell he could concentrate on what she was saying. She'd moved closer to him and was sliding her hand up his thigh.

He tried to think of some way to make her stop, without embarrassing either one of them. He quietly said, "Kayla, we're surrounded by our friends."

Her expression changed, became much more provocative. "Yeah. And?"

He swallowed, "And that's very...distracting."

Leaning very close, Kayla spoke softly, "Teague, do you want to go someplace else?"

Images, memories, crashed into his mind. Bailey, as she'd looked on that misty morning in Indiana, and how she'd sounded when they'd made love. Bailey's smile, the one she gave when she was truly happy, and the way her eyes had rolled back when he'd touched her. Then, Jesse's arms wrapped around her in the middle of the coffee shop.

"Yeah, I think I would." He stood and held out his hand to Kayla.

She took it and followed him out the back door.

At his car she leaned against the driver's door. "Teague, this doesn't have to mean any more than we want it to."

He didn't stop her as she kissed him. Her lips were soft and she tasted like beer. "What do you want it to mean?"

She touched a finger to his lips and whispered, "I'm not looking for anything more than to satisfy my curiosity." That inviting smile was back. "And to satisfy myself."

To his surprise, something about what she'd said, or the way she was looking at him, had him suddenly horny as hell. He grabbed her and pulled her closer. The kiss went from soft and unsure to hard and demanding.

He picked her up and sat her on the hood of the car. She began to fumble with the button on his jeans.

The memory of Bailey, smiling at him from the water at Althea Falls, flashed through his mind. He pulled away. "Stop, Kayla." He took a breath. "I can't do this. I'm sorry."

The seductive smile was back. "Yeah, brah, it's cool." She slid off the car. "If you change your mind, lemme know."

He watched her walk away, up the street and out of sight before he climbed into the car and headed home. His mind wandered as he followed the dark, twisting roads. *I can't keep this up. Seeing them together, Bailey letting him touch her. Like she belongs to him. She does, though, and you knew that. Even if she came back, she'd be on loan. Fuck, that's not okay.*

His preoccupied brain barely registered that there was a car in the driveway and lights on in the house. Cole and Shasta had been at Bailey's when Teague had left, but so many people stayed at the house on their way through town he was used to coming home to strangers. He opened the front door and stopped dead. He'd expected to see family.

Instead, he saw his mother.

He managed a single strangled word. "Mom?"

Priscilla's voice echoed his shock. "Teague?"

He immediately started trying to remember what had been on the coffee table. If his mother would know what a bong was if she saw one.

This can not be happening. But it was, and there was nothing he could do about it. *Just get through it.* "So, Mom, what can I do for you?"

"You can start by shaving and cutting your hair. Then you can throw those clothes in the trash and put on something decent."

"I'm sure you didn't come all the way from Connecticut to critique my personal style choices."

"Until two minutes ago I hadn't thought that necessary." She sniffed. "I see now I was wrong."

He'd been up since five, and had to be up at five the next morning. His night had been seriously fucked up, and all he wanted was to go to bed. "Why are you here?"

"I haven't heard from you in months. I've tried to call you numerous times and no one answers. You haven't talked to your father or your brothers, either."

A wry smile snuck over his face. "I talk to my brother every day."

She snapped waspishly, "I didn't mean Cole."

Teague stared levelly at her. He'd made it a habit to never talk to anyone in his family unless he had a good, solid reason. "Is there something going on with Shea or Callum that I should know about?"

Her eyes narrowing slightly, she said, "What Shea and Callum are doing is irrelevant. I want to know what you're doing." Seeming like an afterthought, she added, "And what Cole's doing."

Absolutely sure she didn't want to hear about it, he said, "I have no idea what Cole's doing. I'm going to bed. If you'd like to continue this conversation tomorrow, I'd be happy to. I have to be at Bailey's at five-thirty, then I'm usually back here by ten." He started towards the stairs. "Feel free to stay, sleep on the couch if you want. All the beds are taken. If you leave, don't lock the door. Cole never remembers his keys."

He left her gaping after him and went to his room. He was relieved when he heard her car start and the crunch of gravel as she left.

Chapter 46

Teague took a swig of orange juice straight from the jug and thought about the fact that his mother had been in the house alone the night before. He had a few minutes to spare before he headed to Bailey's and he used it to look around for drugs and paraphernalia.

He didn't see anything incriminating in the living room or kitchen. Back upstairs, he checked that his bowl was exactly where he'd left it; under his shirts in his drawer. The whole thing pissed him off. His mother being there made him feel like child, sneaking around hiding things.

At the shop, he greeted Bailey and went to work. She didn't even turn around. He didn't expect more. But when they both turned at the same time and stopped face to face, Teague couldn't help noticing that she looked horrible. "Bailey, are you okay?" She was pale and there were dark circles under her bloodshot eyes.

She smiled thinly, "Yeah."

Not fooled, he asked, "How was your night?"

Her voice unnaturally quiet, she said, "Fine. How was yours?"

He ached to tell her about his mother showing up. Instead, he said, "Great."

She looked down at the floor and whispered, "Glad to hear it."

I miss her. He turned back to his dough wishing they could talk and knowing they couldn't.

When he brought the first batch of bagels out she was standing at the back counter staring at a coffee cup, not moving, and there was a line of people whispering and pointing at her. He quietly went to her. "Bailey."

She jumped. "Oh, hi."

It didn't matter what had happened between them, she needed him. "Go up to bed. The customers are talking about you."

"I've gotta work."

"I've got it. Just go."

She looked at the people standing in line, then back at Teague. She nodded. "Okay. Just for half an hour, then I'll be back."

He took the cup she was holding. "Take as long as you need." He filled the cup and went to take care of the people waiting at the counter.

Teague liked working at Bailey's. He knew most of the customers, at least by sight. It was cool to have them come in and say, "Hey, Teague. How's things?" or whatever. And he loved that customers were asking specifically for his bagels.

He got a nasty surprise, though, when his mother walked in. At the counter she folded her arms, tapped her manicured fingers, and in her cold clipped tone said, "Well, Teague. This is a surprise. Tell me, please, how exactly does one go from being a respected lawyer to serving coffee in some hick town in Vermont?"

Teague's mood had improved significantly over the course of the morning and he had no intention of letting her screw it up. "Can I get you a cup of coffee? The Kona is excellent."

She lifted her chin and made a 'humph' sound. "Since I'm here. Do you get a break or something? So you can explain this to me?"

He ignored her and turned to make the coffee. As he handed her the cup, he asked, "Can I get you anything else?"

"No."

A she reached for her wallet and he said, "It's on the house."

She took the cup and sat at a table.

When he had a minute, he sat with her. "Mom, what can I do for you?"

"When are you planning to return to your career as an attorney?"

Teague smiled a little. "I'm considering my options before moving forward." The door opened behind him. "And today, as you pointed out, I'm working here. Excuse me." He left her to stew and went back behind the counter.

As he filled orders, he smiled at his mother's sour expression. He'd spent a huge part of his childhood wondering how the hell Cole could so blatantly ignore their parents and all their rules. For the first time, he thought maybe he understood. It wasn't nearly as hard as he'd imagined, and it was somewhat entertaining to realize his mother was helpless to do anything about it. And to see her so totally frustrated.

When Cole and Shasta came in, Teague quietly said, "We've got company."

Cole glanced at his mother. "What the hell is she doing here?"

"I don't fuckin' know."

"Let's dose her coffee."

Teague grinned. "Fuck yeah." The thought of his mother wandering around listening to the trees talk was awfully tempting.

More seriously, Cole said, "Mom doesn't just show up in Vermont."

"She said she wants to know what we're up to."

Cole snorted. "No she doesn't. If we told her she'd have a heart attack."

"No doubt. She was at the house last night when I got home. Sitting on the couch."

"Fuuuuck."

"Yeah, right. Anyway, you want coffee?"

"Can I have a large organic blend. Did you make bagels?"

Teague got their order and Cole asked Shasta, "You ready to meet my mom?"

Teague asked, "You sure you want to do that to her?"

"I don't have much choice, do I." They walked to the table Priscilla was sitting at.

Teague watched Cole greet his mother, then introduce Shasta. He felt terrible for her; Priscilla didn't bother to hide the look of disgust as she shook Shasta's hand. Worse, he knew that not that long ago he'd have had the same reaction. Now, though, he considered Shasta a friend. Someone who made his brother happy and who he actually really liked.

Priscilla's voice started to rise uncharacteristically. "You mean to tell me he gave up his career to come work at some dirty, stinking coffee shop, serving a bunch of useless hippies *for free?*"

People turned to look at her. Teague walked over to the table and calmly said, "Mom, I'd appreciate it if you'd keep your voice down and your opinions to yourself. We don't tolerate that kind of attitude here. If you can't stay quiet, you'll need to leave."

"Mom, it's been real." Cole turned and sauntered away.

Shasta mumbled, "It was nice to meet you," before she followed Cole to the other side of the room.

Teague chose not to say anything more. Back behind the counter he smiled and talked to customers. He took orders and made coffee. He kept an eye on his mother.

When Matt came in, Teague greeted him. "Hey, Matt, how's things?"

"Good, you?"

"Not too bad."

"Right on. Are you coming out tonight? We're doing a full moon party."

"For sure. What time?" They talked for a few minutes, Teague got Matt's coffee, and he left.

A little later Teague was wiping down tables when Ellen and Aria came it. Aria ran to him, squealing, "Teeaaague!!!"

He scooped her up and hugged her. "Hey, girl!" He spun her around and rubbed noses before he moved her to his hip.

Her voice rang through the coffee shop. "I missed you."

He grinned, his heart feeling like it was going to explode. "I missed you too."

"Nannie wants you to come to dinner."

Teague glanced at Ellen. She was standing by the counter, smiling slightly. He looked back to Aria, wishing so badly that he could accept the invitation. "I'll have to see what's up, okay?"

"Okay."

He put Aria down and she scampered back to her grandmother. Teague followed. "Hi, Ellen." He kissed her cheek.

"Hi, Teague. How are you?"

"Good, thank you."

Looking around, Aria asked, "Teague, where's Auntie Bailey?"

"She didn't sleep good last night, so she was real tired today. She went back to bed."

"Aww. I wanted to see her."

"I'm sorry. I'll tell her you were here." He looked back to Ellen. "Do you need something, or were you just here to see Bailey?"

"A dozen bagels, if you've got them."

"Let me see." He checked the bagel bin. "I only have four. Do you need them right now?"

"No, I was going to freeze them for the week."

"I can make a batch and bring them over to you, as soon as Katelyn comes in."

Ellen shook her head. "You don't have to go through all that trouble.

I can come back later this week."

"It's no trouble. I'm going out to Matt and Lucy's tonight, I can swing by on my way."

"That would be fine." She asked Aria, "Do you want a muffin?"

"Yes please, Nannie."

Teague got her a muffin and a cup of chocolate milk. "Why don't you take this and sit with Cole." She took the plate and cup and skipped to the couch.

Ellen watched her until she was seated, then she looked back to Teague. "She misses you."

"I miss her too." He glanced at the little girl, happily eating her muffin while Cole did a magic trick with a coin for her. "But with things the way they are, it just doesn't work."

Ellen sighed. "I know." She glanced back at Aria. "I'd be more than happy to have you over for dinner."

"You don't need to go out of your way." He didn't want to complicate things more than they already were. "Can I get you anything right now?"

"A cup of coffee would be great. The organic one from the rain forest, if you've got it." She stopped him as he started to turn away. "Teague? Is Bailey okay?"

He didn't know how to answer that. "Things are different now." He poured Ellen's coffee.

She took the cup and called to Aria, "Aria, come on."

Aria hugged Cole before skipping to Ellen. "Oh, Nannie, wait." She ran to Teague. He picked her up and gave her a bear hug. "I'll see you a little later, girl."

She kissed his cheek and he put her down.

Teague went back to wiping down tables. When he got to Priscilla's table, he asked, "Mom? Can I get you a refill?"

Her expression tight, she said, "What you can get me is my son back."

Teague dropped into the chair opposite her. "You know what, Mom? For the first time in my life, I'm happy." He smiled slightly, realizing he was telling her the absolute truth. "I have no idea what I'm going to do. Maybe take the Bar here, go into practice on my own. Or maybe not. But no matter what I decide, it'll be my decision, and I'll make it when I'm ready."

Priscilla's nostrils flared for a moment, the only indication that she was angry. "Fine. If you're going to stay here, you're going to have to start paying rent."

Raising an eyebrow, Teague simply said, "Let me know how much and where to send the check."

Priscilla stood, spun on her heel, and stalked out. Relieved that she was leaving, Teague watched her go.

At noon Katelyn came in. She and Teague talked for a while about coffee shop business. Then he went in back to make Ellen's bagels. He'd just started kneading the dough when Kayla came in.

"Hey, Teague."

He looked over his shoulder. "Hey, Kayla."

She leaned against the counter. "Are you going to Matt and Lucy's tonight?"

"Yeah, are you?"

"Yeah."

"Do you want to go with me?"

He draped a towel over the bowl to let the dough rise, then turned around. "Kayla, I think you're really cool, and smart, and I like hanging out with you. But I told you last night, I don't want to lead you on. I can't be more than friends."

"I know. It's nice to have a friend, though. Don't you think?"

The smile she was giving him lacked the seductive quality of those from the night before. The idea of having someone with him definitely had appeal. "Yeah, I do."

* * *

Bailey woke slowly. She felt someone next to her and for a moment thought it was Teague. *Not Teague. He won't even talk to you anymore.*

Teague had taken Kayla home the night before. She'd seen them leave together. *She's always had a thing for him. But why'd he have to take her up on it?* Bailey's heart ached. *Because you left him. That's why.*

Jesse rolled over and put his arm around her. She opened her eyes. He smiled at her. "Hey."

"Hey."

He brushed her hair back from her face, slid his hand down her arm to her waist and pulled her closer. He kissed her gently. "I miss waking up with you."

"I have to get up early."

"I know. But I miss the days you didn't."

She closed her eyes and moved to him. *Take what you can while you have it. He's with Kayla anyway.* She needed to be held, to be wanted, so badly. Jesse caressed her shoulder. She'd almost forgotten what it was like to be in his arms. "Jesse, I missed you. Why'd you stay away for so long?"

"I don't know, Bailey. I wish I hadn't." He kissed her, gently at first then with more feeling. "Are you mad?"

She sighed. "Yeah, a little."

He kissed her again. "Are you still?"

She could never stay mad at him. "No. But it's hard that you aren't here very much."

"Can I make it up to you?"

Bailey hesitated. Suddenly, the idea of being with Jesse freaked her out. *You can't tell him that.* She lied, "I've got my period."

Jesse smiled softly. "Well, at least we know you're not pregnant."

She put her head on his chest, more to hide her face than anything else. If she was, it'd be Teague's. And she couldn't help thinking she wouldn't be upset about that.

* * *

Bailey had to close the shop, so she and Jesse were late getting to Matt and Lucy's. When they finally got there, she was shocked to see Teague sitting at the fire next to Kayla.

She felt betrayed. Completely, utterly, betrayed.

She sat next to Jesse and tried to tell herself she had no right to feel like that. She and Teague had had a thing, and now Jesse was back so that was over. That's the way it had always been.

But as she sat there, surrounded by her friends, carefully not looking at Kayla's smiling face as she talked to Teague and Sage, Bailey knew that was a lie.

When Teague got up to get a beer she followed. "Hey."

He glanced at her. "Hey."

"What's up?"

He took a swig of his beer. "Nice night for a bon fire."

"Yeah."

He walked away, back to Kayla. She felt like crying. She wanted to be the one sitting with Teague, to have him laughing and talking to her.

You're with Jesse. That's what you've always wanted.

She stood there for a long time, watching her friends. There was so much going on, so many people together and happy. She thought she should have been happy too. But all it took to make her miserable was one look at Teague.

How had she gotten so fucked up?

She went back to Jesse. She rolled a joint, grateful that he always had kind. She let her mind wander, let herself forget everything for a little while other than the feel of the fire and the beat of the drums. She made sure she didn't let that feeling end all night.

Chapter 47

Teague finished shaping bagels and draped a towel over them. While he waited for them to rise, he washed the dishes he'd dirtied. He put a huge pot of water on to boil the bagels in, then went to get himself a coffee.

Bailey smiled weakly. "Hey."

"Hey." They stared at each other, neither knowing what to say.

"So, um…"

The space between he and Bailey seemed to have grown even more. "Can I have a coffee, please?"

"Oh. Yeah, sorry." She turned away.

Teague took his mug, the one Bailey had had made for him, and went back to the kitchen. He remembered when she'd made it, and the day she'd given it to him. He wished fervently that he could go back to that time.

Once the bagels were done, he thought about leaving. There was no reason to stay there. Even if Bailey came and sat with him, they wouldn't talk. But as he put the last pan away, he heard his name as Aria ran to him. He scooped her up and swung her around. "Hey, girl."

She rubbed noses. "Teague, are you staying here today?"

"Yup. I sure am."

"Can we go to the playground?"

Grinning, he said, "Yes, we can. Right now." He squatted, "Hop on, I'll give you a piggy back ride."

She climbed onto his back. "Yeah!!!"

He 'trotted' up to the counter. "Bailey, Aria and I are going to the playground. I'll take care of her lunch and have her back in time for dinner." He didn't wait for permission. He wasn't going to let anything stand between him and Aria.

On the way to the playground, she told Teague all about what she'd been doing since the last time he'd seen her. He soaked it in, relishing being let into her world.

As soon as they got out of the car, she said, "Teague, Mallory's here!" She twirled through the gate and ran off.

Teague spotted Katelyn sitting on a bench and went to sit with her. "Hi, Katelyn."

She smiled, "Hi, Teague."

"It's a beautiful day for the park."

"It is." She eyed him. "What have you been up to?"

"Nothing. What about you?"

"The usual." She turned to him. "I'm really glad to see you here with Aria." He raised an eyebrow and she continued, "She misses you. She asks Bailey every day if you're coming."

Guilt stabbed through him. "I miss her, too. It's not my choice not to be there."

"Yes, it is. Bailey would never keep you from seeing her."

"It's more complicated than that."

Katelyn sighed. "It shouldn't be."

Frustrated with everything, Teague retorted, "Do you really think this was how I wanted it?"

She didn't return his snippy tone. Instead, calmly, she said, "No, I don't. And believe it or not, I don't think this is how Bailey wants it either."

"She's sure got a fucked up way of showing it."

Katelyn put her hand on Teague's arm. "Teague, Bailey's..."

She sounded tired and Teague felt more guilt. "I'm sorry, I didn't mean to snap at you."

Giving him a small, tight-lipped smile, she said, "I know." She turned her attention back to Mallory and Aria who were engaged in some sort of elaborate pretend game. "I love that Mallory and Aria have each other. It reminds me of when Bailey and I were small."

Surprised, Teague asked, "How long have you known Bailey?"

"My whole life. Our parents were friends even before we were born."

"She never told me that."

"Bailey never tells anyone much of anything." Katelyn mused, "Even when we were little, she was quiet. You could almost forget she was in the room. Especially with Peyton around."

This whole idea, that Katelyn had known Bailey for her entire life, was so new Teague hadn't thought as far as to realize she'd have known Bailey's sister, too. "What was Peyton like?"

Katelyn watched Mallory and Aria as they chased each other around the playground. "She was," she smiled sadly, "a ball of energy. Always talking, planning, always doing something. And she had this smile, it dazzled." She looked at Teague. "When she gave you one of those smiles, you couldn't tell her no. She knew it, too, and she used it. She was going to be a famous singer. If things had been different, she'd have made it. She had that spark, ya know? I've always thought that was part of why Bailey left. It was impossible to outshine Peyton."

Thinking about the way Bailey radiated calm, how she was so completely comfortable with herself, Teague said, "Bailey doesn't need to outshine anyone."

Katelyn shook her head. "You don't get it. Peyton was older, she did everything first, and she was so good. She got straight A's, she was a cheerleader, all the boys fawned over her. There was no way to compete with her." She shrugged, "Like when Bailey came in first in the Regional Arts competition. She was so excited to tell her parents, but she never got the chance. That same day Peyton had gotten an acceptance letter from Juilliard. She hadn't just been accepted, either. She'd won an academic scholarship. It was all anyone talked about."

Teague was surprised. "I can't see Ellen not listening to Bailey."

"I don't think it was like that. It was that Bailey didn't feel like her news was as impressive as Peyton's. Even when she was accepted into Paier, she felt less than Peyton because she didn't get a scholarship, too."

Teague was stunned. Because of Callum, he was well aware that Paier was one of the most prestigious art schools in the country. "I didn't think she went to college."

"She didn't. She..." Stopping short, Katelyn said, "You should probably talk to her about this."

He snorted. "Yeah."

Keeping her gaze focused on the girls, Katelyn said, "Teague, I know it's easy to be angry with her for being with Jesse."

"Nope. Bailey's free to be with whomever she chooses."

She gently chided him. "Teague, give her time."

Bitterly, he said, "She's had time. I've been here since January. You think eight months isn't enough?"

"Not for Bailey. She's been with Jesse for years."

Teague shook his head. "She made her choice."

Katelyn turned to Teague, pivoted her whole body, so he really paid attention to her. "Teague, look, I'm not going to tell you what to do."

He grunted. "Yeah, you are."

She smiled slightly. "Okay, yeah, I am. Give her a chance. Let her figure out what she's doing."

"Then what? Just forget that she's with Jesse?"

"No. She went to Jesse, because she always has. But when she realizes she wants you, she'll leave him."

"And I'm supposed to just forgive her for walking away from me? Forget that she's sleeping with him?"

Katelyn gave him a dubious look. "Aren't you sleeping with Kayla?"

Uncomfortable, he said, "We're just friends."

Surprise flickered over her face. "Does Bailey know that?"

"Does it matter?"

"It shouldn't. Bailey's always been very… I guess open would be a good word. It's pretty common with family in general." She searched his face for a moment before saying, "For her it's just sex. But with you—" she shrugged. "I don't know, Teague."

Chapter 48

Bailey was finishing cookies when Jesse sauntered into the kitchen much earlier than usual. He wrapped his arms around her waist and kissed her cheek. "Hey, babe, do you have a cigarette?"

She lifted a cookie off the pan and set it on the cooling rack, then put down the spatula. She closed her eyes and let the familiar feel of Jesse sink into her.

"Bail?"

Opening her eyes, she mumbled, "Jesse, I don't smoke."

"Can I get a couple of bucks then?"

Taking a deep breath, she said, "Yeah. Hold on." She moved away from him, went into the shop and got money from her cash register. When she came back to the kitchen she noticed that Jesse was standing in the middle of the room, waiting, and Teague was at the counter, doing whatever it was he did. She handed Jesse the bills. "Buy a couple packs."

Jesse went out the back door and Bailey stood there, watching him go. She looked towards Teague. He still kept his back to her, but she knew he'd heard everything.

She turned the radio up and finished moving the cookies to the rack.

After he'd finished the bagels, Teague sat and read a book. Bailey wondered what he was reading, and she thought maybe if she went and asked him about it they could talk. She brought fresh coffee back and topped off his mug. Then she stood there, hoping he'd acknowledge her. Without looking up he muttered, "Thanks," and continued reading.

When Aria came in, Bailey watched helplessly as she ran to Teague. She didn't blame her niece. Bailey had to work, she could only set up things for Aria to do, then check on her when she had a few minutes. Teague, on the other hand, could dedicate all his attention to her.

It still stung.

By the time Katelyn came in, Bailey wanted so badly to be alone. Having to pretend everything was great was too hard. She went to the back of the shop and held her hand out to her niece. "Aria, come on. Let's go have dinner."

"Can Teague come?" She gave her winning smile, the one that usually got her ice cream.

Bailey looked at Teague. He was putting the game they'd been playing away but paused at Aria's question. Their eyes met, and Bailey thought she saw hurt that mirrored her own.

Breaking their gaze, Teague said, "Aria, we talked about this, remember?"

"I know." She pouted. "You'll be here tomorrow?"

"Of course. And we'll practice Devil Sticks."

He held out his arms and she hugged him before taking Bailey's hand.

Upstairs, Bailey asked, "Aria, what do you want for dinner?"

"Something that's not complicated."

Bailey turned from the refrigerator and looked questioningly at Aria. "What's complicated?"

"I don't know. But I don't want it."

She closed the refrigerator door and squatted down, taking Aria's hands. "Sweetie, what are you taking about?" Aria looked nervous, so Bailey assured her, "It's okay. You can tell me whatever you want."

Still looking unsure, Aria said, "I asked Teague why he couldn't come to dinner with us anymore and he said cuz dinner's complicated." She fidgeted. "And when Nannie's tired she makes grilled cheese cuz it's not complicated, so I just thought, if you made something like that, he could come."

Bailey grabbed Aria and hugged her, fighting back tears. "Oh, baby. I wish it were that easy."

"You're squishing me."

"Sorry." She let Aria go. She sat on the floor and pulled Aria down into her lap. "It's not about what I cook, sweetie. It's about grown up stuff."

"Did you guys have a fight?"

Bailey sighed. "Not really. Maybe. I don't know." This was way too hard to explain.

"Tell him you're sorry and take turns doing what you each want."

"It's not like that."

Aria's face scrunched in confusion. "It should be. When me and Mallory got mad and yelled at each other, cuz I wanted to swing and she wanted to play dolls, Nannie said to say sorry and swing for a little while, then go play dolls. So we were both happy."

Bailey's heart ached. "If it was that easy, baby, I'd have done that already."

They had grilled cheese after all, then read books while they waited for Ellen. Once Aria was gone, Bailey was free to do what she wanted. She knew if she went back down to the shop there'd be family there, but she wasn't in the mood to hang out. Jesse had never come back that day, which was more of a relief than anything. But that also meant that Bailey was completely alone.

She opened her art closet and looked at half-finished paintings. She thought she really should finish them. There was one of Aria and Mallory, sitting on a river bank. That one was based on a photo her dad had taken of her and Peyton many years ago. She'd started a scenic of Greyhound Rock, but never bothered to finish. And there was the fairy princess painting she'd started for Aria's room.

Running her fingers over the paint, feeling the texture of the fairy wings, she wondered if Aria knew she slept in Peyton's old room. Bailey had never told her. Had never explained that Ellen's study used to be her bedroom, and the room across the hall was Peyton's.

Bailey picked up a sketchbook and a pencil and left the closet. She sat on the couch and began to draw. She rarely took time for this anymore and she missed it.

Her mind wandered back in time. It took three days to drive cross-country, and Ellen had already moved all of Aria's things to her house by the time Bailey got home. Her crib had been set up in Ellen's room, partly because Aria still needed constant care, and partly because Peyton's room had become a storage area so there was no place else to put a baby. Bailey had needed something to keep her mind occupied during those first weeks and cleaning out that room had provided distraction.

She hadn't opened any of the boxes or bags that had been piled in the room. She'd known, without looking, that she'd find things that would bring back memories. Bailey had already become adept at forgetting.

Painting over Peyton's pink walls, hiding anything that would remind her of her sister, had been exactly the right thing to do. Decorating a nursery, and taking care of an infant, had given her purpose, during the day at least.

At night, she lay with Jesse and couldn't stop her mind. She'd cried, what seemed to be endless tears, and he'd held her. He never said anything, but he was there.

Bailey wiped a tear from where it had dripped on the paper. Her sister's face, that smile everyone loved, was beginning to shine off the page as brightly as it had in life.

That smile. The Peyton glow. Bailey remembered it so well. She could see her sister, in the kitchen, morning light streaming through the windows, Peyton's voice ringing through the house as she sang arias.

Everyone was always talking about how Peyton was destined for fame. She had *presence*. When she walked into a room, everyone knew it.

Bailey had spent countless holidays at relatives' houses sitting in a corner with a book, listening to conversations. They were always about what Peyton was doing; winning singing competitions, the lead in the school play, prom queen. The things she did were always big.

Not like Bailey. She liked to sit in the woods and draw what she saw. She liked to pretend there were fairies, long after she was old enough to know it wasn't true. She liked to sit on the patio with her dad and watch the birds that came to feast at the feeders he'd built.

Her dad had always been the only person who understood Bailey. When she brought paintings home from school, her mom would exclaim that they were beautiful and hang them on the fridge. But her dad would look at them, ask Bailey what she'd painted, talk about the techniques she'd used and why she'd chosen certain colors or subjects.

Bailey dropped the sketchbook on the coffee table and stood up. Peyton's smile, her beautiful, perfect face looked up at her. She turned on her heel and practically ran from the room. Grabbing her purse, she flew through the door and down the stairs.

In her van she cranked the radio, but it didn't stop her thoughts.

Jesse was the first person who'd ever told her she was pretty. She could see him, his hair still short, too young to grow a beard, as he kissed her the first time. It hadn't taken long for them to move far past kissing.

It hadn't been much longer before his hair had started to grow out, either.

Peyton had harassed him about it. She'd harassed Bailey, too. If Bailey dressed better, did her hair and make-up, she'd be so much prettier.

But Jesse knew people who looked like he and Bailey did. And when Bailey was with them, she didn't feel plain and boring.

Bailey parked and got out of the van. She didn't go to bars, and she sure as hell didn't go alone, but she *needed* this. There was no one she could talk to, no one who would understand.

She took her first beer and sat at a table in the corner, hoping the mass of people out on a Saturday night would distract her. She nursed her drink and remembered.

Beers on the lot were a dollar, if they were domestic. It was two bucks for an import. But if Bailey wanted a Heineken, she could get one for a buck. All she had to do was smile and ask the brother selling them if he'd give her a deal. That was the thing with being on the lot. Her smile wasn't lost in Peyton's shadow.

She'd noticed it at her very first show. There were a million people, and they were all smiling. But their smiles were happy. Not super model glamorous. They didn't outshine anyone, they just were. They dressed however they wanted. And no one ever told Bailey she needed to do her hair if she wanted to be pretty.

As she started on her second beer, she remembered this guy at Taco Bell. It seemed like so long ago, though it couldn't have been more than a couple years earlier. He'd looked into Bailey's eyes, long and hard, then smiled and said, "You've got the most beautiful kaleidoscope eyes."

She'd stood there and watched him walk away, smiling. Some

complete stranger had just told her she had beautiful eyes. *Take that,
Peyton.*

* * *

Cole shook Teague hard. "Bro, *get the fuck up.*"

"What time is it?" He squinted against the light Cole had turned
on.

"I don't fucking know. Two? Bailey's drunk and she needs you to
get her."

"*What?*"

Sounding exasperated, he said, "Dude, go talk to the guy on the
phone."

Teague rubbed sleep from his eyes as he yanked jeans on and
headed downstairs. He ignored the people in the living room. Since
they'd been home from summer tour he'd gotten used to the constant
presence of Cole's friends. In the kitchen he picked up the phone
and asked, "Hello?"

"Teague?" a man's voice asked.

"Yeah?"

"You know a woman named Bailey?"

"Yeah."

"She said to call you and you'd come pick her up. She's had too
much to drink and I can't let her drive."

Teague pulled his fingers through his hair unconsciously. "Where
is she?"

The man gave Teague the name of a bar and directions from his
house. On auto-pilot he pulled on the shirt he'd worn the day before,
stuck his feet in his Birks, and grabbed his wallet and keys.

Walking into the empty bar, he saw Bailey sitting on a stool with a
beer in her hand. She looked at him, smiled drunkenly and slurred,

"Teeeeeague, you here to drink too?" She almost fell off the stool.

He'd seen her stoned, tripping, but never like this. "Jesus, Bailey. What did you do to yourself?"

The bartender came out of the back. "You here for her?"

"Yeah, thanks for calling. Does she owe you anything?"

"Nah, she's all set. You can leave her car here."

"Thanks." Teague turned back to Bailey. "Let's get you home." He wrapped his arm around her waist, anticipating her inability to walk.

Once Bailey was in the passenger's seat of his car, Teague buckled her seat belt and shut her door. As he got in the driver's seat he said, "Bailey, if you feel sick, you tell me and I'll stop the car. If you throw up in my car I'll never forgive you."

She mumbled back at him, "Shit, Teague, I'm Irish. I can hold my liquor."

He grunted. He wasn't so sure.

As he drove towards town, Bailey asked, "Where are you taking me?"

"Home."

"Your home?"

"No, your home."

She suddenly looked panicked. "No, I wanna go home with you."

Teague sighed. "Bailey, Jesse's probably worried sick about you."

She put her head back and it rolled a little against the seat. "Nah, he prolly doesn't even notice I'm not there."

Teague didn't respond.

"Pleeeeeaaaasssssseeee don't take me there."

"Whatever. I'll take you to my house." In one way he was glad, his house was closer and he was worried that she'd vomit on his leather seats. Not that he gave a shit about the fucking seats anymore, but he'd have to clean it up.

He was relieved when he pulled in the driveway and she hadn't been sick. He walked around to her door and helped her out. He briefly worried that he'd have to explain her presence to whoever was there, but the living room was dark and the only sound was snoring from whoever was sleeping on the couch.

Halfway up the stairs, she said, "I'm gonna puke."

Teague half carried, half dragged her to the bathroom. She just made it. He stood with her, holding her hair and rubbing her back, as she was violently sick.

When she was done, she sagged against him. He said, "Let's get you changed and into bed."

He dug out a new toothbrush from the back of the bathroom closet, helped her brush her teeth and wash her face, and then changed her out of her clothes into one of his t-shirts.

"Heeey, you saw meeee naked" she giggled.

"Yeah, and it was great." She was too drunk to pick up on his sarcasm.

He tucked her in, then sat on top of the covers next to her. She curled up in a ball facing him. "Teague?"

"Hmm?" He put his head back against the headboard and closed his eyes.

"What's wrong with me?"

"You're drunk off your ass, Bailey."

"No, what's wrong with *me*. Am I ugly? Am I not nice?"

"You're probably the nicest person I've ever met. And you're absolutely beautiful."

"D'ya mean that? 'Bout bein' beautiful?"

"Yes."

He could barely hear her now. "Do you love me?"

He opened his eyes again. This was one hell of a night. "Yes, Bailey. I love you."

"No one else does."

"Of course they do. Lots of people love you. Your mom and Aria, Katelyn and Liam. Rain." He purposely left out Jesse.

"Not like you do."

He squeezed his eyes shut. "No, not like I do."

"Teague?"

"Hmm?"

"Will you hold me? Like you did in Pittsburgh?"

He looked down at her, wondering why she'd chosen that particular night. "No."

"Why not?" She kept her eyes closed.

He brushed the hair off her face. Nothing that had happened had changed the way he felt about her. "Because you're not mine."

"I knew you'd leave me."

"I'm right here."

"But you won't hold me."

It was useless to argue. Even to point out that she'd been to one to leave him.

Barely loud enough to hear, she said "I love you anyway."

Teague sat for a while looking at her. She looked so peaceful. More like the Bailey he'd first met than the Bailey he'd seen for the last couple weeks.

He thought of the night she'd woken screaming. It felt like years ago. It was impossible to believe it had been just weeks earlier.

Caching a glimpse of the clock, he was surprised that it was quarter to five in the morning. He sat up, realizing he had to leave. Someone had to take care of Delilah and open the shop. Bailey was in no condition to do anything, and no one knew she was there except him.

He got up, changed into clean clothes, and left.

At the shop, he used Bailey's hide-a-key to let himself in. He went up to her apartment first. Someone, probably Jesse, was asleep on the couch. They didn't budge as Delilah sniffed him as he rubbed her head. After he took her out and got her breakfast, he went to make the muffins. He'd never made muffins but he'd seen Bailey do it. And he could follow a recipe.

Since it was Sunday he had an extra hour to get ready, and he needed it. Bailey could almost do this in her sleep but Teague needed to read the recipe and follow it carefully. He was relieved to see the first batch of muffins come out of the oven looking like Bailey's, and more relieved to find that they tasted almost as good.

He opened the shop on time. He served coffee, sold muffins, and made small talk with people he'd come to know. A lot of people asked where Bailey was. He didn't want to tell anyone she'd drunk herself under the table, so he just said she wasn't feeling well. It was the truth, basically.

At nine he called Katelyn. He'd been up since two-thirty and wasn't going to be able to stay awake much longer.

***

"Bailey. Bailey?"

She tried to ignore the noise.

Louder, "Bailey."

She groaned.

"Bailey." This time with authority.

Her head was pounding and she wanted Katelyn to shut up. She whispered, "What?" She rolled onto her back and tried to open her eyes. "Katelyn?" She didn't quite know why, but she didn't think Katelyn should be there. Then she realized she was in a strange bed. "What the hell?" She struggled to sit up but her head was screaming. She whispered, "Aspirin."

She could hear Katelyn in the bathroom. She brought a couple aspirin and a cup of water back. She took the pills and water from

Katelyn gratefully.

Gently, Katelyn said, "Go back to sleep, let that kick in. I'll go see about coffee." She left Bailey to her misery.

By the time Katelyn got back Bailey felt a little better. At least, until Katelyn started talking.

"This is an interesting turn of events. Miss Bailey Malloy sleeping in Teague Gallagher's bed and Jesse Levasseur home alone."

Bailey cringed and whispered "Katelyn, shhh, please."

Katelyn sat on the edge of the bed and handed her a styrofoam cup of coffee. "Teague doesn't have a coffee pot. I had to go to the gas station."

Bailey grimaced. "He has coffee with me every day."

"Is that the only thing he has with you?"

Not in the mood for anything other than being alone in a dark, quiet room, Bailey snapped, "What the hell kind of question is that?"

Instead of responding to that, Katelyn asked, "Bailey, how'd you end up in Teague's bed?"

Bailey put the cup down on the nightstand, leaned back against the headboard, and closed her eyes. "I couldn't drive last night."

"Why didn't you call Jesse?"

"He doesn't have a car."

"We both know he could have borrowed one."

Irritated at being interrogated, Bailey said, "I don't know. Maybe I forgot he was home."

Softly, Katelyn said, "I've been friends with you my whole life. You can't fool me."

Bailey squeezed tears back. "Katelyn, you're so lucky. Liam loves you, and you love him, and you both know it." She opened her eyes and looked at her friend. "Isn't that the way it's supposed to be?"

Katelyn moved to sit next to Bailey. "Sometimes it's not like that."

"It is for you."

"Because me and Liam work at it. When we have problems, we don't just ignore each other or drink ourselves stupid."

"Ya know, I've always been jealous of you guys."

Smiling crookedly, she said, "You're jealous that we screwed up and had a baby at sixteen, and all we do is struggle?"

Shaking her head, slowly so the world didn't spin, she said, "You have the most amazing relationship. You give Mallory the best home any kid could ever want."

A smile softening her expression, Katelyn said, "I'm pregnant." Quickly, she added, "On purpose this time."

Shocked, she said, "I didn't think you guys…" That was so rude, she stopped.

Katelyn shrugged. "We've been talking about this for a while. We were so young when we had Mallory. It's kind of exciting," she blushed a little, "to do it on purpose. But it's still scary."

Bailey sat up despite her pounding head and hugged her friend. "I'm so happy for you."

"Thank you."

Settling back against the headboard, Bailey said, "If you need anything, time off or help with anything, just ask."

They sipped coffee in companionable silence. After a while, Katelyn said, "Are you going to tell me why you're in Teague's bed?" She glanced at her friend. "And wearing his shirt?"

"No." Bailey looked at Katelyn and wished she could tell her. She wanted, so badly, to talk to someone. Instead, she asked, "Why are you here, anyway?"

"To take you to your car. And then I'm going to work at your coffee shop so Teague can go back to sleep."

"Oh my god! The shop! Delilah!" Bailey sat up and began looking frantically around the room for her clothes.

"Calm down. Teague took care of everything."

"Why'd he do that?"

"Because he's Teague."

Bailey was overwhelmed. That was so simple, and so true. And suddenly, she knew she'd screwed up so bad. "Katelyn, oh my god, I've made such a mess." She felt the sting of tears. "What am I gonna do?"

"You're going to get up, get dressed, get your car, and go home to sleep the rest of this off."

"About Teague. And Jesse."

Katelyn sighed, "First of all, you have to decide what you want."

"I can't have what I want."

"Why?"

Feeling completely hopeless, she whispered, "He's sleeping with Kayla."

Irritation coloring her voice, Katelyn said, "Do you really think that matters?" Bailey didn't respond, so she went on, "Tell him how you feel, Bailey. You both know it, everyone who's ever seen you two together knows it, but Jesus Christ, you have to say it." Matter-of-factly, she said, "And you have to tell Jesse."

Her voice barely audible, Bailey said, "I can't."

Katelyn shrugged, "Then you're going to lose Teague."

Panic erupted in the pit of Bailey's stomach, but she shook her head. "I can't."

"Can't tell Jesse? Or lose Teague?"

"Both."

For the first time, Katelyn looked truly sympathetic. "You've got to make a choice. Jesse won't care if you're seeing Teague on the side, but you know Teague isn't going to be okay with that. He's not Rain. He wants you all or none."

"How do you know he wants me at all?" Bailey hated that she couldn't hide the desperation in her voice. "After what I did."

"What'd you do?"

"You know."

Katelyn folded her arms and gave Bailey a look.

Bailey couldn't hold her gaze. Looking at the sheets piled in her lap, her voice strangled with unshed tears, she said, "I walked away from Teague." She looked up at Katelyn, pain searing her heart. "I let him be part of me, I wanted him to be. I—" Her voice cracked, "We—" It was ridiculous, that she couldn't say out loud that she and Teague had had sex. But she held that close, kept it in her heart. "Then I turned my back on him."

She lay down, hugged Teague's pillow, and cried. Katelyn sat with her, rubbed her back, until she was done.

Bailey looked up, "I let him take me, let it be just us."

Katelyn reprimanded her softly, "You know better than that."

"I know, but I didn't care. I didn't even count days. Never, have I ever done that." Fresh tears starting, she said, "It was like," she shook her head, "I don't know. I can't explain it. It was just... perfect."

Sighing, Katelyn said, "Bail, I get it." Her voice heavy with concern, she asked, "Are you pregnant?"

"No. I got my period the next day." Bailey struggled. She had to tell someone. It was driving her crazy not to. She sat up and swallowed before telling Katelyn, "I couldn't let Jesse." She choked back another sob. "At all."

Shaking her head, Katelyn said, "Bailey, you've gotta deal with this."

Chapter 49

Bailey forced herself awake. She lay shaking, drenched in sweat. It was that goddamn dream again. And again, it had been Teague dying in front of her.

She rolled over, away from Jesse.

She had to tell him.

He slipped an arm around her. "Baby, did you have a nightmare?"

"Sorry. I didn't mean to wake you."

"It's okay. Come here." He pulled her to him and held her tight. "I thought you didn't have them anymore."

"I don't, usually."

He brushed his hand over her hair. "It must be because of Brent. Just relax, I'm right here. I'm not gonna let anything happen." He caressed her back. "I love you, Bailey."

"Jesse—" How could she even think about making him leave?

He held her tighter. "Remember when we went to the Yuba River? We sat on the rocks, and the water was so clear."

She wanted to let herself drift, to relax into his embrace, lose herself in his words. Once upon a time, she'd have relished hearing about the Yuba River. She'd have let herself dream of going there again, with Jesse.

Now, being reminded of those days hurt. She'd never go there again, and she knew even if she did it wouldn't be with Jesse. "Jesse, it's okay. I'm fine."

He settled behind her. It didn't take long for him to fall back to sleep.

Bailey lay awake. All she could think about was that Teague had said he loved her. It hadn't been spontaneous, something said in the passion of the moment. Or something said out of habit. It'd been a response to Bailey's question.

Somehow, that made it more real.

* * *

Bailey couldn't keep her eyes off the door. Teague had left the second Katelyn got to the shop the day before, not giving Bailey a chance to talk to him. After some thought she'd tried calling him, but he didn't answer.

She'd stopped short of driving back to his house.

After a long, sleepless night she worried that he wouldn't come in. Then, he was there.

Relief flooded through her. Maybe she could fix this. Smiling, she greeted him. "Hey, Teague."

He paused, nodded, and went to work.

Bailey's throat closed as she choked back tears. The only sound was the radio, Bob Seeger singing about night moves.

* * *

Bailey was aware of Teague. He was there, but keeping his distance. When Jesse came down Bailey was reminded of why things were the way they were.

He came to the counter, carrying a frame pack. "Bail? Got a minute?"

She came around the counter, knowing that the pack meant he was leaving. The torrent of sadness, anger, and relief made it impossible for her to speak.

Jesse set the pack on the floor and pulled Bailey to him. He brushed her hair back over her shoulder and touched his lips gently to hers. "I gotta go. I'll be back soon. After Madison Square Garden they're going to Europe."

Bailey didn't say anything.

"Maybe I'll see you at a show?"

After a moment, she pulled away. She went behind the counter and came back with a thick envelope. "Here."

Jesse took the envelope and opened it. His face broke into a huge smile. "Bail, seriously?"

"Yeah. There's none for Columbus, because I knew I wasn't going to those, but there's four for all the other fall shows."

Jesse grabbed her, picked her up and swung her around, put her down and kissed her. Then, his smile faltered. "Four?"

She nodded.

"Don't you need one?"

"No." Her heart feeling like it was being squeezed out of existence, she said, "I'm not going."

His smile turning to puzzlement, Jesse said, "Um, I guess I won't see you, then."

Flatly, she said, "I guess not."

Jesse carefully put the envelope in his pack and put the whole thing on his back. He looked at Bailey for a lingering moment. Then he walked out.

The rest of the day went past in a blur. Bailey buried the pain and turmoil deep inside and forced herself to smile and chat with people. She reminded herself over and over that the whole reason she stayed with Jesse was because she knew he'd leave, and because of that their relationship never had to progress past where it was right then.

It wasn't until late at night, alone in her own bed, that she sobbed uncontrollably. Jesse didn't love her. She'd been hanging on to a memory, nothing more.

When she'd cried all she could, she got up.

Jesse was gone, for the last time. Even if he came back, she wouldn't let him in.

She stripped her bed and put the sheets in the wash. While the first load ran, she went through her dresser. All the jeans were hers; Jesse had taken all his. Most of the shirts were hers, too. She took the few that she considered Jesse's and bagged them. She'd pass them on to someone who needed them.

She noticed some of hers were missing. That was fine. A couple shirts was a good trade for finally moving on with her life.

Wanting to make sure all traces of Jesse were gone, she looked around her room. There was nothing of his. She knew the only things he owned were clothes and a sleeping bag. Living the way he did, he didn't need anything else.

She went out to the living room and looked around. There was nothing of Jesse's there, either. Barely even his memory. She could more easily see Aria and Teague. She remembered them reading on the couch, playing Guess Who after dinner, the time they'd made a "restaurant" and served her lasagna.

Opening the box she kept on top of the bookcase and looking at the contents, she thought it would be so easy to float away. A tear trickled, landed on the baggie. She couldn't take the easy way out. She'd brought this on herself, she deserved to suffer.

She shut the box.

* * *

After school let out, Aria danced into the shop. She hugged Bailey then continued to the couches. "Hi, Teague."

He scooped her up. "Hey, girl." He held her close, rubbed noses, and tried to ignore the ache in his chest that he knew was overpowering love for this little girl. He'd started to wonder what would happen if he ever had his own child. If he loved Aria this much, he'd probably die of love for his own.

He set her down and asked, "Do you have homework?"

"Nope. Not yet."

"Do you want to play Candy Land?"

"Sure." She got comfortable in a seat while Teague found the game and set it up. He noticed Aria looking at him, a worried look in her eyes. "Hey, girl. What's up?"

"Teague, Auntie Bailey said Jesse left."

He shuffled cards. "Yes, he did."

Nervously, she asked, "Are you leaving?"

"No. I'm not."

"You don't wanna go to shows?"

Setting the stack of cards on the game board, he said, "I do, but it's more important to me that I'm here with you."

Relief replaced the worry. "Okay, so I wanna be yellow." She gave him a wicked grin. "And I get to go first cuz I'm youngest. The rules say that." She picked the first card and moved the yellow person to the first green space.

Teague had spent enough time with Aria by now to know that she could change gears quickly. "You like rules, do you?" There was a hint of teasing in his voice.

"Yes. Don't you?"

"I do. That's part of why I became a lawyer."

Curiously, she asked, "What's a lawyer do?"

Drawing a card and moving his candy person to purple, Teague said, "They use laws to try to help people."

"What'd you mean?"

"Well, sometimes people do bad things, and it's the lawyer's job to make sure they get in trouble. Or sometimes, someone says someone did a bad thing, but they didn't, so a lawyer makes sure they don't get in trouble."

They played board games. They talked, the kinds of conversations he and Aria had. But throughout the afternoon, Teague continued to think about Aria's questions. Later that night, alone in his own bed, Teague was still thinking. He'd lied. He was a lawyer, but he hadn't done either of the things he'd said. He'd just used every piece of information he could to get the absolute most from the person his client was divorcing, or to make sure they got as little as possible out of his client.

He thought back to when Cole had been in jail. He hadn't deserved to be there. If he hadn't been Teague's brother, if their mother wasn't loaded, he'd still be there.

And that wasn't okay.

Chapter 50

Bailey stood at the counter. She didn't sing, even though the radio was on. She didn't talk, even though there were people there.

After a while, she pulled a sketchpad from under the counter. She flipped past lots of pages of crayon scribbles to an empty page. She picked up a pencil. Not one of the special ones she'd bought at the art supply store; just a regular #2 pencil.

She started to draw.

Her first page was a disaster. Flowers grew in the middle of the sheet with no rhyme or reason, then she absently drew boxes around them, colored in petals completely black, made a bunch of squiggly lines that didn't go with anything, and then for some reason she couldn't explain, put a great big dancing bear in the corner.

She flipped the page, hoping no one ever saw what she'd done.

The next page was marginally better. She tried to create something decent, giving it thought before starting. She ended up with a pretty acceptable fairy sitting on a daisy. It was technically very good, but it lacked life.

As it did so often now, her mind began to wander. She and Teague weren't speaking. It was so hard to have him there, but never be able to talk. It was worse than when he'd first started showing up every day, sitting at the same table, reading his paper. Then, he'd been a mystery. This yuppie guy who didn't belong there, but *was* there every day.

Now, she knew who he was. Not just that yuppie guy, but the person he was underneath. The curious, kind person who had been hiding under hair gel and attitude.

She looked at her current drawing; Teague at his usual table. She was glad she'd chosen pencil. The monochromatic tones made Teague's serene expression more pronounced. She smiled as she added a beard, changed his hair to curls. This was Teague now, and that was how she wanted him to be. She gently erased the title she'd put on the paper in his hands, The New York Times, and in its place drew the logo of Dupree's Diamond News.

"Why don't you talk to him?"

Bailey jumped, tried to cover her drawing. "Hi, Katelyn."

Katelyn took the sketchbook. "Bailey, this is beautiful."

Her face hot, she tried to brush it off. "I was just doodling."

Handing the book back, Katelyn quietly said, "It's been weeks. You guys need to talk."

Teague sat at a table with a book. Not a novel; even from across the shop Bailey could tell it was a textbook. She sighed. "He's busy. And he doesn't want to talk to me anyway."

"How do you know that?"

Bailey didn't have an answer. She closed the sketchbook and slid it back under the counter. "I heard the new keyboardist is good. Not Brent, but good."

Katelyn's eyes bore into Bailey's, as if she could see what was going on in Bailey's head. She nodded, though, and finally said, "Yeah. I heard that, too."

* * *

It had to be at least the tenth time Teague had read the same line.

School had never come easily to him, things had changed in the years since he'd last studied for exams, and many of the laws in Vermont were different. Although, it would have been different even if he'd been in Connecticut.

Criminal law was an entirely different thing than structuring divorces.

He rubbed his eyes, picked up his mug and took a swig. His coffee was cold. He brought his mug up to the counter.

Bailey stood with her back to him, making a fresh pot of the house blend. Teague knew that's what she was doing, because that pot was all the way to the left. Sometimes he was still astounded at the things he'd learned, the things he now took for granted.

He watched as she moved, deftly doing her job. Her hair hung straight down her back, and Teague remembered that when he'd first seen her she'd had a hair wrap. She'd never gotten another. Sometimes he missed it, and the sound of the silver bells she'd had back then. When she turned around he thought how much he loved to see her, and how he didn't notice anymore that she had a stud in her nose.

"What are you smiling at?" For a moment, the old Bailey was there. Then she was gone.

Teague shook his head. "Nothing. Sorry." He set his mug on the counter. "Can I get a coffee, please?"

Bailey poured it, handed it to him. "Teague..."

He waited, but she didn't say anything more. Neither did he. He took his mug and went back to study.

* * *

The morning rush was over. Bailey washed coffee pots and snuck glances at Teague, sitting at his table, drinking his coffee and studying.

When the phone rang they both jumped.

Bailey picked it up. "Bailey's."

An unfamiliar voice said, "This is Mrs. Stein, the nurse at Easton. I need you to come down. Aria's had an accident and you're going to need to bring her to the emergency room."

Bailey felt the blood drain from her face. "What happened?"

"She fell off a swing. She's going to need an x-ray of her arm."

"I'll be right there." Bailey hung up the phone, flashes of hot and cold making it impossible to think. She took a couple steps towards the back, then realized she couldn't just walk out.

Teague stood up. "What's wrong?"

"Aria's hurt. I have to go." She could hear the panic in her own voice.

"What do you need?"

"I don't know." Forcing herself to think, she said, "Call Katelyn, see if she or Diana can come in." She called Delilah and brought her upstairs.

* * *

Teague immediately began clearing out the few people who had been there. He looked for a piece of paper to make a sign. He found a pad under the counter and flipped through it, looking for a blank sheet.

Despite the worry firmly lodged in his stomach, he smiled as colorful drawings, childish and adorable, flipped past. Half way thought there was a page of really ugly flowers, a bear, and a bunch of dark lines. He stopped flipping, realizing instantly that this wasn't Aria's. He turned the page to a fairy on a flower. He recognized Bailey's work from the painting she'd been working on all those months ago. It was still sitting in her closet, half-finished. He saw it every time he and Aria painted.

There was one more page, and as he stared at it he felt his chest constrict. It wasn't that he liked looking at himself, he didn't really think too much about himself or how he looked. It was that this drawing was spectacular. He could feel the calm in the set of his jaw, see the contentedness in the easy way he held Dupree's Diamond News.

This was how Bailey saw him.

He heard her coming down the stairs at a run. He tore the next sheet of paper out and jammed the pad back where it'd come from. He called to her, "I'm coming." He scribbled on the paper, 'Closed for Family Emergency'. "Bail, I need tape."

She came around the counter and grabbed a roll of Scotch tape. "Here."

He took the tape, stuck the sign to the door, and led Bailey to the back. "Diana's going to stay with Mallory when she gets home. Katelyn's on her way in. I locked the front door, put a sign up until she gets here."

Numbly, Bailey nodded. She didn't argue as Teague led her to his car. He started the engine, but before he shifted into reverse he turned to her. "Bailey, if it was life or death they'd have called an ambulance first, and told you to go to the hospital."

Disbelievingly, she asked, "How do you know that?"

"I've got three brothers."

After a moment she nodded. "Okay."

Neither of them spoke other than for Bailey to give directions. At the school they checked in with the office and were directed to the nurse.

Aria was sitting on a bed, her arm in a makeshift sling, her cheeks tear streaked and her breath hitching occasionally. Bailey sat on the bed and draped her arm gently around Aria's shoulders. Teague stood next them and Aria put her good hand in his. He leaned over

412

and quietly said, "Hey, girl," as he kissed the top of her head.

The nurse came out of the back room. "Mr. and Mrs. Malloy?"

Bailey jumped up and held out her hand. "Yes, I'm Aria's aunt."

"I've called the hospital, they're expecting you. Please sign here." She pointed to a notebook on her desk. Bailey signed her name, Teague grabbed Aria's book bag, and they left.

Bailey sat in the back seat with Aria. As Teague pulled away from the school he said, "Bailey, you'll need to give me directions."

"Head back towards the shop. I'll tell you when to turn." She sat forward in the seat. "I'm so glad she was at school, and not at home. If she'd been at my mother's, it'd take forever to, turn right at the next light. My mom lives so far out, I swear I don't know how she does it. Although it's nice in the summer, to have the windows open and hear nothing but the peepers. But in an emergency, there's no one—"

"Bailey." He could still hear panic in her voice.

"Huh?"

They stopped at a light and Teague turned back to her. "Hey, it's okay." He reached for her hand, gave it a quick squeeze, and turned back to wait for the light.

* * *

Realizing she'd been babbling, Bailey sat back. She had to get her own panic under control, or she wouldn't be any use to Aria. She closed her eyes, forced her emotions to the back of her mind. This was what she was good at: shutting off what she didn't want to, or couldn't, deal with. The car started moving and she opened her eyes. "It's the next street on the left. The parking lot is right after the main entrance."

Once they were in a room, they had to wait. Aria leaned against Bailey and started to cry softly. Bailey rubbed her back. She needed something to use as a distraction. "Do you want to play I Spy?"

"Uh uh."

"The Rhyming Game?"

"No."

"Twenty Questions?"

"I want a story."

Bailey smiled a little. "Yeah, okay. Once there was a little girl named," she paused to think of a name, "Daisy."

Aria snickered. "That's Mallory's dog's name."

"Shhh, listen. Her name was Daisy, because she was as beautiful as a flower. She wore her long blonde hair in braids intertwined with her namesake."

"What's that mean?"

"It means she had flowers in her hair." Bailey ran a hand down Aria's hair. "I can braid flowers into your hair, if you want."

"Okay. Can you draw Daisy?"

Bailey looked around the exam room. "There's no paper."

Teague immediately offered, "I'll go find some. Be back in two seconds."

Bailey waited, thinking about the story so she'd be prepared when Teague came back. It took him less than a minute, and he had a stack of copy paper on a clipboard and a fat pen with four colors of ink. Bailey took them, wondering how he'd managed that.

"Daisy loved to walk alone in the woods. She knew all the trails on the mountainside behind her house." As she spoke, her voice soft, almost like she was talking to herself, she drew. In minutes the blank page became a wooded hillside, the figure of a girl with flowers in her hair following a winding trail.

Bailey wove a fantastic tale of talking animals, a daring quest, and a creative, resourceful girl. One drawing became two, then three. As she finished each page, she handed it to Teague. Aria was brought for an x-ray, then had to wait for the film to be developed and a doctor to look at it. Between doctors and nurses visiting, Bailey continued the story while Aria's arm was evaluated, set, and casted.

Once they were done, Aria's arm in a bright white plaster cast, they were allowed to go home. Teague carried Aria out to the car.

As he set her in the back seat, she said, "I'm hungry."

Bailey sat in back with her again. "How about McDonald's?"

Usually Aria would have cheered at the prospect of being allowed fast food. Instead, she leaned against Bailey. "'Kay."

* * *

Teague watched Aria, next to Bailey on the other side of the table, as she picked at her French fries. He hated to see her looking so unhappy. He picked up his soda. "I propose a toast."

Bailey raised a curious eyebrow, but picked up her cup anyway.

Aria, too, picked up her cup.

"To Aria's first cast. May she never have another." They moved their drinks together, being careful not to smush the paper cups.

Bailey said, "Here, here," and they all drank.

Aria asked, "Teague? Will you sign my cast?"

He went to the counter, talked to the cashier for a minute and came back with a Sharpie. "How about right...here." He pointed to a spot on the underside of the cast.

"No, I can't see it there." Aria looked at the cast, then pointed right at the middle. "Here. Nice and big."

Teague took his time. He turned the hook on the g into a smiley face.

Aria beamed at him. "Now you, Auntie Bailey. Where I can see it, okay?"

She painstakingly wrote her name, then decorated around it with hearts and flowers.

Teague returned the marker to the cashier and got Aria an ice cream.

Aria fell asleep on the ride home. Teague parked and whispered to Bailey, "I'll get her, you get the doors."

Even though she kept her eyes closed, Teague suspected Aria wasn't really asleep as he carried her upstairs. She snuggled into his arms and looked like she was trying a little too hard to keep her face slack. He didn't care. He'd have carried her whether she was asleep or not.

Upstairs he lay her on the bed and Bailey pulled her shoes and socks off. She kissed her on the forehead and she and Teague left her to sleep.

In the living room Delilah nosed Bailey. "Oh, sorry, honey." She looked up at Teague. "I have to take Delilah out." Then she added, "And I should really check on Katelyn." Looking distinctly uncomfortable, she asked, "Do you think you can stay here for a little longer? In case Aria wakes up before I'm done?"

"Yeah, of course." Bailey left with Delilah and Teague looked for something to watch on TV.

Chapter 51

Teague jerked awake when the bedroom door opened.

"Teague?" Aria's voice sounded so tiny.

"Hey, girl. What's wrong?"

"My arm hurts. It woke me up."

He rubbed his face, trying to wake up, too. "I'll get Auntie Bailey."

Her lip trembled. "No, I want you."

"Okay." He glanced around in the fading light, wondering how long he'd been asleep, and where Bailey was. "Sit here, I'll be right back." He tucked blankets around her and went to find the prescription the doctor had given them. He came back a minute later with a pill and a glass of water. He helped her swallow the pill then put the cup on the coffee table.

"Come on, let's get you back to bed."

"I don't want to go back to bed. I want to stay out here with you."

"Then you can sit here with me." He knew Ellen would be coming soon, it wouldn't hurt to let her stay there until then.

Snuggling next to him, Aria asked, "Did you ever break your arm?"

She looked up at him, her face so innocent. He adored her. Sometimes he wished she was his. *Not sometimes. You always wish she was yours.* "Yes, actually I did."

"Did you fall off a swing too?"

"No, I fell out of a tree."

417

"Why were you in a tree?"

"Did you know I have three brothers?" She shook her head no. He told her, "You know Cole, he's my little brother. But I also have two older brothers."

"You're lucky. I don't have any brothers or sisters, and I can't because my mother died when I was a baby and no one knows who my father is." She said it so matter-of-factly, Teague was surprised. But then, she'd never known anything different.

"I think you're pretty lucky. You have Nannie and Auntie Bailey who both love you so much. I have three brothers, and a mom and dad, but I never had half as much love as you do."

"How come?"

"That's complicated grown up stuff. Do you want to hear how I broke my arm?"

"Um hm."

"Well, I have two older brothers, Shea and Callum. Shea dared me to climb the big old tree in our back yard. I didn't want to, it was huge and I was scared. But he said if I didn't it meant that I was a baby. Cole was the baby, not me, so I climbed the tree. I got so high up I couldn't see the ground. I yelled down to Shea to ask if that was high enough, but he didn't answer. So I went higher. I yelled down again, but he still didn't answer. So I went higher. I wanted to make sure he knew I wasn't a baby. Then I could see the top of the tree, so I decided that was high enough. I started to go down. I don't know how far I got, but a branch broke and I fell."

"Did you cry?"

There was no way in hell he'd have cried in front of his brothers. They never would have let him live that down. But he remembered, vividly, Aria's tear streaked face in the nurses' office. He lied easily, "Heck yeah. It hurt super bad. And my mom was real mad. She got all four of us in the car and drove me to the hospital. She yelled the

418

whole way. She yelled at me because I'd been in the tree and at my brothers for daring me."

In awe, she asked "Did they call you a baby?"

He grinned. "No, they thought I was pretty cool after that."

"I was trying to go highest on the swings. Mary Parker thought she could go higher, but I knew I could. I did, too. But then I guess I went too high because I fell. I cried, too. And the boys were laughing."

Anger surged thought Teague's veins at the thought of Aria, broken and in pain, and kids laughing. He was glad he'd lied. "Don't you worry about them. Boys are stupid sometimes."

"It's not nice to say stupid."

"That's true, but sometimes it's also true that people do stupid things." He added, "Especially boys." He couldn't help thinking that he was in the midst of something pretty stupid himself, with Aria's aunt.

"Do you think the kids at school will think I'm cool cuz I broke my arm?"

"I bet they will. I'll get you a Sharpie and all the kids can sign your cast."

Her eyes fluttered, closed for a moment before she yawned and opened them again. "Can you tell me a story?"

"Real or made up?

"Made up."

"Okay." He got comfortable, let her snuggle him. "Once upon a time there were four brothers."

"I thought you were going to make it up."

"I am. Just listen. There were four brothers. The oldest brother was super smart, so smart he could answer any question anyone asked and he was the advisor to the king. The next brother was really good at making things and the king hired him to build his new castle. The youngest brother didn't work for the king, but he was happy with who he was and what he was doing. The problem was the third brother. He wasn't really smart, he couldn't build things, and he wasn't happy with who he was. So, one day he decided to go on a quest, to find what he was good at and what made him happy. He left his brothers and started through the woods. A little ways in, where he could still see the sun, he came upon a fairy. She was flitting from flower to flower, giving them each love so they could grow. He stopped to talk to her, but she flew away."

Soon he felt Aria relaxing, then her breathing even out. He stopped talking and started counting to himself. He thought he'd count to five hundred, then put her in bed.

Somewhere in the two hundreds he stopped counting.

* * *

Exhausted from the stress of the day, Bailey stumbled down the stairs. She was barely through the door when Katelyn anxiously asked, "What happened? Is she okay?"

"She fell off a swing and broke her arm. She's okay. Or, at least, she will be."

"Your mom called, freaking out because the school left her a message, but not what had happened. I didn't know, either. All Teague said was you had to go get her, you were taking her to the hospital, and could I come here."

Bailey went behind the counter to use the shop phone. It wasn't private, but upstairs she'd risk waking Aria and she didn't want to do that. It took her a few minutes, but she eventually assured her mom that Aria was okay. When she hung up, Katelyn was looking at her.

"You and Teague finally talked?"

"No. Why?"

Leaning against the counter and crossing her arms over her chest,

Katelyn said, "You just told your mom that he's upstairs with Aria."

Bailey poured herself a cup of coffee, an excuse not to answer right away. She turned back to Katelyn. "Teague is the next best thing to me or my mom."

Katelyn nodded slowly. "So him being here has nothing to do with you?"

"No."

Narrowing her eyes, Katelyn asked, "Why not?"

"Because he's here for Aria."

Katelyn pulled out the sketch pad Bailey kept under the counter. Silently she flipped to the drawing Bailey had done of Teague and slid it on the counter towards Bailey. Gently, she said, "Bailey, I swear to god, if you don't go talk to that man, I'm going to lock you both in a closet until you work this out."

Bailey's eyes flickered to the drawing. Her voice trembled slightly. "He doesn't want to talk to me, Katelyn. I've tried."

"You really want me to believe that he spends all that time here, comes in at five-thirty every morning and stays until you close, because he likes making bagels for free?"

Picking up the sketch pad, Bailey slid a finger over Teague's face. "I don't know how to make it better."

In her no-nonsense way, Katelyn said, "You start by apologizing. Then you tell him how you feel. Exactly how you feel. And you don't hide a thing."

More afraid than when she'd gotten the call from the nurse, Bailey asked, "But what if it doesn't work?"

"Then you learn to move on."

Although Katelyn was there, Bailey stayed in the shop and kept herself busy until Ellen got there. Her mom came rushing through the door, not looking like her usual calm self at all. "Where is she?"

"Upstairs with Teague." Joining her mom to go upstairs, Bailey said,

"She's got to stay home from school at least for at least a day or two."
She updated Ellen on everything as they climbed to her apartment.

When she opened the door Teague was sound asleep, sitting up on
the couch, with Aria in the crook of his arm, sleeping with her head
on his chest.

Bailey had the most insane thought. This could be her family.

Then Ellen was walking to them, and Teague was opening his eyes.
He moved, which woke Aria. "Nannie?" Her voice sounded young
and scared.

"Hi, sweetie." Ellen knelt in front of her. "How are you?"

"Can I stay here?"

Ellen glanced at Teague, then back at Bailey, before answering.
"I'm going to take you home, but Auntie Bailey's going to take you
tomorrow all day."

Turning to Teague, Aria asked, "Will you be here, too?"

"Of course. As long as you need me to be." He looked to Bailey,
making her wonder if his words had a double meaning.

Bailey got Aria's things together, kissed her niece goodbye, and
gently closed the door once she and Ellen were down the stairs. She
turned back to Teague.

Chapter 52

Bailey stared at Teague awkwardly.

He started for the door. "I'll be in tomorrow, and I'll stay as long as Aria needs me."

There was a time when he'd have been there to see Bailey. She knew that if she wanted that back she had to do something. Katelyn's words running through her mind, she said, "Teague, I miss you."

There was a flicker, too quick to pinpoint. He said, "I miss you, too."

That was better than I expected. She continued, "I'm sorry."

Bitterly, he said, "Yeah, me too." He went towards the door again.

She stopped him with a hand on his arm, determined to make this right. Her voice very soft, she asked, "Can we talk?"

It took a moment for him to answer, during which he stared at her, his expression unreadable. "Bailey, you had nine months to talk to me."

She pleaded, "I want to fix this."

"You can't."

"If you'll just let me explain."

He waited in silence.

She took a deep breath, "I love you. I am in love with you, Teague."

"You've sure got a fucked up way of showing it."

"I made a mistake."

Turning back to face her fully, he glared at her. "A mistake? Bouncing a check is a mistake. Running a stop sign is a mistake. What you did, Bailey, was so far beyond a mistake. You can't just pay a fine and go on like nothing happened. You can't just *fix* this."

Her own anger flaring at Teague's refusal to accept her attempt to make things right, she retorted, "So what you're saying is that we're not friends anymore?"

"Friends? Is that what we were? Because I thought we moved pretty fucking far past that." Cold and calculated, he narrowed his eyes. "Oh, wait. I forgot. As far as Bailey's concerned, friends are just the guys you sleep with when yours isn't around."

Bailey's eyes narrowed in response. "Yeah? That's the pot calling the kettle black."

"What the fuck is that supposed to mean?"

Hot rage fueled by hurt boiling over, Bailey screamed, *"You slept with Kayla!"*

Teague snapped, "So what if I did?"

"How could you do that?"

"Because *you chose Jesse!*" He started towards the door.

"You're such a fucking hypocrite! Who's leaving now?"

He stopped and turned back. He growled, "If I don't leave we'll both regret it."

Cheeks wet with tears, Bailey picked up one of the books that happened to be piled on the coffee table and yelled, "What are you gonna do, throw something through my window? Punch a couple holes in the wall? What the fuck? You think you're the only one who can throw a tantrum?" She flung the book as hard as she could. It hit the wall, leaving a hole in the sheet rock. Picking up another book, she threw that one, too. Hysterically, she shrieked, *"How's that? Is that enough damage?"* She sank to the floor and covered her face. Her shoulders shook as she cried.

He sat next to her, the anger gone from his voice. "Bailey?"

Her voice muffled by her hands and distorted by sobs, she said, "Go away."

He ignored her and instead pulled her to him. He brushed his hand over her hair and held her. At first she tried to move away, but after a minute she relaxed and leaned against him. Quietly, he said, "Bailey, we can't keep going like this."

Moving to lay on her side, her head in Teague's lap, she sighed. "I want things to go back to how they were."

He ran his hand over her shoulder, pushed her hair back from her neck, touched her cheek. "That can't happen."

"I know." She rolled to her back and looked up at him. "Can we fix this?"

His jaw clenched. He shook his head, an almost imperceptible movement. "I don't know."

Barely a whisper, she said, "I want to try."

His expression softened. "Can we get off the floor?"

"Yeah." She stood and held her hand out to him.

He hesitated, then took her hand. She pulled him up and they stood facing each other, her hand still in his. He moved his other hand to her face, brushed a tear, and very gently kissed her.

She closed her eyes. Even though the kiss had been just a brush of lips, she savored the feel of Teague; his fingers intertwined with hers, his body close enough that she could sense him there. She opened her eyes slowly to see him looking down at her. She reached up, ran her hand over the side of his face. Her heart felt like it was going to beat out of her chest as hope that they could get past this, fear that they wouldn't, and love so big it hurt, vied for a space inside her.

He led her to the couch. They sat, facing each other, and he took her hands. "Bailey—"

"Teague—"

They smiled as they spoke simultaneously. But their smiles were brief, the seriousness of their situation keeping their mood somber.

She swallowed. Her voice barely above a whisper, she said, "Teague, I never meant to hurt you."

"Yeah, but you did."

"I know."

"Why, Bailey? He's never here. He doesn't care. If he did, he wouldn't leave you like that."

Her shoulders fell and she looked down at their hands. As long as Teague stayed there, as long as his hands held hers, they could be okay. She had to keep him there, had to tell him anything he wanted to know, no matter how bad it hurt.

She raised her face to his. "Because when I needed him, he was here." He started to speak, but she didn't let him. "Teague, I know he doesn't love me. I've known for a long time. But it never mattered, because I don't love him either. I don't know when it started, probably the first time he left after Peyton died, but by the time you got here I knew I was letting him stay because it was easy." She paused, then said, "Jesse's been part of my life for a long, long time. There's things he understands, that I don't have to explain, because he was there when they happened."

A flicker of anger passed over his face. "If you told me I'd know, too."

"It's not that easy."

Teague pulled his hands from Bailey's. "Ya know, Bailey, I learned more about you in the last month from Katelyn and Kayla than I have from you in all the time I've been here." He got up; paced. "You tell me nothing. *Nothing*. The few things I know about you, I know either because someone else told me, or because I dragged it out of you."

She stood, hands clenched at her sides. "Oh, yeah, and you're

Mister Spill Everything?" As soon as it was out of her mouth she felt completely stupid. That was the dumbest thing she ever could have said.

"I never hid anything from you. I'll tell you whatever you want to know. Just ask."

"When did you decide to take the Bar here?"

"A couple weeks ago."

"Why didn't you tell me?"

"Because you seemed quite happy with Jesse and I didn't figure you'd care what I did."

Her lip trembled. "Well, I do."

Raising an eyebrow, he deadpanned, "I'm planning to take the Bar here."

"You're staying in Vermont?"

"Yeah, I am."

"When did you decide that?"

"The day my mother barged into your coffee shop and demanded to know what I was doing with my life."

"When did that happen?"

"The day you and Jesse came down the stairs holding hands, all smiles. The day I realized that you running to him wasn't just a knee jerk reaction."

"The day you started sleeping with Kayla."

Teague shook his head. "You are so fucked up. I don't know what to say to that."

She sat back on the couch, curled up in the corner. She could hear him as he went to the kitchen, heard the faucet turn on. When he came back to the living room he said, "Bailey, I'm leaving. Like I said before, I'll be here for Aria."

She mumbled, "See? I knew you'd leave."

"What the hell do you want from me?"

Frustrated, she yelled, "I don't know!"

"This is stupid. I've got a life to put back together. I've wasted enough time." Teague turned and headed for the door.

Panicked, Bailey begged, "Teague! Please, don't."

He demanded, "Don't what? Don't try to get close to you? Or don't leave? Don't ask about you and your life? Don't tell you how much you mean to me? Or don't give up and turn to someone else?" Annunciating each word, he spat, "I can't do any-fucking-thing right with you."

"It's me. It's all me. I'm sorry. I can't… I just…" She sobbed, "It's too hard to…"

"To what?"

"If I love you, if I let it happen, you'll leave, and I'll be alone."

"I've stayed with you all this time. I've been here every fucking day. What the fuck would make you think I'd leave now?"

"Because you said you were."

"Now. I'm leaving *now*, Bailey. But for Christ sake, I can't stay away. If I were really leaving I'd have done it already."

She got up and went to the bathroom. She blew her nose and washed her hands. When she came out, Teague was still standing in the same place. "You're still here."

He snorted. "Yeah, I am."

"Why?"

"I don't goddamn know."

Slowly, afraid to mess up yet again, Bailey moved towards him. He stayed where he was. When she was close enough, she took his hand and looked up at him. "Teague? Will you come sit?"

"Will you tell me why the fuck you're so attached to Jesse?"

Bailey swallowed, a tear escaped from the corner of her eye. She nodded, then spoke. "It's not that I'm attached to Jesse. It's that I'm scared to be attached to anyone else. Teague, I lost my dad and my sister two years apart. No one expects to lose their dad when they're seventeen." She tried to strangle a sob, but couldn't hold it. Her eyes began to water as she asked, "Do you know what it's like to watch someone die? To know what's happening and not be able to do a goddamn thing to save them?" The tears overflowed. "I loved my dad so much. I was seventeen, Teague. We were home alone, and I didn't know what to do."

He wrapped his arms around her, held her head to his chest as she cried. When her knees buckled he scooped her up and carried her to the couch. There, he kept her in his arms, brushed her hair, rubbed her back, until she finally quieted. He kissed the top of her head, but didn't say anything.

She appreciated him being there, and not pushing. "My mom took Peyton shopping. She was going to New York for some stupid interview, and she wanted a new outfit. Me and my dad were in the kitchen, making dinner. He...he had... had a heart attack. When my mom and Peyton came in I was sitting on the floor, his head in my lap. I knew he was dead, but I didn't know what to do, who to call, so I just sat there and cried. My mom freaked out, she grabbed him, started screaming his name. Peyton—" She had to stop.

"It's okay, Bailey. You don't have to."

She sat up and moved so she could see Teague. He brushed tears from his eyes, making her feel even worse than she already did. *Finish it. You have to.* "No, I want to. I want you to understand."

He wiped her tears, then his own again. "Okay."

"Peyton blamed me. She said if I had called an ambulance, if I'd known CPR, if I'd done something besides sit there like an idiot, he'd have lived. It wasn't true. I know, because," she gulped, then continued, "I saw him. He was standing there, then he was on the floor. It wasn't chest pain, he didn't grab his arm and say it hurt. It was a *massive* heart attack. He dropped like a stone. The doctors told my mom he'd have died even if he'd been in the ER when it happened. But Peyton didn't care.

"My mom was devastated. My sister was angry. I was alone. The only person I had was Jesse. He stayed with me, all the time. At night he'd leave, then he'd sneak back in and stay with me. Maybe my mom knew and just didn't care. Or maybe we really were good at hiding it. I don't think it matters either way. What does matter was that if he hadn't been there, I'd have been lost."

Teague took her hands and held them gently. "I'm really glad you had someone. Bailey, I wish it could have been me."

She smiled a little. "That's really sweet."

He spoke softly, "My beautiful butterfly Bailey."

She looked down, her lips twitching but not quite smiling. "No, I'm not. At the most I'm pretty." She looked back up. "Peyton was beautiful. If you'd seen her, I never would have stood a chance with you." Smiling wryly, she added, "And she'd have been all over you. The way you looked when you first came here? She loved guys like you."

Shaking his head, Teague said, "Bailey, there's no one but you. It's not about what you look like, what I look like. It's about who you are and how you make me feel."

Grinning, Bailey said, "That's only because you never did see her." Her smile faltering, she went on. "She was going to be famous, was already well on her way. If my dad hadn't died, you and everyone else in the world would have known her face. But you only get one shot at something like that, and they don't care why you're canceling. It didn't matter anyway. Once things settled down, she couldn't bring herself to leave. She wanted to be close to my dad, to where he'd lived." Bailey laughed harshly, "It's funny, when he was alive she didn't seem to care much. But once he was gone," she shrugged. "People react to death in strange ways."

"What about you?"

"Me?" Trying to avoid looking at him, she said, "I wanted to move on. He was gone, my life was destroyed, why bother staying here?"

Gently, Teague asked, "Is that why you went on tour, instead of going to college?"

Puzzled, Bailey asked, "College?"

He smiled apologetically. "Katelyn told me you were accepted into Paier."

"I guess. I mean, it was always my dad who encouraged me to follow my dreams, and," she sniffled, "I couldn't really bring myself to..." She sat straighter, smiled awkwardly, and said, "I don't regret that. I loved touring, I loved the life I lived. I never wanted to stop."

"You don't have to. You can still go to shows."

Shaking her head, she said, "I have obligations. The shop, Aria. And my mom's been through enough. When I'm not here she worries.

"When, um, when Peyton died, I..." She'd never told anyone this. Not even Jesse. "When Peyton died, I felt so awful. I felt like I should have been here. Like maybe if I had, things would have been different. Or at least I'd have spent more time with her." She laughed bitterly, then sarcastically rolled her eyes and said, "Because she and I willingly spent so much time together." Sadly, she added, "It's so stupid. She and I never understood each other. We were so different, she used to tell me I was adopted, since we obviously couldn't have come from the same parents. If she'd lived maybe she'd have forgiven me for my dad dying. And maybe we'd eventually have had a relationship. But she's gone, and I can never have my sister back." Her voice shook. "I'm sorry, Teague. I shouldn't dump all this on you."

"Yes, you should." He squeezed her hands.

She pulled her hand from his, absently wiped her eyes as she sniffled.

Teague pulled his t-shirt off and handed it to her.

"What's this for?"

"Your nose." She raised a questioning eyebrow and he told her, "Unless you want me to go get you tissues."

She didn't want him to leave, even for a second. She blew her nose on his shirt. "I'll wash that for you later."

He smiled, "It's fine. I can take care of it." He took her hands again. "I want to take care of you." He touched her face, gently ran his fingertips across her cheek.

She laid a hand on his, keeping it pressed against her face. "I can take care of myself."

"I know you can. But you shouldn't have to."

"Teague— "

He stopped her, laying a finger on her lips. "Bailey, I'm not leaving." He dropped his hand, picked hers up and held them between his. "I thought about it. You have no idea how many times I told myself that I should, that you had what you wanted and I was an idiot for staying here. It didn't matter. The idea of not being here, of not seeing you, of you not being part of my life, literally made me want to vomit."

Bailey got up. She walked to the other side of the room and wrapped her arms around herself, her back to Teague.

He followed, slipped his arms around her and held her close.

Refusing to look at him, she said, "That's exactly what I don't want."

"What?"

"I don't want that kind of attachment." She turned in his arms, forcing him to let go. She stepped back so he couldn't touch her. "If you love like that, it hurts so much when it's over."

"You can't live like that, Bailey. You can't just not feel because you're scared."

Obstinately, she demanded, "Why not? It's worked so far."

"No, it hasn't." He stepped forward, halving the distance between them. "You love Aria."

"Of course I do. But she's a child. She'll be here long after I'm gone."

"You know that's not a guarantee." When she didn't say anything he continued, "You love your mom." He moved closer, nearly touching her. "And, Bailey, I love you." He took her face in his hands and kissed her, pulled back and looking into her eyes. "I'm not willing to stop living now because some day I'm going to die. I'm not willing to not love you, because I know that someday I may lose you. I grew up without love. A life like that isn't worth living."

She wanted to let him hold her, comfort her, keep her. Instead, she pulled back. "You don't understand. I saw what my mom went through when my dad died. It was horrible. She didn't just lose her husband. She lost her life. I can't go through that."

"Do you think that if your mom could do it all again, she'd not fall in love with your dad? Do you think she'd give up having you and Peyton? Not have Aria? So she could spare herself pain?"

Through tears, Bailey shook her head. "No."

"No. Of course not. Everyone loses people. Everyone has pain. But you can't let that stop you from living."

Bailey crumpled. Teague caught her, held her as she sobbed. "Will you stay?"

Instead of answering, he picked her up and carried her to her bed. He carefully laid her down, pulled her shoes off, took his own shoes off, and lay next to her. She turned to him and put her head on his bare chest. He wrapped his arm around her and held her close.

She traced her fingers over his skin. "I really missed you. Teague, so much it's scary."

"I know."

She pushed herself up to see him. In the soft light spilling from the living room through the door he'd left open, she looked at him. Tears dripped, landed on his chest. She ignored them, smiling sweetly. "I love you."

"I love you, too." He kept an arm around her back, kept her close. "There's only one thing that can ever take me from you."

"Let's not think about that." She kissed him. Parting her lips, she gently touched his lips with her tongue. He responded, sucking her lip gently before tasting her in return.

Time seemed to stand still as they held each other. Bailey ran her hand down Teague's chest. She wanted to feel his skin against hers. She pulled her shirt off and straddled him. He moved her, brought her breast to his mouth.

She arched her back as his tongue pressed against the swell of her breast. He sucked and hot pleasure shot through her. She could feel him, hard between her legs. She ground against him, wished they weren't wearing anything.

Moving his hands down her body, he began to mess with the button of her jeans. He shifted, rolled her to her back, and looked down at her. As he slid a finger along the top of her jeans she rocked her hips. He undid the button, then slowly pulled the zipper.

She closed her eyes, felt his breath warm against her as he kissed her stomach. She shuddered as he kissed lower, pushing her jeans down. She raised her hips as he struggled to get her jeans off. He stood next to her and she unbuttoned his jeans. She sat up and kissed him, as he had done to her, and he inhaled sharply. She smiled and kissed lower.

She pulled at his jeans. Once he had them off, he lay next to her. She moved above him, lay with her bare skin against his, and kissed him. He ran his hands up her back, down to her bare ass, and she felt him throbbing with need beneath her. She wanted him in her.

She leaned over the edge of the bed, dug in the drawer in the bedside table, and handed him a condom. "I'm not on the pill."

Teague turned the packet over in his hands. He flicked his eyes back to her. "We didn't use one before."

434

Her face got hot. "We should have." She squirmed. "I'm always really careful."

He put the condom down and brought Bailey to lay next to him. He held her tight, kissed her long and well. When he broke the kiss, he whispered, "I don't want that. I want you."

"We were just lucky last time. I got my period the next day. But it's not safe."

He brushed her hair back from her face. "I want you. All of you, and everything that means."

Nerves tightened in her stomach. She'd thought about this, a lot. Actually admitting it out loud was a whole different thing. "I think that's something we need to really think about before we make that kind of decision."

"I've thought about it. Too many times to count. There's no doubt in my mind that I want to spend the rest of my life with you, and I want everything that includes." He paused, then told her, "But I've waited this long. I can wait until you're ready, too." He smiled a little, "If you want, we can wait until we're married."

Surprised, she asked, "You want to get married?"

Smiling a little, he said, "Isn't that what people do?"

"I guess maybe lawyers do. Hippies don't usually."

He shifted. "Wait, so are Matt and Lucy married?"

She shrugged. "I don't know. I never asked."

"What about Katelyn and Liam?"

"I don't think so."

Teague laced his hands behind his head. "Fuck. I guess that pretty much ruins my plans."

"What plans?"

"To open a practice here. I mean, if no one gets married, no one gets divorced, either."

"That's very practical, Teague."

"I guess I'll have to study up on criminal law instead. There may not be a need for divorce lawyers, but it seems there is a need for defense attorneys."

She put her head on his chest. "Are you serious?"

"Yeah. Do you have any idea how few choices I had when I was trying to find someone to defend Cole?"

"I meant about us. About having a family."

He traced her shoulder. "Yeah, I am. Being with you and Aria, seeing how you and your mom are, it's amazing to me. I never had that. I can't tell you how many times I've wished..." He kissed the top of her head. "All I want is to be here with you, and with Aria. Every second of every day. If there was a way I could... I love Aria, Bail. And I love you."

She slid her leg over him, trailed her fingers down his side. Visions of her and Teague, a family of their own, danced through her mind. She moved, lay on him, looked into his dark eyes. She wondered if their children would have his eyes.

She kissed him, felt him harden between her legs and press against her. She rocked her hips, the need growing deep in her. Teague would stay with her. She knew, in her very bones, that he would.

Reaching down, she pushed him against her. He whispered, "Bailey..."

She covered his mouth with hers, slipped her tongue to meet his. She wanted to be with him in every way possible. As she pushed him into her, his sigh was lost in their kiss. She started to move, slowly, concentrating on the feel of him.

His fingers found her hips, dug into them as he moved against her.

She wrapped her arms around him, held him close, and buried her face against his neck. She inhaled the scent that was Teague and whispered, "I love you."

He wrapped his arms around her back and squeezed her close. She

436

pushed herself up, kept her eyes locked on his, and began to move faster. She could feel him, every time he slid into her, pushing deeper, straining against her.

He grabbed her hips and pulled her onto him. He watched her face, shifted to go deeper, saw the flicker of pleasure, felt it in the way she tightened around him, the sudden heat, and the slick wetness that coated him. He knew he was going to come.

He tried to stop it, to hold out for her. Then, she moaned, and he lost control. He slammed into her, as hard as he could, needing to touch her deep inside, needing to feel her around every inch of himself. He felt his cum as it shot up through him and into her, felt as he pushed into the wetness again and again, and there was nothing in the world except her around him, squeezing, pushing, her cries echoing his.

Bailey felt the change, knew Teague was there. He arched against her, pushing into her deeper than she'd ever felt, and still she wanted more. Bearing down on him, she took him. His throbbing filled her as she clenched around him, harder and harder, until suddenly she was releasing. Over and over, she pushed him into herself, every thought in her mind blown away by the sheer power of the pleasure Teague gave her.

She collapsed, quivering, on him. Her insides clenched again, and Teague throbbed in response. Trying to calm her jagged breathing, she gulped air. It didn't help, instead it made her move, which made Teague move, which made her clench again, which made him throb again. She didn't care, it felt so good she wanted it to go on forever. She slid him out, just a little, then pushed back onto him.

He wrapped his arms around her, his heart beating way too fast. He needed her. Needed her to stay with him. So badly it was scary. He silently prayed she'd never leave him.

* * *

The sudden draft of Bailey moving woke Teague. He mumbled, "Where are you going?"

"I have to take care of Delilah." She pulled her shirt back on, then stood to find her jeans.

"That sucks."

She leaned down and kissed him. "Just wait until we have a baby. At least Delilah waits until I'm ready."

Teague rolled to his side and propped himself up on an elbow. "Do you think we did that?"

Bailey sat back on the edge of the bed and ran her fingers through his hair. "I don't know. Are you having second thoughts?"

He pulled her back into bed. "No." Kissing her, taking his time and making sure she was well kissed. Against her lips, he said, "No, Bailey. I have no second thoughts with you." Then he grinned. "Just thoughts about seconds. And thirds." He reached under her shirt and caressed her breast.

As much as she loved what he was doing, she had responsibilities. "You're gonna have to wait on that." She left him to take care of the dog.

While he lay in her bed, waiting for her to come back, he thought about everything that had happened that night. It was completely crazy. What they'd been through, what they'd done, all of it.

He realized he was going to have to introduce her to his mother. Then he grinned. He may be introducing her to his mother as the mother of his child.

That was the most extraordinary thought.

Epilogue

Bailey sang along to "China Rider" as she wiped down the tables. She told Teague, "Sometimes I still miss having riders."

"I'm sure Cole would be happy to catch a ride to Giant's Stadium with us." He left the papers he was working on scattered at his usual table and took her in his arms.

"Your brother is always welcome." She tipped her chin down, "Although, to be honest, when we're alone I definitely don't miss people opening doors at inopportune moments."

"We're never alone anymore."

She grinned. "Nope. *And* it doesn't matter anyway because you promised Aria we'd take her."

"How could I not? I mean, if we left her behind who'd make sure I brought my toothbrush?"

The bell over the front door jingled. Bailey turned to greet customers. The words died on her lips.

Jesse stood just inside. He looked from Bailey to Teague, then said, "Hey."

Bailey turned all the way around, breaking Teague's embrace. She folded her arms across her chest and stated, "It's been a long time."

He looked embarrassed. "Yeah."

She waited for the feelings to come rushing back, then smiled because she knew they wouldn't. "Too long."

Teague slid one arm around Bailey's waist. "Jesse." He nodded at the other man.

"Teague."

From the corner, where the porta-a-crib was set up, Maggie whimpered. On his way to get his daughter, Teague petted Delilah. He picked up Maggie and brought her back to Bailey's side.

Jesse's gaze shifted from Teague to the baby to Bailey. "Congratulations."

Bailey said, "Thank you. Can I get you a cup of coffee? Or a bagel?"

"No, thanks. I was passing through and thought I'd stop in."

"Well, if I can get you anything please let me know."

He turned and left, the door swinging behind him.

Teague said, "Are you okay?"

"As long as I have you, I'm always okay."

The baby squirmed. "I think she's hungry."

Bailey laughed. "I told you babies had much worse timing that dogs." She took Maggie and sat at Teague's table to nurse her.

Teague kissed the top of Bailey's head before taking the chair next to her. "Do you think we should have gone with Magnolia for her first name?"

"No. Absolutely not. Do you have any idea how hard life would be for a girl named Magnolia? Can you picture her having to fill out job applications?" She rolled her eyes. "And I love that we know what her name means, and some day we can tell her, but no one else would ever put it together." Her smile faltered. She suspected he'd revived their dispute on purpose, to distract her from what had just happened. She adjusted her grip on Maggie so she could free one hand, then she reached for him. "I love you."

He carefully leaned forward and wrapped his arms around her and their baby. He kissed her neck and whispered, "Bailey Jean Malloy Gallagher, I love you, too."

The first notes of "Brokedown Palace" drifted through the shop. Bailey sang softly.

"You like this song."

"Mmmmm. I do."

"I can tell. You've got goosebumps."

She smiled against him. "That's not the song, Teague. It's you."